The screaming c

"I'll handle this,"   ne
audience parted b   Sea before
Moses, revealing a hysterical Ramona Houdeyshell
sprawled on the floor amidst the ruins of an antique
wooden trunk and something else. Something white
and filmy and frothy.

"Oh, my God, Alice-Ann," I screamed. "It's a veil.
A bridal veil."

I reached Mrs. Houdeyshell's side just as two of the
Barn Door Swingers pulled her to her feet. She fell,
sobbing, into Billy Boy's arms, giving us all a clear
view of what she'd been lying in. Not only a bridal
veil with a crown of silk roses, but shreds of shattered ivory silk, decorated with seed pearls and crystal beads. And we also saw the real reason for
Ramona Houdeyshell's screams: a skull grinning up
at us from the tattered bridal finery.

Emily Rakestraw had come home.

★

Also from Worldwide Mystery by VALERIE S. MALMONT

TORI MIRACLE AND THE TURKEY OF DOOM
  in FEAST OF CRIME (anthology)

DEATH, BONES, AND STATELY HOMES

Valerie S. Malmont

TORONTO • NEW YORK • LONDON
AMSTERDAM • PARIS • SYDNEY • HAMBURG
STOCKHOLM • ATHENS • TOKYO • MILAN
MADRID • WARSAW • BUDAPEST • AUCKLAND

For Nathaniel Malmont

DEATH, BONES, AND STATELY HOMES

A Worldwide Mystery/May 2005

First published by Perseverance Press/ John Daniel and Company.

ISBN 0-373-26528-X

Printed in U.S.A.

Acknowledgments

As always, my thanks go to my critique partners, Françoise Harrison and Helen O. Platt, for their invaluable assistance. I also want to thank Brad Gsell of the White Tail Refuge for providing a fascinating insight into deer farming. Last, but certainly not least, my thanks to Shirley Katusin for supplying me with authentic Pennsylvania Dutch recipes.

ONE

In the darkness, I grabbed my bedside phone to stop the annoying ring and was surprised to hear Garnet's voice all the way from Costa Rica. He sounded warm and loving, not exasperated and cold as he had when we parted in January. "I have something important to tell you," he began.

In my eagerness to hear what he was going to say, I sat straight up. The phone rang again, and I remembered with great disappointment that there was no phone by my bed; it was the alarm clock I was clutching to my ear. In anger, I hit the snooze button.

"Come back," I called, trying to recapture my dream, but the voice was gone, and I wanted to cry from the frustration of not knowing what he was going to tell me. A dream, only a dream, and yet it had seemed so real. Fred meowed in his sleep and moved closer to me. I stroked his soft orange-and-white tummy for a moment until the alarm sounded again. The best time for sleeping, I've always found, is in the early morning, so I closed my eyes and pulled the covers over my head.

"Tori. Tori Miracle. Aren't you up yet? Your clock's been going off for half an hour." My landlady's voice, outside my bedroom door, had all the subtlety of a chain saw. "It's nearly seven!" she continued.

I opened one eye and looked toward the window. Sure enough, morning sun was streaming through it.

"You've got to get up now. The exterminator's coming this morning, and I want to make sure he does your room. All that junk food you've got in your dresser has got to be attracting ants."

Recently I'd discovered the Philadelphia delicacy called Tastykakes. Since they were neatly wrapped in plastic, I doubted they'd attracted anything from the insect kingdom. As I rubbed the sleep from my eyes, I became righteously indignant. How did Ethelind know what was in my dresser?

"Hurry up," the chain saw rasped. "He'll be here soon." I heard her sensible shoes clumping down the hall as she hurried toward the front stairs. Reluctantly, I put my feet on the braided rug beside my bed, gathered my clothes together, and headed to the bathroom.

All winter, I'd been the housesitter for Ethelind Galland and I thought she'd be gone for a full school year, but she returned from her sabbatical in England much sooner than I'd expected. She hadn't really had time to learn everything there was to know about contractions in Middle English, but I think she was worried that her house wouldn't stand up for nearly a year under my charge. She'd forgiven me the fire, but the collapsed front porch still irritated her. Knowing my apartment in New York was still sublet, she told me I was welcome to say as long as I wanted. "I enjoy having company, and this is a huge house for just one person."

It was indeed huge, and for one thing I was very grateful. With Ethelind home, I would no longer be paying the oil bill. That was particularly important since P.J. Mullins had resumed her rightful position as publisher/editor of the Lickin Creek *Chronicle* and kindly allowed me to stay on as part-time reporter, even though I'd lost a lot of her subscribers due to the Civil War-reenactment fiasco last fall. "They'll be back," P.J. assured me. "We're the only paper in town."

She'd even given me a week off with pay in January, and I used that time to fly to Costa Rica to visit Garnet Gouchenauer, the former Lickin Creek police chief who was now a police adviser in Central America. That week had not been what I hoped it would be. Although the beach resort on the Pacific coast was beautiful and the weather had been warm and sunny, a nice change from the cold, gray skies of Pennsylvania's winter, our visit was strained at its best moments and miserable at the worst. Garnet seemed very different away from his natural south-central Pennsylvania habitat. More self-assured. Busier. Even happier. His life was full, and there didn't seem to be much room for anybody else in it, even me. He did say he wanted me to stay with him, but since he knew I had obligations back in Lickin Creek it didn't mean much. When we kissed good-bye at the airport in San José, I knew it was for the last time.

During the next few months, I finished revising proofs of my second novel, a fictionalized account of what could have happened to the USS *Eldridge* in 1943 when it was rumored to have been teleported from Philadelphia to Norfolk, Virginia, during government experiments with invisibility. With great relief I mailed them to the New York publisher of my earlier book, *The Mark Twain Horror House,* and hoped she hadn't forgotten who I was.

My mistake was dropping in on Alice-Ann MacKinstrie, my best friend, to tell her I was done.

"Now that your book is finished and you're only part-time at the paper, you'll have time to help me out with the June house tour," she said. We were sitting at the round oak table in her country kitchen, drinking coffee from blue splatter-glazed mugs, and she had just finished telling me that she'd agreed to co-chair the annual fund-raiser for the Caven Country Humane Society.

"What do you want me to do?" I asked, reaching for another doughnut hole. "With my reputation for having houses fall down around me, burning down the historical society headquarters and the courthouse, and killing Senator Macmillan, if anybody knows I'm involved they'll back away in a panic."

"Don't be silly, Tori. You didn't burn down the courthouse." If that was said to make me feel better, it didn't. I knew the blame for that disaster was still on my shoulders, even if I hadn't lit the match.

"Since you're a writer, you can write the descriptions of the houses we're going to show. For the tour book. That doesn't sound too difficult, does it? And besides, it will show the townsfolks how much you want to fit in here." Alice-Ann had been my best friend since college, and she knew exactly how to manipulate me.

"But isn't it the first weekend in June? That doesn't give me much time."

"You can get it all done this week. The printer only needs a few days. Besides, the same people go on the tour every year, so there's not any real need to sell tickets in advance."

I'd used up all my excuses, and my desire to be known as more than "that gal what burnt down the historical society," or even worse, "that New Yorker who got dear old Mack Macmillan blown to smithereens," was the clincher. I agreed to help her. Secretly, I was rather flattered. Poking about in old houses and writing about them would be a nice change from the routine my life had slipped into. "It might be fun," I said. That had been enough. In the next instant I was on the committee.

The chain saw outside the bathroom door interrupted my thoughts. "Aren't you nearly done with your shower, Tori? I need to run the dishwasher."

"Done," I called, turning off the water. There was no heat in the room, and despite it being mid-May, my teeth chattered from the cold. I quickly dried myself and pulled on jeans and my NYU sweatshirt.

"Not staying for breakfast?" Ethelind sounded disappointed as she watched me jam my arms into my blue jacket. "I've got some nice kippers."

"Thanks, but I promised Alice-Ann I'd meet her at eight," I said.

"You will be here for dinner, won't you? I thought I'd fix

a beef and kidney pie. It's a recipe I picked up at a charming pub called The Whole Hog, in a little town outside of…"

I waved and was out the door before she finished. Once Ethelind-the-Anglophile got started on stories about her favorite country, she could and would go on for hours.

Garnet's blue monster-truck waited for me in the circular driveway. I'd have to give it up soon, I knew, but figured I was doing him a favor by keeping it running while he was gone. I drove it downtown to the Humane Society Thrifte Shoppe, located on Main Street in what used to be the Woolworth Building.

When I tapped on the window, Missy Bumbaugh, the manger, looked up from the pile of clothes she was sorting, screwed her face up in displeasure, unlocked the door, and let me in. "Good morning," she said coolly, eyeing my casual outfit with disdain. In keeping with her position as wife of the president of the borough council, she always dressed as if she might be called to a meeting at the White House at any time. Today she wore a light blue suit with a white silk bow at the neckline. And high heels, of course, not sneakers like me. "You're late. Everybody else is already here."

Alice-Ann's cheery voice called out a greeting from the darkness in the rear of the store. "Come on back," she called. "We're just getting started."

I pushed aside the curtain that covered the door to the workroom and saw that the other members of the committee were already seated around the long table. Except for Alice-Ann, all the women present wore spring suits in pastel colors. Alice-Ann was slightly more casual in beige linen slacks, yellow silk T-shirt, and a matching cashmere sweater. That she could dress differently and get away with it spoke of her position in Lickin Creek society as a member, by marriage, of the town's first family.

Once again, I was inappropriately dressed. How did they know, these citizens of Lickin Creek, what the dress of the day was to be? Did they have some sort of secret events calendar that told them what to wear on every occasion? And where could I get a copy?

I was glad to see Maggie Roy, the town librarian and my good friend, at the table. She patted the empty chair next to her. "Saved you a seat, Tori. And I brought sticky buns and coffee. Help yourself and sit down."

I put a large, gooey bun on a paper plate, doctored some coffee with artificial sweetener and creamer, and joined her. The reek of mothballs emanating from the boxes of used clothing behind me would have put me off my feed, if I hadn't been quite so hungry.

Adelle Ashkettle, a dainty woman with eyes as round and cold as blue marbles, rapped on the table with the large gold-dome ring on her forefinger and announced that the meeting was called to order. "Mrs. MacKinstrie and I are delighted to have so many committee members here this morning. Bless you all for taking time from your busy schedules to be here today. It's less than two weeks until House Tour Day, so it's time to buckle down and put our shoulders to the wheel. Let's start with a moment of silent prayer."

Everyone bowed their heads, so I did, too. I heard Adelle shuffling through some papers, and after a very brief moment, she said, "Amen. Let's see, Alice-Ann, do you have chair-women lined up for each house?"

Alice-Ann nodded, stood, and read a list of names. "Does everybody know what's expected of them? You contact the owner of the house you're in charge of and go through it, making note of which rooms are not to be open to the public. At the same time, you ask the homeowner to show you what items of interest she would like the tour guides to point out. And you determine whether or not you will need runners to protect the carpets. I'm sure you all remember what happened to the Laudermilch house last year—cleaning that rug took a good bite out of our profits. You also need to decide how many tour guides you will need positioned inside the house. And it is your responsibility to enlist them and make sure they show up. Please remind your guides that they have to keep an eye on visitors, to make sure nothing is removed or damaged. Any questions?" When nobody responded, Alice-Ann sat down.

"Who's the refreshment lady this year?" Adelle asked.

A woman at the end of the table raised her hand. "It's me, again. Same as every year. Everything's organized. We plan to serve cookies and punch in each dining room as the visitors leave."

"No red punch, I hope," Maggie Roy said.

"Of course not. When I think of that lovely sofa at the Bighams'…" The refreshment lady sighed. "I've contacted the Giant Big-Mart bakery manager, and he has offered to give us the cookies for free. Part of the company's community outreach program, I think."

"You've done a wonderful job, Martha." Adelle smiled. "Let's move on to traffic control. Since nobody volunteered, I have shouldered the burden here and arranged to have the West End Volunteer Fire Department directing cars in the downtown area. Does the chairwoman of the ticket committee have anything to report?"

A woman stood and said, "I can't do anything about ordering the ticket books until Janielle Simpson finishes the sketch of Morgan Manor for the cover. And I still need the house descriptions."

Everyone turned and stared at me. "I'll get right on it," I promised.

"Good," said Adelle. "I think that covers just about everything. Are there any questions?"

A hand rose. "What if it rains?"

"It won't. It never has. Any other questions?"

"How did you manage to get permission to show Morgan Manor?"

"I have my ways. Since it's the first time we've shown the manor, I expect it to be the centerpiece of the tour." One of the women at the table spluttered an objection. "Don't worry Mrs. Houdeyshell, the Bride's House as always plays an important part of the tour. After all, it sets the tone—romance, June brides, all that. I only meant that since it has been shown every year, and since very few people have ever been inside Morgan Manor…oh never mind. If there are no more questions, the meeting is adjourned. We'll be back here next week at the same time. Until then, put your noses to the grindstone and get busy. We only have a short time to pull all this together."

One hesitant hand went up. "Has the flower committee contacted someone about supplying plants for the houses?"

A nod came from an elderly woman. "Fowler's Flowers will do it as usual, and there'll be no charge if we get a mention in the program booklet. You house chairs need to let me know what you'uns want pretty soon. We gots to order stuff in, you know."

I was in the process of preparing to leave, when Maggie Roy beckoned to me.

"Look what I found," she said in a low voice, as though trying not to be overheard. Maggie had knocked over one of the odoriferous boxes behind her when she scooted her chair back, and she was gazing at the spilled contents as if they were the jewels of Araby.

"What?" I saw six or seven sweaters in pastel colors, pretty but nothing to get excited about.

"Cashmere, all of them," Maggie said. "And in large sizes, too. This peach would look gorgeous on you, Tori."

Although I resented her implication that I needed a large size, I couldn't resist taking the sweater she held out to me.

"Perfect color," came Alice-Ann's voice from the other side of the room. "You should buy it, Tori."

I wanted it. Really wanted it. I wanted to look like Alice-Ann did in her cashmere sweater and linen slacks. I wanted to

VALERIE S. MALMONT 15

look as if I belonged. I wanted to look tall, thin, and blond. "I can't afford cashmere," I began, but the manager interrupted me.

"Of course you can. All our sweaters are three dollars. How many do you want?"

I had ten dollars in my wallet, so I took three. Maggie bought thc rest.

TWO

Morgan Manor, originally known as the Matteus Morgan farmhouse, is located on a ten-acre portion of the original farm and is dramatic in size and appearance. It has remained in the ownership of the Morgan family since it was built in 1796 of native limestone.

The fifteen-room farmhouse is built in the Federal style, which is reflected inside and outside the home. The porch with the Ionic columns was probably a later addition. As you stroll around the exterior of the house, please take notice of the finely chiseled masonry surface and narrow mortar joints on the front of the house, and the coarser stonework on the side and rear elevations. As you enter the home, the molded fanlight over the entranceway lights the center hall. Please stay on the plastic runners to protect the original pine floors. There are two staircases; the most formal curves upward from the front hall, while the smaller service staircase leads from the kitchen to the third-floor servants' quarters. Be sure to take note of the walnut grandfather clock in the living room, a Morgan family heirloom. Use caution as you climb the staircase; there is a slight list and we don't want anyone getting hurt. On the second floor, there are six bedrooms with adjoining baths, which were added about forty years ago. Just imagine the luxury of soaking in a Jacuzzi in an eighteenth-century house.

Maribell Morgan, the present owner, has made it her life's work to restore the home to its original beauty. This included getting all twelve closed-off fireplaces to work. Although much

*of the original furniture was sold during the Great Depression,
Miss Morgan has spent her entire lifetime collecting appropriate
period furniture to make the house as authentic as possible.*

*Morgan Manor is rightly listed on the National Register
of Historic Places. The term "Manor" does not refer to the
house, but was the word used to designate land awarded to
the descendants of William Penn.*

*The present property includes the house of native limestone,
a frame bank barn built in the late nineteenth century, and a
one-and-a-half-story springhouse, which still supplies water to
the Manor house. The springhouse will not be open for the tour.*

I STOPPED TYPING, leaned back, and closed my eyes. The memory of what we'd found today in that springhouse was haunting me, and I couldn't write any more. I decided I'd done enough, without going through the boxes of scrapbooks and diaries I'd found in the attic, and I turned off my computer before my conscience led me to pick up the telephone and call the police.

Earlier, as soon as the meeting of the Thrifte Shoppe was over, Alice-Ann had suggested we start visiting the houses, so I could begin writing the tour book. "We can do Morgan Manor first, since nobody's living there, and I have a key. We'll take my car," Alice-Ann said, leading me to her beige Volkswagen Beetle, which had carried us to many an adventure during our college days. "It still runs," she said, noticing my doubtful smile. "And I can't afford to replace it. Not until I get Richard's debts under control."

Richard had been her husband, the last surviving member of Lickin Creek's founding family, and a scumbag of the first order. When he was murdered, leaving Alice-Ann to raise her small son alone, he also left her with myriad debts. Because Lickin Creek "takes care of its own," as I'd heard often enough, she had been given a lot of leeway and extra time to pay back the money he owed. And she'd been allowed to keep the historic family home, which Richard had mortgaged to pay for some stupid land scheme he'd been involved with.

"Is your house going to be on the tour?" I asked her, as the engine sputtered and refused to start.

She shook her head. "Come on, baby, you can do it." The Bug must have liked the tone of her voice because it started instantly. "You have to know how to talk to them," Alice-Ann said with a grin. "In answer to your question, no. Since the theme of the Humane Society tour is June and romance, it doesn't seem appropriate to show my house. Not after what happened to Richard. But it will be shown on the AAUW historical home tour in the summer."

"Another house tour? How many are there?"

"There were four last year. Every organization in the borough jumped on the bandwagon when they saw how successful ours was." After a moment's thought, she said, "More like three and a half. The Garden Club only lets visitors wander around the outsides of the houses, so I guess that shouldn't really be called a house tour."

"Everyone acted surprised when they heard the Morgan house was going to be on the tour," I said. "What makes it so special?"

"It's never been on the tour before," Alice-Ann said. "Maribell Morgan was asked a dozen times, but always refused."

"Why did she agree this time?"

"She didn't exactly." Alice-Ann's grin was wicked. "She's been in the Sigafoos Nursing Home for a couple of months, and her nephew is the one who authorized its use. Evidently he's her conservator or trustee, or something like that. He's planning to put the house on the market in the spring, and I think he's hoping someone on the tour will see it and make an offer. That happens quite often, and owners like it because it saves on realtors' commissions."

We were driving on one of Lickin Creek's notoriously confusing one-way streets, when Alice-Ann swerved to avoid a stove in the street. "People should be more careful," she muttered, but she didn't seem particularly surprised by finding a stove in the street.

Now, I began to notice that there were many large objects sitting on the sidewalks: refrigerators, rolled-up carpets, old wooden dressers, chairs, complete dining room sets, even an iron gate or two. When I saw a woman dragging a leather sofa out her front door to the edge of the curb, I asked, "What's going on with all the furniture on the sidewalk?"

"Bulky Trash Pickup," Alice-Ann said. "Once a year the borough schedules a pickup of all the big stuff people don't want anymore. It gives everyone a chance to clean house. Look." She pulled over to the curb and pointed to a truck that was slowly cruising down the street behind us.

"They're sidewalk shopping," she said. As we watched, the truck stopped, two men jumped out and a moment later the leather sofa was in the bed of the truck.

"By the time the borough actually gets its pickup trucks out, most of the stuff is gone. It's a great way to furnish a house for nothing. And antique dealers from miles around stock their stores from what they find here."

Another odd local tradition for my Lickin Creek journal, I thought, as I watched a brand new SUV pass us, slow down, and then stop. A little boy climbed out, ran directly to a bicycle propped against a telephone pole, and screamed with delight. Within seconds, he and his mother had stowed the bike in the backseat of the SUV and resumed their cruising. It wasn't such a bad tradition at all, I thought. If I had a place of my own, I might have been tempted to do some sidewalk shopping myself.

Morgan Manor was on the edge of town, and even with the slow-moving trucks and vans clogging the streets, it didn't take us very long to reach our destination. Alice-Ann slowed down before pulling into the driveway, so I could get a good look at the house.

Morgan Manor was an enormous structure of gray lime-stone, built in what I'd come to recognize as the Federal style. It sat well back from the road, about halfway up the side of a hill. Between the house and the road ran a small brook. We drove across a one-lane bridge spanning the water to get onto the property.

"Not a bad little shack," I commented, after we'd gotten out of the VW.

"It was built by Matteus Morgan, one of Lickin Creek's earliest and wealthiest settlers. Local lore claims he was a descendant of William Penn."

"Undoubtedly someone who was in the wagon with your former husband's great-great-something-or-other when the wheel broke," I laughed, recalling a local legend about the town's founder who, when he couldn't fix his broken wagon wheel, decided it would be easier to stay put and build a town instead.

Alice-Ann nodded agreement. "I believe Matteus was in the second wagon, but apparently he was no better with his hands than Great-great-grandpa MacKinstrie." I laughed again, and she joined in. She wiped her eyes with the back of her hand. "Let's go inside."

I followed her up three steps to the front porch, which had a roof supported by a row of Ionic columns. "Obviously the porch isn't original," Alice-Ann murmured. "Be sure to mention that in the booklet."

While she unlocked the front door, I pulled my notebook from my fanny-pack and began to make notes.

In the front hall, dust motes swirled in the rays of sunlight coming from the fanlight over the door. "We'd better get a cleaning crew in here before the tour," Alice-Ann remarked. "Isn't it amazing what happens to a house when it has been vacant for a few months."

Noticing the tattered plaster that hung from the front wall in three or four places, I nodded.

Alice-Ann followed my gaze. "That can be fixed easily. It even happens in my house—something about the plaster reacting to the limestone in the walls. But dear old J.B. is going to have to pay for it. Our committee can absorb the cleaning costs, but not repairs."

"J.B.? Is that J.B. Morgan, president of the Old Lickin Creek Bank?"

"And charter member of the Old Boys' Club," Alice-Ann chuckled. "You can count on him to try to save a few bucks on the realtor's commission."

I followed her voice into the living room, which was large and sunny and filled with beautiful furniture. "The clock's supposed to be an heirloom," she said. "J.B. wanted to be sure that was mentioned in the tour book. Just in case an antique dealer comes through carrying a wad of money."

We entered the dining room, which was almost as large as the living room. "Nice antiques," I commented. "Are all these original to the house?"

"For the most part, no. Maribell collected period furniture. Had to, after some loser ancestor sold everything off to pay his gambling debts."

The kitchen was as small and gloomy as the public rooms had been large and cheerful. It did, however, feature a stone fireplace big enough for me to stand upright in. A small room off the kitchen had been turned into a den, complete with knotty-pine paneling. "Forties redux," Alice-Ann sniffed. "My house had the same stuff in it. There must have been a hotshot pinewood salesman in this area, sixty, seventy years ago." A quick peek into the small, dark adjoining bathroom told us it should not be shown on the tour.

"That's the service staircase." She pointed to a narrow door beside the kitchen fireplace. "It's so narrow, I doubt that most of the Lickin Creek community could squeeze through. We'll keep the door shut and use the front stairs for the tour."

I followed her back into the front hall, scribbling madly in my notebooks as I went.

She was halfway up the stairs when she warned, "Hang on to the railing. The whole thing sags to the left. Makes you feel like you're going to fall off."

Climbing it was a little like being in a fun house; the list was enough to throw my balance completely off-kilter, and I fought the strong gravitational pull all the way up. "I'd better put a warning about this in the booklet," I said. "It wouldn't look good to lose a visitor."

"Good idea." Alice-Ann had reached the relative security of the landing and began opening bedroom doors. The first three were elegantly furnished alike with mahogany four-poster beds, highboys, Oriental carpets, ladder-back chairs, and enormous quantities of silk and lace. "Lots of dusting and vacuuming needed up here," was Alice-Ann's only comment. Adjoining each bedroom was a bathroom, which apparently had been created by chopping up other bedrooms. In the bath next to the largest bedroom, Alice-Ann chuckled, "I'll be darned. Maribell had a hot tub. Who'd have guessed."

Alice-Ann opened a fifth bedroom door. We stopped in the doorway, surprised at what lay in front of us. No period furniture or original oil paintings here. Instead, it was filled with cheap furniture from the sixties: beanbag chairs, a sofa bed heaped with orange and turquoise pillows, an unpainted bookcase untidily filled with book, posters and a shaggy orange-and-red rug.

"Oh my God," Alice-Ann said. "It's never been touched, like a shrine—she never changed it after…"

"After what?" I had stepped into the room and was looking at the contents of the bookcase. Amidst the biographies of classical composers and stacks of yellowed sheet music I noticed several books of photographs. I pulled one out, opened it, and hastily replaced it. "Come on, Alice-Ann, tell me what you know about this room. Was erotica Maribell's secret vice?"

There was no answer, and I turned around to discover Alice-Ann was gone.

"I'm in here," came her voice. "In the closet. The stupid door slammed behind me. Can you pull from the outside?"

I had to brace one foot against the wall while I pulled to get some leverage. Even with Alice-Ann pushing from the inside, it took several long minutes to get the door open.

Her face was flushed and her blond hair was streaked with cobwebs when she stomped out of the closet. "The house must have sagged to make that door swing closed like that."

"Anything interesting in there?" I asked, peering into the dingy interior.

"Some very dated clothes on hangers, and a box. Way back in the corner. Let's see what's in it. Hang on to the door while I pull it out."

With the cardboard carton now on the bedroom rug, Alice-Ann gingerly folded back the top flaps. "Hope there's no spiders in there," she said, poking it open with one foot.

"Or snakes," I added, mentioning my worst fear.

"Sneakers," she said, staring down at the box. "It's full of old sneakers."

I looked in, too, and noticed something odd. "There only seems to be one of a kind."

Alice-Ann dumped the contents onto the floor. "You're right," she said. "Why do you think someone would save one sneaker out of a pair?"

"They're different sizes, too." While all were men's shoes, the sizes ranged from small enough to fit my size-seven foot to something Michael Jordan's size.

Alice-Ann put the sneakers back in the box and shoved it into the closet. "Maybe he was a collector," she said.

"A sneaker collector? And who is it you are talking about? Who lived here? It looks like a teenager's room. Did Maribell have a son?"

"No, she never married or had children. This must have

been the room she rented to the high school teacher. I think he lived here for about ten years. Back in the sixties, I believe." She read his name from the framed Penn State diploma on the wall. "Rodney Mellot."

"And Rodney up and left without taking any of his belongings? Didn't anybody think that was odd?"

"Not really. He left on his wedding day, and everyone assumed he'd developed cold feet. Emily Rakestraw, the poor bride-to-be, was left standing at the altar in the most expensive wedding dress this town had ever seen."

"How dreadful. But why do you know so much about it?"

"Because of the Bride's House being on the tour for the last ten years. That's where Emily Rakestraw, the deserted bride, lived. And the story is now part of local folklore."

"What a sad story."

"Not as sad as you might think," Alice-Ann said. "Rodney came back a few weeks later, and they eloped."

"So this is one legend that has a happy ending."

Alice-Ann grimaced. "I only hope their marriage was happier than mine. Maybe it was, because they stayed away from Lickin Creek. Settled in Texas, I think."

"Still," I said, "it does seem strange he wouldn't have taken his belongings with him."

She shrugged. "Maybe they wanted a fresh start. Her parents never really approved of him. I heard it broke her mother's heart when they ran off together." She looked around the room and giggled. "Maybe Emily wouldn't let him bring this tacky stuff. She was an art teacher and probably had halfway decent taste."

"You're not going to have this room open on the tour, are you?" I asked.

Her eyes opened wide with surprise. "Of course we will. It ties in so nicely with the Bride's House Legend. People will love to see it."

We left the bedroom, and I followed Alice-Ann to the foot

of the narrow steps, which I presumed led to the attic. I was still thinking about Rodney Mellott. "Why did he live here? Did Maribell Morgan need money badly enough to take in boarders?"

"Are you still talking about the music teacher? I've heard that there weren't any apartments available, and Maribell graciously offered to let him stay here until he found a place. He was very popular in town, and evidently she decided he was worth keeping. She must have been in her fifties back then and not too bad-looking, and he often was her escort to parties and concerts. I guess she liked having a younger man around as a companion. We should all be so lucky in our middle age."

Alice-Ann started up the stairs. "Aren't you coming?" She looked down at me, over her shoulder.

"Do we really need to check the attic? Visitors won't be going up there, will they?"

Alice-Ann shook her head. "I want to make sure there haven't been any leaks. Or birds trapped up there. One died in my attic once. It smelled—"

"Never mind the graphic details," I interrupted. "I'll wait here."

She smiled, and I knew she was thinking I was being lazy and didn't want to climb any more stairs. Let her assume what she wanted, I thought, it was my private business that I was terrified of bats, and I knew all the old houses in Lickin Creek had attics full of the nasty mammals.

After a few minutes, the attic door swung open, and Alice-Ann came out carrying another cardboard box. "It's an antique dealer's paradise up there. I'd better tell J.B., so he can start getting some quotes. I found some boxes full of really old scrapbooks and notebooks in an enormous walnut wardrobe. I brought one down for you to look through. Maybe you can find some juicy tidbits for the tour book."

After putting the box in the trunk of the VW, we strolled down the hill toward the springhouse. Flagstones had been laid to create a narrow path and even steps where the hill grew steep. The little limestone building had a slate roof, and one shuttered window on the side facing the manor house. The door was on the left side, facing away from the road. Weeping willows and cattails grew along the water's edge.

"How charming." I paused at the top of the steps to take in the view, while Alice-Ann gingerly climbed down the flagstone steps.

"Oops!" Alice-Ann's feet slid out from under her.

"Are you okay?"

"Yes, but be awfully careful. The stones are covered with slippery moss." She picked herself up, determined that nothing was broken, and stretched a hand out to me. With her help, I climbed down safely.

Alice-Ann unlocked the door and we entered a dim room. Little light was admitted by the louvers of the shuttered window, but Alice-Ann found a wall switch, and in a moment a carriage lamp that swung from an overhead rafter brightened the good-sized room. Above us, it was open to the slate roof, with exposed beams showing. The walls and floor were of the same limestone as the exterior, but only the floor was softened by a worn and dusty Oriental rug. In one corner stood an old cast-iron wood-burning stove. Seven or eight folding chairs stood in a semicircle. Metal music stands stood before the empty seats as if waiting for a sepulchral orchestra to enter.

"I think I heard that Rodney taught private music lessons here," Alice-Ann whispered. For some reason, it seemed right to whisper, although there was nothing there to be disturbed except a few spiders.

I shivered and wished the stove were working. Then I realized it wasn't so much the damp cold that bothered me as the eerie vibrations I was receiving from the empty room. Here it was, exactly as it had been nearly forty years ago, waiting for musicians who would never come. "I don't like it here," I whispered.

"Me either." Then Alice-Ann added in a normal voice, which made me jump, "We're being silly. Come on, let's see what's downstairs."

An open staircase of wood slats led through a black hole in the floor to the lower level. I wasn't anxious to climb down into unknown territory, so I didn't demur when Alice-Ann announced she'd go first. After all, she did have a flashlight.

"Watch your head," she called out, shortly after I heard a nasty thump and a squeal. "I'm looking for a light switch... Here it is."

Suddenly the stairs were bathed in golden light, and I was no longer afraid to go down. I managed to evade the beam that had left a large red spot on Alice-Ann's forehead and stepped onto a mossy green ledge. Before us lay a large, black pool, the surface of which bubbled gently from water splashing into it from the spring in the far corner of the room.

"This is where the house water comes from?" I asked. "I'm glad I didn't help myself to a drink."

"According to J.B., the water's fine. They had problems some years back, he said, but that's when they put in an ultraviolet sterilization unit. That took care of it." She leaned against the wall and lifted one foot to look at the bottom of her shoe. "I think I've got a rock or something stuck in here." She began to dig at an unseen object.

The sterilization unit was on the wall directly in front of me, and I stepped forward to examine it. The little dials were spinning, so I assumed it was running although I had no idea of how it worked. "I don't need to mention this in the tourbook, do I? I don't even think you should let visitors come down here. Those flagstone steps outside are a disaster waiting to happen."

From behind me came a crash and Alice-Ann's cry, "Oh sugar."

I cringed. Alice-Ann was a klutz by nature, and today she seemed to be in top form. "Are you okay?" I asked, turning around. Where Alice-Ann had been standing, there was now a huge hole in the rocky wall.

"I'm fine," came her weak reply from inside the hole. "Oh, no!" Her voice rose to a scream.

"Oh my God!" I yelled. "What have you done? Are you okay?" I rushed to her, nearly losing my balance on the slippery floor, and peered into the hole. I could barely see Alice-Ann sitting in the corner, with her knees drawn up under her chin and her eyes closed.

"Alice-Ann, you're not dead are you?"

She opened one eye. "I wish I was. Look over there." She flapped her left arm in the air for a moment, then returned to clasping her legs tightly against her chest.

"I can't see anything."

"My flashlight. Wait a sec. I think I'm sitting on it." She squirmed a little and retrieved it. "Here. Turn it on and tell me I didn't see what I think I saw."

I played the light beam on her face first to make sure there was no blood. She waved it away. "Only my dignity is hurt."

The circle of light fell upon an unrecognizable bundle against the wall. Alice-Ann moaned and covered her face with her hands. "There's nothing there, is there?"

"There's something, but I can't tell what it is. Just a second, let me get a closer look." I stepped through the opening in the wall. "Looks like a bunch of old clothes… Oh my God."

"It's a body, isn't it?" she whimpered.

My mouth was so dry no words would come from it. I swallowed cotton a few times, then whispered, "I think it is." Actually, the grinning skull on the floor left no room for doubt.

I couldn't bring myself to touch the gruesome bundle, so I nudged it with one foot. An arm flopped forward and a skeletal hand protruded from a black cloth sleeve.

Now that I had determined it really was a body and not a figment of her imagination, Alice-Ann pulled herself together, rose from the floor, and stood next to me.

"It's a skeleton," I said. "Obviously it's not someone who died recently."

Alice-Ann seemed relieved by that.

I nudged the bundle again, and this time I uncovered a man's shoe. Thankfully, there was no skeleton foot inside so I gingerly picked it up, and after I wiped a half-inch of dust from it, found it was black and shiny.

"Patent leather," Alice-Ann said. She seemed to have recovered from her initial shock, because now she dropped to her knees and touched the bundle of rags and bones. "Look." She held something in one hand. The flashlight beam revealed a metal clip with shreds of black, silky fabric hanging from it. "I think it's a bow tie," she said. "Richard wore one like it at our wedding… Give me the flashlight." She turned back to the skeleton, and examined it more closely.

After a minute or two, she stood up and handed the light back to me. "I think it's wearing a tuxedo. The silk parts have kind of rotted away, but I could see a stripe down the side of the pant leg where it was. And there's a shirt with ruffles. At least I think they're ruffles." She wiped her hands on her slacks, leaving nasty smudges in their wake. "This is awful."

"It is." I agreed. "Let's go back. This cave is giving me the creeps."

Back in the basement, we sat on the steps and breathed hard for a few moments. "No wonder the water went bad," I said, after I'd somewhat recovered. "Decomposing bodies aren't the healthiest thing to have around your water supply."

"Are you thinking what I'm thinking?" Alice-Ann asked. "That it's the missing bridegroom—Rodney Mellott?"

"But you said he came back and eloped with Emily What's-her-name."

"Emily Rakestraw. That's what I've always understood. But a body in a tuxedo—that can't be a coincidence."

"We'd better call the police."

"We can't," Alice-Ann said.

"Of course we can. There's got to be a phone in the manor house."

"I mean we shouldn't, Tori."

In answer to my questioning look, she added, "If we call the police, they'll have to close up the house and investigate who this body is and why it's here. It will ruin the house tour. Everyone in town is eagerly waiting to see Morgan Manor. Without it, we'll be lucky to sell half a dozen tickets."

"What are you suggesting?"

"Only that we lock up the springhouse and don't tell anyone about the body until after the tour."

"You can't be serious." I felt myself splutter with indignation. "You can't hide something like this."

"Somebody hid it for a long time, I'd say from the looks of the body. What's a few more weeks?"

"But…"

"It's not like someone we know was murdered, or there's a killer hiding in the house. This guy's been dead for years. Nobody has to know right away. Tori, think of all those little animals who need shelter. Without the money from the tour, the Caven County Humane Society might have to close down. We'd have to destroy all those sweet little puppies, those darling kittens…"

Deep inside I knew what she was proposing was wrong, wrong, wrong. But her plea to save the animals was the way to my heart, not my head. "Only until the day after the house tour. Then we have to tell. Agreed?"

"Agreed. Help me put the stones back."

THREE

THE BRIDE'S HOUSE is a stately Victorian mansion, built entirely of brick in 1879. The exterior remains basically untouched and is a reminder of more elegant times. Enter the spacious grounds through the wrought-iron gates and stroll up the curved brick path to the gracious front porch. Pause here for a moment to imagine a more leisurely lifestyle, where you might have sat on wicker furniture, drunk lemonade, and waved to friends in passing carriages.

The grand foyer, with its wide-planked pine flooring, is unusual for its size and for its marble European fireplace. The kitchen has been kept in its original state, with only a small gas heater in the fireplace added as a concession to modern comfort. Think of how charming it must be to have breakfast at the round oak table set in front of the enormous wood-burning stove.

Follow the magnificent chestnut staircase to the second floor where you will see many bedrooms filled with oversized Victorian furniture. Throughout the house, many of the windows are stained glass reputed to have been made by the famous Tiffany Studios.

Come down the back staircase and visit the twin living parlors and Victorian dining room, which are furnished with lovely antiques from the late 1800s and early 1900s. Please notice the walnut Eastlake sideboard, which displays a collection of old lusterware pitchers.

The front parlor is where, forty years ago, Emily Rakestraw, a beautiful young debutante, waited in her wedding gown for her bridegroom who never came. Her bouquet has been preserved under glass and is displayed on the marble-topped table by the front windows. Over the fireplace is a portrait of her fiancé, painted by the talented bride, who was employed by the Lickin Creek High School as an art teacher after her graduation from Bryn Mawr College.

Although Emily Rakestraw was reputed to have been heart-broken, her mother was not, having said publicly she thought her daughter was better off without him. Emily continued with her teaching and her charity work around town. Less than a month after her fiancé deserted her at the altar, he returned and the couple eloped. The bride's mother died shortly after, some say from a broken heart, and the house was sold to the first of several owners, who took no pride in the historic home.

In 1990, the property passed into the hands of the Snyder family, who restored it to some of its past grandeur. Recently, it was purchased by Tom and Cathy Ridgely, who are planning to turn it into a country inn. This house tour coincides with the grand opening. We wish the new owners of the Bride's House Bed-and-Breakfast the best of luck with their endeavor.

I TURNED OFF the computer and thought back on the day's events.

I'd had a sleepless night, worrying through most of it about the skeleton in the springhouse and whether or not I had done the right thing in agreeing not to tell anyone until after the house tour. I was grateful when the sky finally lightened and I could get up. Ethelind expressed shock and disbelief when she came downstairs in her fuzzy pink bathrobe and found me in the kitchen and the coffee ready.

"I've got a lot of things to do today," I explained, not wanting her to know about my guilt-ridden night, "so I got up early. I'm going to visit the Bride's House today."

Ethelind sniffed as she poured a cup of coffee. "Makes me

sick to hear them making such a fuss about that story every year. The only thing that boyfriend of hers did that was wrong was to come back. He should have kept on running."

"Did you know them?"

"Everybody in town knew Emily Rakestraw. Everywhere you went in town, there she was. She thought she was something special because her dad had money and they lived in that big house. She and her mother used to serve on committees where they didn't do anything except lend their name as if they were members of the royal family. As if anybody cared a hoot who she was. And she was always a party girl. Even back in high school. Debutante, her mother liked to call her, but if being a deb meant hanging out in every bar in town and screwing all the members of the football team, and not even caring if they were some other girl's boyfriend or not, then I'm glad my father was just a poor machinist. Not that there's anything wrong with being a machinist, mind you. *His* father did come from England."

I did some quick mental calculations and decided Ethelind must be about sixty-four. That put her and Emily's graduation back in the fifties, before the great youth rebellion of the sixties. Had Ethelind been one of the girls who had lost her boyfriend to Emily Rakestraw? It was hard to imagine Ethelind as a teenager, dating and doing all those things teens did back in the fifties, but I knew it was naive of me to assume she'd sprung from her father's brow as a full-grown college professor.

"It's not my choice," I said, sensing she was somehow blaming me for something I didn't even know about. "I'm doing the tour booklet as a favor to Alice-Ann, that's all."

"Hmmph," Ethelind sniffed. She sipped her coffee, emptied her cup in the sink, and started another pot. I grabbed my things and left.

Unlike Morgan Manor, which had been on the outskirts of Lickin Creek, the Bride's House sat on a large lot in the Historical District, only a block and a half away from Garnet's house. I went the long way around so I wouldn't have to see the Gochenauer home.

On the brick sidewalk, outside the Bride's House's iron fence, sat an enormous pile of trash and a row of old-fashioned porcelain toilets. A woman, who didn't seem a day older than nineteen, dropped a box containing chipped clay flowerpots and wiped her forehead with her sleeve. "For some reason, it doesn't seem as chilly as it did half an hour ago," she said with a smile.

I acknowledged the trash heap with a nod in its direction. "You must be cleaning house for the tour."

"That…and getting ready for our grand opening."

I extended my hand. "Tori Miracle. I'm doing the tour booklet. Grand opening of what?"

She shook my hand, leaving a little grit in my palm. "Our bed-and-breakfast. We bought the place about three months ago from the Snyders. I'm Cathy Ridgely."

"Is there enough tourist traffic in town to make a bed-and-breakfast worthwhile?"

From the startled look in her eyes, I gathered she hadn't thought about that.

"We're depending on a lot of town folks coming here because of the Legend and all. When they see what we've done, they'll recommend it to their friends and relatives when they come to visit. Come on in. I'll show you around."

As we approached the house, I noticed the brick facade was badly in need of repairs.

"I know," she sighed, although I hadn't said anything. "There's so much to do with an old house. And it's all so much more expensive than you think it's going to be. We're concentrating on remodeling the inside, first."

"I love your porch," I said, after we had climbed the steps. It was full of charming white wicker furniture, and flowers were beginning to bud in the planters along the railing. A large truck roared past, drowning out her answer.

Inside the foyer, which was already cramped because it held a grand piano, stood another row of toilets, but unlike the ones on the curb, these looked brand new.

"We're going to add a bathroom to each of the guest bedrooms by boxing in one corner of each room. It's not the best solution, but it's all we could think of. Let's go upstairs. Be sure to mention the woodwork is chestnut—you don't see wood like this anymore." She patted a carved newel post before climbing the stairs.

The bedrooms on the second floor were all being reconstructed, with the framework for the new bathrooms partially completed.

"This one will be Victorian style," she said as she opened a door. I only had an instant to peek inside before she had another door open across the hallway. "This one will have Art Deco furniture. We've been going to auctions and flea markets picking up vintage furniture." She kept moving and opened another door, revealing a sunny room. "This used to be Emily Rakestraw's studio. I wanted to keep it that way, sort of a memorial, but my husband said we needed rooms to rent more than we needed a shrine. I plan to do it in pinks and whites, like a little girl's room. We'll have extra cots in case anybody brings children with them. We haven't exactly begun work on the third floor yet, but this one will be ready for the tour."

Even though I thought it was a lot of work to accomplish in about nine days, I kept my doubts to myself and asked, "Is the third floor where you live?"

"Oh no. We've made a bedroom out of the storage room behind the kitchen. It's small, but cozy. It used to be Emily's darkroom."

With all the mess, it was hard to envision what the bedrooms would look like, so I decided not to say much about them in the tour book. "Let's take a look at the downstairs," I suggested.

"As you can see, this is the kitchen. It hasn't been changed at all. Don't you just love the big fireplace? That used to be where all the cooking was done. The stove was probably added in the twenties. Isn't it a beautiful antique?"

The hideous small gas heater sitting on the hearth and the enormous black, cast-iron stove with a wood box beside it were not my idea of beauty.

"It's so cozy having breakfast in here, with the woodstove going. We've been thinking of putting a window in someday. And maybe one in our bedroom, too."

"Are you really planning on cooking breakfast for guests on a woodstove? What a lot of work."

She ignored me and went through an archway into the dining room, which was by far the largest room I'd seen in the house. The long, narrow walnut table could seat eighteen comfortably. "I picked the sideboard up at a flea market," she bragged. "You should have seen it. I had to scrape ten layers of paint off it. It's Eastlake—that's a Victorian style, you know. I keep my lusterware pitcher collection on it. Isn't it pretty?"

The shiny gold, silver, and bronze pitchers on the hideous sideboard were indeed pretty, and they brought some much needed lightness into a very dark room.

"We're eventually going to change those," she said, pointing to the tasseled red velvet drapes that nearly hid one wall. "But we still will need heavy material to cut down on the traffic noise.

"Here in the front parlor, we've got a display having to do with the Legend of the Bride's House. That's Emily Rakestraw's bridal bouquet under the glass dome near the window. And over the fireplace is a portrait she painted of her fiancé. She was the art teacher at the high school, and he was the band director. A very talented couple, from what I hear."

I crossed the room to look closely at the portrait of the man whose body, I feared, was hidden in the springhouse at Morgan Manor. Emily had painted a fair, slightly plump man, with blue eyes, pink cheeks, and a pouty lower lip. He wore a shiny tuxedo jacket, a ruffled shirt, and a bow tie.

"Did she paint him in his wedding outfit?" I asked.

"I think that's what he always wore when he was directing the band. There's a scrapbook over there on the coffee table that we found in the attic, and there's a lot of pictures of him in that same suit. Or one just like it. Emily was a photographer as well as an artist, and they are apparently all her work."

Cathy crossed over to the table and picked up a small cardboard box. "There's postcards from Emily and Rodney in here, donated by various people who received them over the years."

I took the box and opened it. Inside were more than a dozen postcards, mailed from a number of overseas locations. They all seemed to bear a variation of the standard "having a lovely time" message. Cathy reached around me and selected one of the cards. "Here's the one Emily sent to her parents telling them she'd eloped to Texas." She handed me the card from Laredo, Texas, so I could read it. The delicate, feminine writing on the back said only, "Mumsy and Daddy. Rodney and I are married. We're living in Texas. I know you'll be angry, so I'm not sending my address. Emily."

"What about Emily's wedding dress? Do you have that to put on display?"

"I wish. Either she took it with her, or her father kept it when he sold the house after Emily's mother… Have you seen enough? I have to get back to work."

"What were you going to say about Emily's mother?"

"Only that she died a few weeks after Emily left. Part of the legend is, she died of a broken heart caused by her disappointment over the elopement, since she'd been delighted when Rodney skipped out. Apparently she'd hoped Emily could do a lot better socially."

"I guess I'm done," I said, starting toward the foyer.

"Wait a sec. Could you give me a hand with a few things? They're just too bulky for me to get them out to the curb."

I grabbed one end of a mattress and we wrestled that to the street. Then we went back for a wooden chest with rope handles. "It's not heavy. Just awkward to get hold of and I don't want to scratch the floors. We just had them refinished. It's the original wide pine planking."

"Cracks and all," I commented, deciding I'd better warn visitors to walk with caution.

There was a ton of stuff to take out, and after about six trips back and forth to the street, I conveniently remembered another appointment. "Would it be all right if I took the scrapbook along? I'll take good care of it. Maybe I can find some human interest bits about the couple to spice up the booklet."

She didn't look too pleased with the idea, but she fetched the scrapbook anyway. "Be sure I have it back by tour day. I want to display it."

I hoisted myself into Garnet's truck and was surprised to see that it was nearly noon. I hadn't had any breakfast, and I was starved. There was a Waffle Shoppe on Main Street, downtown, which I'd been meaning to try, so I drove in that direction.

I despaired of trying to find a legal parking place, and parked in a loading zone in front of the Scene of the Accident Theater. It was only a block and half away from the Waffle Shoppe, but it was a block full of boarded-up storefronts and pool halls. Ignoring the catcalls from some teenagers who should have been in school, I walked up the street. Standing before the restaurant, I tried to look through the window to see if it looked appetizing, but years of grease, and smoke-filled air had taken their toll and I could see nothing.

Inside, I found it to be a narrow room, with a row of booths along one side and a counter with stools along the other. The ceiling fan overhead didn't make a dent in the cigarette smoke. There was only one stool left at the counter, so I sat down and looked at the speckled menu. Pecan waffles leaped off the page at me. If there's one thing I love, it's pecan waffles. "And coffee," I told the waitress.

I sipped my coffee while I waited for my order and tried to ignore the man on my right who kept staring at me. I could almost feel his breath on my arm. Finally, I couldn't take it anymore, and the New Yorker in me came to the fore. "Look, buddy," I began, turning toward him. "You're in my personal space."

Face-to-face with him, I wasn't sure I really minded. He was extremely handsome, in a rugged, down-to-earth way. Even though he was dressed in the usual Lickin Creek male attire of jeans, plaid shirt, and boots, at least there wasn't a backward-facing ball cap on his head. Blue eyes twinkled in a tanned face. His light brown hair was short, almost a buzz cut.

"Sorry, ma'am, I was trying to figure out where I've seen you before."

Ma'am. He called me *ma'am*. He couldn't be much younger than me. Where did he get off with that *ma'am* stuff?

"I know," he said with a huge grin that revealed straight, slightly yellow teeth. "Christmas Eve."

I stared blankly at him.

"You'd run off the road into a snowbank, and I pulled you out of your car. I remember you had something funny on your head."

Now I remembered everything. "It was a tea cozy," I told him. It was his turn to look blank.

"It's a…thing to keep a teapot warm… I was trying to stop my forehead from bleeding… Oh, forget it. You were driving an eighteen-wheeler, and you took me into town. You were trying to get to West Virginia for Christmas, weren't you?"

"Yup."

Gary Cooper or Jimmy Stewart? Cooper, I decided, he was my favorite of the two old-time Western stars.

The waitress brought my waffles, a scoop of butter big enough to fit in an ice-cream cone, and a bottle of warm maple syrup. "No wonder this place is so popular," I sighed, after taking a bite.

"I eat here every morning I'm in town," said my new friend. "By the way, my name is Harley."

"I'm Tori Miracle. Is Haley your first or last name?"

"Both."

I couldn't think of anything appropriate to say, so I speared another piece of waffle with my fork. The man on my left chose that moment to light a cigarette, and smoke drifted under my nose. I slammed my fork down and snarled at him. "Kindly put that cigarette out or take it outside."

He inhaled deeply and smoke curled slowly from his nose. He was dark, with a short beard, and narrow lips. "You got a problem, lady?"

"Yes, I do. You're polluting the air and ruining my appetite."

Without any warning, he reached forward and ground his cigarette out right on top of my pecan waffle.

"You happy now?"

I'm not often at a loss for words, but all I could do was stare at my ruined waffle and gasp in disbelief.

That's when Haley twirled his stool around and stood up. Even from where I sat, I could tell he was well over six feet tall. "I don't suffer fools gladly," he rumbled ominously, and with one quick movement, he grabbed the man by the back of his shirt and pulled him from his stool. He didn't stop pulling until they were out the door. The other diners, who up till then had watched in silence, began to cheer, and many of them rushed out the door behind Haley and my tormentor.

After only a minute, the crowd outside roared, the door flew open, and Haley paused in the doorway and said, "'How are the mighty fallen,' Second Samuel." He was followed by a dozen men who were all trying to slap him on the back.

"That's enough," Garry Cooper said shyly. "Just remember that pride goeth before a fall."

He straddled the stool next to me. "Sorry you had to see the dark side of me, ma'am."

"It wasn't a dark side, at all. You were protecting me. I'm not used to that, and I liked it. Thank you."

He blushed but refrained from saying, "Aw shucks."

"Miss Miracle, this might seem kind of bold of me, but I wonder if you'd like to socialize with me some evening?"

"Why…thank you. That would be very nice." I'd never heard the word *socialize* in this context before, but I assumed it was a synonym for date.

"Great." He swung around and stood. "I'll be out of the state for the next few days. How about Friday? I'll pick you up at six, six-thirty. We can get a bite to eat. You still living with that college professor?"

I nodded and was distracted by the waitress bringing me a fresh waffle. It didn't occur to me until later to wonder how Haley knew where I lived. But by the time I thought of asking, he was gone.

FOUR

OUTSIDE THE RESTAURANT, I took a deep breath to cleanse my lungs and started to gag. Instead of fresh air, everything smelled like grape juice. It coated my nostrils, and I even imagined I could taste the grapey flavor on my tongue. From somewhere came the sound of tinny, rhythmic drumming. Now what? I wondered. I thought I was familiar with most of Lickin Creek's idiosyncrasies, but this was something new.

I returned to the truck in time to stop Luscious Miller from writing a ticket for illegal parking. Luscious, who was the acting police chief in Garnet's absence, was trying very hard to do a good job and to be nice to me because he still thought of me as the chief's girlfriend. "Please don't park like this anymore," he pleaded. "Next time, it might be one of the part-timers writing tickets, and more'n likely they won't tear it up."

"I promise I'll never do it again," I swore with my fingers crossed behind my back.

"Thanks, Tori. How's things going for you?"

Guilt washed over me. Just fine, I could have said, I found a skeleton yesterday, and I'll probably give you the details in about three weeks. Instead, I said, "Can't complain. How about you?"

"I've got nearly four months of sobriety," he said, his sallow cheeks flushing a little.

"Congratulations. That's quite an accomplishment."

He pushed the three strands of hair back over his bald spot and smiled shyly. "I owe it to you."

Now it was my turn to blush. "You don't owe me anything, Luscious. All I did was give you a talking-to. You did the hard part. By the way, do you happen to notice a grape juice smell in the air?"

He looked surprised, turned his face upward, and sniffed. "Sure do. It's for the crows."

"I've heard of feeding the birds, but giving them grape juice seems a little extreme."

"Sounds silly, I know, but Marvin Bumbaugh read somewheres that crows don't like grapes, so he sprayed all the trees in the square with grape juice to try to scare them off before they nest. And he's got kids from the middle school beating on pots and pans and shooting off firecrackers down there by the fountain. One way or the other, he's going to keep the streets clean this spring. Not to mention protecting all of us from the West Nile Virus."

"What on earth is West Nile Virus?"

Luscious shrugged. "Don't exactly know, but it's bad news for people and horses. And we've got plenty of both in Lickin Creek."

He saluted and marched down the street, shoulders squared, looking inches taller.

The clock on the Old Lickin Creek National Bank chimed once. I decided to drive out to Alice-Ann's house and get the keys to another house.

"YOU MADE A DATE with who? I mean whom," Alice-Ann, the English major, screamed. "A truck driver you only met this morning? Tori, you're crazy."

"Actually I've known him for several months," I told Alice-Ann, not mentioning that our earlier encounter had been a brief ride through a blizzard on Christmas Eve.

"That's better," she said. "I thought he was a perfect stranger. Did you say he was in the trucking business?"

"No, Alice-Ann. I did not. I said he was a trucker."

Her shoulders stiffened, but she was savvy enough not to say anything snobbish.

"I know what you're thinking," I couldn't resist saying.

"Tori, I'm sure he's a nice man, whatever he is."

I waited in her kitchen while she slammed things on a tray: glasses of iced coffee with lots of fresh cream, a plate of chocolate mint Girl Scout cookies from the freezer, sugar in a red ceramic bowl, and long-handled spoons. "Grab some paper napkins, will you please? I can't fit anything else on here."

I followed her through the center hallway into the living room. This was a large room, nearly fourteen feet high, with tall, uncurtained windows across the back that looked out upon trees still bearing the soft pastel-green leaves of spring.

Alice-Ann's decorating taste was "country," and by that I mean rickety-looking chairs, a three-legged carpenter's bench used as a coffee table, and cracked pottery pieces full of dried weeds sitting in every corner. Old bean pots and canning jars served as lamps. Duck decoys and dried herb bundles dangled from the ceiling, while blue-and-white enamel cookware, full of holes, hung on the walls. Rag rugs were scattered over the polished pine floors. Even though it was May, a small fire burned in the great stone fireplace.

Alice-Ann nudged aside a copper bowl full of dried yellow flowers and placed the tray on a wooden bench sitting in front of the fireplace. I moved a half-dozen hand-quilted pillows off the red-and-white checked loveseat to make room for us to sit down.

We faced the fire and sipped our iced coffees. "This is so cozy, Alice-Ann. Makes me almost want to nest."

"Maybe someday you and Garnet will have a place of your own," she said. Apparently she had decided my trucker date was inconsequential.

I hadn't told her Garnet and I were through. It was too painful a subject. "Maybe," I said.

Alice-Ann looked over the notes I'd made while touring the Bride's House earlier that morning and had a few suggestions to make. "You don't need to mention anything about the exterior. Hopefully, with the trees in full leaf, nobody will see how bad it looks. And do be sure to mention the stained glass windows. They're supposed to have been made by the Tiffany Studios." I hadn't even noticed them, but duly made an addendum to my notes.

Alice-Ann read to the end and began to chuckle.

"What's so funny?"

"What you say here about Mrs. Rakestraw dying of a broken heart."

"That's what I was told."

"I guess if you want to get technical, every heart that stops is broken."

"What are you trying to say?" I asked.

"She committed suicide. But her husband didn't want anyone to know. Apparently she had some sort of mental disorder the family wanted to keep quiet. I suppose that part of the legend has been conveniently forgotten. It wouldn't do for potential B and B guests to know she hanged herself in the closet of one of those charming bedrooms the Ridgelys are hoping to rent out at exorbitant rates."

"I can see where that might be bad for business," I acknowledged. "I have time to look at another house today. Which one do you recommend?"

"The Zaleski House on Magnolia Street. It's small and won't take long." She glanced at her watch and frowned. "I'd go with you but Mark gets home from school around three. I'll call the owner and see if she's home."

She lifted the straw beehive on the end table and revealed a very modern-looking telephone. Her glare silenced my giggle, and she dialed. "Hello, Mrs. Bonebrake? Alice-Ann MacKinstrie here." The next few minutes were spent in ritual conversation about health, weather, and family. I emptied my glass and waited patiently. She finally got around to asking if I could come right over. "Wonderful, Mrs. Bonebrake. Her name is Tori Miracle." She paused and listened. "Yes, that one.

Please don't hold that against her. It was an accident." Another pause. "So was that."

She hung up and re-covered the phone with the beehive. "All set." She grinned.

"What did she ask about me?"

"Oh, the usual… Aren't you the one who planned the Civil War reenactment at the women's college last fall? And didn't you have something to do with the courthouse and the historical society burning down?"

"Is that all? Did she forget I'm supposed to have killed Senator Macmillan?"

"She didn't even mention him. You're going to have to stop being so paranoid, Tori."

She gave me directions to the house, the kind I'd fondly come to think of as Lickin Creek directions. "Go downtown, turn right at Second Street, hang a left where the railroad station used to be, go a few blocks and turn right just before you come to the oak tree in the middle of the road, go about a mile past where the Roadcaps used to live. The house will be on your left. You can't see the Lickin Creek from the street, but it runs past the back garden."

"What's the house number?" I asked. I should have known better. Nobody in Lickin Creek knew anybody's house number. Houses were identified by the name of the first family to have lived there. Thus was Mrs. Bonebrake's home still known as the Zaleski House. For a newcomer like me that made finding any place doubly confusing. Not only did I not have a house number to go by, but the name on the mailbox was unlikely to be of any assistance.

"You can't miss it. It's the only Queen Anne on the block."

"It would help if I knew what Queen Anne looked like."

QUEEN ANNE, I discovered an hour later, meant a house with a gingerbread front porch, a front door set to one side, and a tower on the other side covered with fish-scale shingles. At least that's what it meant in Lickin Creek. The part that wasn't covered with fish scales was red brick. A moss-green picket fence, the same shade as the fish scales, surrounded the front yard.

I entered through the gate and found myself in a happy little garden full of tulips, hyacinths, and other spring flowers whose names I didn't know. The door burst open, and Mrs. Bonebrake filled the porch. She was an imposing woman, nearly six feet tall, with longshoreman's shoulders and a mustache.

"Come in," she said curtly. "I'll show you around, but you'uns got to be quick about it. I've got an orthodontist appointment at four." Perhaps her need for orthodontia was why she didn't smile at me.

I entered a tiny foyer, brightened by a window veiled with lace curtains on my right. Ahead of me was a staircase, to my left the front parlour. "Let's start here," I said, pointing to the parlor.

Mrs. Bonebrake went ahead of me. The room was sparsely but elegantly furnished with Victorian antiques. The walls were painted a delicate pink, which perfectly matched the faded Oriental carpet covering most of the dark wood floor. And there were more lace curtains filtering the afternoon light.

"The fireplace works," she said, nodding toward what appeared to be a black marble mantel. Closer examination proved it was wood painted to resemble marble. I made a note of that and followed her into the dining room. Over the rectangular walnut table hung an antique oil lamp. "It's original," Mrs. Bonebrake told me. "I like the way it looks at night, so we never replaced it."

The kitchen was engaging. It had modern appliances while still retaining most of the old-fashioned feeling of yesteryear. Here, the knotty pine I'd seen in so many Lickin Creek homes seemed to fit.

"Back stairs," she said, opening a narrow door. "Come on." I was glad I didn't have to turn sideways to get up the staircase. Mrs. Bonebrake did, and I wondered how often she used these stairs.

She opened a door at the top, and we stepped out onto a landing that overlooked the front staircase and the foyer. "There's two bedrooms up here," she said. "Used to be three, but we took one out to make the bathroom larger."

As she spoke, she opened the middle doorway and held it open so I could look. It was a dream bathroom, with an enormous claw-footed porcelain tub as the centerpiece. A modern shower with glass on two sides had been inserted into one corner. It had enough ferns and rubber plants set around to create its own ecosystem.

"Lovely," I murmured.

"Aren't you going to write anything down?" she asked, looking suspiciously at my closed notebook.

I flipped it open and scribbled something about a bathroom that combined the old and the new.

The spare bedroom was in the back of the house. It was painted pale blue and the antique iron bed was covered by a quilt in delicate shades of blue, lavender, and rose. Sheer white curtains fluttered in the breeze. A doorway led to a small balcony overlooking the backyard. "You can go out there," she said. "It's solid."

On the balcony was a white wicker table-and-chair set surrounded with more plants. I had a view of the long backyard and saw, beyond the garden, the sparkling waters of the Lickin Creek.

Reluctantly, I went back in and followed Mrs. Bonebrake across the landing to the master bedroom, which ran the whole width of the building, making it the largest room in the house. The walls were a soft cream, the bedspread a yellow-and-white quilt. The furniture was all walnut and on the marble top of the dresser sat a crystal vase holding fresh flowers. The tower I had seen from outside contained a comfortable-looking armchair, a small table, and a floor lamp. Beneath the windows were built-in bookcases.

"It's my reading area," Mrs. Bonebrake said.

I sighed at the pleasurable thought of having a "reading area" of my own.

"Yep, there's a lot of Velma Bonebrake in this house," she said. "I'm going to hate leaving it."

"You're leaving? Why?"

"The usual reason. Harry Bonebrake needed time to find himself. And what he found was a tootsie. He wanted out so bad, he let me have the whole kit and caboodle in the divorce, and I'm selling it and moving to Florida. It's going to be sun and surf for Velma Bonebrake's golden years."

"I'm so sorry," I murmured.

"Don't be. Let her deal with his hemorrhoids, bunions, and arthritis for a while. I had the good years." When she smiled her blue eyes twinkled, and I realized she was really quite attractive. "Let me show you the garden."

FIVE

*THE ZALESKI HOUSE has long been a charming part of Lickin
Creek's history. Built in the Queen Anne style in approxi-
mately 1890, it has been lovingly restored by Mr. and Mrs.
Harry Bonebrake. You may feel as if you've traveled back in
time when you walk though the picket fence into the English-
style cottage garden. Step onto the vine-shaded porch and
please note the original spindles and brackets at its cornice
and the rail carried by turned balusters. Imagine yourself sitting on the porch swing in the Victorian era.*

*The front door is to the right of the swing. After you ad-
mire the stained glass panel, open the door and enter the small
but appealing foyer. The living room is decorated in soft pinks
and roses; the beautiful fireplace is faux marble.*

*Throughout the entire house are delicate lace curtains,
and to complete the effect an oil lamp still burns over the dining room table. The kitchen has been modernized, but still re-
tains the charm of yesteryear. Upstairs, there are two lovely
bedrooms, one of which overlooks the back garden and the
Lickin Creek. The master bedroom, done in creams and yel-
lows, has a reading nook in the tower. A recent life-change
has prompted the Bonebrakes to put their historic home on
the market.*

I PAUSED AND REFLECTED what it might be like to live in a house
with a reading nook, lace curtains and two bedrooms, one of
which would be perfect for my study. I could learn to garden,
I was sure. It couldn't be too hard. Lots of people did it.

Mrs. Bonebrake had told me what she wanted for it. Compared to New York prices it seemed a mere pittance. I was positive that it would be sold before the house tour was over.

I clicked the laptop off. It was time to dress and report for work at the *Chronicle*. As I filled the bathtub, I couldn't help but think about Mrs. Bonebrake's spacious bathroom with the claw-foot tub. The running water reminded me of the sparkling stream that was the Lickin Creek, flowing past her back garden.

Stop this, I scolded myself. You're going to make yourself miserable wanting something you can't have. I sprinkled some of Ethelind's English bath salts into the tub and watched the water foam. But was the house really something I couldn't have? I could visit the Lickin Creek National Bank and see if I qualified for a loan. That way I'd know for sure I couldn't afford to buy a house. After all, a chat with a banker wouldn't oblige me to buy the house. Besides, I wanted to talk to J.B. Morgan about Morgan Manor's history and judge his reaction. Someone had to have placed that body in the springhouse. Maybe he knew something about it.

A real house. My own house. I sighed and lowered my body into the water. Just think, in a month I could be lying in my own tub... Of course, I couldn't afford to furnish it with real antiques the way the Bonebrakes had, but in time...

I came to my senses with a start to find myself lying in tepid water. The bubbles had disappeared, leaving only a slimy oil slick on the surface. Oh no, I was going to be late for work again.

P.J. Mullins, the longtime editor and publisher of the Lickin Creek *Chronicle,* and the only reporter until I'd come along, was tapping her teeth with her fountain pen when I ran in the door. That was usually a bad sign.

"I'm sorry," I apologized. "I had a little problem at home, and..."

"Tori. Your whole life is a problem."

That was so unkind.

"Sit down. I've got some stories to go over with you."

I plopped down on the folding chair in front of the card table I used as a desk. "Shoot," I said, whipping out my reporter's notebook.

P.J. busied herself for a moment or two digging through the papers on her rolltop desk, giving me a chance to study her. She had always reminded me of Katharine Hepburn. Today, as usual, she wore khaki men's slacks, a white cotton shirt over a turtleneck jersey, and had a blue silk scarf tied around her throat. Her short hair was steely gray, and she wore little half-moon glasses perched low on her nose. For the first time, I noticed how much thinner she was than she'd been when I met her nearly a year ago.

P.J. was one of those people who used to have two cigarettes going at one time and a filthy ashtray on her desk, but since her operation the butts in the ashtray had been replaced by a bowl of mints, which she sucked on all day long.

"Here's what I want you to work on," she said, handing me a fax. "We can feature it in next week's paper."

It was an FBI Most Wanted poster, with a blurry photograph of a man who appeared to be middle-aged, although it was hard to tell. The accompanying text said he was a prison escapee, who had been convicted of blowing up several clinics. He was considered armed and dangerous.

"Can you tell me what I'm supposed to be looking for?"

"It would be nice if you could find him. But since that's hardly likely, I'll take interviews with family and a background story instead. He's a local boy. Escaped a few days ago from a county jail in Louisville, Kentucky, where he was awaiting sentencing. There's a chance he might have headed back this way. He used to have a cabin in the woods near the Appalachian Trail."

"I'll get right on it. Anything else?"

"The landfill was closed last Thursday when it reached its monthly limit of 9,999 tons. Try to get a story about what the borough's going to do with its garbage. You can tie it in with something about Bulky Trash Pickup Week, since all that extra stuff is what put it over the top."

"But the borough hasn't even picked up all the trash from the streets," I said. "What is it going to do with all of it?"

"That's what I want you to find out, Tori. I'd also like to continue with the series on local businesses. Why don't you choose a couple and write articles about them?"

That was an order, I knew, and not a question. "Anything else?" I asked with a frown. P.J. only paid me to work three days a week. How could I possibly get all this done in that time?

"Yes, there are some anthills on the Appalachian Trail. If you get a chance, go take some pictures."

I closed my notebook. "And maybe I can kill two birds with one stone and find the escaped convict hiding in his cabin at the same time."

"Good idea. Now scoot. You have no time to waste." Her voice was raspier than usual, and as I walked into the outer office I overheard her coughing frantically.

"I thought the operation was supposed to take care of that," I said to Cassie Kriner, the office manager, as I paused in the doorway.

Cassie's blue eyes were cloudy with tears. "I think it came too late."

Outside, I leaned my back against the bricks of the narrow *Chronicle* building and used my sleeve to rub grape juice off the brass plaque, which said BUILT IN 1846, while I pondered my next move. I had options. Too many, as a matter of fact. I had to find out about an escaped convict, write stories about local businesses, Appalachian ants, and the landfill, and I also needed to write up two more houses for the house tour booklet before Friday. Several explosions from the direction of the town reminded me that I could also do an article about crows and the disease they spread. West Nile Virus, I thought it was called.

Procrastination is my middle name. Actually, it's Livingston, but the *P* word would be more appropriate. With everything I needed to do, I made the decision to visit the Lickin Creek National Bank instead and do a little investigating about the body in the springhouse.

"TOBY MERKLE, good to see you. Have a seat." J.B. Morgan, the bank president, welcomed me heartily, getting both my first and last names wrong as usual.

"It's Tori Miracle," I gently reminded him.

"Of course. Please forgive me. Now, what brings you to my humble little office?"

The humble little office he referred to was about as large as Ethelind's enormous living room, with antique chestnut paneling, alabaster light fixtures, and an Oriental carpet the size of Libya.

He smoothed his silver hair and smiled, revealing perfect teeth that probably looked even whiter than they really were because of his tan. When I sat across from him, I noticed his eyes were blue-green and rimmed with thick black lashes. I wondered if he were married, then I wondered why I wondered. Sure, he was handsome, but he was also years older than me. How many? I mentally calculated he must be about fifty, maybe fifty-five. Much older than my thirty-plus years. Stop this immediately, I told myself. Just because you have no man in your life, doesn't mean you have to start looking at every man you meet as a potential beau.

"Is there something wrong, Toby?" J.B. asked. "You seem…distracted."

"No. Nothing. I was only thinking about something unimportant. Actually, I came here to ask you a few questions about Morgan Manor."

His eyes narrowed, making him look a little like the older, sophisticated Cary Grant. "What kind of questions? And why?"

"I'm writing up a description of the house for the house tour booklet, and wondered if you could give me any background information that could make it more interesting."

"For goodness sake, I'd nearly forgotten the house tour was coming up. I'll be glad to help you out. But to be honest, I don't know a whole lot about the history of the house."

"Didn't you grow up there?"

"Nope. I grew up in a nice split-level in the South Hills development. That's south of the borough," he added unnecessarily, since I knew South Hills was Lickin Creek's most exclusive and expensive suburb. "Aunt Maribell is my father's sister, and since she didn't have kids I never had much reason to visit her, except when she held her annual summer picnics and Christmas dinners." He gave a little shudder, but grinned to show he was being funny. "Not exactly my idea of fun. 'Don't touch this. Don't sit there. Be careful on the stairs. No running. No jumping. Stay away from the stream. No fun allowed.' You know the drill."

I certainly did. It was quite similar to growing up in an ambassador's home.

I felt a little embarrassed at continuing, but still I did. "I am trying to link Morgan Manor and the Bride's House together. Thought it might generate some local interest."

His eyebrows raised as if he hadn't thought of that. "How so?"

"The runaway groom...what was his name...?"

"Rodney Mellott?"

"That's it. He lived with your aunt, didn't he?"

"He rented a room from her. That's not quite the same as living with her."

"I wasn't suggesting they were linked romantically," I apologized. "I simply wondered if you had ever met him?"

"Of course I met him. He was the high school music teacher. I had him for band."

I'd forgotten that. "What was he like?"

"You know something, Miss Merkle, I was just a kid. It was forty years ago. How do I know what he was like? All I remember was, he was kind of a pudgy guy with pink cheeks. Oops. Nearly forgot. He had a tendency to spit when he talked rapidly. Does that help?"

"That's not exactly a description of a romantic character," I said. "I think I'll leave his looks to people's imaginations. I couldn't help noticing the springhouse. It's quite charming. Anything you can tell me about it?"

"Yes indeed. It's made of limestone, it sits over a spring, and Aunt Maribell used to worry about it being full of snakes. Anything else I can tell you?"

"Snakes! If I'd known that I never would have gone in. Alice-Ann mentioned something about the water having gone bad once. Is it all right now?"

"Over my aunt's objections, I had a UV water purifier installed. She didn't want to spend the money, but I thought, better safe than sorry. Lots of dairy farms around here causing pollution. Now I have the water tested every year, and it is always clean. Anything else?"

"Thank you very much for your time, J.B. I'm sure I have enough information. By the way, how can I find out if I qualify for a home loan?"

He whipped out a ballpoint pen, produced papers as if by magic, and within half an hour, I had applied for a loan.

"I see no reason why you shouldn't qualify, Miss Merkle. After all, the Zaleski House is small and not very expensive. I can safely say you are preapproved for a mortgage. Go make your offer." He winked, a coconspirator, my buddy. "Offer five grand less than the asking price. I happen to know Mrs. Bonebrake is very anxious to get far away from Harry and his tootsie. The sooner the better."

We shook hands, and I left his office in a daze. What had

I done? I stumbled down the street, worried, until I came to the realization that just because I had applied for a loan didn't mean I was committed to anything.

SIX

THE WYNDHAM-CRATCHITT Gristmill lies on the southwestern border of the borough of Lickin Creek at the confluence of the Lickin Creek and the Green Spring. Built in 1820, it was once the business center of Caven County, but the mill became less important to the community as farms shrank in number. Finally, the mill stopped operating full-time in 1979. Bill Wyndham and Elmer Cratchitt are cousins who inherited the mill from their grandmother in the late 1980s. Bill had the idea of bringing the mill back to life, and the two men have hand-crafted many of the parts in order to restore the mill to working order. They open one day a year to grind cornmeal, and they sell it once a week in the old mill office, where the pot-bellied stove sits as a reminder of the olden days when farmers gathered around it to visit, chew tobacco, and talk politics.

Above the working mill, the second and third floors of the enormous building have been turned into a spacious home, occupied by Bill Wyndham's family. The huge living room, which runs the width of the building, is on the second floor. The wide plank floors are original, as are the limestone walls. The windows, overlooking the falls that run the mill, have been enlarged to take advantage of the breathtaking view. When you sit at the dining table, you feel as if you are floating in an aerie high above the treetops. The kitchen, with its beamed ceiling, is dominated by a walk-in fireplace.

The sound of the waterfall is constant and soothing at night to people sleeping in the six third-floor bedrooms, and even reaches the children's playroom in the attic. An out-

building has been turned into a sun-drenched studio where Annette Wyndham, Bill's wife, produces her acclaimed paintings. The studio will be open throughout the tour and paintings will be available for purchase.

AFTER MY VISIT to the bank, I had used my lunch hour to visit what was commonly called the Mill House. Looking at it had taken only a little more than an hour, and I hand-wrote my report while sitting in the truck, then stopped at the library to show it to Alice-Ann, who worked there part-time as the children's librarian.

She and Maggie Roy invited me into the back room for a cup of coffee. While I doctored mine liberally with imitation cream and sugar, Alice-Ann made room for us at the table by moving aside piles of books and plastic book covers, then looked over what I'd written. She laughed when she reached the end. "Good old Annette, never lets an opportunity go by to sell her dreadful paintings. And when I visited the mill last year on cornmeal-selling day, the waterfall noise reminded me of Frank Lloyd Wright's Fallingwater. It's enough to drive you crazy. Night and day: splash, splash, splash. It never stops. And the smell of mildew is overwhelming."

"It is pretty, though," I said. "And I didn't smell any mildew."

"Maybe I'm exaggerating," Alice-Ann said. "Are there any doughnuts left?" She got up and crossed to the refrigerator where she found a Dunkin' Donuts box. "Aah, good," she sighed. "Jelly doughnuts."

"I think it's a beautiful place," said Maggie, bringing the subject back to the mill. "I wouldn't mind living there. It would be so much fun to furnish with antiques from the Civil War period." Maggie's fiancé was an avid Civil War reenactor, so it was only natural she would think of that period first. But I knew the mill actually was built forty years before the war. Historical accuracy was beginning to become important to me. If I should buy the Zaleski House from the Bonebrakes, I'd be sure to decorate authentically.

"Very nice, Tori," Alice-Ann said, putting my description of the mill in a folder labeled HOUSE TOUR. "All four descriptions have been perfect. Only one more house to go. And Trinity Evangelical Church, of course. That's where we let people use the restrooms." She glanced at her watch. "I'd better get back to work."

I followed Alice-Ann through the reading room and down the basement steps to the empty children's section. She went immediately to the low picture-book shelves and began to straighten the books. I wondered why she had complained about the mildew smell at the mill. It couldn't be worse than what she lived with on a daily basis down here in the basement.

"Alice-Ann, I've got to talk to you. About…you know… what we found in the springhouse." I didn't want to say the word *body* out loud. "I'm feeling bogged down with guilt."

She sighed but didn't look at me. In fact, she seemed totally engrossed with arranging the picture books in alphabetical order by the author's last name. "Don't get me confused," she said.

"As if the kids care," I said grumpily.

Alice-Ann stood and wiped dust from her hands onto her slacks. "It makes it easier for me to find what they ask for. Please don't worry about the *you-know-what*, Tori. In less than two weeks the house tour will be history, and then we'll report it. You know it doesn't make any difference to the *you-know-what*. He's…you know."

"I don't like this. I don't like it at all. It makes me feel guilty. As if I…you know…What if someone finds it? They'll know we were in there, and they'll know we found…"

"We filled in the rocks in the hole in the wall. And the door is securely locked. Quit worrying."

"But we don't know…" I began to laugh at the absurdity of our conversation. "Remember that silly thing we used to say when we were kids? Something like: Who knows what the nose knows. That's what we sound like. I'll try to finish the write-ups tomorrow. See you then."

I bade Alice-Ann good-bye and left her to alphabetize her books, marveling at how she could be so unconcerned about the *you-know-what* in the springhouse.

My next stop was the Lickin Creek police station, which was actually a room in the back of Hoopengartner's Garage. This was convenient for Henry Hoopengartner, since he was the elected county coroner, and it also provided a service to the community. Since Hoopengartner's was open twenty-four hours a day, there was always someone there to answer calls for help. The garage was Lickin Creek's own version of 911 service. Historically, the teenaged girls whom Hoop usually hired to answer the phone seldom got the messages right. But that little detail didn't bother the borough council, which paid the rent. A bargain was a bargain.

Today's secretary and police dispatcher looked a little older than what I was accustomed to seeing behind the gray army surplus desk, but that might have been because she wore her blond hair in an enormous beehive, the likes of which hadn't been seen since 1965. Her eyes were heavily rimmed with black kohl. Her lips were the color of dried blood, and as I walked in she licked lipstick from her front teeth, reminding me of a vampire movie I'd seen recently.

"Looking for Luscious?" she asked. Without waiting for my answer, she jerked her head toward her right shoulder. "He's in there. Probably taking his after-lunch nap."

I entered the office and found Luscious diligently working at his computer. "You should leave the door open," I told him, "so that girl outside will know how hard you work."

"Who care what she thinks," he said with a bravado that was new. "I get my work done, and the council knows it. That's all that matters. Do you think Garnet's going to stay, or will he go back to Costa Rica?"

"What are you talking about?"

"Garnet. He's coming back for the wedding, I'm sure. And I'm hoping it'll be for good."

"Oh, that," I said, as if I knew what he was talking about. *What wedding?* I wanted to scream. *Who's getting married?* The thought suddenly came to me that Garnet might be coming back to get married, himself. Oh my God! I didn't care, did I? I mean, I knew it was over when I left Costa Rica. Didn't I? Would he really have found someone to marry that quickly? Wouldn't he have let me know?

Luscious was looking at me strangely. "Can I get you a cup of water? Your cheeks looked flushed."

I shook my head. "I'm fine, and I'm here on official business. I need to find out everything you know about the escaped convict."

"That's easy." He shuffled through the papers on his desktop, found what he was looking for, and handed several to me.

I read through them quickly and learned the escapee was one Vonzell Varner, also know as Big Guy. He was forty-one years old, and he had been convicted of murder and federal weapons charges after blowing up several abortion clinics, one with a doctor and nurse inside. He had a long record of arrests and convictions going back to when he was a teenager growing up in Lickin Creek, and had spent time in a juvenile detention center, several county jails, and the State Correctional Institution at Graterford. He was six feet tall, 170 pounds, and had brown hair and brown eyes. No distinguishing facial features, but his arms and hands were heavily tattooed. On his right arm was a map of Pennsylvania. On his left, a severed man's head with a heart beneath it that said MOM. From left to right, the fingers on his right hand spelled out KILL, while the left hand fingers had WWJD tattooed on them.

"WWJD?" I asked.

"What Would Jesus Do. It's a popular phrase around here, mostly with teenagers."

He'd escaped from a jail in Kentucky where he was being held pending sentencing. Vonzell Varner last had been seen in Maryland, heading toward Pennsylvania in a stolen truck, and it was thought he might be coming to see his ex-wife and five children, who lived right here in Lickin Creek. He was known as a mountain man, who could survive long periods of time in the wilderness. He was considered armed and dangerous. The FBI also warned that he might be attaining "folkhero" status with fringe groups.

The picture showed a rather ordinary and pleasant looking man. He had the kind of face you wouldn't notice in a crowd.

"Wow," I said when I had finished. "How did he escape?"

"Picked a lock, climbed through an air-conditioning hatch, and walked away. He claims to be invisible."

"What about federal agents? Shouldn't they be on the lookout for him?"

"I've had a few in here this morning. They've staked out his cabin up near the Appalachian Trail." Luscious laughed. "They're the people in the brand new, expensive outdoor gear. Not like the real hikers, who look like hell by the time they reach our area."

"Have they staked out his ex-wife, too?"

"Of course. If he comes to Lickin Creek, he'll be caught."

"May I take these papers along?" I asked.

"Help yourself."

I walked back to the *Chronicle* building, feeling the full heat of the day. The weather had gone from too cold to too hot with no transition period. I was grateful to get into Garnet's truck and turn on the air conditioner.

The ex–Mrs. Varner lived in an area of the borough that was filled with small, inexpensive town houses. Most had been covered with aluminum siding, but their tall windows and gingerbread trim were reminders that the buildings dated back to the nineteenth century.

For the most part, the little houses were well maintained. Several small children played marbles on the sidewalk. With the exception of a fairly new green van, the only vehicles parked on the street were aging pickup trucks. The van had tinted windows, making it impossible to see if anyone were inside, but I thought I saw a shape in the front seat, and I assumed it was a federal agent.

The woman who answered the door was tall and thin, middle-aged, I guessed, with fair hair straggling around her haggard face. Dark circles surrounded her pale blue eyes. Jenny, as she asked to be called, invited me inside, where it was only a few degrees cooler than outside.

"Sorry about the heat," she apologized. "I don't have no air-conditioning. I can get you an iced tea, if you like."

"Thank you. I would like."

While she was in the kitchen, I checked out the living room. While the mantel held an array of framed photos of children of various ages, there were none of Vonzell Varner. A gun cabinet served as a divider between the living room and the adjoining dining area, but it was locked. More telling than what I did see was what I did not see; there were no books or magazines in the room, nor were there any toys scattered around as one would expect in a house where five children lived. I heard the clink of ice cubes against a glass in the next room and sat down. There had been no sign of Big Guy, but then there wouldn't be if he were invisible, I thought with a silent chuckle. He could even be sitting right beside me on the couch.

"Here we are," Jenny said, putting a wet glass on the coffee table in front of me. "Nothing like a cold drink on a hot day. You know I wouldn't of let you in if I didn't know you was that reporter lady from the *Chronicle*. And I feel safe because the feds got the place staked out. I suppose you'uns is here to ask about my ex. Right?"

I stirred the tea, looked around for a place to put my spoon, and finally dropped it back into my glass. "What can you tell me about him?"

"What do you want to know?"

"What kind of man is he? What was his motivation for the clinic bombings? How long were you married? Anything you want to tell me." I opened my notebook and licked the point of my pencil. "Are your children in school?"

"I've sent them away. And I'm not telling you or nobody where they are. It's safer that way."

"Safer? Are you afraid Vonzell would hurt them?"

"I think he'd do anything to get back at me. And he knows my children are the most important thing in my life."

"Why would he want to get back at you? What did you do to him?"

"I turned him in. He blames me for his incarceration. He doesn't think what he done has anything to do with him being in jail." A tear dripped down her right cheek, seemingly unnoticed.

I said nothing, just waited.

"I never thought I'd end up marrying a crazy guy and fearing for my life and my kids' lives. I came from a nice family, Tori. Both my parents worked hard so we could live in a classy neighborhood. I was a sophomore in high school and kind of a nerd. You know the type: glasses, braces, arms and legs too long for my body. I never felt like I belonged in any of the groups in school. When I bumped into Vonzell at Sheetz one day after school, everything changed. He made me feel pretty and smart. Pretty soon we was making out at my house after school while my mom was at work, and the next thing I knew I was pregnant.

"Mom didn't want me to marry him because I was still in high school and he was fifteen years older, but I thought I knew better. Besides, with a baby on the way and me being so young I didn't know what else to do. Vonzell didn't want to at first, but when I found out I was going to have twins, my dad went after him and made him 'do the right thing.' At least that's what Dad called us getting married.

"It wasn't too bad at first. I had to quit school because of being so big, and it was fun having a place of my own and a husband coming home at night. But after the twins were born, he stopped coming home most nights and I was alone with the babies and all of a sudden it wasn't so much fun.

"The boys were only a few months old when I got pregnant again. That's when he started beating me up, blaming me for the pregnancy. I had our little girl, and I thought everything would be okay because he really loved her. The boys he didn't care so much about, especially when they started walking and getting into everything. And I was too tired to clean up much, so when he did come home he'd yell at me and call me a pig." She paused to wipe her nose with a tissue.

"Sorry," she said. "I thought I was done with crying. Anyway, I got pregnant again and had another boy. So now I was seventeen and had four kids. I found out Vonzell was using and dealing."

She was not as old as she looked. I realized she was probably younger than me. "Dealing what?" I asked.

She allowed herself a smile, as though she couldn't believe my naiveté. "Crack. Heroin. Ecstasy. You name it. And I found out he had a record a mile long he hadn't bothered to mention during while we'uns was dating. One night, we had an argument about drugs, and Vonzell hit me and I fell down the stairs. I didn't even know I was pregnant that time, till I woke up in the hospital and the doctor told me I'd lost the baby.

"After that, Vonzell went real crazy. He decided the reason I'd lost the baby was because God was punishing us for allowing abortions to happen. He said we had to have another baby right away to make up for the one who died. He called it 'atonement.' I didn't want to, but he forced me. He wouldn't let me take any of the kids out of the house. Said the devil was out there. Hid all our shoes every time he went out. By the time my fifth kid was born, he'd been gone for a month, and I was glad.

"When I heard about the bombing at the first clinic, it never occurred to me that Vonzell done it. He came home about that time and swore he'd finished with the drugs. One night, I woke up and found him gone. That was the night of the clinic bombing in Harrisburg, where some people was killed. When he came home early in the morning, he was high from cocaine.

"The next day he went out drinking with some buddies, and I went through his stuff looking for the dope. I was going to throw it out and take whatever he dished out. Down in the basement, I found the explosives and bomb parts. I didn't waste no time calling the feds 'cause I was furious mad at him, keeping things like that in a house where small children lived.

"They searched his cabin up in the mountains, too, and found a diary where he'd written all about the bombings. He'd even done a couple I hadn't heard of.

"I didn't even go to his trial. I never wanted to see him again, and I haven't. He's written me threats from prison, saying exactly what he's going to do to me when he gets out. First he's going to torture the kids in front of me, and after they're dead he'll kill me. I don't care none about me, but I'm not going to let him get the kids."

"Wasn't he in a county jail somewhere waiting to be sentenced when he escaped?"

She nodded. "After he finished his term at Graterford, he was rearrested on other charges. That's why he was in Kentucky."

I'd stopped writing in my notebook before she was half finished. What a horrible life the poor woman had. "Do you have a weapon?" I asked. "To protect yourself in case he gets in?"

"I got a shotgun under my bed. He shows his head in here, I'll blow him through the wall."

When Jenny walked me to the door and opened it, I was surprised to find a beautiful, sunny day outside. Inside, I'd been overwhelmed by the darkness. The green van pulled away as I stood blinking on the porch.

"Where do you think your bodyguard's going?" I asked Jenny, wondering why the feds would leave the house unwatched.

She looked at me wide-eyed. "The federal agent is in the black truck over there."

For the first time, I noticed a black pickup with a man sitting in the cab reading a newspaper.

I said good-bye to Jenny, climbed into the truck, and started the engine, and suddenly a question popped into my head. If the man in the black pickup was the federal agent, who had been in the green van?

SEVEN

I HAD CHOICES. I could go back to the office and write up what I'd learned about Vonzell Varner. Or I could visit one of the local businesses on my list, interview the owner, then go back to the office.

However, I knew I was only about six blocks away from the Zaleski House and it was calling to me. The truck turned in that direction as if it had a will of its own.

"Hi there, Tori. Good to see you. Come on in. I was just getting ready to have an iced coffee in the garden. Now, I'll have company," Mrs. Bonebrake said. She held the door open for me, and I had the feeling that my visit was not a total surprise.

She led me through the house, which was dim but cool despite the heat outside and no running air conditioner. In the kitchen, she poured coffee into a glass, added a large dollop of real cream and two teaspoons of turbinado sugar, then said, "This is how I drink mine. I should have asked first. Is this okay with you?"

I stopped salivating long enough to nod and accept the glass.

At the bottom of the garden, three Adirondack chairs faced the creek, a picture-postcard setting. At Mrs. Bonebrake's invitation, I sat on one and immediately sank down so far I thought I'd never get up again. My chin practically rested on my knees.

Once I was down, she asked, "What can I do for you, Tori? I thought we covered everything about the house the first time you were here."

I couldn't stop myself from blurting out, "I want to buy your house, Mrs. Bonebrake."

We stared at each other for a long moment, me in shock, her with a growing smile on her face.

"How marvelous. I would feel so good about it going to someone who would love it as much as I do. Hold on a minute." With that, she struggled out of the chair and went inside the house.

What have I done, I thought, over and over. But the sight of the iris in full bloom, the little dock at the bottom of the garden with its upside-down canoe, the buzz of the bees, all calmed me into thinking I'd made the right move.

"She'll be right over," Mrs. Bonebrake said, when she returned carrying a pitcher full of creamy coffee and an empty glass.

"Who will be right over?" I asked, as she refilled both our glasses.

"The real estate agent. She just lives down the street. In fact, here she is now."

I turned, as best I could in the deep chair, and saw a woman coming through the gate in the picket fence. She closed it carefully, then waved. "Sorry to take so long," she called.

I glanced at my Timex. It couldn't have been ten minutes since I'd said those fatal words. What did she consider quick?

Although she teetered down the garden path on three-inch heels, not one blond hair of her upswept 'do moved. She seemed to be balancing herself by dangling an enormous purse from one hand and a huge brown briefcase from the other. When she reached us, she put her purse on the table and extended her hand. "Howdjado. I'm Janielle Simpson. With Simpson and Simpson Real Estate."

"Howdjado, yourself," I responded. She was perfectly made-up and dressed in a blush-pink suit. I wondered if she sat all day like that, waiting for a call. "I don't think we've ever met, have we?"

She shook her head, and all but disappeared into another Adirondack chair.

"Your name is familiar," I said. "Wait a minute. Aren't you the artist who's doing the cover for the house tour booklet?"

"Why yes, I am. And you're the writer who's supposed to be doing the write-ups, aren't you? Are you nearly done? I have to get the book to the printer soon."

"One more house to go," I said. I didn't mention that the church still needed to be written about also.

"Good. You can give everything to me on Friday. Before the pre-tour."

"What pre-tour?" I asked, feeling very much like an insecure high school girl looking in at a meeting of popular cheerleaders. Why didn't I know what everybody else took for granted?

"I'm sure Alice-Ann told you we meet at the church, go over last-minute details, then we get on the trolley and tour all the houses. It's the only way the people who are working the day of the tour can see them."

Alice-Ann had not mentioned it, I was sure of that, but just like the insecure high school girl I was at heart, I didn't want to admit I didn't know something, so I said, "Oh, yes. The pre-tour," as if I knew what the heck I was talking about.

Abruptly changing the subject, Janielle said to Mrs. Bonebrake, "There was a green van I've never seen before parked in front of your house when I came in. Do you have company?"

"A green van?" I'd seen a green van only an hour or so before, parked on Jenny Varner's street. At that time, I'd thought it might be her husband spying on her. Now, I wonder if he was watching me, curious as to why I'd been visiting his wife. I hoisted myself out of the chair, said I'd be back in a minute, and ran up the hill to the garden gate. If there had been a green van there, it was gone now.

"Odd," I said, as I dropped back into the chair.

"Indeed it is," Janielle said. "This is the kind of neighborhood where everybody watches out for each other. You'll love living here, Tori." And thus she deftly brought the subject around again to real estate. "Now, the first thing you'll need to do is apply for a loan."

"I've already been almost pre-approved," I said. "J.B. Morgan, at the bank, said there should be no problem."

"Good," she said. "But I'll still put a contingency clause in the contract."

"What is that?"

"It's an escape clause for you. If you can't get a loan approved in the set amount of time, you are let out of the contract. Except for your earnest money, of course."

"I hadn't really thought about a deposit."

"Ha, ha, ha." It was not a laugh of amusement. It was the kind of laugh kids use when they know a peer is lying to them.

"Since you're known to the seller, I'll take a minimum deposit of five hundred dollars. A check will be fine."

I found myself writing a check for every last cent in my bank account and thinking, It's a good thing Friday is payday.

Janielle tucked the check into her briefcase as she pulled a cell phone from it. "I'll call the bank and start the loan process." She pushed one button, waited a second, then said, "J.B., please. This is Janielle." After another second, she handed me the phone.

His booming voice was effusively cheerful as he asked, "Did she accept the lower offer?"

"Oops." I'd been so excited with the prospect of being a home-owner, I hadn't thought to offer less than the asking price.

"That's all right," he said soothingly. "It's still a good price. Put Janielle back on, please. And congratulations, Toby."

By that time, Janielle had reopened the briefcase and extracted a sheaf of papers a good six inches thick. She thumbed through them, marked spots with an *X*, then said to me, "After you read through these, you can sign each page where I've put an *X*."

I leafed through them, pretending to read, but the legal jargon blurred before my eyes. I took the pen she handed me and signed in at least two dozen places.

"Keep the pen," she said, as I handed everything back to her. I put the five-hundred-dollar pen in my purse and watched anxiously as she checked my signatures.

"I'll get the paperwork started immediately," Janielle said, rising from the chair with a move that was almost graceful.

"I thought what we just did was the paperwork," I commented.

"Ha, ha, ha. This is just the beginning. I'll get back to you in a week or two. In the meantime, you can arrange for the termite inspection. Oh, and don't forget I'll need the house tour descriptions on Friday. See you then, Tori."

I spent the next day and a half busily trying to make up for everything I hadn't done the day before for the *Chronicle*. When I dropped by the office before noon on Friday with my articles neatly typed, P.J. uttered a little grunt of astonishment.

"Pretty good," she admitted after reading my report on the escaped convict. "That poor woman must be terrified of what he'll do to her if he comes home."

"The feds are outside her house, and she's got a shotgun if he gets in. She's sent the kids away. Won't tell me where they are."

"Keep your eye on it," she said. "We could always put out a special edition if he shows up."

She looked at my business report. "The Yummy in the Tummy Bakery? I've never heard of it."

"It's new, but they've got big plans for making potato rolls. I thought people might enjoy reading about it. And I got several good pictures. See, here's the outside of the plant, and here's another of the assembly line."

"I guess it's all right, but there *are* more exciting businesses around. And a lot of them are advertisers."

"I've already called a few and made appointments to visit them."

"Where's the landfill article?"

"I didn't have time…"

"Oh, Tori," she sighed, making me think of the many times I'd disappointed my mother.

"Don't worry, P.J., I've written something about Bulky Trash Pickup and another article about scaring away the crows on the square, plus a research article on West Nile Virus. You'll have enough news to plug any holes."

"You won't forget to cover the Hissong wedding Sunday evening? The bride's mother calls every five minutes to remind me."

"I'll be there. Where did you say it was being held? Just joking."

I made my escape before she thought of anything else for me to do. I made a quick stop at the drugstore, known more for being the local big-shot hangout than for having edible food. Several heads turned as I entered the dim room, made even murkier by the layer of cigarette smoke hanging low over the booths. I'd been in Lickin Creek long enough to recognize the Good Old Boys at the counter. J.B. Morgan from the bank, Judge Fetterhoff, Marvin Bumbaugh of the borough council, my dentist, and several attorneys who appeared to have been stamped from the same mold as Steve, the man who, in another lifetime, had been my fiancé. Other movers and shakers filled about half the booths. Almost everybody looked up to see if anyone of importance had come in. When they recognized me they turned back to their conversations and lunches without bothering to greet me. Only Wilbur Eshelman, the drugstore owner, stopped what he was doing and nodded pleasantly. I smiled back at him, grateful that he was always nice to me, and found an empty booth, slid across the cracked yellow plastic, and waited for the waitress in a pink nylon uniform to take my order.

After a quick chicken salad sandwich and a Coke with cherry syrup in it, I glanced at my Timex and realized it was a little later than I thought it was, and there was somewhere I had to be.

EIGHT

A BUNDLE OF FILTHY RAGS in the alley next to the drugstore scared me half out of my wits when it stirred and then sat up. "Hey, Mizz Miracle," it said.

If the brick wall of the bank hadn't stopped me as I staggered backward, I probably would have fallen to the pavement.

"Don't be scared. It's jest me, Bob."

I recognized the wide face, low brow, receding chin, glassy eyes, and fanglike teeth, at about the same time his body odor reached me. It was bad enough to choke a skunk. Big Bad Bob was the town's best-known homeless man. As long as Big Bad Bob caused no one grief, he was left alone to sleep where he wanted, eat whatever garbage he could scrounge, and drink whenever he could panhandle enough money to buy a bottle of cheap booze from the state store. When last I saw him, at Christmas, he'd been sleeping under a bridge near the old cold-storage building. I hadn't known he'd moved downtown. I wonder if I should give him some money for food, and after a moment's thought offered him a dollar.

"No thanks," he said. "You probably need it more than I do."

Leaving Bob in the dim alley, I stepped out onto sunny Main Street. Fine thing, I thought, when a homeless man worried more about me than himself. There had to be a lesson there. Somewhere.

I strolled down the street to Trinity Evangelical Church where the house tour committee members were to gather. I was a little early after all, but I could use the extra time to look the place over and write my description of it for the tour booklet.

The bulletin board outside the church announced that orders were being taken for sugar cakes, which could be picked up the day of the house tour. I wondered what sugar cakes were. Wasn't there an old song about someone baking a sugar cake for her husband to take to work? "Tea For Two," that was it. I hummed it as I pushed on the Gothic-style oak door.

The door didn't move. I tried it again and realized it was locked. I knew there was a door from the alley on the side of the church, close to the pastor's office, so I decided to try it.

The modern aluminum-and-glass door swung open easily when I pulled on the handle, but after I stepped into the gloomy waiting room a gust of wind slammed it shut behind me, with a loud crash that echoed through the church. When all was finally quiet, I was struck by the silence. Surely, someone should have looked in to see what had caused the noise.

"Yoo-hoo," I called out, feeling foolish. "Anybody here?" This was a silly question. Through the open door to Pastor Flack's office, I could see both his desk and his secretary's, but no signs of people anywhere.

When there was no answer, I tiptoed into the cool medieval-style sanctuary. Brilliant rays of colored light streamed through the Tiffany windows to illuminate the stone floor, but even they failed to warm the room. From high above came the cooing of mourning doves, who appeared to have taken up residence among the beams that supported the arched ceiling.

As I walked down the aisle, I remembered that this was the church that Garnet's family attended. If things had worked out for the two of us, this might have been the very aisle I walked down in my bridal gown. I tried to picture Garnet waiting for me at the altar, but my imagination wasn't working very well. When I reached the altar, I turned around to face the empty pews, just as Garnet and I would have faced a congregation of his friends and relatives. But of course there was no one there.

A puff of white smoke drifted past me. Incense! I closed my eyes, inhaled deeply, and coughed. Something was burning, and it wasn't incense. I looked desperately around for a fire extinguisher, as if I expected to find one on the altar, right next to the brass cross and the silk flowers. I knew I'd better find out what was burning, although I figured that perhaps someone had simply forgotten to remove a sugar cake from the oven.

I passed through an arched door nearly hidden behind the organ and entered a narrow hallway where dozens of blue choir robes hung from brass hooks along the walls. There was a single door at the end, and when I opened it I discovered a flight of stairs leading down to the basement. I'd been here before, at Christmas time, and knew that below the sanctuary were the nursery, meeting rooms, an auditorium, and a kitchen. My natural instinct was to run from the building, find a phone, and call the fire department, but even more immediate was the thought that someone could be trapped downstairs. I ran down the steps, calling loudly, "Anybody here? I smell smoke. Yoo-hoo."

Black smoke swirled near the ceiling, its acrid smell causing me to cover my nose with the hem of my T-shirt. Although I continued to call out, nobody answered. I appeared to be alone in the huge building.

At the end of the hall, a red glow shone through the open auditorium doorway. I knew I should turn back, but still I was afraid that someone could be in there, overcome by the smoke, needing immediate assistance. And it was up to me, as the only person around.

As I ran down the hall toward the auditorium, I was relieved to see that the light came not from fire, but from the overhead fluorescents, glowing dull orange-red through the clouds of black smoke lapping at the ceiling tiles.

The smoke was streaming into the room from the kitchen area behind the counter.

"Anybody in here?" I yelled as I rushed forward. Again, there was no answer.

A fire extinguisher was prominently displayed on the wall next to the door, and I grabbed it, pulled the pin, and sprayed a foam pathway in front of me as I charged into the kitchen.

The source of the smoke was obvious. Someone had been fixing lunch, placed a pot on one of the stove's six burners, then walked away leaving it unattended. After the contents burned away, the aluminum pot had melted.

I sprayed the area thoroughly then turned off the burner, opened a couple of the windows set high in the wall, and switched on the ceiling fan. Within seconds, the air began to clear.

"What the hell…? What have you done, girl?" Reverend Flack stood in the doorway, unpreacherly mouth agape, glaring at me as if I had done something awful instead of saving his church from a fiery doom.

"I smelled smoke upstairs and traced it down to this." I pointed to the stove with the metallic ruins of the melted pot cooling on the front burner.

"Good grief. Did you put it out, Tori?"

I nodded.

"Then I apologize for yelling at you. It was just such a shock walking in here and finding this mess…and you… Well, you know your reputation for burning things down."

"The historical society fire was an accident, and I wasn't even there when the courthouse burned. You know that was arson, and who caused it."

"Sorry," he murmured, not looking at all contrite. He walked past me and looked down at the stove. "Ruined! I'd better call the insurance company."

"Where is everybody?" I asked. "The church was deserted when I came in."

"It's my secretary's birthday, so we walked down to the ice-cream shop to have a celebration lunch together. We're the only people here on Fridays."

"You didn't go out and leave the church unlocked, did you?"

"Of course not. How did you manage to get in?"

"Through the side door. You must have forgotten to lock it when you left."

"Absolutely not, Tori. We have too many valuables in here for me to leave the church unattended. I can't imagine why it was open."

"What if someone needed to come in?" I asked. After all this was Lickin Creek where nobody locked their doors for fear of seeming unfriendly.

"We only take an hour for lunch. If it's important they could wait. Thank you so much for what you did, Tori," Reverend Flack added. "Your quick actions just might have saved Lickin Creek's most historic church. God put you here at just the right time." Now that he had regained his composure, he was definitely sounding like a proper minister should. "And speaking of God putting you here, just why *are* you here?"

"I thought you or the secretary would be available to show me around so I can get information to put in the house tour book about the church."

"Of course. I'd nearly forgotten about that. If you come by my office I'll give you a brochure that tells all about the history of Trinity Evangelical. Please don't forget to mention the genuine Tiffany windows."

He raised one hand as if to bless me, but opted instead to merely wiggle his fingers at me. "Must get back upstairs. God's work is never done." He left the room, and I heard his footsteps clicking down the tiled hallway.

I started to follow him, and that's when I noticed the empty soup can on the counter, along with a jar of peanut butter, an unwrapped loaf of bread, and half a sandwich with a large bite taken from it. After touching the bread and finding it fresh, I trotted down the hall calling Reverend Flack's name.

He turned with a peeved frown on his face, but replaced it with a serene smile in an instant. "Yes?"

"Someone was in the kitchen. Fixing lunch. And it couldn't have been too long ago."

"That's impossible, Tori. I've already told you that only my secretary and I were in the building, and we went out to eat. Maybe someone had lunch here yesterday and forgot to clean up."

I dragged him back to the kitchen. "See," I said, pointing to the evidence. "The bread is fresh, so it couldn't have been out long. Someone was here. Oh my God…"

"What is it?" the minister asked.

"The escaped convict…it could have been him."

"He," Reverend Flack corrected.

"He, him, whoever. I'll bet he saw you leaving, sneaked into the church to get some food, heard me upstairs, and ducked out, leaving the pot of soup on the stove."

"Oh dear. I think I should call the police," he said, heading toward the doorway.

"Don't leave me alone down here," I said. "What if he didn't leave? What if he's hiding?"

"Come on, then," the minister said. "Let's get out of here."

Keeping one wary eye on the door in case the escaped convict showed up, I read the church brochure while we waited for the girl at Hoopengartner's Garage to locate Luscious. Reverend Flack spent most of the time rocking in his chair and saying things like *"tsk, tsk,"* and "Who'd ever think this could happen in a town like Lickin Creek," and "My, oh my." The church secretary, who wore a flowered cotton dress and had tight gray curls all over her head, feigned working on Sunday's bulletin, but from the sniffs coming from her I assumed she wasn't getting much accomplished.

Soon the office was filled with women, all members of the house tour committee, and all full of questions about the smoky smell that had greeted them.

Into the confusion stepped Luscious and his freckle-faced assistant, Afton Finkey. I managed to hide my surprise at see-

ing that Afton was still on the Lickin Creek police force,
which was a way-station for grads of the nearby junior college's criminal justice program who put in a little time here
to get some police experience under their belts before they
moved on to "real" jobs elsewhere. What was surprising about
Afton Finkey was that he was actually quite competent and a
great help to Luscious, who tended to react to situations rather
than act on them.

After hearing from Reverend Flack what had happened,
Luscious asked the obvious question. "Wasn't the door
locked?"

The minister sighed heavily. "Of course it was. And Mrs.
Liverberger can vouch for that. I locked it with my key, and
as usual, she tugged on it to make sure it was locked."

The church secretary nodded. "I only wanted to make sure."

"Does anybody besides you have a key to the church?"
Afton asked.

Reverend Flack's eyes opened wide with surprise that
someone would ask such an obvious question. "Of course,
Mrs. Liverberger, could you get the key list from the file,
please?"

Mrs. Liverberger wiped her eyes, blew her nose, and
opened the file cabinet behind her desk. "Here you are," she
said, laying several sheets of paper on the minister's desk.

"Thank you so much, Mrs. Liverberger." He slowly ran his
finger down the list. "Funny, I thought he died. Didn't the
Heindmans move ten years ago? And I see you have a key,
Luscious. Why?"

Luscious flushed. "You gave it to me when I was elected
to the building committee."

"Of course. How silly of me to forget." He turned to Afton
with a smile. "There are fifty-six keys out, officially. In reality, there are probably a lot more than that."

Luscious nodded in agreement. "I made ten copies of mine
alone."

"You did what?" I asked.

"I had permission. I gave them to the members of my Alcoholics Anonymous group, so whoever gets here first can open up and make the coffee."

"And there are many other groups who meet here at the church, who have been given permission to copy their keys, too," Reverend Flack said. "The Boy Scouts, the Girl Scouts, Overeaters Anonymous, the divorce support group, the women's auxiliary, the—"

"So there could be hundreds of keys out there," I interrupted, flabbergasted. "Why not just leave the doors open?"

Nobody seemed to think that was a question worth answering.

"Do you want me to show Luscious and Afton the kitchen?" I asked the minister, who was totally surrounded by the house tour women.

He threw a grateful smile at me. "Please."

I took the two policemen downstairs, showed them the kitchen, and told them of my escaped convict theory.

"You could be right," Luscious said, smoothing his strands of blond hair over his balding forehead. "Afton, look around and see if there's any sign of him."

The assistant policeman scurried out of the kitchen, and Luscious turned to look at the stove. "Damn shame," he said. "It was practically brand new."

"Is that important?"

He turned wounded eyes toward me. "Of course it is, Tori. I'm on the building committee here, so I know how much that stove cost, and it's only a few months old."

"Boss," Afton called excitedly. "Come here. I think I've found something."

He stood on the stage, a piece of cloth dangling from his hand.

"What did you find?" Luscious asked.

"In the Boy Scout locker, behind the stage. Someone's been living in there, by the looks of things. There's a bed roll spread out, some dirty clothes in the corner, and a big mound of McDonald's hamburger wrappers."

By the time he finished telling us what he'd discovered, we were in the small room the Boy Scouts used for equipment storage.

"Oh, no," Luscious moaned. "The flag's on the floor. It'll have to be burned."

Afton and I sighed in unison. "There's more important things going on here than the desecration of the flag," I pointed out.

"I know that," Luscious sniffed. "Wonder what I should do?" This he mumbled, nearly under his breath, as though he were questioning himself.

But still I answered. "Call the FBI," I snapped. "Maybe they can identify the clothing. See if it belongs to Vonzell Varner and not a junkie looking for a place to hole up."

If I didn't know better, I would have said Luscious frowned at me. "There's no junkies around here, Tori. This is Lickin Creek."

The look of incredulity on Afton's face was priceless, and I had to turn my back on him to keep from laughing.

"But I'll call them right away," Luscious said, oblivious to our reactions to his naiveté. It was one thing to be in love with your hometown, another to be totally oblivious as to what was going on in it.

"Since you seem to have everything under control, I'd better be off," I said. "The house tour bus will be leaving soon."

"Thanks for your help, Tori," Luscious said. He then added, rather coolly I thought, "I'll be in touch if there's anything you should know."

My eyes smarted, and I left the room quickly before he could see how hurt I was. What did he mean he'd be in touch if there was anything I should know? I, who had been at his side countless times since Garnet left him in charge. I, who had selflessly given my assistance, even when I wasn't asked. I was nearly at the stairs, when I heard Afton calling my name.

"Yes?" I paused, but didn't turn around.

Afton's hand touched my shoulder gently. "He didn't mean anything."

My cheeks were so hot I knew they were flaming. "He was rude to me. What did he mean by that crack about getting in touch if there's anything I should know? I've helped him out over and over since Garnet left. Why did he suddenly turn on me? What did I do wrong?"

"Nothing. Absolutely nothing. Except I think Luscious has finally come to realize you're playing on the other team now."

"What other team? What are you talking about?"

"You're a newspaper reporter. Everything he says or does around you goes immediately into the *Chronicle*. He's beginning to resent that. That's why he told you there are no junkies in Lickin Creek. If he admitted he knew the borough has a problem with the homeless and with addicts, you'd print it, and he'd be on the hot spot at the next council meeting."

"I'd never disclose anything told to me in confidence," I said with self-righteous indignation.

Afton's only reply was a small smile.

"Well, hardly anything," I said, lamely.

"Don't let him upset you, Tori. He still needs you. But he's growing in the job and has to find his own way."

"You're quite the philosopher," I said. I sounded grumpy but I knew he was right.

"I hear the trolley bell," Afton said. "Don't miss your ride."

NINE

SEVERAL YEARS BEFORE I'd ever heard of Lickin Creek, the borough council had purchased a used trolley from a town in Texas. It was really a bus on wheels, designed to look like the old-fashioned trolleys that used to run through the borough on tracks that are still set into the streets. Supposedly, it was so charming and reminiscent of old Lickin Creek that the council thought it would be a draw for the tourists who always seemed to skip Lickin Creek in favor of Gettysburg. And it was also going to provide public transportation where there had been none. Unfortunately, nobody in the borough seemed to have any idea of where it was supposed to stop or where it was going, and the riders never appeared. Therefore, a few months ago the council voted to end the borough's attempt at providing transportation and rent the trolley out for civic groups and wedding parties. Today was the first time I'd actually seen it being used.

Alice-Ann stood before the green-and-yellow trolley, waiting for me. Through the open windows, I could see the house tour committee already on board.

"I was afraid you weren't coming," she said. "I've done everything I could to keep the bus, I mean trolley, from leaving."

I smiled. "Even throwing your body in front of it?"

"Of course. Anything for you. Let's get on."

The trolley lurched forward before we'd taken our seats.

"Must be in a hurry," I remarked.

Alice-Ann slid in and patted the bench next to her. "We're twenty minutes late getting started."

"Sorry," I said, trying to ignore the aggravated stares of the women around me. "It wasn't my fault."

"Never mind, Tori. Have you got the information on the church and the last house written up yet?"

"They'll be finished before the afternoon is up." A small groan escaped from Alice-Ann's mouth, but her lips never ceased to smile. I whipped out my notebook and began to copy from the church brochure I'd picked up, adding what I'd learned from Reverend Flack.

Trinity Evangelical is one of the oldest churches in Lickin Creek, having originally been founded in 1785. The present building on the square was erected in 1869. The beautiful stained glass windows in the sanctuary came from the famed Tiffany Studios of New York. Behind the church is a cemetery where the ancestors of many of Lickin Creek's most noted citizens are buried. Also to be found in the cemetery are the graves of several members of the Delaware Indian Tribe. Trinity Evangelical is well known throughout the area for its annual Christmas pageant, which was written yearly by Oretta Clopper until her untimely death last year. The spire is closed to the public, but if you could climb it you would see a panoramic view of Lickin Creek, very similar to that which was sketched in 1877 by W.W. Denslow, best known as the illustrator of that classic book The Wonderful Wizard of Oz. *A print of that panorama is on display in Reverend Flack's office.*

House tour participants are invited to tour the church and use the restrooms in the basement. Sugar cakes will be available for purchase, the proceeds to benefit the church building fund.

BY THE TIME I'd finished scribbling my description of Trinity Church, the trolley had stopped before the one house I hadn't yet visited.

"Are you coming?" Alice-Ann asked me.

"Yes, Just one second more, please. I'll bet you didn't know Lickin Creek has a *Wizard of Oz* tie-in."

"You'd probably find a *Wizard of Oz* tie-in if you were in the middle of the Sahara Desert, Tori."

"Funny you should pick the Sahara Desert, Alice-Ann. L. Frank Baum and his wife Maud visited Egypt in 1906. Maud wrote a book about the journey called *In Other Lands Than Ours.* And the underwater city of *Glinda of Oz* resembled the ruins of Philae, which were underwater when they were there…"

Alice-Ann's giggle stopped me. "I should have expected something like that from you."

I turned my attention back to what I'd written and compared it to what was in the church brochure, then handed the paper to Alice-Ann.

She glanced at it. "Couldn't you type it?"

"Not on the trolley. If you want to wait a few more days, I can type it neatly for you. However, if you want to meet your deadline…"

"That's all right." Alice-Ann folded the paper and put it in her purse. "Is that all of them, then?"

"Actually, I haven't quite finished the description of this house." I waved one arm in the direction of the mansion where the committee members had gathered on the porch. "Pretty elegant place. What is it, anyway?"

"Don't fib, Tori. You haven't even started to write it, have you?"

"I confess. But I'll have it written by the time we reach the next house. Come on. Let's go in. I don't want to waste any time."

Half an hour later, back on the bus, I wrote:

The Benjamin Koon Funeral Home is located in one of Lickin Creek's oldest and grandest houses. Originally the residence of Benjamin Koon's great-grandfather, Dr. William Koon, and built in 1807, it is a fine example of Flemish Bond brick style.

(I had no idea what that meant, but it sounded important when Benjamin Koon said it, so I decided I'd better stick it in.)

John Brown, the abolitionist, is reputed to have visited the home in 1859 shortly before his ill-fated attack on Harper's Ferry. General Robert E. Lee's forces commandeered the house to use as a billet on their way to Gettysburg. It is ironic that at that same time, the house was also serving as a stop on the Underground Railroad.

During the terrible influenza epidemic of 1918, the house was used as a hospital. In 1937, it was sold to three nurses who turned it into a maternity home. That closed after 15 years, when the Lickin Creek Medical Clinic was built, at which time the house came back into the Koon family and was turned into Lickin Creek's most elegant funeral home.

While the front parlors have been turned into visitation rooms where services are held, the Koon family resides in the rest of the spacious home, which you will tour today. Please note the antique furniture, all original to the house, as well as Mrs. Koon's delightful collection of ceramic owls. The stained glass windows are from the Tiffany Studios of New York.

The mortuary is located in the basement and will not be shown today, but Mr. Koon states that special tours for small groups can be arranged at any time. It is extremely popular with middle school students, who visit every year.

If a viewing should be going on during the house tour, please speak softly as you pass by out of respect for the deceased and relatives.

"I'M DONE," I announced cheerfully, ripping the pages from my notebook as the trolley neared Morgan Manor.

Alice-Ann looked at what I'd written and frowned. "Are you sure they're real Tiffany windows?"

"I'm no stained glass expert, my friend. All I know is what Benjamin Koon told me. And he said they were Tiffany."

"All right," she said through pursed lips. "We'll have to go with it, then. But doesn't it seem there are an awful lot of windows reputed to be made by Tiffany Studios in one small town?"

"Maybe Tiffany had a really good salesman in the area."

I'd had to skip touring the Bride's House with the group to get the article finished, but that didn't bother me since I'd seen the house only last Tuesday. When the committee had come back to the trolley, I heard a lot of conflicting comments. There were those who thought turning the house into a bed-and-breakfast was a wonderful idea. Then there was the very vocal majority, which expressed horror at defacing historic property for commercial use. These were the women who did not appreciate the rooms being chopped up into oddly shaped spaces in order to put a toilet and sink into each guest room.

The arguing had gone on until the trolley stopped in front of Morgan Manor. The women poured from the trolley, chatting excitedly in anticipation of finally getting to see the famous Morgan Manor for the first time. Alice-Ann put a hand on my arm, holding me back until the trolley was empty.

"I'm going to check the springhouse," she said, "and make sure nothing's been disturbed. Do you want to come?"

I recalled that J.B. had mentioned snakes in conjunction with the springhouse. If there's one thing I'm afraid of it's snakes. Bats, too. And heights. But snakes are number one. "Good idea. But I'll wait for you in the house."

I caught up with the group in the front hall. Apparently J.B. had heeded Alice-Ann's suggestions about the need for repairs and cleaning, because many changes had been made. The house looked good enough to move into. And no doubt that was what he had in mind, because a silver tray sat on a table next to the staircase, and on it was a stack of small white cards, all of which said, "If you are interested in purchasing this part of Lickin Creek's history, contact J.B. Morgan at the Lickin Creek National Bank." Below that were six numbers in small, discreet print. Not enough digits for a phone number. Then I realized that was the price. I looked around the hall in awe. I had no idea that there was a house in Lickin Creek worth half a million dollars. I knew that in New York City it would barely pay for a small apartment. But who in this small farming community would have that kind of money to spend on a house?

Mrs. Houdeyshell, the woman who had been designated as the hostess here on the day of the tour, suggested we begin upstairs. She forgot to warn us of the slope, and several women teetered a little near the top of the stairs and had to grab onto the railing.

Amidst a chorus of *"oohs"* and *"aahs,"* I peeked into each bedroom. The windows had been washed until they glistened, the curtains and bedspreads were no longer dusty, and the air smelled of lemon-scented furniture polish.

On the closed door at the end of the hall, a brass plaque had been attached since my visit there last Monday. "Rodney Mellott's Room," read Mrs. Houdeyshell, "As you know, the runaway bridegroom lived here with Maribell Morgan for several years."

The women pressed forward into the room and expressed admiration for the way the sixties had been so carefully preserved. The shag rug was clean, the orange-and-turquoise pillows had been plumped up, and even the beanbags almost looked inviting. The unpainted bookcase held several neat stacks of LP records and piles of yellowed sheet music, but the pornographic books had vanished.

No one was paying any attention to me, so I pulled open the closet door to see if someone had taken care of the sticking door. It would be terrible to lose a tourist in there on the big day, but thankfully the door swung open with no trouble at all. The interior had been freshly painted with bright white paint, and the dated clothes were gone, as was the box of unmatched sneakers.

"Tori. *Psst.* Tori." I swung around to see Alice-Ann in the doorway, her face as white as the closet wall.

"What's the matter?"

"Shhh." She waited until the room was empty. Then she whispered, "It's gone."

"What's gone?"

"The…you know…it's gone. There's a big hole in the wall where we put all the stones back, and there's nothing inside."

"That's impossible."

"Oh no, it isn't. I know what I saw."

"We've got to report this," I said.

"No!"

Mrs. Houdeyshell poked her head in the door. "Is anything wrong?"

Alice-Ann bared her teeth in a semblance of a smile. "Certainly not. Do you want us to turn out the lights when we leave?"

Mrs. Houdeyshell looked doubtfully at us, while we tried to look like a couple of innocents. "I'll wait here and outen them after you'uns leave."

"The very idea," Alice-Ann sniffed on her way down the back stairs. "You'd think she didn't trust us."

"Imagine what she'd be like if she knew about the…you know." We were alone in the kitchen. Laughter drifted in from the dining room, an indication that the other women would soon be here.

Tears welled in Alice-Ann's eyes. "Please come back with me. Maybe I overlooked him." She lifted the key from the hook next to the back door.

"Is that where the key was kept?"

Alice-Ann nodded.

"We shouldn't have left it there after we found the…you know."

"But if I didn't put it back, somebody might have wondered where it was, and that would have attracted attention. And then somebody might have gone down there to see if everything was all right. And found the…"

"I see your point. But it seems to me there are an awful lot of keys floating around Lickin Creek." I was thinking of the hundreds of keys to Trinity Evangelical Church as well as the key or keys to the springhouse.

I followed Alice-Ann out of the house. After we looked over our shoulders to determine nobody had seen us leave, we dashed down to the stream, slipping and sliding on the mossy steps until we reached the shelter of the little limestone building.

"We're safe now," she said. "They can't see us down here."

I bent over and struggled to catch my breath. "I'm too out of shape for this," I puffed, while Alice-Ann unlocked the door.

"Come on," she urged. I stepped inside, and she slammed the door shut behind me.

The room looked exactly the same as it had when we'd first seen it. The chairs and music stands still waited for the ghostly orchestra, which hadn't yet appeared.

"Don't turn on the light," I warned. "Somebody might see it and come to investigate."

"I've got a flashlight with me. Come on," Alice-Ann insisted again as she disappeared through the dark hole in the floor. Her voice was shrill, on the verge of panic. "Ouch. Be careful of that overhead beam."

I realized Alice-Ann had bumped her head on the same beam that had slowed her down the first time we were here. I didn't want to follow her, but I also didn't like being alone in the strange room with only spiders for company, so I took a deep breath and descended the rickety staircase. My head easily cleared the beam by several inches, but I am nearly ten inches shorter than Alice-Ann.

Alice-Ann had switched on her flashlight, so I could see her rubbing her forehead.

I also could see that about half the rocks we'd carefully stacked up to hide the opening to the cave were strewn all over the ledge. "That's not a good sign," I said.

She threw an exasperated look at me and pointed the flashlight beam into the hole. "Tell me he's there, Tori. Please tell me he's still there."

I took the flashlight from her shaking hand, and ignoring all my basic survival instincts including my dread of snakes, scaled what was left of the wall and dropped into the void. The circle of light revealed nothing. Absolutely nothing.

"Sorry to tell you this, Alice-Ann, but there's nothing here."

Her groan of disappointment echoed off the limestone walls of the cave, but she bravely climbed in to stand beside me.

"Oh my God. What are we going to do?" she moaned. I watched as she dropped to her knees and began to dig in the dirt with her fingers.

"What are you doing?"

"Maybe there was a cave-in, and he got buried…"

I put my hands on her waist and pulled her to her feet. "He's gone," I told her. "Somebody moved the body."

"Who, Tori, who? We were the only ones who knew the body was here. What should we do?"

The look of panic on her face made me think she was going to pass out, and I felt bad that all I could offer was, "Call the police."

"No!" Her cry was pure agony. "We can't. We can't tell anyone. Not until after the tour. Don't you remember you promised to keep it a secret?"

"But that was before someone moved the body, Alice-Ann. That's a crime."

"How about concealing a murder? That's what we did. That's got to be just as bad as moving a body. Maybe even worse. Think of how bad we will look if we report a body is missing, Tori. We'd have to admit we knew it was here before. We'd probably go to jail."

I couldn't think of a retort. At the time I agreed to keep the discovery of the body a secret, I hadn't thought of what we'd done as a crime since the body had obviously been in the cave for such a long time, but murder was murder, and there was no statute of limitations.

"How did you plan to break the news," I asked, "without letting on that we knew for weeks it was here?"

"I planned to say we came here to clean up after the tour, and that's when we discovered it. Nobody would have to know how long ago we really found it."

"I don't know. I really think we ought to confess and take the consequences."

But Alice-Ann hadn't stopped talking. She was begging me to keep the secret a little longer. "Just till after the tour. Please, Tori. Then I'll do whatever you say. But think of all the precious cats that will have to die if we don't raise any money. There's Ben, and Tiger, and Casper, and Shadow. And the dear little dogs, Harry, Lacey, Sadie, and the twin husky puppies, and…"

"Stop. Please." I covered my ears. "I don't want to be responsible for what would happen to the animals."

Alice-Ann's worried frown had disappeared now that she knew she had me convinced. "Thanks, Tori."

"There's something we haven't talked about that we have to consider, though."

"What's that?"

"We have to think about who moved the body. Even though we did a fairly good job of replacing those stones, that wall didn't look the same as it did before we knocked it down. So someone who knew the body was in there must have noticed and had reason to fear its discovery."

Alice-Ann's hands flew to her mouth. "You mean the killer, don't you?"

I nodded. "And since everyone in town knew you and I were here looking the place over a few weeks ago, the killer would assume we were the ones who'd been in the cave. He could be coming after us right now, to keep us quiet."

As if to prove me right, from overhead came a creaking

sound. Alice-Ann grabbed my hand and pointed above us in alarm. "The door," she whispered.

"Shhh," I cautioned. I grabbed the flashlight from her dangling hand and switched it off.

We heard footsteps now, coming down the wooden staircase, drawing closer and closer to us.

We pressed our backs against the limestone wall. I prayed for it to open up and swallow us, but no such luck. I also prayed there would be no rattlesnakes nesting in crevices behind me.

A bright light shone through the opening, played on the back wall, then moved slowly across the ground to where we stood. Terror stopped my breath.

"There you are," Mrs. Houdeyshell said. "I thought I saw you two heading in this direction."

My breath whooshed out of me as my knees turned to jelly, a reaction to relief.

"What is this? A cave? Why are there rocks scattered everywhere?" She directed the flashlight to my face, nearly blinding me. "The springhouse isn't supposed to be open to the public." Her voice grew shriller and more and more irate as she threw questions at us. "Did the place look like this when you came down here? Is this your work, Tori Miracle? What have you done? How could you?"

Funny how a local person finding Alice-Ann and me in a cave with our backs against a wall and the ruins of the entrance around our feet would immediately put the blame on me. But it wasn't a surprise, since I was the outsider who had single-handedly destroyed such landmarks as the historical society and the courthouse, prevented the low-level nuclear waste dump from bringing prosperity to the valley, and murdered that beloved congressman Mack Macmillan by my irresponsible sponsorship of a Civil War reenactment.

Alice-Ann squeezed my hand reassuringly and spoke up. "It looked like this when we came down," she said truthfully.

"Maybe there was an earthquake," I offered.

"Come out of there right now. The ladies are on the trolley, waiting for you."

We climbed out and apologized, but she paid no attention to our excuses. "I'll have to send for someone to repair this," was all she said.

"I'll pay for it," Alice-Ann said.

"I'm sure you will."

The women on the trolley greeted us with outraged silence as we boarded. We were both covered with dirt, Alice-Ann's skirt was torn from climbing over the rocks, and most of her fingernails were broken. Guilt, both real and imagined, bowed my shoulders as I trudged to the back of the bus.

Mrs. Houdeyshell stood next to the driver, counting heads, and it suddenly occurred to me that despite her fuss over discovering us in the springhouse, despite all her angry questions about who was in the cave and demanding to know who had made the mess, she had never asked us why we were there. That struck me as exceedingly odd. If I came upon two women cowering in a cave in the basement of a springhouse, the first thing I'd ask is why. I suddenly realized that despite the simple cotton dress, the gray hair neatly pulled into a bun and covered with a white net bonnet, and the steel-rimmed glasses, she was a very strong woman, with the broad shoulders and muscular arms of an active farmer. The kind of woman who would have no trouble moving a body.

Then I remembered that what remained of Rodney Mellot really wasn't a body at all, but simply some bones held together by an old polyester tuxedo. Rodney probably didn't weigh more than a couple of pounds now, if that.

TEN

AFTER EVERYTHING that had happened today, I nearly forgot I had a date with Haley Haley, the knight in shining armor who'd defended my honor at the Waffle Shoppe. But Ethelind hadn't forgotten. Apparently she had my date marked on her kitchen calendar, which showed how rare it was for me to go out. She took one look at my bedraggled appearance and ordered me to hurry upstairs and get ready. "He should be here in an hour."

I wasn't particularly excited about the date, but since it had been more than a year since I'd gone out with anyone other than Garnet, I had to start somewhere. I decided to dress with care. It wouldn't hurt to make a good impression.

Ethelind had a fine collection of English lotions and potions that she'd told me I was welcome to use. I never had, but today I splashed a few drops of Pure English Lavender Oil into my bath. Afterwards I used her English Soothing Foot Balm Blended with Witch Hazel and Peppermint to scrub some of the dead skin off my feet and finished with an Oil of Roses Face and Body Cream that Ethelind claimed was responsible for her peaches-and-cream complexion.

As I pulled on pantyhose for the first time in months, I noticed that they were a wee bit tight. In fact, I could barely tug them up over my hips. It couldn't possibly be that I'd put on a few pounds from a steady diet of Pennsylvania Dutch cooking? Of course not. I was always careful to begin every meal with a salad. The pantyhose must have shrunk in the wash.

I wasn't quite sure what to wear, but finally decided on a

sleeveless navy blue linen shift with white trim at the neck. It had been my favorite summertime "dating" dress in the city. I put it on and studied myself in the mirror. Absolutely perfect, I thought. Its simple lines were sophisticated but certainly couldn't be considered too citified, even by Lickin Creek standards.

A pair of pretty white shoes with straps and two-inch heels nearly completed my ensemble. All I needed was a white purse. I was tired of being thought of as that "New York gal," when what I really wanted was to blend in. Matching shoes and handbag would help. I flung open one dresser drawer after another until I found one I'd bought on sale at Bloomingdale's in another lifetime.

Not bad, I thought, as I spun around in front of the pier mirror in my bedroom. Then I paused, mid-spin. Was that a protruding tummy I saw? It was, despite the control-top pantyhose, and I solemnly vowed to start a diet tomorrow.

"Nice," Ethelind grunted when I entered the kitchen. "Do you want to borrow a sweater? Your arms might get cold. And be careful in those shoes, you're liable to break your neck. I never wear anything but sensible shoes, myself. When I was in London, I walked all the way from Marble Arch to—"

Mercifully, the doorbell interrupted her.

"Good-bye," I said, grabbing my purse.

"Better leave me a number where you can be reached."

"I haven't any idea where we're going," I said gaily. Instead of being annoyed, I found it rather flattering that she cared enough to worry about me.

"Don't wait up," I warned. "There's no telling what time we'll be home."

"Ten o'clock," Ethelind said. "You'll be home by ten, ten-thirty at the latest. There's nothing to do in Lickin Creek past ten."

I could think of several things I hadn't done in a long while, but I simply smiled and left the kitchen.

By the time I'd trekked through the pantry, the dining

room, the library, the billiard room, the music room, and several parlors, and finally reached the entry hall, I was limping and wished I had worn the sensible shoes Ethelind had suggested. But it was too late to hobble back upstairs now. Through the glass panel on the left side of the front door, I could see my date waiting on the porch.

I squared my shoulders and flung open the door.

The welcoming smile on my face froze. Why was Haley wearing black leather motorcycle chaps and matching leather jacket? Certainly he didn't expect me to ride on a motorcycle. I looked over his shoulder to see if there was a motorcycle in the driveway, and what I saw made me wish there was.

"What is that?" I demanded.

He turned around to look as if he had no idea what I was talking about. That's when I saw that the back of his jacket had a cartoon-like painting on it of a man looking through bars and below it the caption JAILBIRDS FOR JESUS.

"Oh…that?" he said, as if he was seeing for the first time the gigantic eighteen-wheeled truck parked in the road. "That's my semi," he said. "Shall we go?"

He offered me his arm, which I was too dazed to reject. If I'd been in my right mind I would have twirled on one of my white heels and disappeared right back into the house. But I didn't.

As my father used to say, "If you had brains, Tori, you'd be dangerous."

It got worse. As we walked toward the semi, I saw that the trailer had a small cupola with a white cross on it, and painted on the side of the trailer were the words JUMPIN' AND JIVIN' FOR JESUS."

"Oh, my…" I whispered.

"Wait a minute," he said. "I want you to see this." He swung himself into the cab and flicked a switch. Immediately, little white Christmas lights lit up the cross.

Looking up at him in the gigantic truck, I said, "Haley, I'm not sure I want to do this."

I meant, I wasn't sure I wanted to go on a date with him, but he must have thought I was hesitant about climbing up into the cab of his truck. He jumped down, took my hand, and led me around to the passenger side of the truck. "Just grab hold of that bar on your right, and I'll give you a boost."

As if I were in a dream, no, make that a nightmare, I let myself be shoved through the door of the truck. When I'd recovered my balance and some of my dignity, I looked around the cab. I'd never been in a semitrailer before, but I had been in the cockpit of a transcontinental jet, and this setup of dials, levers, and knobs looked almost as complicated. One thing I was sure of, no dummy could drive one of these.

He put the truck into gear and slowly moved around Ethelind's circular driveway. "You look awfully nice," he said. "Lots better than you did earlier. And you smell good, too."

I thanked him, pleased that my extra effort had been noticed.

With me scrunched down in the front seat so nobody I knew would see me, he drove his church on wheels through the historic district. Passing Garnet Gochenauer's family home, I felt the familiar pang of loneliness I'd felt so often since we broke up. I hoped I wasn't becoming obsessive, but I couldn't help thinking what my life would be like if we'd stayed together. Certainly, I wouldn't be barreling down Lickin Creek's brick streets with an ex-convict. There was safety in a steady relationship. That was something I hadn't realized in my youth, which had lasted in fact right up till last year, but of course I was much older and wiser now.

While I was philosophizing internally, Haley suddenly began to downshift, eliciting groans of protest from under his enormous vehicle.

"What's the matter?" I sat higher in the seat so I could peer through the window at what was going on.

"The borough's got its bulky trash pickup crew out. I can't get by. We'll have to wait."

It seemed to take forever before the truck stopped.

Haley said, "It takes a full football field-length to bring one of these big rigs to a stop." The truck groaned and stopped only a foot or so away from another large vehicle, this one with a giant metal bucket on the front.

"What is it?"

"It's the borough's front loader."

From my vantage point I had a great view of the front loader. Its enormous scoop reached down to the sidewalk, where it caught up a sofa, several cardboard boxes, and a sled with only one runner. The scoop lifted everything high into the air, swung back toward the street, and dropped the items into the bed of a pickup truck.

"You'd think somebody could use that stuff," I remarked.

"It's all been thoroughly picked over. Anything good has found a home. I found a couple nice chairs myself this week."

"For your apartment?"

"I don't have an apartment. I live here."

"In your truck?"

"Sure. There's a bed right in the cab, behind us. Why pay rent for some place I wouldn't spend any time in? I'm either on the road driving a big rig for someone, or I'm taking the church to one truck stop or another."

I slumped into my seat. Not only an ex-con, but one who was homeless. Could I sink any lower?

In an effort to break the awkward silence and find some common ground, I asked Haley where he was from. That brought a five-minute description of a small town in West Virginia, which actually sounded rather charming.

"And where were you in jail?" I asked.

"How did you know...? Oh, I nearly forgot my jacket. I was in Graterford State Correctional Institute, outside of Philadelphia."

I must have looked ignorant, because he explained, "It's Pennsylvania's largest maximum-security prison. And I already know the next question you're going to ask, so I'll ask it for you. What was I in for? I was caught dealing cocaine. Took the rap for the big guys, who never get caught. I'd probably be dead now if I hadn't been incarcerated. That's where I found Jesus. He saved my life."

"Wow," was all I could think of saying. "That's a real success story. How long ago did you get out?"

"Been nearly a year. And I've been clean and sober for four years. 'Course it's easier to stay clean in jail than outside, you know."

"I can imagine," I said softly. And to my surprise I found I really could.

The front loader finished cleaning the street, and within minutes we were on the interstate, heading south.

"Where are we going?" was my hopeful question. I tried to make myself look very small in the hope that no one would see me.

Why? I asked myself. Why am I embarrassed by this? Was I feeling guilt over the fact I never went to church and now I was riding in one? Was I diminished by someone else's strong faith? Did it make me nervous to be in the company of a former convict? I answered yes to everything, which didn't exactly make me feel proud.

He pulled into the major highway truck stop, a place identified by huge signs advertising Family Cooking, Free Showers, Diesel Fuel, and Laundry Facilities.

"This is it," Haley announced. He went through a series of impressive manipulations, which moved the big rig through the parking lot and brought it to a stop.

"Now what?"

"I call the faithful to worship, of course."

"I should have thought of that."

"Come back with me," he said. "I'll show you around before the service."

It was another humiliating experience, but I had to let him help me get out. I'd never realized those cabs were up so high.

He flung open the wide double doors on the back of the truck and pulled a small flight of steps out.

"After you," he said with a sweeping arm gesture.

Even with the steps, I needed an embarrassing boost up.

The interior of the truck had been converted into a small chapel. The sides were paneled in dark walnut, on which the stations of the cross had been painted in bright acrylics. For pews there were four short wood benches bolted into the floor. In the front was a lectern decorated with a cross, and on either side of it were two potted palm trees. Behind it was a paneled wall, a storage area, I guessed from the handles and hinges that broke the expanse of wood.

Haley flipped a switch. I expected lights to come on, but instead an invisible organ blasted "Amazing Grace" into the air.

"Now we wait," he said, leaning on the lectern. "You can have the front pew."

The chapel was hot and stuffy, and I found myself wishing I hadn't worn pantyhose or the blue-and-white dress that had always been the appropriate choice for city dating but seemed so wrong right now.

The chorus of "Amazing Grace" was repeating for the third or fourth time when the first worshipper climbed into the truck. His rolled-up white T-shirt sleeves revealed burly arms covered with tattoos. I was entranced by the skull with a dagger protruding from it because beneath it was the word MOTHER.

After three more men joined us, Haley checked his watch and winked at me. "Here we go," he said. "Good evening, gentlemen and lady. Welcome to Church on the Go. Tonight's sermon is based on Romans six, twenty-twenty-three, 'For when ye were the servants of sin, ye were free from righteousness.' Where will you be on Judgment Day? In Heaven or in Hell? The choice is yours."

It bothered me that I found his performance fascinating. And performance it was. Haley was a cross between television evangelist Benny Hinn and Mick Jagger, as he strutted, pounded the lectern, waved his arms, roared, whispered, laughed, and even wept. He shared his "experience, strength, and hope" as he told of his years in prison, finding salvation at AA meetings there, and finally his conversion to Christianity and the discovery that he had been called to the ministry. There wasn't a dry eye among the worshipers, and that included myself, as Haley finished his sermon with, "'For the wages of sin is death, but the gift of God is eternal life through Jesus Christ our Lord.' Let us sing his praises."

He bent over and pushed a button on the boom box that was nearly hidden behind one of the potted palm trees, and a gospel choir sang out "By the Waters of Babylon."

Sweat poured from his brow as he danced and sang along with the music. His small congregation joined in the singing with more enthusiasm than ability, and often punctuated the refrain with "Amen, brother," and "Hallelujah." I felt myself carried away by the genuine emotion in the chapel and was exhausted when Haley finally paused.

He raised his arms signaling for silence. "Remember the words of the Lord Jesus, 'It is more blessed to give than to receive.' There is a basket by the door. Please give generously so that we may carry the message to others less fortunate then ourselves. And don't forget there are both AA and NA meetings at the truck stop every night at eight. I urge you to take advantage of them."

The men filed out, but not before each had deposited a good-sized roll of bills in the basket.

Haley emptied the basket, counted the bills, and said, "Let's go eat."

"Do we have to take the church with us?"

"Would you rather ride my motorcycle?"

"Yes," I said. Anything would be better than pulling up to a restaurant in his tractor-trailer.

He slid open a panel behind his pulpit and wheeled out a

large black Honda. "Just slide that board over to the back and drop it," he said, pointing to a long plank along one side of the truck. He rode the motorcycle down the makeshift ramp, shoved the board back into the truck, slammed the doors shut, locked up, straddled the motorcycle, and said, "Mount up."

No longer was Haley the shy Gary Cooper/Jimmy Stewart clone I'd met in the Waffle Shoppe. Now he was a combination of Marlon Brando's *Wild One* and James Dean's *Rebel Without a Cause.*

I hoisted my skirt as far up as the law would allow and threw one leg over the seat behind him. There went the pantyhose.

With me clinging to his waist, my cheek pressed against the JAILBIRDS FOR JESUS jacket, we sailed onto the interstate.

A few minutes later, we were back in Lickin Creek, where he turned into the parking lot of one of the town's many bowling alleys. Lickin Creek had not only a plethora of churches, but more bowling alleys than the rest of the tristate area of Pennsylvania, Maryland, and West Virginia.

By now I felt as if I'd lost all control of my life, and I meekly followed my date inside.

For once, more people seemed to know me than him. Ordinarily being recognized in my chosen hometown was gratifying, but tonight, for the first time, I longed for the anonymity.

The latest girl to serve as the receptionist for the Lickin Creek police force looked surprised and scratched her scalp through her enormous platinum beehive, and when she leaned over to whisper to her companion her eyes never left my face.

Cassie, from the Lickin Creek *Chronicle,* was there with a gaggle of preteenage girls. "My niece's birthday," she said when she came by to plant a kiss on my cheek.

Despite her obvious curiosity, I didn't introduce her to Haley.

I saw my dental hygienist, who reminded me it was nearly time for my checkup. I saw the clerk from the convenience store where I often picked up my morning cup of coffee. I recognized two of Greta's AA friends, a shoe salesman from Sears, and the director of the Sigafoos Home for the Aged. For every person I recognized, it was obvious that a dozen more knew who I was. That city slicker was out for a night on the town. That gal what burned down the historical society. You know her, the one who got dear old Senator Macmillan killed.

Haley claimed an alley. "What size shoes do you wear?" he asked, gazing down at my scuffed white heels.

"Seven."

"Funny, I'd have thought your feet were bigger than that. At least they looked bigger when you was wearing sneakers."

He walked over to the counter to rent bowling shoes for us, and I sat down hard. His words about my shoes reminded me of what he'd said shortly after picking me up tonight. Something about my looking better than I had earlier. How did he know what I'd looked like? When had he seen me in sneakers? What was going on?

I asked him when he came back, and he smiled and said he'd been to Morgan Manor earlier to pick up the wife of a friend. Hadn't I seen him there? I hadn't, and although I wasn't satisfied with his answer, I couldn't think of any reason why I shouldn't be.

Dinner was a slice of pizza and a soda eaten between frames. With a little coaching from Haley and a dozen raucous onlookers, I managed to get the ball down the alley more than half the time. Haley chivalrously said gutter balls didn't count against me, but from the guffaws and hoots of the bowlers around me, I gathered he was making that rule up.

I decided to stop and rest on my laurels when I finally scored over sixty on a game. We shared a soda, he personally bade good-bye to each and every person there, and then he drove me home. At the front door he looked expectantly at me. Was he hoping for a kiss? I didn't wait around to find out.

"Thanks for a lovely evening," I said robotically as I just

about leaped through the door. I slammed it shut behind me, threw the dead bolt for probably the first time since it had been installed, and pressed my back against the door. I stayed that way until I heard the motorcycle roar down the road. Only then did I realize I'd been holding my breath. "What a night," I said to myself. "It just can't get any worse than this."

The grandfather clock in the hall chimed. As Ethelind had predicted, I was home by ten.

"Tori? Tori? Is that you?" Ethelind's shrill voice drifted through the empty rooms and assaulted me in the hallway.

Before I could respond, she was there, looking even more frazzled than usual. "Oh Tori. I'm so sorry…" She threw her arms around me in a bear hug.

I pulled back from her unexpected embrace. "It was an awful date," I said, "but it wasn't that bad."

A look of horror swept over her face. "Oh my dear, you don't know…you haven't heard…"

"What?" I snapped. "What are you talking about?"

She took my hand and pulled me into the parlor where she watched TV every evening in a blue haze of cigarette smoke. The set was on, turned to one of the twenty-four-hour news stations.

"It's been on all evening. I thought you'd know. Sit down, my dear." She turned the volume up.

I stared at her first, then the TV, trying to figure out what the heck she was talking about. That's when the announcer read, "And this just in from the Department of State. There is still no word on the fate of Ambassador Grantham Livingston Miracle, his wife, and their six-month-old baby. Members of the rebel forces who have assassinated the king and taken possession of the royal palace say they have no knowledge of the family's whereabouts. More in half an hour, but first a look at cholesterol. Is it really as bad for you as your doctor says?"

Did I hear correctly? "This is a dream, right? I'm sleeping, and I'm going to wake up and everything's going to be okay."

"I'll get some tea. And one of your Snickers bars, too." Ethelind patted me awkwardly on the shoulder and scurried out of the room.

ELEVEN

THE NEXT FEW DAYS sped past in a blur. The TV was on constantly; the news never changed. My father, his new bride, Tyfani, and their baby, Billy, were still among the missing. The embassy was under siege, the Marine guards had been taken prisoner. Whoever said, "No news is good news" hadn't been in the situation of wondering what had happened to her family. Any news, even if it were bad, would have been better than the nightmare of not knowing.

I was interviewed by telephone several times by different networks, but the small African nation where my father was U.S. ambassador was not considered important enough to bring a TV crew to Lickin Creek, and for that I was grateful. I didn't need news teams on the front lawn to make the tragedy any more real.

Besides the telephone interviewers, I was surprised that many Lickin Creekers called to express their concern and offer support. People from other areas of my life also called. Murray Rosenbaum, my New York neighbor and best friend there, was the first. After telling me how sorry he was to hear of my father's predicament, he told me my subletter had temporarily moved a family of six into my two-room apartment. "But they're all very nice, and I'm sure they'll be gone before your landlord finds out."

Former classmates in Bali, Okinawa, and Laos telephoned. Even my editor rang to say she was rushing my book to print to take advantage of the publicity.

I spoke to Haley once, but when he kept calling, I asked

Ethelind to tell him I was out. She counted twelve attempts to reach me, each ending with "I'll pray for you." The thirteenth time I took the receiver from her, and told Mr. Haley Haley never to bother me again. When he asked why, I told him the truth. My emotions were so raw and close to the surface by that time that I didn't care if I hurt his feelings or not. I told him we had absolutely nothing in common, I didn't want to see him again, and he was annoying the bejeezus out of me. He did not try again, so I guess I got the message through. And I felt terrible. He was a nice guy and didn't deserve to be treated so rudely.

After that I let the answering machine take messages, rather than one of us running to the phone every time it rang.

Greta, Garnet's sister, was the first person to leave a message. After telling me how sorry she was to hear the bad news, she continued, talking mysteriously about black cocktail dresses and how she knew I had a nice one. And why was I so fearful of making commitments?

P.J. left a message telling me the Hissongs were furious that I'd missed covering the wedding, but she understood I was under a lot of stress, and that I should take some time off, but could I please write a short article about how all this was affecting me for the next week's edition.

There was only one person who hadn't been in touch. And that was Garnet. Even though I knew we were no longer a couple, it hurt me that he didn't think enough of me to console me during the worst moment of my life. If the situation had been reversed, I would have called him. At least I was pretty sure I would have.

By Monday, Memorial Day, nothing had changed except that my father had become old news. He was apparently not significant enough to even rate a mention on the evening news, and even the Harrisburg newspaper gave the story only an inch on the bottom of the third page.

I hadn't slept since Thursday night and had eaten next to

nothing. Ethelind had done her best all weekend long to distract me by preparing some of her specialties. But not even her famous toad-in-the-hole, bubble and squeak, steak and kidney pie, or bread pudding could tempt me to eat. She finally threw her hands in the air at noon on Monday and ordered in a couple of pepperoni pizzas.

"This hits the spot," I said gratefully, as I picked up a fourth slice.

She sighed as she lit her tenth or twentieth cigarette of the day. Obviously, to her, I was an unrefined slob of uneducated tastes. "I'll fix some coffee for you," she said. "Then I've got to be off to my office to finish some research." Ethelind was a professor of early English literature at the college. Her actual classroom time seemed to occupy only a few hours a week, but she took offense the time I commented on that and reminded me of how much time she devoted to class preparation and researching material for her book on the use of contractions in medieval literature.

Revived by real food and several cups of coffee, I decided work would take my mind off my worries. I'd write up that article P.J. wanted for the *Chronicle*. Putting my feelings down on paper was always an emotional release for me.

Alone at last. I drank a last cup of coffee and enjoyed the silence and absence of cigarette smoke. After a few peaceful minutes, I decided it was time to get to work. Ethelind kept a mug full of sharpened pencils on the counter and paper in one of the top drawers. "Never know when an idea will pop into my head that I need to jot down," she'd said. Rather than hike through miles of corridors and up the stairs to my bedroom to retrieve one of my own notebooks, I decided to use her supplies. I opened the drawer, and stared aghast at the tangle of tape, string, pens, paper clips, and miniature pencil sharpeners. I pulled out two staplers, a hole puncher, a roll of thirty-two-cent stamps from several years ago, a tin box of breath mints, and some ancient *TV Guides* before I finally found a dog-eared tablet. It had been a long time, I thought, since Ethelind had been seized by an idea she needed to jot down.

I flipped through the tablet, hoping to find some sheets near the bottom that didn't look quite so worn, and as I did, a square envelope, which had been stuck between two sheets of paper, fell to the floor.

I started to put it back into the drawer, when I took a closer look at the envelope, which appeared to have been handmade from a grocery bag, and saw it was addressed to me. "What the…?" I quickly opened it and extracted a card made of the same brown-bag paper.

What it was, was an invitation to the wedding of Greta Gochenauer Carbaugh to Buchanan McCleary. I glanced at the wall calendar and saw the date was the third Saturday in June. A note was included, on recycled paper according to the imprint on the back of the page, which asked that in lieu of gifts, donations be made to Trout Unlimited or the Lickin Creek Greenaway Association. And penciled on the bottom of that note was a personal note to me. "Tori," I read, "why haven't you called me back? There are other people I can ask if you don't want to do it. Greta."

The handwritten note attached to the wedding invitation I'd never seen was nearly as mysterious as Greta's phone call had been, so I picked up the phone and punched in her number.

"Tori. What a surprise." Greta's voice was so cool and distant that I knew immediately I'd done something wrong, but I had no idea what it was.

I explained about finding her wedding invitation in Ethelind's stationery drawer. "And I'm sorry, but I don't understand the note you wrote."

"Are you telling me the truth, Tori?"

Annoyed, I snapped, "Why would I lie to you? Will you please tell me what's going on? If you're upset because I haven't RSVP'd, I'm sorry about that, but I really never saw the invitation until two minutes ago. And of course I'll come."

"But why didn't you call me back after I left all those messages?"

"What are you talking about?"

"I called several times, a month ago, but you were never in. I finally told Ethelind I wanted you to be one of my bridesmaids. She said she'd make sure you returned my call right away, but you never called to say yea or nay or even go to hell, not even after I called half a dozen more times. That's what I'm upset about."

I was stunned into silence for a moment. At last I said, "I never got any messages, Greta."

"Really?"

"Cross my heart."

"Why wouldn't she have given you the messages?"

"I don't know," I said. "Maybe she forgot. Who knows what else I've missed."

"Then I forgive you," Greta said. "And can you be a bridesmaid? Please say yes. It would mean so much to me to have you there."

Once, back in my college days, I'd been a bridesmaid. I still had nightmares about the way I'd looked waddling down the aisle in five yards of turquoise taffeta, of which at least two yards made up the puffed sleeves, while two and a half more yards billowed from my waist and made me look a mile wide through the hips.

Greta noticed my hesitation. "I'm not requiring my attendants to wear a matched set of bridesmaid's dresses. I've told everyone just to wear a black cocktail dress of their own choosing. Everybody has one. I know you do. I've seen you wear it several times."

"Of course I'll be a bridesmaid. Thanks for asking."

After hanging up, I tried to get started on the article I'd promised P.J. I'd write, but I could not concentrate. I kept wondering if Ethelind had intentionally kept Greta's wedding a secret from me, and if so...why?

The words about how I felt about my father's disappearance did not flow onto the paper, even though they were in my heart, and I finally decided to try again later.

So what should I do now? I wondered. I needed something to take my mind off my worries.

That's when I remembered the box of scrapbooks Alice-Ann had taken from the attic at Morgan Manor. I'd brought it home, ostensibly to use as I wrote the house description, but I'd had enough facts without resorting to it. I thought I'd go through it now, though, and if something new and interesting turned up I could phone the new information to the printer.

Up in my room, I emptied the contents of the box, five scrapbooks and a small blue diary, onto my bed. The cloud of musty dust that arose shocked both cats, who had been asleep on the bed and now looked down disapprovingly from the top of the dresser.

Sitting down, I opened the first of the five albums, which I assumed was the oldest because it had an ornate, hand-tooled leather cover. Photo after photo of black-and-white nameless faces smiled out at me. Men in baggy swim suits with white canvas belts flexed their muscles on beach blankets, while women in girlish pigtails and stiff white bathing suits looked on in admiration.

Children stood at attention in parks, on city streets, and in school playgrounds. Others had been photographed waving from tractor seats or while taking a break from tossing the hay, unwittingly posed as caricatures of Grant Wood's *American Gothic*, with pitchforks in hand.

"No names. You'd think someone would have thought to put names under the pictures." I sniffed. Noel sniffed sympathetically.

"All these people are probably dead by now, and there's no way of identifying any of them."

Noel lost interest in the conversation and had turned her attention to cleaning Fred's ears.

I put that scrapbook aside and picked up one that appeared to be newer. My guess was correct, because some of the photographs in the back were in color.

I guessed I was looking at pictures taken in the forties. Slowly, I began to recognize some of the same people. A man and woman who changed very little, and a boy who changed a lot, growing taller on every page, until by the middle of the book he was taller than the man.

They were part of a large extended family, I assumed, for many of the pictures showed the boy admiring various birthday cakes or seated at a holiday table surrounded by many of the same faces.

The birthday cake with a big six on it must have marked an important milestone in the little boy's life, because he stood next to it gazing with rapture at the small violin he was holding. Gift wrappings lay strewn around his feet.

The happy family pictures continued through two more albums until the boy looked to be about twelve or thirteen, and his violins grew proportionately.

Then suddenly they stopped, and the last picture in the book was of a tombstone dated 1945, marking the burial place of Robert and Alameda Mellott.

That was when I realized the box of scrapbooks didn't belong to the Morgan family, but to the long-gone music teacher, Rodney Mellott.

There were some missing years, for the final scrapbook seemed to pick up on Rodney when he was in his late teens or early twenties. Where had he gone after his parents' deaths? To some relative, I imagined, who didn't care enough about him to chronicle any more birthdays.

Yellowed programs from various high school and college concerts took up most of the pages of that last book. The only pictures seemed to be Rodney, much older but recognizable as the child in the earlier albums, posing in front of automobiles. I looked closely at the buildings in the background of these pictures but none looked familiar, so I guessed these were Rodney Mellott's pre-Lickin Creek years.

I tossed the scrapbook to one side, nearly knocking Fred from the bed. "I'm sorry, sweetie," I said, stroking his soft white tummy. "Forgive me?"

He gazed at me with round golden eyes, assuring me I had his unconditional love. For some reason, this made me burst into tears for the first time since Friday night, and after sobbing for half an hour or so, I drifted into a dreamless sleep.

When I awoke, a glance at the clock told me it was nearly five. I must have slept for three or four hours, and I felt much better.

The house was still. Ethelind must not have come home yet, or I'd surely hear the sound of the TV. There was no point in going downstairs, so I picked up the one thing I hadn't yet looked at—the small blue diary. It reminded me of one I'd been given for my twelfth birthday by my mother. "Don't ever be afraid to write your deepest thoughts in here, Tori," she'd said. "It will always be your private place, and nobody can read it because it has a lock and key." The little brass lock, I found out after I lost the key, could be opened with a bobby pin, and since my deepest, most innermost secrets all seemed to deal with what I'd had for dinner most nights, I'd soon given up writing in it.

But this was different, for the handwriting was that of a mature adult, and not a twelve-year-old.

The first entry was dated September, 1964, and chronicled in great detail Rodney Mellott's first day of teaching at the Lickin Creek High School. He had taken an immediate dislike to the principal, who had given him a windowless office, and he was dismayed to learn he would have to lead the marching band as well as teach instrumental music.

I read through the travails of Rodney's first few weeks at the high school, and wondered with him why he had left his position in Pittsburgh. He seemed even less fond of his landlady than he was of his principal, describing her as a "harridan," and a "sex-crazed old woman" who was hot for his body. Recalling the portrait I'd seen of the pudgy young man in his tuxedo I decided his portrayal of Maribell Morgan's lust for him was more wishful thinking than truth.

Boring, I thought, thumbing through to November. By Thanksgiving, Rodney was tutoring music students privately, using Maribell's springhouse as a studio. Even more boring.

I was about to abandon the diary as a waste of time, when I noticed a strange notation at the bottom of one page. "11." Some sort of code Rodney had used, I supposed. I turned a few pages, and found a similar note: "12 1/2 ." And on the next page, "13— the best yet." A code? Yes, but what did it mean? Maybe the numbers were his students' ages. But, what had he meant by the best yet? Was he describing his students' musical abilities?

I read on a few pages more, and realized with disgust that what Rodney was talking about was not his students' ages but their shoe sizes. It was pretty obvious that he had a shoe fetish of serious proportions. Before the Christmas holidays he was cleaning sneakers for various boys and in his own words, "making love to them" before returning the shoes to their owners. After a few weeks, the diary made it obvious that he had progressed to sexually abusing his students.

"Eeeew," I squealed, dropping the diary, and wiping my fingers on the quilt, "this is the most disgusting thing I've ever read."

"What's disgusting?"

"Oh my God!" I clutched at my pounding heart, as I glared at the figure in the doorway. "Alice-Ann, you scared me half to death. I didn't hear you come in."

"I knocked, but there was no answer, so I just came in. Are you all right? You look kind of flushed."

She adeptly caught the diary I tossed to her. "Why aren't you at work?" I asked. "Isn't the children's room open on Monday nights?"

"It's Memorial Day, and I'm off. What's this?" she asked, looking down at the blue book in her hand.

"Take a look at it, staring somewhere in the middle of November."

Alice-Ann sat down next to me on the edge of the bed and began to read.

"Yuk," she said after a few minutes. "Whose diary is this, anyway?"

"It belongs to the town's favorite missing bridegroom," I said.

Her mouth dropped open. "You mean Rodney Mellot… the…you know…?"

I nodded. "That's right. Just think of him as the dead pervert in the tuxedo."

"What do you think of this?" Alice-Ann asked, reading out loud, "'B. brought broken bike by today. Fixed it. Cleaned his size 12s. Showed him how much I love him.' Tori, this is horrible stuff. Those were youngsters. What are we going to do about it?"

"Maybe we should concentrate on finding his body first, then worry about what to do."

She collapsed backward onto the bed and threw one arm over her eyes. "Can you bring me a damp washrag, please. I think I've got a migraine."

TWELVE

A GENTLE BREEZE SWAYED the high grass and rustled the needles of the tall pine trees that bordered the area known as The Flats. Reputed to be a teen hangout at night, up here in the daylight the air in the state forest was clear and cool, and the quiet was unbelievable compared to the traffic noise on the highway on the way up.

I had left the truck next to a log rail that delineated the official parking lot for that part of the Appalachian Trail, and now I stood before a wooden sign, painted brown, which pointed the way north to Maine and south to Georgia. No other vehicles were within sight, although I thought I heard one nearby just as I pulled off the road. I was alone to enjoy the serenity and solitude of the wilderness.

The trail, as far as I could see before it disappeared into the trees, was perfectly flat and didn't look as if it would make for difficult walking. But before I stepped foot on the famed Appalachian Trail, I dutifully read the notices on the bulletin board: Leave no trace. No motorized vehicles. No mountain bicycles. Respect the privacy of property owners along the trail. Don't set the woods on fire. You are here (this last accompanied by a little X on a topographical map).

I chose to go north for a good reason. Jenny Varner had told me where her husband's cabin was: "Hike north on the trail for about a mile and a half, and it'll be the only cabin you see. On private land to the east of the trail. Unless it's raining, you oughta be able to see it easy from the trail. But you have to be watching close 'cause it's dark and blends right into the trees." I thought as long as I was in the area, I might as well take a look at it.

Wouldn't it be great, I thought, if I found the escaped convict hiding there?

"Sure it would," said the chairwoman of the Committee of Good Sense who lurked in the depths of my mind. She didn't often surface, but when she did I usually listened to her. "And just what do you think you would do if you found him there?"

This was not one of the times I chose to listen. *"Valde-ree valderah, my knapsack on my back..."* I sang, trying to drown her out as I trotted down the trail.

Almost immediately, I was overtaken by a young woman bearing a heavy pack on her shoulders and wearing very short khaki shorts and heavy hiking boots.

"Good morning," I said cheerfully. "Where are you from?"

Perhaps she really did answer with more than a grunt, but that was all I heard as I watched her blond ponytail bounce out of sight around the next bend in the trail.

Why was I hiking the Appalachian Trail early on the Tuesday morning after Memorial Day? It had all come about because I had grown frustrated with no news about my father. Even my calls to the Department of State brought only a cryptic, "We'll be in touch with you as soon as we hear anything." I decided going to work was the only thing that would keep my mind occupied during these uncertain times, so I'd headed into the *Chronicle* office early this morning.

Cassie jumped up from her desk, hugged me, and led me to the red plastic sofa as if I were an invalid. "I'm so sorry...if there's anything I can do..." All words I'd heard at least a hundred times in the past four days, but they still brought tears to my eyes.

P.J. came out of her office to greet me, something she hadn't done since the day I first met her. "Are you getting along all right? Is there anything I can do? Have you heard anything?"

I wondered if her questions were from real concern or a need to fill Saturday's front page with Lickin Creek's own connection to an international crisis. Then I was ashamed of myself for being so cynical when she looked so sincere.

I handed P.J. the pages I'd worked on almost all night. "Here's what I wrote about my father, how he was a career foreign service officer who worked his way up to being an ambassador, and what it was like for me growing up in that kind of environment, and how I'm sure he's all right because he's a resourceful man who has been in danger before."

Cassie clucked her tongue against her teeth. Obviously she thought I was delusional.

"It's true," I said. "We were once under siege in an embassy for three days, and all we lost were our household goods. And another time we had a cook who went crazy with jealousy and tried to kill his wife with a machete, and my father overpowered him.

"And when we lived on Okinawa, he went out in a fishing boat, alone, and was lost in the East China Sea for nearly a week. My mother was half-crazy with worry, and then he simply walked in as if nothing had happened. And…" I began to cry. "You can see he's very clever. And careful. He won't let anything happen to the baby," I sobbed. "I can't bear to lose my baby brother. I haven't even seen him yet. Not another brother…"

Cassie stroked my back, while water gurgled in the cooler.

"Drink up," P.J. ordered gruffly, placing a soggy paper cup in my hand. After I'd regained my composure, I told P.J. I wanted to get back to work.

Cassie nodded sympathetically. "Keeping your mind occupied would be the best thing for you. And Tori, I'm sure your family is going to be just fine."

Since Cassie was the head priestess of her Wiccan coven, I had confidence in her ability to know such things. I smiled and thanked her for her reassurances.

In the meantime, P.J. had gone into her office and returned carrying a map. "If you really want something to do, why not get to work on that article about the anthills?"

"I'd forgotten all about them. Where are they located?"

"Somewhere near the Appalachian Trail, Tori. I told you that before."

"Those are rather vague directions, seeing as how the trail is over two thousand miles long."

P.J.'s face reddened as she huffed, and I knew my grace period was up. "There's only one place in this county with an entrance to the trail. Start there. Up in the mountains in the state forest. It crosses the highway up there and the anthills are supposed to be within walking distance of the road."

"North or south?" I regretted asking before the words were out of my mouth.

"I really have no idea. Just go up there and ask whomever you see hiking the trail."

"One more question… How will I recognize them?"

P.J. gave me that smile she reserved for idiots and me. "You look for mounds of dirt about two or three feet high. And if they have ants crawling in and out of them, I think you'll be pretty safe in assuming that they are anthills."

Now, on the trail, the sun was beating down upon me without mercy. That gentle breeze had stopped a while ago. My sneakers threatened blisters on both my heels. The camera hanging from my neck was gaining weight at about a pound a minute. What's the fun in this? I asked myself. Why do people do this to themselves? I was no longer singing. I needed to reserve all my strength for breathing as I trudged down the dusty path.

I kept looking off to my right, searching for the Varner cabin. Good grief, I'd certainly covered five or ten miles, hadn't I? Had I overlooked the place?

I looked at my Timex and found that only fifteen minutes had passed since I first set foot on the trail. "Well," I said to the laughing committee in my head. "Time is relative. And if you go by how miserable I am, then hours have passed, not minutes."

I'd brought no water with me. Perhaps I'd thought the trail would be more like a public park with drinking fountains strategically placed along it. That had been my first mistake. My second was wearing sneakers instead of hiking boots, as if I had any, and my third mistake was starting out on this expedition in the first place.

Then I saw the cabin, nestled in a small clearing in the woods, set far back from the trail. Somehow I'd expected it to be one of those modern cabins I'd seen advertised in decorating magazines, built from cedar logs all turned to the same dimension, with lots of big triangular windows to take in the sweeping view.

Instead, this was the type of log cabin Abe Lincoln would have found homey. Logs of all diameters were held together by great expanses of white plaster. The windows were covered with louvered shutters, but even if the shutters were opened, the windows were too small to permit a view of anything. This cabin had been built by someone who thought of windows as a source of light and ventilation only.

I left the trail and walked toward the cabin, keeping close to the trees, trying to make myself invisible to anyone who might be inside.

When I was only a few feet from the cabin, I paused behind a crepe myrtle bush, peered through the brilliant pinkish-red blossoms, and listened carefully for any signs of occupancy, but I neither heard nor saw anything. The place had a deserted air about it, and I was positive I was alone.

That made me feel more courageous, and I darted toward the cabin, pressed down on the latch, found the door was unlocked, and walked in.

Feathery cobwebs stuck to my face, and I brushed them away as my eyes adjusted to the dark interior, lit only by sunlight filtered through the narrow slits of the shutters that covered the windows.

It took a moment or two before my eyes adapted. Then I saw that the cabin was actually only one large room, divided in half by a fireplace built from massive stones. This side of the fireplace was apparently the living room, I decided, taking in the disreputable couch flanked by two velour recliners before the fireplace, the round oak table directly in front of me with a kerosene lantern on it, and an empty gun case next to the fireplace. I realized the room was also the bedroom when I saw two sets of bunk beds on either side of the front door.

Behind the fireplace was the kitchen. The knotty-pine salesman had been here, too, for the walls were lined from floor to ceiling with cabinets, stained nearly black from the fires that had burned in the great stone fireplace for many years. A woodstove dominated one wall. A fairly modern stainless steel sink had an old-fashioned manual water pump over it. There was no refrigerator, only a Styrofoam cooler in one corner. I checked it out, and found it reassuring that it was home to several families of spiders. I took that to mean nobody had been here in a long time.

Seeing the pump made me remember I was about to expire from dehydration. I pumped until my shoulder was aching, and just as I was ready to give up I was rewarded by a trickle. I quickly stuck a chipped coffee mug under it and caught the water. It smelled like rusty rotten eggs and was the color of weak green tea, but since I knew I'd very likely be dead in ten minutes or less if I didn't get some liquid in me, I held my nose and gulped it down.

There was absolutely no sign that Vonzell Varner had visited his cabin any time in the recent past. Not even the great escape artist he was reputed to be could spend time in a cabin in the woods without disturbing a single cobweb. Wherever he had been hiding, it hadn't been here.

Beneath the sink were some empty plastic soda bottles, and

I filled one with smelly water from the pump. I'd decided I would hike north on the trail for no more than fifteen minutes to search for the anthills. If I didn't find them, I'd go back to the truck and look for them another day on a different part of the trail. There was a limit to what my body could endure. P.J. had said they were within a mile or two of the highway, so I knew I couldn't be far away. If I were going in the right direction, that is! I snapped a few pictures of the cabin, inside and out, and cut across the meadow to rejoin the trail.

Once again, the trail was deserted and quiet, except for the chirping of crickets and the occasional cry of a bird. The trees provided shade, and thanks to the water I'd drunk I felt much cooler. A few times, I was startled by squirrels and rabbits, but otherwise there was no sign of life. Apparently, the hikers who used the trail had taken to heart the warnings about not littering and respecting the wilderness, for there was nothing to suggest anybody had ever walked this path before me. Despite my blisters, I was beginning to enjoy my wilderness trek.

After walking for only about five minutes, I saw the first anthill off to my left. Just as P.J. had said, it was a big mound of bare dirt, rising out of the grass, resembling a miniature volcano. And when I got close to it I saw hundreds of ants climbing in and out of holes in its side. Even a city girl like me could recognize it as an anthill. I pointed the *Chronicle*'s camera at it and snapped several pictures from different angles. Behind it were more hills, some even larger than this one. There were probably hundreds more hidden in the depths of the forest.

I sat down to rest for a few minutes before starting back to the truck. I drank about half the water in the bottle, saving the rest for my hike back to the parking lot, and was just struggling to my feet when something stung my leg. Over and over. Burning worse than anything I'd ever felt. I screamed and jerked my pants up to my knees revealing a small army of ants climbing up my legs, taking large bites out of me as they progressed.

I leaped about, knocking ants right and left, and squealing with fear, disgust, and pain.

"Hold still," someone said. "I'll get them off you." It was the blond girl who'd passed me by earlier.

"Owww," I howled in reply. Within a few seconds, she had brushed them all away and led me back to the trail.

"We should be okay here. There's so much food close to the hill that they don't need to come here. I hope we didn't hurt any of them," said my savior. She told me her name, which I hope wasn't Brunhilda, although that's what I recall.

I didn't really care if we'd slaughtered the entire colony, but I was wise enough not to say so.

Brunhilda was, she told me, working on her degree in environmental studies at the nearest Penn State campus. She knew everything there was to know about the scientific study of ants, or myrmecology, and told it all to me while we stood on the trail, safely away from the nasty little creatures. The ants, she said, were Allegheny mound ants, or *Formica exsectoides*. Among other things, I learned that the formic acid they produced was what had caused the burning sensation on my legs, which thankfully was beginning to fade.

"They don't mean to hurt anyone," she said cheerfully. "It's their method of stunning their prey so they can take it back to the hill and feed the rest of the colony."

When she said I could quote her in my article about the anthills, I pulled my notebook out of my fanny pack and asked her to write down her name, address, and telephone number.

As she handed it back to me, she caught sight of the plastic bottle I'd dropped by the log during my battle with the ants from hell. "Did you leave that trash there?" she snapped.

"It's only my water bottle. I'll get it."

"No. You stay here. I have boots on to protect me. You should never come out on the trail without boots. They protect you from insects and snakes too."

"Snakes! There are snakes on the trail?" This really was a wilderness.

"Of course there are snakes," she said cheerfully. "Rattlesnakes mostly, but there are also…"

I covered my ears. "Please don't tell me. I'm terrified of snakes."

"They're nature's children, just as we are."

"That may be true, but I don't have to like all of nature's children."

She was paying no attention to me, and instead was sniffing the water in my bottle.

"You weren't drinking this, were you?"

"Of course I was. Why do you ask?"

"Where did you get it?"

"From a deserted cabin about half a mile from here. There was a pump in the kitchen. Why do you ask?"

"Because it's obviously polluted. Just look at the color. Didn't you smell it?"

"I noticed a rusty, sulphuric smell."

"It's not rust or sulphur I'm worried about. It's fecal coliform bacteria. If that cottage was deserted, the well probably hasn't been treated in ages. I hope you don't get sick."

Of course, I did. Even before I got back to the borough. I had to pull over and head for the shrubbery on the side of the road. I was so miserable I didn't even worry about snakes lurking in the bushes. In fact, after my third or fourth stop I would have welcomed relief of any kind, even death by snakebite.

Somehow, I managed to get back to Lickin Creek, where I went immediately to the clinic. The nurse practitioner, who was running the clinic until the town found a replacement for Doc Jones, gave me a small vial of pills to calm my burning stomach and a tube of ointment to soothe my burning legs.

Totally bedraggled and miserable from head to toe, I drove though Lickin Creek's frustrating maze of one-way streets until I reached the shelter of Ethelind's Moon Lake mansion.

"Don't ask," I said as she looked at me in amazement. "I'll tell you about it after a bath."

I headed up the back stairs, shed my clothes and a few dead ants in my bedroom, wrapped myself in the luxurious terry cloth robe Ethelind had brought to me from England, and went down the hall to the bathroom.

I pulled open the shower curtain, reached down to turn on the tap, and saw a folded piece of paper lying in the bottom of the bathtub.

"What the…" I opened it and read, without comprehension at first, the words printed there in childlike block letters. I'M WATCHING YOU RIGHT NOW, TORI MIRACLE.

My fingers turned numb, and the paper floated back into the tub. I dropped to the cold tile floor, pulled my robe tight around my body, and hugged my knees to my chest. Who had been in the house? Was someone really watching me right now? Who? How? Why?

THIRTEEN

AFTERWARD, EVERYONE AGREED that this year's house tour would have been the best ever if it hadn't been for what happened to poor Ramona Houdeyshell.

Alice-Ann had wanted to be at Morgan Manor to keep an eye out for anyone behaving in a suspicious manner. Despite my doubts that we'd spy one of the five hundred ticket-holders sneaking down to the springhouse to put Rodney's body back in the cave, I agreed to volunteer to work at the manor house with her. Mrs. Houdeyshell hadn't looked too happy about having us in the house, but she was shorthanded and had no choice, so she assigned us to work the first two-hour shift as room monitors. I think she put me in the dining room because it adjoined the hall where she stood to greet guests, enabling her to keep an eye on me. Alice-Ann unhappily spent her time in the dark paneled, knotty-pine kitchen.

I can't recall how many times I did my spiel, but the facts I recited about the paintings, fireplace mantel, china closet full of Chinese export ware, and the restored murals will probably come back to haunt my dreams for many years to come.

Overheard comments varied. "Lovely, just lovely." "Wonder what it costs to heat a drafty old place like this in the winter?" "My mother had a table just like that but she threw it out in the fifties. It would probably be worth a fortune today." "Where's the bathroom?"

Many had already visited the other houses. I saw quite a few women with large oil paintings under their arms, which they had purchased from Annette Wyndham at the Wyndham-Cratchitt Gristmill. As Alice-Ann had said earlier, the paintings were really dreadful.

I nearly floated to the ceiling with delight every time I heard a remark about how charming the Zaleski House was. My house, I wanted to say. It's soon going to be the Miracle House.

Every now and then, I glanced through the window toward the springhouse, but as I expected no one attempted to visit it.

When Alice-Ann and I were relieved by our replacements, we strolled outside and sat down on the grass under the shade of a giant maple tree to relax and enjoy the music presented by the Downtown Businessmen's Association Band.

"What they lack in talent, they make up for in enthusiasm," Alice-Ann commented. The spectators, most of whom had brought their own folding lawn chairs, seemed to agree with her, because they clapped and cheered loudly after each number.

"Isn't that J.B. Morgan?" I asked, pointing to the bass player.

"Just a minute." Alice-Ann dug around in her purse until she found her glasses, which she always refused to wear in public because they made her look like a caricature of a librarian. Those were her words, not mine.

"Yup. That's him all right. Probably hoping some rich farmer will drop a half million dollars for the house in his lap before the tour is over."

I looked over the DBAB, as it was known. "For goodness sake, that's my dentist. And that one over there, the skinny guy with the toupee, and trombone, isn't that Judge Fetteredhorse?"

"Fetterhoff," Alice-Ann gently corrected me. "Yes, it is."

The drummer, in the back row, waved at me. I waved back. "That's what's-his-name, from the drugstore."

"Wilbur Eshelman. Why do you have so much trouble with names, Tori? It's almost as if you don't even try to get them right."

I'd heard it all before, so I ignored her. "There's Marvin Bumbaugh. I didn't know he was a musician." As if to prove he wasn't, a long, deep, sour note erupted from the end of his tuba. We both laughed, earning some disapproving stares from the people sitting around us.

"I don't know all of them," I said.

"Stick around another year and you will," was Alice-Ann's comment.

From all around us came, "Shhh."

Alice-Ann bought ox-burgers and French fries from the concession cart. About an hour later, I went up and ordered two funnel cakes and two diet sodas. After we'd eaten them, we stretched out on the grass and enjoyed what was left of the afternoon. Too soon, the orchestra members laid down their instruments, and Marvin Bumbaugh stepped up to the microphone, which whistled as he said, "Thank you, ladies and gentlemen. It's always a pleasure to entertain you. I hope you will all attend the concert in the square performed by the DBAB on the third Saturday of this month. We look forward to seeing you there."

Women, and a few men, streamed out of Morgan Manor. It was five o'clock, and the house tour was now officially over.

"Let's go," Alice-Ann said.

"Sure. Where?"

"To the party to celebrate another successful house tour. If we leave first we might be able to get a parking place within a mile or two of the building."

After she had managed with some difficulty to get the old VW running and pulled out onto the road, I heard the sound of a car approaching from behind. Too close for comfort, I thought, and turned to see if I knew who it was. I whimpered out loud when I saw the dark green van with tinted windows looming in the rear window.

"What's wrong?" Alice-Ann asked.

"That van. I think someone's been following me in it."

The driver must have seen me turn around, because he turned right at the next crossroad and was gone in a flash.

"Really?" Alice-Ann sounded doubtful, but then she hadn't seen the van. "Who do you think it is?"

"I have a gut feeling it's Vonzell Varner."

When she looked blank, I explained, "He's the guy who bombed some women's clinics and escaped from jail. The feds think he headed back here to Lickin Creek because his ex-wife and kids live here. I wrote an article about him for last week's paper. Didn't you read it?"

"I don't always have time to read the paper, Tori. Why would he be following you?"

"I don't know. Maybe he saw me at his ex-wife's house and thinks we're hatching something up to trap him. That's where I first saw his van. Outside her house."

"How can you be sure it was him in the van?"

"Who else would it be? Do you think I'm crazy?"

"Not at all…just a tad paranoid." She laughed, but this time I wasn't laughing with her.

"Someone's been in my house," I told her. "And left a note saying he was watching me. I think it must be the same person."

"Now, that's scary."

"To put it mildly."

"Does Ethelind know anything about it?"

"She said she doesn't. She's as nervous as I am. So much so, she's actually thinking of getting some keys made so we can lock up when we're out."

I kept my gaze fastened on the road behind us for the rest of our trip, but the van never made a reappearance. I was so preoccupied that when Alice-Ann turned off the engine and set the parking brake, I was surprised we'd reached our destination so quickly.

When I peered out the front window, I realized I hadn't the slightest idea of what our destination was. "Where are we?" I asked. I knew only that we were in a parking lot behind one of downtown Lickin Creek's Victorian-era buildings. One of the oldest, I judged, from the looks of the sagging wood porches attached to the second and third floors of the brick building.

"Handshew's Hardware," she said, as if that should mean something to me, and took off at a trot down one of the dark, narrow alleys that separated one ancient building from another.

"Where you'uns going?" a deep voice asked from a dark doorway.

I jumped back in alarm.

"Just me. Big Bad Bob. Stores downtown all's closed on Saturday night."

"We know that," Alice-Ann countered. "But we're going to the hardware store."

"Oh," Bob said with a smile that lit up his reptilian face. "I see."

"And there will be more ladies coming along in a few minutes, Bob, so don't you go jumping out and scaring them."

"I won't, Mizz MacKinstrie. Cross my heat and hope to die." He continued to grin at us, radiating cheap booze and sour body odor as well as good cheer.

I'd never been in Handshew's Hardware before, not having seen anything to attract me in the painted message on the dusty window advertising hardware, electric appliances, genuine antiques, chain by the foot, and gifts.

Now, an additional hand-lettered sign said simply BLUE-GRASS TONITE. And below that, PRIVATE PARTY—CLOSED TO THE PUBLIC.

I took a quick look up and down Main Street and was relieved not to see a green van anywhere. However, some cars were coming around the fountain in the center of the square. They had to be members of the committee, for there was no reason for anyone else to be driving into downtown Lickin Creek on a Saturday night. Big Bad Bob had been right; the stores "all's closed."

Alice-Ann grabbed me by the arm and dragged me through the shop's front door. "Let's get good seats before the others get here," she suggested.

Alice-Ann laid claim to two wooden barrels of nails by laying her sweater on one and her purse on the other.

I was still enough of a New Yorker to wince at the sight of her purse lying unattended, but it didn't concern her in the least.

"Don't worry about it, Tori. This is Lickin Creek."

The Lickin creek I knew was full of maniacs stalking innocent women, missing bodies, and escaped murderers. But I envied Alice-Ann her vision of the world. It was really much nicer than mine.

Handshew's Hardware Store was a relic of Lickin Creek's past, with all the features a preservationist could hope for: wood floor, pressed tin ceiling, a wall of small drawers with brass pulls containing screws, hinges, cup hooks, and other things I couldn't identify. An oak-and-glass case to the right of the door displayed piles of pots, pans, dishes, and glassware. On shelves above the case were dusty ceramic teddy bears and angels, dolls dressed as Amish with no features on their stuffed pink faces, and black cast-iron buggies—the gift selection as mentioned on the sign in the window. Covering the top of the display case were untidy stacks of yellowed towels, washcloths, and pot holders.

The back third of the store was devoted to the sale of used bicycles and antiques, mostly furniture from the Victorian era that badly needed repairs. Three-legged chairs were stacked on top of cracked oak tables. Sideboards competed with each other for the Most-hideous-piece-of-furniture-ever-made award. Boxes overflowed with chipped dishes, moldy books, and rusty kitchen tools.

Overhead fans stirred the stale air but did nothing to cool the room. Each new arrival added more body heat to the already sweltering building. The cavernous room was soon filled to capacity and people were still pouring in. Every woman on the house tour committee, every person who'd been assigned to guard a room at a house, every man who'd helped direct parking, showed up. And all of them brought their spouses, their kids, and probably their neighbors, too, judging from the size of the throng. Many carried folding lawn chairs, some grabbed antique chairs, and the rest perched on barrels of nails, the counter, and anything else with a flat surface, while the children sprawled on the floor.

Some antiques had been shoved to the side and were stacked in precarious piles to create a small open area in the back of the room, where four metal folding chairs, four microphones, and a sound system from the early days of electronics waited for tonight's performers to arrive.

The musicians showed up and were greeted by a flurry of enthusiastic applause and whistling as people scurried to their seats. Our barrels were so close to the band, I could smell the corn liquor.

"Ah-one-ah-two-ah-three," said a portly man with a bushy gray beard who was dressed as a common soldier of the Union Army, and all at once the banjo, mandolin, fiddle, and guitar began to produce the most amazing music I've ever heard. The sound seemed to bypass my ears and go directly to my bloodstream, where it became a pulsing part of my body.

"It's glorious," I whispered to Alice-Ann. Both my feet were tapping, my fingers were snapping, and it was all I could do to keep from jumping up and joining the uninhibited children who were dancing with enthusiasm in any empty spaces they could find.

People clapped, pounded the floor with their feet, and sang along with their favorite songs. "Rocky Top," "Turkey in the Straw," "Cumberland Gap."

After a dozen numbers, the Union soldier announced, "I'm Billy Boy Barnes and these guys here are the Barn Door Swingers. We're sure glad to see you'uns here tonight. We're gonna take a little break right now, but we'll be back with some more good old country music in about fifteen minutes. You'uns come back now, hear?"

"Amazing," I said to Alice-Ann, as I bent over to wipe the

sweat from my brow with the edge of my T-shirt. "I've never experienced anything like it. I actually felt as if I was a part of the music, not just a spectator."

Alice-Ann nodded knowingly. "We should come more often. There's a show every Saturday night, and you never know who's going to show up and play with them. Let's get something to drink. I'm dying."

I willingly followed her through the crowd to where cans of soda were cooling in tin tubs full of ice. We helped ourselves to Diet Cokes and went out onto the sidewalk in search of a cooling breeze.

I put the icy can to one cheek then the other and felt my body temperature drop to almost normal.

"It's time," I said to Alice-Ann.

She glanced at her watch. "Uh-uh, we've got almost ten minutes, and they never start on time anyway."

"I'm not talking about the show, and you know it. What I'm saying is, it's time to report the missing…you know."

"Shhh." Alice-Ann looked around furtively. "Someone might be listening."

"What difference does that make now? I promised you I wouldn't tell anybody until the house tour was over. And the house tour is now over, Alice-Ann."

"But since the…you know…is missing, do we really need to report it was there in the first place? Why don't we just wait until it turns up somewhere, then we can…"

I stared sternly at her. "I kept my promise. I'm not going to cover up a crime any longer. I plan to see Luscious first thing in the morning. You can come with me if you choose to."

"He won't be there, Tori. His mother makes sure he goes to church on Sunday mornings."

"Very well, then it will be the first thing I do on Monday morning. Can I count on you to show up and go with me?"

"I don't know. Maybe we should wait and…"

"It's time," I said. And now what I said had a double meaning. It was time to tell the truth as well as time to go inside for the second half of the show.

Another folding chair had been added to the circle, and I was amazed to see Big Bad Bob sitting on it, grinning at me, with a stringed instrument in his lap.

"Hammered dulcimer," Alice-Ann whispered in my ear.

"Welcome back, folks," shouted the jovial host, Billy Boy Barnes. "We'uns had a little nip of refreshments out back, and now we're ready to rock and roll. Ah-one-ah-two-ah-three."

The five men played "Tavern in the Town," and the hardware store really did rock, as people stomped their feet, clapped their hands, whistled through two fingers, and shouted out encouragements. Who'd ever have thought that Lickin Creek's most proper matrons could get so carried away by anything? I was seeing a new, human side to women like Missy Bumbaugh, Adelle Ashkettle, and Ramona Houdeyshell.

The enthusiasm mounted as the pounding music became more insistent. I began to worry that the swaying ceiling fans were going to crash down upon us.

After a particularly boisterous rendition of "Sailor's Hornpipe," Billy Boy announced the Swingers would now perform a medley of songs popular during the war. I'd been in Lickin Creek long enough to know "the war" was the Civil War, which was still being fought in parlors throughout the country. And not only by reenactors, either.

"So you'uns jest lay back, relax, and imagine you're sitting 'round the campfire after a day of slaughter. You done seen boys you went to school with die, and now's the time to reflect on your own mortality and the folks back home. It's the time to ponder on how your mother will weep when she hears you died, and of that sweet little gal you left behind, and then someone begins to sing a love song, and one by one your companions pick it up, and eventually you join in. Here's a ballad that was popular with the boys on both sides."

He began to sing in a sweet tenor voice, accompanied by

Big Bad Bob on a battered recorder. "The years creep slowly by, Lorena, the snow is on the grass again…"

Hankies and tissues fluttered as the ladies in the audience sniffed and patted their eyes. When the last chord faded, the audience waited for a moment in respectful silence, then erupted with cheers, applause, and cries for more.

Billy Boy held up one hand asking for silence, and at that moment, from somewhere off to my left came a crash followed by a piercing, high-pitched scream.

Heads swiveled, and barrels and chairs tipped over as men and women jumped to their feet trying to see what had happened. The word "mouse" was repeated until several women ran from the building, squealing in terror.

The screaming continued unabated.

"I'll handle this," Billy Boy announced, rising. The audience parted before him like the Red Sea before Moses, revealing a hysterical Ramona Houdeyshell sprawled on the floor amidst the ruins of an antique wooden trunk and something else. Something white and filmy and frothy.

"Oh my God, Alice-Ann," I screamed. "It's a veil. A bridal veil."

I reached Mrs. Houdeyshell's side just as two of the Barn Door Swingers pulled her to her feet. She fell, sobbing, into Billy Boy's arms, giving us all a clear view of what she'd been lying in. Not only a bridal veil with a crown of silk roses, but shreds of shattered ivory silk, decorated with seed pearls and crystal beads. And we also saw the real reason for Ramona Houdeyshell's screams: a skull grinning up at us from the tattered bridal finery.

Emily Rakestraw had come home.

FOURTEEN

LUSCIOUS PLAYED HIS FLASHLIGHT OVER the floor, the ceiling, the walls, and every nook and cranny of the little cave.

"Don't see nothing nowhere," was his comment.

While I was still struggling to figure out the real meaning of his triple-negative statement, he said, "Might as well go," and climbed over the rock pile. I was so stunned by his lack of interest that I didn't follow him. But through the hole in the wall, I could see him studying the UV filter. "Looks like it's running good," he announced. "We had to replace ours about a year ago, but I think that's 'cause we bought it secondhand."

"Luscious. Shut up."

He dropped his flashlight in surprise, and of course when it hit the limestone floor of the springhouse the lens shattered and the batteries popped out, leaving us in the dark.

After a few minutes of screwing and unscrewing the back of the flashlight and shaking it furiously, the light bulb came on again. "Glass is broke," Luscious said. "Council's gonna ask questions about this."

"I'll buy you a new flashlight." I had climbed out of the cave while he was fiddling with the flashlight and now stood next to him. "Why don't you tell me what you're going to do about this?"

Luscious smoothed his stringy blond hair back and said, "Do about what, Tori? There's nothing here."

"I know there isn't anything here. Not now. But there was. There was a body here. It was Rodney Mellott. And someone took him away. We have to find him."

Luscious picked at a pimple on his cheek. "I'll play along with you for a minute. Let's say there was a hypo…hypothete…"

"Hypothetical," I offered.

"Right. If there was a body here, how do you know for sure it was Rodney Mellott?"

I told him the skeleton had been dressed in Rodney's famous tuxedo and ruffled shirt. "The very same tuxedo he'd planned to wear to his wedding, which he didn't show up for. Who else could it be?"

"I dunno."

"It has to be Rodney Mellott, Luscious. That's even more obvious, now that Emily Rakestraw's body has turned up, too."

"We don't know for sure that it was Emily."

"How can you be so damn stubborn? How many brides and grooms have disappeared from Lickin Creek?"

"Well, there was that Hissong boy. His folks was Plain and didn't want him to marry an English girl, so they ran away together. Moved to Biglerville. Mom says they bought an orchard there and raised apples, peaches, and kids. That was back in '76, I think. And my cousin's girl got PG about ten years ago and eloped with her boyfriend instead of waiting for the big church wedding my cousin had planned. And in '93, or maybe it was '94…"

"Stop it." It took all my moral strength to refrain from strangling him.

"We better go," was all he said. "Flashlight's flickering. Don't want to get caught down here in the dark."

"Aren't you going to dust for fingerprints or do something?"

"Wouldn't be any use on this rough limestone. Besides…there's no crime if there's no body."

"You do have a body. Emily Rakestraw's bones are in a cardboard box over in Henry Hoopengartner's examining room right now." I knew this to be so, because Henry Hoopengartner, the very same man who owned the gas station that also served as the police station was also the county's elected coroner, and he'd arrived at the hardware store last night, pronounced the body to be dead at "nine-thirty-two p.m.," had bundled the shattered pieces of the trunk, the bones, and the bridal dress up and placed the whole thing in a large cardboard packing case. He'd announced he was taking it to his lab "for later examination." I could have done as much myself, and I haven't even been to coroner's school.

"We don't really know there's been a murder, Tori. We got to wait for Henry's report. He'll tell us."

"I've got Rodney Mellott's diary, Luscious. The man was a pervert. He seduced young boys."

"I don't see what that's got to do with anything that's happening today."

"Do you want to see it?"

"Maybe after I get Henry's report."

I'd had it with him. How could Garnet have gone to Costa Rica and left this idiot in charge of the public's safety? And to think, only a few months ago, I'd thought he was growing in the job.

"If there really was two people murdered, I'll find out. It's my job."

I flashed back to Afton Finkey advising me that Luscious had grown resentful of me. Perhaps I had overstepped my boundaries a few times. Perhaps I should give him a few days to work on this alone before I came down hard on him.

"Okay, Luscious," I said meekly. "I'll stay out of it. However, I am going to write something about the missing couple for the *Chronicle*. And I'm going to put in it that Rodney Mellott was found, then lost again."

"Do you have to?"

"It's what I do," I said, full of self-righteousness.

"Suit yourself," Luscious shrugged. "Now, let's get out of here. I might still have time to meet Mom at church."

I'D BEEN TRYING not to worry about my missing family, but Ethelind's kitchen was a reminder, full of casseroles and pies, gifts that kept arriving courtesy of Lickin Creekers who showed concern by providing food. There were several plates of sugar cakes from the Trinity church fund-raiser. Sugar cakes, I discovered, were really big, chewy cookies. I took a plate of them upstairs to my bedroom, where I worked diligently for the rest of the day on my articles for the *Chronicle*. The one about the anthills didn't take very long, thanks to the information Brunhilda, the environmentalist, had given me. That left me free to write my feature article about the tragic story of Rodney and Emily. I was determined not to make it the Lickin Creek version of *Romeo and Juliet*, because Romeo, as I remembered, was not perverted but only horny.

I began,

The Legend of the Bride's House has long been a piece of Lickin Creek's charming folklore. The story of Emily Rakestraw, the lovely debutante who became an art teacher at the very high school from which she'd graduated, and the popular high school music teacher, Rodney Mellott, was as romantic as any story found in a book. And it had as many twists and turns as one would expect from a good romance novel.

Despite her family's opposition to the match, Emily was determined to marry her true love. When she was deserted at the altar by her fiancé, the jilted bride threw herself into good works and was admired by everyone for her bravery in the face of such humiliation.

In the tradition of the world's great love stories, there was a happy ending. Emily eloped with Rodney. The couple left town for a fresh start in Texas, keeping in touch with friends and family through occasional postcards, sent from various vacation spots in the United States and Europe.

But this week, Lickin Creek learned that the fairy-tale ending to this story was a lie. The body of Emily Rakestraw, dressed in her bridal gown and stuffed into an antique trunk, was discovered Saturday night at Handshew's Hardware Store by Ramona Houdeyshell. The trunk, it now turns out, was found by Charlie Handshew during Bulky Trash Pickup Day in front of the Bride's House itself, now Ridgelys' Bride's House Bed-and-Breakfast. Mr. Handshew had planned to restore the trunk and sell it in his hardware store.

Now Lickin Creek knows the couple hadn't eloped after all. So where, you might ask, is Rodney Mellott? Did he commit this terrible crime? Did he come back after an absence of several weeks and murder the woman who loved and trusted him?

The answer is no. For Rodney Mellott himself was murdered. In his ruffled shirt and tuxedo, still recognizable after all these years, he lay alone in a walled-up natural cave beneath the Morgan Manor springhouse until this reporter found his body two weeks ago. Because he was dressed for his wedding and disappeared on that day, one can assume that what was supposed to have been his wedding day instead became the day of his death.

What was the cause of death? Certainly Rodney Mellott did not commit suicide by walling himself up inside the cave. He was murdered, and his body hidden for almost forty years.

By whom? No one can answer this question, for Rodney Mellott's body has recently been moved from the very spot where it has rested for four decades.

Where is the body now? That is an excellent question, to which there is no obvious answer. In fact, there are many questions that need to be answered, and the Lickin Creek Police Department is now seeking the answers to those questions.

The Legend of the Bride's House has changed from a romance into a tragedy. It has transformed from An Affair to Remember *to Edgar Allan Poe's "The Black Cat."*

Just as in Poe's story, the bricks, or stones in this case, were displaced, the corpse was inserted, and the murderer walled "the whole up as before, so that no eye could detect anything suspicious. The wall did not present the slightest appearance of having been disturbed."

Someone murdered the happy couple, not together, but separately, then hid the bodies and deceived Emily's family into thinking they were traveling and living happily in another state.

And why should someone murder this charming couple? A diary recently came to the attention of this reporter, that chronicled Rodney Mellott's first months in Lickin Creek. And the beloved music teacher was not the man he appeared to be. In his own words, he was a reptile, a disgusting pedophile who preyed on the young boys who came to him for private music lessons.

Did Rodney Mellott's disgusting perversions have anything to do with his and Emily's murders? Did the person or persons unknown who moved his body last week have something to do with Rodney's death? At the present time, there is no way of knowing, but this reporter and the Lickin Creek Police Department will find out. Even though it all happened nearly forty years ago, murder is still the worst crime imaginable, and justice will prevail.

I ATE THE LAST SUGAR CAKE, stretched, and read over what I'd written. A little too dramatic? Was I guilty of pontificating? Had I broken all the rules of journalism by inserting myself and my personal prejudices into it?

The answer to all the questions was yes. But I didn't care.

I was particularly pleased with myself for identifying the trunk from the hardware store as the one I'd seen in front of the Bride's House several weeks ago, put out for bulky trash pickup by the new owners of the house. I smiled as I corrected a few typos, printed it out, and slept the sleep of the just.

P.J. had wanted to publish my article about my father while his whereabouts were still unknown. That, plus the exciting discovery of a skeletal bride in the hardware store, was enough reason to put out a special edition.

P.J. had appeared grateful when I dropped my articles off on Monday morning. By all of us working diligently for the rest of Monday and all day Tuesday, an abbreviated version of the weekly paper was ready to be delivered on Wednesday morning.

Ethelind was sitting at the kitchen table reading it in a blue haze of smoke when I came down to breakfast shortly after ten. "Here you are," she said, quickly stubbing out her cigarette. She and I had had words recently about her smoking around food, and now she only smoked in the kitchen when I wasn't there. She folded the paper and handed it to me. "It's so nice having a morning paper during the week. I do wish you'd talk to P.J. about making it a regular event."

"I'm not sure there's enough going on in Lickin Creek to warrant a semiweekly paper," I said.

"Can I fix you some bacon? Maybe some scrambled eggs?"

"No thanks, Ethelind. I've got a date to meet Maggie Roy for lunch today, so I'm going to skip breakfast. I've got to get started on my diet again."

"You should never skip breakfast, Tori. It's the most important meal of the day. I'll just pour a small bowl of cereal for you."

"Any calls?" I asked hopefully.

She shook her head. "You know I'd have come to get you if there had been. Try not to worry, dear. I'm sure your family will be found safe and sound."

While I ate the cereal and drank the fresh orange juice Ethelind insisted on squeezing, I skimmed the front page. It was all about Ramona Houdeyshell finding the body of the missing bride. Nowhere in it was Rodney Mellott's name mentioned.

Inside, the second page was devoted to my article about my missing father. It was good. Really good. I couldn't wait for him to read it.

On page three was my feature article about the anthills,

with two pictures that could have been anything but certainly didn't look like anthills.

I flipped to page four, the editorial page, and finally found my article about the tragic end of Rodney and Emily tucked away in the lower left-hand corner. Cut to twenty lines with no mention of Rodney Mellott's perversions or diary.

"What's the big idea? How dare you cut my article like that?" I spluttered into the telephone.

"Calm down, Tori. Cassie and I decided it was too inflammatory. You have no proof that any of those things happened."

"I have the proof in Rodney Mellott's handwriting. Mr. Rodney Pervert Mellott's very own diary. Which wasn't even mentioned," I said with indignation.

"Perhaps you read something into it that wasn't really there."

"P.J. He masturbated into kids' sneakers. He described in detail how he taught a teenager with the initial *B* 'the meaning of love.' I didn't read anything into it. I didn't have to."

"Tori, all this happened a long time ago. Why dredge things up if we don't have to? Besides, we really don't know that Rodney and Emily were murdered, do we?"

"Oh no," I shouted indignantly. "Emily probably put on her wedding dress and climbed into that truck and waited to starve to death there. Motivated by grief, of course. As for Rodney, it was probably an accident that walled him up in the springhouse. Maybe he was down there washing up for the wedding and the walls just opened up and swallowed him."

"You are practically accusing someone local of murder, Tori. That's not going to win you any friends."

"I didn't mention any names. I can't even think of a suspect."

"It doesn't matter. Half the people in town would have read that article as you wrote it and suspected the other half of being murderers. At least, the way I've edited it won't outrage too many people."

"The way you've buried it on page four it will be a miracle if anybody even sees it."

"Judging from the irate calls I've had already, Tori, plenty of people have seen it. You've taken a part of Lickin Creek's history that everyone loved and ruined it. And you've insinuated that one or more of our local, upstanding citizens has covered up two murders for forty years. I have just one more thing to say to you."

"What?"

"I'm still the publisher and editor of this newspaper, and you have totally pissed me off! Don't bother to come in for your check. I'll mail it to you." My ear rang as she slammed her telephone down.

HEADS SWIVELLED toward the door as I entered the drugstore. It was twelve on the dot, and the place was filled with the Old Boys' Club members and their cigar smoke. Maggie waved from a booth near the kitchen door, and as I walked back to join her I smiled and nodded to the men in suits and greeted a few of the women in sundresses by name. Nobody returned my greeting.

"What have I done now?" I asked Maggie, as I slid onto the torn yellow vinyl bench.

I could always count on Maggie to be blunt. Today was no exception. "It's that article you wrote," Maggie told me. "The locals are all abuzz about what you said." Maggie picked up the menu encased in greasy, yellow plastic and began to study it.

"I tells it as I sees it," I joked. I picked up the rolled paper napkin containing my tableware and peeled off the tape.

"You should learn how to tell it with a little more tact, Tori. This isn't New York where nobody knows each other. You're writing about real people here. People who have grown up together, are related, and treasure their local stories. They don't like outsiders to come in and make fun of their comfortable lives. What are you going to eat?"

"I wasn't making fun of anything. I was informing the community that it had made a folk hero out of a monster, that's all."

"Perhaps they'd rather not know."

Mildred, the drugstore's veteran waitress who seemed to own an endless supply of vintage fifties-style pink nylon uniforms, hovered over us and interrupted. "You'uns ready to order? Today's special is chicken-fried steak."

"Sounds good, Millie," Maggie said. "I'll have it. With mashed potatoes and gravy, please."

The waitress wrote something in her order pad, flipped the page, and looked expectantly at me.

"I'll have the same thing. With French fries."

Mildred stared me straight in the eye and said, "Sorry, we're all out."

"But you took Maggie's order," I protested.

"That was the last one. Are you ready to order?"

I glanced at the menu, chose a grilled bacon and cheese sandwich, and asked her if she had any fries left.

"Yeah, I think so. You'uns want a red beet egg if we're out of fries?"

"No. Fries or nothing."

She made a notation on her pad, which I assumed said, "No fries," smiled at Maggie, and said, "Be right back."

"Sure is cold in here," I said. Since the inside temperature was close to a hundred degrees, Maggie knew what I meant.

"Did you hear about Ramona Houdeyshell?" When I shook my head, she went on. "She had a nervous breakdown last night. Turns out she's been having nightmares about being chased by an angry ghost in a wedding dress. Her husband had to drive her to Hershey."

"I thought I was the only person who thinks of chocolate as medicinal."

"You're so silly, Tori. That's where Penn State has its medical school and a state-of-the-art hospital."

"I suppose crashing through the lid of a trunk and smashing a skeleton to bits would be rather traumatic."

Maggie nodded as she unwrapped her silverware. "I wonder how Henry's ever going to put the body back together to determine cause of death."

Our waitress presented us with our meals. As I expected, there were no fries on mine, only a few broken potato chips, and a bright, red pickled egg.

"How's everything here, ladies? Everything okay?" Wilbur Esthelman, the drugstore's owner, looked down at us with pale blue eyes magnified by thick glasses. "Nice article about the anthills, Tori. Very nice article. Bet you didn't know Brunhilda, who gave you all that good info about ants, is my niece. My sister's kid, Brunhilda is. Nice girl, though I think it's kind of funny, her tramping round in the woods all the time looking for bugs and things. Didn't Mildred get you anything to drink? How about if I fix you one of my special homemade cherry Cokes? I know you like them. Like them a lot."

He scurried off before I had a chance to answer and was back before I'd finished my chips. "Here you are. With a double shot of syrup. Cherry syrup."

"Why thank you, Mr. Eshelman. That's very kind of you."

"No problem. No problem at all. Anything for my favorite reporter." He gave me a broad wink, patted Maggie on the shoulder, and walked back to the kitchen.

My eyes began to burn, and I dabbed at them with my paper napkin. What was wrong with my self-esteem that one person being kind could bring me to the brink of tears?

"I think I've been fired," I confessed, after eating half my sandwich. It was hard for me to admit.

"You think?"

"P.J. didn't exactly say so, but she did tell me not to come in for my check. She'd mail it to me."

Maggie shrugged. "P.J. is easily annoyed. But she cools down just as fast. By now she's probably forgotten all about it. If I were you I'd just show up for work as if nothing had happened. What did you do?"

I told Maggie what was in the article as originally written, and I unloaded everything I knew about Rodney and Emily. It felt good to get if off my chest.

"Oh, my," Maggie said. "No wonder P.J. was upset with you. By the way, have you noticed I've lost twelve pounds?"

I congratulated her on her weight loss, finished my lunch, and looked for the check.

"On the house, Tori," Mr. Eshelman called from behind the counter. "On the house. My thanks for doing such a good job for the paper. Really good job. If you ever want to write an article about the drugstore for that local business series, you just see me. I'll be happy to talk to you. Very happy."

"I'll be in touch, Mr. Eshelman." I left Mildred a generous tip, hoping she'd be more hospitable the next time I came in, and left with Maggie.

After the dimness of the drugstore, the midday sunlight was unbearably bright. I blinked, while Maggie sneezed. "Bright sun always does that to me," she muttered.

Several shots rang out, causing me to grasp Maggie in alarm.

"It's just the kids shooting firecrackers to scare the crows," she said between sneezes. "Nothing to be scared of. Got to get back to the library. How about next week, same time, same place?"

I gave her a hug. Friends like Maggie were to be treasured.

"Just keep in mind, Tori, that what happened to Rodney and Emily occurred a long time ago. Some things are best forgotten."

"I can't do that."

"Dog and bone. That's you. Gotta run."

I'd left the truck behind the building, and to get to it I had to walk down the alley between the drugstore and the bank.

"Third time's the charm," said a voice, coming from somewhere down near my ankles.

This time, because it was daytime, Big Bad Bob didn't startle me half as much as he had the last time I encountered him in an alleyway.

His snakelike head and then his shoulders arose from a window well, and I saw that he was wrapped in a heavy khaki blanket.

"Warm enough for you?" I asked. It was Lickin Creek's traditional summertime greeting.

"Got thin blood," he said. "Have to stay bundled up or I gets sick."

He smelled of vomit and wine, and I covered my nose.

"You all right there, Mizz Miracle? You look kinda pale. Not gonna be sick, are ya?"

"I'm fine, thanks." It touched me that one of the few people who was concerned about me was the town drunk. If he hadn't smelled so bad, I might have hugged him. Instead, I smiled and said, "I enjoyed your music Saturday night, Bob. I didn't know you played."

"I play seventeen instruments, Mizz Tori. Just came naturally to me, I guess. I could hear a song, then play it on whatever was nearby. Was in the band, back in high school, 'fore I dropped out. Want me to play you a song? I got my recorder right here."

"Maybe another time. I have to get to the office now," I fibbed. "It's been nice talking to you, Bob."

"You, too. Not too many people 'round here see Big Bad Bob. It's like I'm invisible to 'em. But you always take notice."

He pulled back into his hole, and I continued on to where I'd left the truck, thinking he and I had a lot in common. We were both unpleasant blotches on the serene Lickin Creek landscape. Stains to be ignored in the hope they'd go away. Or, as in Bob's case, have the good sense to become invisible.

I strolled casually into the office as if I weren't scared to death of what my welcome would be. Cassie sat at her rolltop desk in the outer office, looking exquisite in a simple linen sheath that skimmed her body. Her silver hair was pulled back into a French twist, and around her neck hung the silver and amber necklace that symbolized her position as leader of the local coven. It was only because she was a third-generation Lickin Creeker that her unorthodox beliefs were tolerated. If word got out that I'd attended a few of her coven meetings, I'd probably be burned as a witch.

"Is it safe to come in?"

Cassie nodded. "The worst is over. Just watch yourself, though. Try not to rile her up any more this week. Her blood pressure's through the roof already."

"Is she here?"

"Nope. Gone home for a nap. But she did leave some assignments for you."

That was a relief. It meant she hadn't seriously fired me, not this time.

Cassie riffled through the scraps of paper that littered her desk. Amazingly, the woman always knew where to find things. "Here." She handed me a notecard. "P.J. says, be sure to visit the Laughenslagger farm this week. It's a unique business in this area, and the council is counting on it to bring in big bucks."

Since when was a farm news? In fact, when had any farm in the area brought in more than a bare existence for its owners? But who was I to argue. "Her wish is my command," I said. "I'll do it now. I need to stay busy to keep my mind off of things."

"I'll call and tell Bruce Laughenslagger you're on the way. Have you got your notebook handy? I can give you directions. You can't miss it. Oh, I nearly forgot. This was on my desk when I came in this morning. It's got your name on it." She handed me a folded piece of lined paper torn from a three-ringed binder.

I stared at it in dismay as if she'd handed me a scorpion.

That paper looked familiar. It was exactly like the note I'd found in my bathtub.

Almost in a trance, I unfolded it and read the message there: YOU ARE NEVER ALONE.

"What's the matter, Tori? You're as white as a ghost. It's not bad news about your father, is it?"

"It's nothing." I crumpled the paper and stuffed it into the pocket of my slacks. "Nothing at all."

FIFTEEN

As USUAL, I got lost shortly after leaving the borough. Cassie had given me directions in typical Lickin Creek fashion. "Turn right at the second-to-last traffic light on the Marshallville Road (how was I supposed to know which light was second to last without driving all the way to Marshallville and turning around), go about five or six miles (it turned out to be eight) until you come to where the Seven Star Fruit Stand used to be (used to be?), turn there (she hadn't mentioned whether it would be a right or left turn, which gave me another opportunity to get lost for half an hour), drive past three barns, a house, and a cornfield, then turn left at the second farm road and keep going till you see the pond. (It was dried up and looked nothing like a pond.) Go around it, to the right, I think, and just keep driving up the side of the mountain till you reach the green fence. Keep blowing your horn there, and eventually someone will come to let you in."

It was late afternoon, and the sun had dropped behind the pine trees when I finally reached the green fence Cassie had mentioned. Fence was hardly the word I would have used, for although it was made of chain-link, a screen of dark green netting behind it made it impossible to see through. And I estimated it to be at least ten feet high. A few weeks ago I had watched *King Kong,* the original Fay Wray version, not the new one, and this tall, dark fence was reminiscent of the wall that protected the islanders from Kong and his prehistoric buddies. If this farmer kept cows in there, he would never have to worry about them getting out and wandering onto the highway, as happened in Lickin Creek about twice a week in the summer.

I pressed the horn, waited, and wished again that Garnet's truck was air-conditioned, even though he'd told me several times you didn't need air-conditioning in Pennsylvania. I was steaming, both physically and emotionally as I pressed the horn for the tenth or maybe even the hundredth time.

One more toot and I'm out of here, I thought, just as the enormous gate slowly swung open.

"Howdy. You Tori Miracle?" The man who came toward me through the opening was well over six feet, but dwarfed by the height of the fence. He had gray hair pulled into a ponytail, which protruded from the back of his green John Deere tractor cap.

"Sorry to take so long," he said, leaning his arms on the passenger's-side window. "I saw you coming on the security camera, but I thought I'd save myself the hike and wait till the other guy got here."

"What other guy?"

"Go ahead and drive on in and wait for me. I'll close the gate."

"What other guy?" I repeated.

"There was a van coming up the road about a mile, mile and a half behind you. I thought maybe you were traveling together. But it turned off a few minutes after you parked here."

An alarm sounded in my head. "Was it a dark green van?"

"Dunno. Could have been. Looked black to me, but my security monitor's black-and-white. Now hurry up, please, and drive in so I can close the gate."

I waited while the gate closed. He opened the door and swung himself into the seat beside me with a grace I wouldn't have expected from a man of his age. Which, I judged, to be about sixty, although perhaps I overestimated because of the lines that seemed to be permanently etched into his deeply tanned face.

"What would you like to see first?"

"Cows? Corn? I really have no idea. Why don't you surprise me?"

His green eyes sparkled as he looked at me, and I lowered my age estimate by a decade. "You're not going to see any cows here. Go that way."

After driving for a few minutes through dense forest, we came upon several buildings in a clearing.

Bruce led me to the largest of the buildings, which was of dark wood, two stories high, and in an uninteresting style. He should have spent the extra bucks and hired an architect, I thought. But when he opened the nondescript white door and I looked inside, I was overcome with the magnificence of the interior. Instead of the two-story building I had expected, there was a great room that soared up to a beamed cathedral ceiling. One whole wall was native limestone, with a fireplace set in it that was big enough to walk into. There were several groupings of huge white leather sofas, draped with Indian blankets, and coffee tables of heavy oak.

The other side of the room was devoted to dining and kitchen areas, which were set under a balcony. There was one door leading onto the balcony, and I could tell from where I stood that it was a bedroom. Several other doors opened off the great room.

But what was most dumbfounding of all was the display of animal heads high on the wall. There must have been a hundred; mostly deer, but also elk and wild boar.

A stuffed wildcat was draped on a ledge above the fireplace. A hawk, or maybe it was an eagle, spread its wings as if preparing to soar across the room. A pair of squirrels cavorted in an endless dance on a coffee table. Small dead animals lurked in every corner.

"Welcome to the BL Deer Hunting Preserve."

I nodded, too dumbfounded to speak.

A man was sitting at the dining area table, with a laptop computer in front of him and a portable telephone held to his ear.

"Meet Sal," Bruce said.

The man glanced up and nodded, then clicked off the phone. "Got a couple of bucks lined up for you to take a look at."

"Where?"

"An Amish farm in Ohio."

"Good. We can fly over on Monday to see them."

"That's what I told him. And I've got two more hunts booked for October."

"I don't know what I'd do without Sal," Bruce said as he slid open the glass door and gestured for me to step outside.

The view from the deck took my breath away. I hadn't realized I'd come so high, but now I was looking over the treetops, at the Tuscarora Mountains on one side and South Mountain on the other.

In the valley below lay Lickin Creek, resembling a small, charming village like the ones people put under their Christmas trees. Miniature church steeples reached skyward over the borough's two- and three-story buildings. On the outskirts of town, farms were a patchwork quilt of greens and golds.

"Too bad it's so hazy," Bruce said. "Otherwise you'd be able to see all the way to Maryland."

"This is quite enough for one day," I told him.

"I hope you'll come back another time." There was something in the tone of his voice that made me wonder if he were making a pass.

We reentered the great room, and I crossed over to the dining area wall, which held a number of photographs and certificates. Most of the photos were of men holding up deer's heads with huge antlers, but one was of a small country-western band. Bruce noticed what I was looking at and said, "That's me in the middle, with the guitar. Once I actually thought I might make a career out of music. Come sit down."

We sat on facing sofas. "I understand this is for a feature for the *Chronicle*. Am I right?"

"Yes." I took out my notebook and a pen and waited.

"Questions?"

"Just tell me what you do here, in your own words."

"I raise deer for hunters who want trophies. In order for a deer to grow a trophy-size rack, it takes about four years. Most public areas around here are so overhunted that a hunter is lucky to bag a two-year-old."

"How much are people willing to pay for the bigger antlers?"

His answer caused me to drop my pen. By the time I'd retrieved it from beneath the couch, I'd recovered enough to ask, "What kind of person has that kind of money to spend on a hunting trip?"

"Movie stars, NASCAR racers, CEOs of Fortune Five Hundred companies. There's a lot of people out there with a lot of money."

I was astounded. "I've never seen a celebrity in Lickin Creek."

"They don't go into town, Tori. They come directly to the BL Hunting Preserve, stay here, hunt, and go home with their trophies."

"Can you give me some names?"

Bruce shook his head. "Sorry. My client list is confidential. They pay for privacy as well as trophies." He was interrupted by the arrival of a young man, who paced impatiently while Bruce was speaking. "This is Kevin, Tori."

Kevin nodded in my direction and smiled, showing me he was missing several front teeth. His black hair was shoulder-length and his goatee was sparse, and he had bright blue eyes rimmed with black lashes.

"Kevin's in charge of the grounds. Another invaluable employee."

"You wanted to see me, boss?" Kevin broke in.

"You'd better come outside, Kevin, and see what I've got in the truck. I'll be right back," Bruce said to me. "Sal will get you some coffee."

Before I had an opportunity to decline, Sal had a mug of

steaming coffee in front of me. He sat on the sofa Bruce had vacated and smiled at me.

"How long has this ranch been in operation?" I asked him.

"About six years."

"And how big is the ranch?"

"Fifteen hundred acres, more or less."

"I had no idea there was a property that large near Lickin Creek."

"Not many locals know about it. That's why the boss thought it would be a goodwill gesture to get it better known."

"It must have cost Bruce a fortune to buy a piece of property this large."

"It would have, but he didn't have to buy it. It's been in his family for years. He's the third, no, fourth generation of Laughenslaggers to own it. Used to be they just used it for their own hunting place, but Bruce was the one who thought it could be a moneymaker."

The front door slammed as Bruce entered, followed by Kevin. There were two red spots of anger on Bruce's cheeks.

"Damn coyotes," he muttered. He unlocked a gun case, removed a rifle, and handed it to Kevin, along with a box of shells.

"Go get him," he snapped. "Can't afford to have any more bucks killed."

Kevin nodded and left with the gun.

"I'm sorry," I said, feeling inadequate.

"We do what we can, but one gets in every now and then. They're worse than bears." As he spoke, the red spots began to fade. "Ready to go for a drive?"

"I'd love to."

Outside, instead of walking toward the parking area, he turned right and led me to a small outbuilding with a chain-link fence around it.

"This is where we bottle-feed the fawns." He tapped on the

fence, and immediately about ten adorable little baby deer came bounding out of a small opening in the side of the building.

They came right up to the fence, and I was even able to touch one of them on its soft little nose.

"They are so cute!"

"We'll put them in the large pens with the other young deer when they get a little bigger."

A fence enclosed a large area behind the fawn house, and now I saw it contained a dozen or more deer.

"We keep them there till they are two, then move them into the back fields."

"How can you tell how old they are?" I asked.

"Notice the little tags the fawns have in their ears? Different color for each year."

As we walked toward his four-wheel-drive vehicle, he pointed to several other small outbuildings. "Butchering room there. Cooler next door."

"Do you do your own taxidermy?"

Bruce shook his heard. "There's a local guy we recommend if people ask, but lots of people like to take their trophies home and have them mounted by their own man." He held the door open for me and closed it once I was in the vehicle. A real gentleman, I noted with a small smile.

The forest was thick and dark overhead, but the lower branches of the trees were bare. The road was little more than a trail, and I hung on with both hands to keep from bouncing to death. "Sorry about the bumps," Bruce apologized.

"It's okay," I said through clenched teeth.

"There's some," he said slowing down and pointing to the left.

At first I couldn't see the deer because they blended in so well with the background, then gradually they took shape. A tree branch became an antler, a sun-dappled clump of bushes turned into a face, a fallen log was really four deer huddled together. As my eyes adjusted, I saw more and more animals. "Beautiful," I said. "They are so beautiful."

"Bad rack on that one. Nobody will want to hunt him," Bruce said, pointing to one of the deer. "Gonna have him for dinner soon."

We continued through the forest, seeing hunting blinds, feeding stations, a large lake full of waterfowl, and eventually coming to the fence that encircled the area. A large gate stood open, and Bruce cursed and slammed on the brakes.

"I've told them a hundred times to keep these gates closed," he snarled. "Can you help me swing it shut?"

I nodded and got out of the truck. The gate was heavy, and it took both of us, putting all our weight on it, to push it shut. I watched while Bruce made sure it was secure, then locked it. At that moment, something whined by my head and slammed into a tree behind me, sending splinters in all directions.

"What was that?" I spun around, saw the shattered tree trunk, and realized I had narrowly missed being shot. Another bullet whizzed past me, and I dropped to the ground with my hands covering my head, as though that would protect me.

"Tori. Tori. Are you all right?" Bruce was on his knees beside me, trying to help me sit up.

My head hurt, and when I touched my forehead I felt something sticky. "I think so. Am I bleeding?"

"Let me check." Bruce parted my hair and stared intently at me. "A scrape," he said. "You must have hit something when you fell. Stay down. I'm going to find who did this."

Terrified, I huddled next to the tree, hoping no more shots would come my way. Thankfully, nothing else happened. After a wait that felt like an hour, but was probably only a few minutes, Bruce returned, accompanied by Kevin.

"Look what you did, you idiot. You almost killed her."

Kevin hung his head and looked sheepish. "I'm sorry, ma'am. I thought you was a coyote."

"You thought my head was a coyote? Five feet above the ground?"

"I'm really sorry, ma'am."

"I could have been killed." I didn't mind stating the obvious.

"God, I am so sorry, Tori." Bruce said. "I'm very proud of our safety record here. Very few of my employees or hunters have ever been shot."

I wondered how many "very few" actually were and was glad I hadn't become one of them. Then I realized he was probably trying to inject a little humor into the situation. I didn't appreciate it.

Bruce and Kevin hauled me to my feet. My legs wobbled like jelly, and I needed to hang onto both men to walk to the truck.

Back at the lodge, I transferred to my truck. Bruce got in and rode with me to the gate. Before he got out, he cleared his throat and asked if I'd go out to dinner with him some time. "I'd really like to show you how sorry I am."

"I'm seeing someone," I fibbed. I actually found his rugged, tanned face and lean athletic build quite attractive, but he was nearly as old as my father. Besides, after my disastrous date with Haley Haley, I wasn't ready to chance another dating fiasco.

"YOU LOOK RATHER PECULIAR," Ethelind said from her armchair in front of the television, as I entered the parlor. "What happened to your head?"

"I had a little accident," I told her, which explained nothing. "All I need is a shower."

Fred followed me upstairs, entranced by the bits of twigs and leaves that dropped from my clothes. "Scoot," I said, shutting him out of the bathroom. "I don't need an audience."

I almost didn't have the courage to draw the shower curtain, but this time there was no note in the bathtub.

I scrubbed the dirt and deer smells off my body, then shampooed my hair three times before I felt clean. When I pushed aside the shower curtain, I found the bathroom door ajar and Fred sitting on the sink with a superior look on his face. He was my Houdini cat, who had taught himself to open a door by jumping up, grabbing hold of the doorknob, and hanging onto it until the door opened.

"Hi, Mr. Show-off." I thrust my arms into my terry cloth robe, grabbed Fred up in my damp arms, and carried him down the hall to my bedroom. By the time I dropped him on the bed, his purr had come to a roiling boil.

He stretched out on the antique quilt, rolled onto his back, and waved his paws in the air until I gave in to his demand. "Okay," I acquiesced, "just a quick tummy rub, then I have to get dressed."

A few minutes later, with both of us feeling rather pleased with ourselves, I gave him a gentle swat on the rump, our signal that playtime was over. He closed his eyes and instantly fell asleep.

I pulled the drawer in the mahogany dresser where I kept my underwear, and my heart nearly stopped as I saw the folded note.

Maybe there are fingerprints, was my thought as I used two fingernails to pluck it from the drawer.

I slowly unfolded it, taking care only to touch the edges. It was the same lined notebook paper as before, torn from a three-hole binder.

PRETTY PANTIES, it said. I screamed, dropped the paper, and woke up Fred.

"Come on!" I grabbed all my underwear out of the dresser and fled downstairs with my arms full and Fred behind me. I washed my clothes twice before I could bear to put anything on my body.

Before we went to bed, Ethelind made sure the doors and windows were closed and locked. It was probably the first time in the old mansion's history that it had been so tightly secured.

SIXTEEN

"WHERE'D YOU get this, Tori?" Luscious leaned back in his desk chair, stretched his long legs out on the desktop, and dangled Rodney Mellott's diary from his bony fingers. Garnet's desk, I thought resentfully. It hadn't taken Luscious long at all to move his belongings to the more prestigious location in the back of the room. My resentment was unreasonable, and I knew it. Luscious was acting police chief and had every right to sit there.

It was Thursday morning, and I was trying to enlist Luscious's help in finding a killer.

"I told you. It was in a box of old scrapbooks Alice-Ann found in the attic at Morgan Manor."

"Pretty active imagination for a music teacher."

"It wasn't imagination, Luscious. This is a diary."

"How do you know he didn't make it up?"

"Would you make up things like this and keep it where your landlady might find it?"

"Probably not, but it would be even worse if she found it and it was the truth, wouldn't it? He could have been arrested if he really did molest those boys."

"I'm glad you agree with me that what he did was a crime."

"I'm not saying that's so, Tori. I'm only saying that if it was true it would be criminal, but I'm not so sure that was the case. My dad was in high school back in the sixties. I don't like to think…" His voice trailed away, as he drifted off into the gentle days of Lickin Creek's past. After a moment he shook himself slightly, focused his eyes, and rejoined me in the Lickin Creek Police Department, the back room of Henry Hoopengartner's Garage.

"Besides, he'd have had to be some sort of an idiot to keep a journal like this."

"Maybe he was."

"But he taught at the high school," Luscious argued, as if only geniuses and the pure of heart were allowed to be instructors in Lickin Creek High School's hallowed halls.

"So you don't want to keep it?"

Luscious handed the diary back to me. "Can't see any reason to. No mention of Emily in there, and I only have your word that Rodney was murdered."

"Alice-Ann saw him, too," I protested.

"Funny thing. You say that, but I've called to corbotorate your story and left half a dozen messages on her machine, and she ain't returned them yet."

"Corroborate." After I corrected him I wished I hadn't, for he looked so dejected. Poor Luscious, he really was trying to do his best in Garnet's absence. I knew I shouldn't be so hard on him.

"What about the box of sneakers in Rodney's closet?" I asked.

"I didn't see no box."

It was time to change the subject. "Have you heard any more about Vonzell Varner?"

The policeman's eyes brightened. "Matter of fact, I have. He was spotted the Monday before Memorial Day in a Giant Store in Washington County, Maryland. Stole a van from a used care dealership. Walked in, bold as you please, and asked to take it for a test drive. Never came back. Left a Chevy Tahoe with Kentucky license plates behind. Turned out that was stolen, too, from a sheriff's deputy, of all people. He's on the top of the Bureau of Alcohol, Tobacco and Firearms' Most Wanted List, not to mention the U.S. Marshal's list."

I had been scribbling in my notebook, but something he had said registered and stopped me. The back of my neck tingled unpleasantly. "A dark green van?"

"Let's see." Luscious shuffled papers. "Yup. A '98 Plymouth Grand Voyager with privacy glass. How'd you know it was green?"

"Lucky guess. I hope the feds are still watching Mrs. Varner's house."

"I dunno. It's been a long time. He'd probably be here already if this was where he was heading."

"Maybe he is here, Luscious. I've seen a green van around town several times. It could be the one he stole."

"Sure. There's only one in town, right?"

"Only one that appears to be following me," I snapped back. "I saw it for the first time right after I wrote the first article about Vonzell Varner for the *Chronicle*. No, take that back. I saw it for the first time outside Jenny Varner's house, even before I wrote that article."

"Next I suppose you'll be asking for police protection. Well, I have to tell you Afton and I ain't got time to…"

"I know. And I'm not asking. I'm simply telling you, on the off chance that it might be useful information. Wouldn't it be a feather in your cap to catch an escaped convict?"

Luscious appeared to like that.

"And wouldn't it also be a triumph if you found out who murdered Emily and—"

Luscious swung his feet to the floor with a crash. "I've got a lot of work to do, Tori. You feel free to drop by any time, hear?"

Since I'd stopped making notes right after Luscious had mentioned the stolen van, I asked, "May I take that latest bulletin about Varner with me? I can use it to corrob—to check my facts when I write the Police Blotter."

He shrugged to show me it wasn't important. "Help yourself."

I already had.

In the truck, I looked over the bulletin. Vonzell Varner had escaped from a county jail in Louisville, Kentucky. I knew that. But I hadn't known he'd done time in Graterford. I'd heard that name fairly recently. From Haley Haley, and I couldn't help wondering if there was some sort of connection between the two men. I dismissed the thought. There must be thousands of convicts at Graterford; that didn't mean they all knew each other.

I went into the office and helped P.J. and Cassie lay out the pages of this week's newspaper. P.J. told me she liked the article about the deer preserve, but wanted to leave out the part about my nearly being shot. "No need alarming people," she said, peering over her half-moon glasses. "Hunting accidents happen all the time."

I would have argued with her, but she was overcome by a coughing fit, and I could only watch helplessly while Cassie got her a cup of water and rubbed her shoulders.

We worked into the late afternoon, with only one short break when Cassie went out for sandwiches. We left the front page blank for late-breaking developments. The inside pages were filled with farm news; the Extension Agent's advice; comics; the police blotter; lists of divorces, marriages, hospital admissions, and real estate transfers; some syndicated columns we subscribed to; club news; and sports, lots of sports. The editorial page was also left half-blank, waiting for P.J.'s editorial of the week.

"That's it," P.J. announced. "See you both back here early in the morning to finish up."

I left quickly before she thought of anything else for me to do. I glanced at my watch and saw it was not as late as I thought. There was still time to do something I'd been meaning to do ever since I found Rodney Mellott's diary.

After showing a photo ID and signing a book, I was allowed into the Lickin Creek High School. It was the closest thing to a security measure I'd ever seen in Lickin Creek. What a shame it had to be in a school. It wasn't always that way; there was a time when schools were safe places, I thought, then stopped short as I recalled Rodney Mellott, whose diary proved that danger sometimes came from unex-

pected places and that it was always necessary to be aware of
its hidden presence.

The librarian looked a little surprised when I entered his
office, but he still greeted me warmly.

In response to my question, he said, "Yearbooks from the
sixties? Of course. We have a complete collection." He opened
a closet door and pointed to many rows of books. "They're
supposed to be in order by year, but sometimes they get put
back wrong. If you have any problem finding what you need,
let me know."

I settled down at the worktable in the office with several
yearbooks from the early sixties. It was my intention to find
out who "B" was, the boy who was mentioned in Rodney's
diary. And after I figured out who he was, I was going to determine whether he knew anything about Rodney's demise.

It only took a few minutes to find pictures of Rodney Mellott with both the orchestra and the band. Rodney was posed
in his tuxedo and ruffled shirt, looking both serious and proud.
Other faces stared out at me from long ago. Young boys with
Elvis pompadours, girls with either long straight hair or enormous beehive hairdos. All looked so much alike, I had to
look at the captions below the pictures to identify them.

As I scanned the list of names. I realized there were a lot
of names beginning with *B*, and I saw the names of many of
the borough's now-established citizens. Bruce Laughenslagger, millionaire owner of the BL Deer Hunting Preserve.
Benjamin Koon, funeral home director. Billy Barnes, of the
Barn Door Swingers. Even Buchanan McCleary, the borough
solicitor, soon to be Greta Gochenauer Carbaugh's husband.

Others, who didn't begin with a *B*, but whom I recognized
were Edward Fetterhoff, now a judge; J.B. Morgan, president
of the bank; Wilbur Eshelman, who owned the drug store;
even a Luscious Miller, who I guessed was the father of our
acting police chief. Others with whom I was familiar were
Charles Handshew, owner of the hardware store where

Emily's body had been found, and Marvin Bumbaugh, the president of the borough council.

There were few girls in the music program, I noticed. Things had certainly changed for the better in that regard. Last time I'd been to the symphony in New York, more than half of the orchestra had been female. As I stared at the picture, I noticed a face that looked somewhat like a snake. It was Big Bad Bob, who apparently hadn't always been a homeless alcoholic.

Which one of the young people in those pictures was the mysterious "B"? And how many of the others had Rodney Mellott tried to corrupt? The secrets of the band director were not revealed in the innocent faces of his students.

It suddenly occurred to me I'd seen no pictures of Emily Rakestraw and had no idea what she looked like, and so I flipped pages of the yearbook until I came to a double-page spread devoted to the art department.

Emily looked nothing like what I'd imagined. Because of the romantic legend that had grown up around her, I had expected her to be quite glamorous. Instead, she was a plain-looking woman, a little overweight, with a hairdo that must have been disastrous even in a decade of bad hairdos. I knew I shouldn't judge character based on appearance, but looking at Emily's pictures, I couldn't help but understand a little better why she had agreed to marry the unattractive music teacher.

Just for fun, I opened an annual from the mid-fifties. I quickly found Ethelind Gallant's senior picture. The years had been fairly kind to my landlady. She had hardly changed at all. She'd been big and mannish-looking then, and she was still big and mannish, only now her hair was gray instead of dark brown or black.

Ethelind once mentioned that she'd known Emily Rakestraw in high school, and I found Emily's senior picture on the next page. She looked pretty much like all the other girls. In the index, I found her name listed a half dozen times. Emily had participated in a lot of extracurricular activities. She'd been a cheerleader, worked on the yearbook and the school newspaper, was a member of the art club, and she also was a "Booster," whatever that was.

"Do you have a copy machine?" I asked the librarian.

He nodded, not even looking up from his book, and pointed to a corner of the office. I copied the two photos of Rodney Mellott with his band and his orchestra. I also made a copy of the faculty photo of Emily.

"Thank you," I said. "I'm going now."

"You're welcome. But I advise waiting a few minutes. School's letting out, and you might get trampled in the rush."

I watched through the windows as hundreds of students streamed toward the cars in the parking lot. "Doesn't anybody ride the bus anymore?"

The librarian smiled wryly. "They're supposed to, unless there's a good reason like after-school jobs, activities, or sports practice. Apparently most of the students have something important to do right after school lets out."

Within a couple of minutes the parking lot was nearly deserted. That's when I noticed about a dozen men walking toward the school building carrying large coolers. I recognized one of them as Wilbur Eshelman from the drug store. I tapped on the window, and when I had his attention waved at him. He looked up surprised, then smiled and nodded, unable to wave back because his arms were full.

Soon, Wilbur was standing in the doorway to the library office. "What are you doing here?" he asked with a warm smile.

I pointed to the yearbooks. "I've been trying to identify former students who might have known Rodney Mellott and Emily Rakestraw," I said.

Wilbur put down the cooler he'd been carrying, came over to the table, and stared down at the yearbooks. "How?" he asked.

"By determining who was in band and orchestra."

"Why?" he asked.

I didn't want to tell him about the diary, so I simply said, "Maybe someone who knew him might know something about his disappearance."

"He didn't disappear, Tori. Didn't disappear. He eloped…" Wilbur's voice trailed off as he remembered that Emily's body had been found a few days ago. "Good grief. Do you think…do you think Mr. Mellott had something to do with what happened to Miss Rakestraw and then killed himself? The newspaper said you found his body in a cave. I am confused, Tori. Really confused."

I noticed he had reverted back to the high-school way of speaking of teachers. There had been no mention of the diary in what P.J. had left of my article, and I couldn't tell him about it. "I don't think so," I said. "Maybe."

Wilbur shook his head. "Hard to think of Mr. Mellott doing something like that…something awful like that."

He seemed lost in contemplation, so to break the mood I asked, "What are *you* doing here, Wilbur?"

"Chicken and Slippery Pot Pie dinner tonight. The Downtown Businessmen's Association holds it once a month to make money for our projects."

I should have remembered that. I'd been sent by P.J. often enough to cover the monthly event.

"Why don't you stop by and join us? Please do," Wilbur said.

"I just might," I said, thinking I had no intention of eating another fried, starch-filled meal.

Wilbur paused in the doorway, looking nervous.

"Yes?"

"Tori, I like you a lot. A lot. And I don't want to see anything happen to you."

"That's very kind of you, Wilbur. I assure you I'm taking good care of myself."

"I meant…just be careful, will you?"

After he left, I put the photocopies I'd made into my purse and the yearbooks back in the closet. I was thoughtful, trying to make sense of Wilbur Ethelman's words to me. No doubt about it, they'd sounded like a veiled warning. Maybe even a threat.

SEVENTEEN

ETHELIND GREETED ME with a cup of hot cocoa and a stack of phone messages. I flipped through them, determined that most were from strangers, and pulled out the ones I wanted to answer immediately. The most pressing was one from someone at the State Department, and I called on the chance that a civil servant might be working late. I was correct.

He wanted to tell me that the American embassy where my father was presumably holed up was still under attack. No supplies were allowed in. At least three local hires had been killed. He couldn't tell me anything about my family. He wasn't very encouraging that things would work out. When I hung up I was in tears. The ordeal had gone on for nearly two weeks.

Ethelind handed me a tissue, and I wiped my face and blew my nose. No point in crying, I thought. Not until I know for sure what has happened.

There was also a message from my dental hygienist. Last time I'd seen her, at the bowling alley during my disastrous date with Haley Haley, she had reminded me that I was nearly due for a cleaning and checkup. The receptionist sounded a little cranky when I called, saying the office was officially closed, but yes, they had a cancellation tomorrow afternoon and could work me in.

On Friday morning, I went into the *Chronicle* office to help finish the paper. Cassie waited until I was seated, then handed me a folded piece of lined notebook paper with my name on it. "It was inside the front door when I got here," she said. "Looks like someone slid it under the door."

I unfolded it and read, "I'M NEAR YOU RIGHT NOW." For a moment I couldn't breathe.

"Anything I can do?" Cassie asked, looking worried.

I shook my head. "Just some crank writing me notes," I explained.

"Maybe you should take it to the police."

"Good idea," I said, thinking it was no such thing. But I folded it and put it in my purse as if that were my intention.

All morning, I wrote whatever was necessary to fill in the holes, added a long article about local club meetings, and by noon the paper was on its way to the printer. Thankfully, P.J. had said no more about my being fired. Either she'd forgotten or she knew she needed me. Regardless, I was grateful to still have a job.

I grabbed a quick bite to eat at the newest pizza joint to open on Main Street, then got the truck and drove to the dentist's office.

"I'm so glad you could come in on such short notice," Megan said. She was the hygienist who had cleaned my teeth the last time I'd been here. "It's rare we have a cancellation. Dr. Gelsinger suggested I try to call you since he knows you have Friday afternoons free."

I grunted, which was all I could do with my mouth full of her hands.

She x-rayed, chipped, scraped, and finally polished. "All ready for Doctor," she said brightly.

Again, all I could manage was a grunt. She stepped back, and Dr. Gelsinger came in. He was a man in his mid-fifties, well tanned as if he'd just stepped off the golf course. He put his hands where hers had been. "How are you today?" he asked.

"Grunt, grunt, grunt." I intended it to mean, "Pretty good, thank you."

"Tut, tut."

My mouth was reflected in his glasses. "Grunt?" Meaning, "What?"

"Bad cavity. If you've got time I'd like to fill it today."

"Grunt, grunt?" Meaning, "Is that really necessary?"

How he understood me, I'll never know, but he answered, "The tooth could break if I don't do something. Then you'd have to have a root canal, crown…"

"Grunt." Meaning, "Go ahead."

"Do you need me here, Doctor? If not, I have another patient waiting."

"It's all right, Megan." He was preoccupied with my mouth. "I can manage."

For the next century, or perhaps half an hour, I lay back and grunted while he worked. Finally, he stood back, pulled off his rubber gloves, and announced he was done. "It was even bigger than I thought. I'm going to call a prescription into the drugstore for you. Be sure to take it as directed. We don't want you to get an infection. I'd advise starting it tonight."

"Which drugstore?"

"The one downtown," he said, as if there were no other worth mentioning.

"How about something for pain?" The novocaine was wearing off.

Dr. Gelsinger shook his head. "Take Tylenol. I don't want you getting addicted to anything."

He was dialing as I left the office.

It was rather later in the day, but I thought I'd best go to the drugstore and pick up my prescription, since Dr. Gelsinger had been so adamant about my starting it right away.

Lickin Creek, like a lot of Pennsylvania towns, had long ago turned its back on its scenic wonders, and so the pretty bubbling stream that was the Lickin Creek was bordered by paved parking lots and the unattractive backsides of most of the town's Civil War-era buildings. In the twilight, they looked dilapidated and sadly in need of paint. I parked in the lot behind the drugstore and ran down the alley, hoping Mr. Eshelman would still have the pharmacy open.

Inside, the dinner crowd had already gathered. It looked exactly the same as the lunch crowd. The lawyer types from the courthouse often met here with the members of the Old Boys' Club for the day's last chat before heading to their respective homes for the evening.

To get to the pharmacy, I had to walk through the dining room, but this time nobody looked up. When I reached the window, I found that a louvered shutter was pulled down over it. The sign said BACK LATER.

Mildred, the waitress, spoke so close behind me that I jumped. "He went home for dinner," she said.

"Food here not good enough for him?" I thought I was being funny, but she didn't crack a smile.

"He always goes home at this time, after making the bank deposit. He should be back in about an hour. Do you want me to get you something to eat?"

"Maybe he left a prescription for me," I said, hopefully. "Could you check behind the counter?"

If her sigh was meant to make me feel bad, it didn't. I waited patiently, while she ducked under the counter. I heard her rummaging through paper bags. In two minutes, she was back. "Nothing there for you," she said. "Do you want to order dinner now?"

"No thanks. My dentist really wants me to get started on the medicine right away. Isn't there someone here who can fill it for me?"

She shuffled through a very small pile of papers. "The cook's a part-time pharmacist, but there's no prescription written down here for you. Your dentist must have forgotten to call it in."

"I'll come back for it tomorrow."

She shrugged. "Suit yourself."

I walked slowly back to where I'd left the truck, half keeping an eye out for Big Bad Bob. I didn't particularly want him scaring me again, but this time he wasn't in sight. I was also preoccupied with feeling irritated at Dr. Gelsinger. If he thought my taking antibiotics was so important the least he could have done was call in the prescription. I'd thought that was what he'd been doing when I left the office, but now I realized I was mistaken.

I had gotten as far as getting into the truck and turning on the engine, when I noticed a 1960 Oldsmobile at the far edge of the lot. I recognized it as Mr. Eshelman's car. There weren't too many of that vintage around.

My first thought was that he'd just returned, and I'd give him a minute to get into the store, then follow. But after several minutes went by and nobody had gotten out of the car, I began to get worried. After all, he wasn't a young man, and his skin had that grayish pallor I associated with sick people. What if he were in there, sick, maybe dying?

I turned off the engine, climbed down, and hurried over to the car. I peered in the window and saw that the car was empty. When I tried the door, I found it unlocked just as I had expected. People who don't feel it's necessary to lock up their houses when they go out certainly wouldn't lock their cars. How could he have gotten past me without my seeing him? The only way in to the drugstore was through the alley.

I slammed the door, and started to turn to go back to the truck, when I felt something nasty beneath my feet. "Dog-doo," I muttered. "There ought to be a law." I lifted one foot to stare at the sole of my shoe. It was wet and slimy, all right, but it neither looked nor smelled like dog-doo. I appeared to be standing in a puddle of oil.

I gingerly walked to the edge of the parking lot to wipe the offensive material off on the grass. It came off easily, leaving reddish stains that made me feel uneasy. I knelt to examine them and touched a blade of grass with one fingertip. The stickiness turned my stomach, and the smell assaulted my nose. An unpleasant, old-penny smell that was unmistakable. It was blood I'd stepped in, not oil.

My first thought was that someone had hit a deer in the parking lot, which wasn't uncommon. But if so, where was the carcass? Had the driver taken the unfortunate animal home for supper? As I stood up, I was able to see over the bank down to the river's edge where a bundle of old clothes was visible, half-covered with leaves. But somehow I knew, without even exploring further, that it was not just clothing. I slipped down the riverbank and nudged the bundle with one foot. My gentle prodding uncovered a hand, which seemed to reach out as if pleading for me to help.

"Oh my God. It's a body." I wanted to run, but then reason checked me. It could be someone who fell down the embankment and hit his head. Big Bad Bob leaped to mind. As drunk as he usually was, he could have taken a tumble.

I actually managed to talk myself into believing that maybe the hand protruding from the pile of clothes belonged to a person in need of assistance, so I knelt next to it and touched my fingers to the wrist. The hand was icy cold, and there was definitely no pulse. It belonged to a dead person, I was sure of that, but now that I'd actually touched it I was no longer frightened by it. I brushed away some of the leaves and twigs that covered the bundle until I saw a face looking up at me.

"Mr. Eshelman," I whispered. "Oh no. Mr. Eshelman." Tears streamed down my cheeks while I brushed the dry vegetation from his face.

"Hey!" somebody shouted from above. "What's going on?" I looked up and saw the silhouette of a man.

"Call the police," I called. "There's a dead person down here." The man disappeared.

I sat with Mr. Eshelman as purple evening shadows fell around me, and the surrounding air turned cool. "I'm sorry," I kept repeating. "I'm so sorry." Although I hadn't known him well, he'd always been nice to me, and I felt awful that this had happened.

And suddenly Luscious was beside me, along with several EMTs from the volunteer fire department.

One of them knelt next to the body, listened for a heartbeat and a pulse, then shook his head. "Nothing."

Luscious whipped out his cell phone, pressed a button, and muttered a few curt words. "Henry'll be right here," he said.

"Looks like he was shot," the EMT said. He lifted a branch covering Mr. Eshelman's chest, revealing a gaping wound.

I gagged and threw up.

"Please be careful, Tori. You're messing up the crime scene," Luscious scolded.

When the coroner arrived, he was accompanied by most of the customers from the restaurant. They stood on the edge of the parking lot, looking down at the gruesome scene.

"You'uns just stay put," Henry Hoopengartner warned. "Don't want nobody doing nothing down here till I've had a chance to look things over." He nodded at me, then turned his attention to the body. I watched the clear water of the creek splash over a bed of small stones. Every now and then a large fish swam by in water so shallow that its back would actually break through the surface. One of the native brown trout the creek was so famous for, I thought, trying to keep my mind off what was happening.

"Time of death, six forty-two," I overheard Henry say. "You'uns can take him away now."

"Tori," Luscious's voice was gentle. "How did you happen to find him?"

I explained the chain of events that had led me to Mr. Eshelman's side, starting with my trip to the dentist and ending with the discovery of the body. Through tear-blurred eyes I watched Luscious write everything I'd said in a notebook, just as I had once suggested he should.

"Did you see anybody around here?"

"Not a soul. The parking lot was empty."

"Let's get out of here," he said. He extended a hand and

helped me up the grassy hill. I was grateful for his assistance, as my legs were shaking and unsteady.

The ambulance carrying Mr. Eshelman's body pulled out of the parking lot, leaving the area filled with a crowd of curious onlookers. Mildred stood off by herself, sobbing heavily. I went to her and put my arms around her. I half expected her to push me away, but she only leaned her head on my shoulder and continued to cry. After a few minutes, she straightened up, dug in her apron pocket for a tissue, and blew her nose.

"It's awful," she whispered.

"He was a nice man."

Mildred nodded. "It must have been someone after the money bag. I told him he oughta leave it in the safe overnight. I coulda made the deposit in the morn—morn—morning." Her sobs resumed.

"Luscious, come here, please," I called.

Looking somewhat annoyed, Luscious joined us.

"Mildred says Wilbur was carrying a money bag to make a night deposit. She thinks he might have been killed for the money."

Luscious shook his head no. "Found the money bag lying right next to him. It's full. Don't look like nothing's missing. We'll count it later and compare it with the deposit slip."

"Was it an accident, then? Someone shooting at a deer in the woods, maybe?"

"Henry'll be able to tell us what kind of bullet it was what killed him. But if it was an accident, there wouldn't be any reason to drag him down the hill and try to cover him up. Accidents happen all the time, but I don't think this was one."

It was true that hunting accidents happened frequently in the Lickin Creek area, but as Luscious spoke I was sure he was right. This had not been an accident. But if it hadn't been a robbery, either, why on earth had it happened?

"You run on home, Tori," Luscious said, rather condescendingly. "Get some rest. You look terrible."

I meekly agreed to leave. Luscious and Henry seemed to have everything under control, and there was no need for me to hang around.

Ethelind was at the kitchen table, smoking, when I walked in. As I walked in she quickly ground the cigarette out in a flowery Royal Doulton saucer and looked up with a smile that faded to a worried frown. "What's the matter with you?" she asked.

I dropped onto an oak chair and told her what I'd found.

"Such a kind man," Ethelind murmured. "And so young, too."

For the first time in hours, a smile crossed my lips. Mr. Eshelman had been a few years behind Ethelind in school. I guess that's why she thought of him as "young."

Ethelind brewed tea in a Staffordshire pot, her cure-all for the evils of the world, and poured a cup for me. She even provided real sugar and milk instead of the powdered calorie-free substitutes I used when I was alone.

The cats crept in one by one, and Noel settled herself on my lap while Fred claimed Ethelind's lap as his own. After finding a dead body, there's nothing as comforting as a cup of tea and a cat for company, I thought.

When the phone rang, Ethelind and I stared at each other. Which of us would disturb her cat to answer it? When she stood up, Fred gave a little chirp of disgust and stalked from the room, while Noel gave him her smug I-won look.

"It's for you," Ethelind said. "Don't get up. I'll bring it to you."

I half expected to hear Luscious's voice, but it wasn't.

"Miss Miracle?"

I recognized the voice of J.B. Morgan from the bank.

"Yes, J.B. How are you?"

"I'm fine," he said brusquely. "But I'm afraid I have some bad news for you."

My heart sank to my shoes as I anticipated his next words.

"Your loan application has not been approved. I'm very sorry."

"But…I don't understand…. You said there wouldn't be a problem."

"These things are out of my control, Miss Miracle. The problem doesn't lie with us."

"Isn't there something I can do?"

"You could try another bank, but I don't think you'll do any better. It's your credit rating. It's one of the worst reports I've ever seen."

EIGHTEEN

SATURDAY was newspaper day. All over Lickin Creek, people were enjoying their morning coffee and catching up with news about friends, enemies, and neighbors who could be either. I found our paper caught in the rosebush to the left of the front door and brought it into the kitchen where Ethelind already had prepared coffee and a hot tray of sticky buns, part of her Saturday morning ritual.

Of course, poor Mr. Eshelman's death had occurred too late to be included. And by next week it would be considered old news, probably not even worthy of the front page. What did surprise me was, there was no mention of Rodney Mellott nor Emily Rakestraw. And even the latest reports of Vonzell Varner's escapades were buried in the middle pages. The front page, which we'd saved for late-breaking news, was filled with my article about the BL Deer Hunting Preserve. I folded the paper and handed it to Ethelind. "I'm going into the *Chronicle* office," I told her. "There are a few things I need to get straight."

Ethelind smiled. "It's not your idea of what a paper should be, is it?"

"I know what you're going to say," I said. "It's the kind of paper people in Lickin Creek want."

"Exactly. Aren't you going to get dressed?"

"I am dressed, Ethelind." I glanced down at my pink T-shirt, jeans shorts, and sandals, which I thought were perfectly appropriate to be wearing while visiting a nearly deserted newspaper office on a hot summer Saturday morning.

I left Ethelind poring over the paper, coffee mug in one hand, her freshly lit cigarette poisoning the air. At least she'd begun waiting till I left the room before lighting up.

Cassie seldom worked on Saturday morning, and P.J. had not yet come in when I arrived at the *Chronicle*. Before she'd left the office yesterday, Cassie had prepared the electric coffeepot, so all I had to do was push the ON button. I then used the quiet time to pick up the phone and call Dr. Gelsinger about my prescription.

He was contrite. "I'm sure I called it in," he said. "I can't imagine what happened. And isn't it a shame about Bill? I still can't believe it. Such a good man. A real pillar of the community, he was. I can't imagine what's going to happen to the Chicken and Slippery Pot Pie Dinners now that he's gone."

I interrupted his soliloquy. "Can you please call my prescription into another drugstore? I'd really like to get started taking it."

There was a pause, then he asked, "How are you feeling this morning?"

"Fine," I said.

"No pain? No fever? No unusual aches?"

"No to all the above."

"Then I really don't think you're going to need an antibiotic after all, Tori. I can call it in for you, of course, but it costs about a hundred dollars, and if it's not really necessary for you to…"

"Thank you," I said. "I'd just as soon not take a drug if I don't need to."

"You found him, didn't you?"

"Yes, I did."

"It must have been awful for you. Did you see anything suspicious? Like someone lurking around the building, who might have done it?"

"No. I didn't. Look Dr. Gelsinger, I really don't want to talk about it."

"Of course you don't. That was insensitive of me. I told

him he shouldn't carry that deposit bag around like that. No point in turning yourself into a target."

I hung up, relieved I didn't have to listen to him anymore, and also relieved I'd been saved from spending money I didn't have.

My next call was to Janielle Simpson, the realtor. She sounded shocked when I told her my loan request had been denied. Then she switched to her optimistic voice.

"Don't worry about it, Tori. I'm going to find you a loan if I have to go to the National Bank of Timbuktu."

"How reassuring."

"We'll get you into that house, one way or the other."

Although she had been very upbeat and positive, I was downcast after I hung up. My little dream house was going up in smoke. It was as if it had never really been meant to be mine.

While the office was still quiet, I wrote about discovering Wilbur Eshelman's body and tried to describe, without going into graphic details, the horrific gunshot wound in his chest. Why had it happened? I mused. Who could have done such a terrible thing to such a nice man?

P.J. came in around noon, looking groggy. This lateness was a sure sign she wasn't feeling well. As long as I'd known her, she'd always made it a point to come in early.

I poured a mug of coffee and handed it to her along with my article about Wilbur. When I was close to her, I saw that her eyes were red and swollen. "Have you been crying?" I asked in surprise. P.J. never showed emotion. She said it was the mark of a good newspaperwoman not to.

She nodded. "I've had a hard time accepting Bill's death," she said. "He was a good man."

"I've heard that from everybody who knew him," I remarked. Then what she'd said caught up to me. "You called him 'Bill.' So did Dr. Gelsinger. Are we all talking about the same person? Wilbur Eshelman?"

P.J. sipped her coffee, then nodded again. "Bill's what we called him back in high school. When he went into business, he didn't think it was dignified enough, so he switched back to his full name of Wilbur."

"Speaking of high school. I brought in some photos I copied from the yearbook, showing Rodney Mellot and his music students." While I spoke, I was walking out to the front office where I'd left my bag. "Here they are," I said as I returned.

P.J. barely glanced at them. "So?"

"So, I'm saying one of these students was the boy Rodney called *B* in his diary. There could be a tie-in with his death. If I can just identify which one he was…"

"Drop it, Tori."

"What?"

"I said, drop it. I've never had so many complaints called in as I did this week after that inflammatory article you wrote. Nobody wants to read that kind of stuff. Especially about people they grew up with. Here…" She handed me my article about Wilbur Eshelman. "Nice job. Put it on Cassie's desk."

I started to take the pages over and noticed P.J. had changed the headline. Instead of what I'd written, which was LOCAL BUSINESSMAN MURDERED, it now read ROBBERY GONE WRONG.

"It wasn't a robbery, P.J. Nothing was taken."

"That is exactly why it was a robbery gone wrong, Tori. Probably the thief was startled by something and ran away before he could get the money."

"I don't think so—"

"I do." The look she gave me silently added, "And it's my paper."

I heard the front door burst open and went out into the front room to find Luscious covering his bald spot with what was left of his hair.

"Hi, Luscious," I said. "Any leads yet on who killed Mr. Eshelman?"

He ignored my question. "Beautiful morning, ain't it? Is P.J. here?"

I pointed to the archway that separated the two rooms. "In there."

He entered P.J.'s inner sanctum, and I followed close behind him.

"What's up, Luscious?" P.J. asked.

He glanced at me, as if wondering if he should ask me to leave, then apparently decided against it. "There's some guys from the state health department down here, looking for places mosquitoes can hatch."

"I know that," P.J. said. "They're trying to stop the spread of West Nile Virus. It's not exactly news, Luscious."

"You don't have to be condescending, P.J." Luscious said.

"Ooh, Tori, did you hear that big word?"

"Cut it out, P.J. I'm trying to broaden my vocabulary by learning one new word a day and using in three times in conversation. Read about it in Mom's *Cosmopolitan*."

"Sorry." She didn't look sorry at all.

"Anyway, what I'm going to tell you is news, P.J., so listen up. Can I have a cup of coffee, Tori?"

He lowered his voice to a low rumble as I left. If he thought he was gaining privacy, he was wrong, because from the next room I could pick out some of the words from some of his sentences. "West Nile Virus. Tire pile. State crew. Human bones."

I burst back into the room, splashing myself with coffee. "What are you talking about?"

P.J. glanced at Luscious, who nodded his okay. "Luscious has just told me that there's a crew from the state health department down here spraying to kill mosquito larvae."

"I knew that already. What about the human bones?"

"You know the tire pile out on Funkhauser Road, don't you?"

Everybody knew about the tire pile. About thirty years ago, a local farmer, Adam Funkhauser, thought he was going to make a fortune selling old tires, only after he collected a half million or so he learned nobody wanted to buy them, and now his heirs were stuck with an environmental disaster to clean up.

"The bones," I persisted.

"The crew was working out there last night and found a plastic garbage bag with human remains in it," Luscious said.

"Were these remains wearing a polyester tuxedo and a ruffled shirt?"

After another exchange of glances, Luscious bowed his head slightly. "That's kinda what it looked like."

I felt so triumphant I was almost ashamed of myself. I'd come to think of this particular corpse as *my* body, even when nobody believed he existed. Now there could be no doubt.

"You don't need to look so happy, Tori," P.J. snapped.

"I'm going to call Henry and ask him what he thinks the cause of death was," I said, already dialing the number for Hoopengartner's Garage, Police Department, and Coroner's Office.

"Hoop's," said the female voice on the line.

"Henry, please."

Henry came on the line so quickly I knew he must have been right next to the receptionist.

He listened quietly while I asked my questions. Where? When? How? What? Who? Why?

"Funkhauser's tire pile. Last night. Crew was spraying for mosquitoes. Big green plastic bag, the kind you use for outdoor trash. It is Rodney Mellott. I've compared the skull to his dental records. Cause of death was multiple stab wounds. How can I tell? Because there are marks on several bones where the knife went deep into the body. Anything else you need to know?"

"What about Emily Rakestraw's body? Have you finished examining it? How did she die?"

"I can't tell, Tori. No signs of trauma. Maybe she suffocated in the trunk."

"You're saying, maybe she crawled in, wearing her wedding dress, and the lid fell down and locked?"

"Stranger things have happened. I've reconstructed the

trunk, and there are scratch marks on the inside of the lid, Tori. They could have been made by Emily as she tried to break out of the trunk."

The horror of how Emily might have died stunned me into silence, and I quietly hung up.

"What's wrong?" P.J. asked.

"Henry thinks Emily might have been alive when she got into the trunk. That perhaps she was knocked unconscious by the lid falling, then couldn't get it open."

"Dear God," P.J. said. "What a nightmarish thing to happen."

"Do you want me to write this up?" I asked.

P.J. shook her head. "I think I'd better do it. I'd rather you got busy on the feature article I asked you to do."

"What article? You didn't mention any article."

"There's an assignment in your box."

I walked over to my pigeonhole and pulled out a piece of paper. It hadn't been there when I left yesterday at noon, I was sure of that.

"You didn't mention this earlier, P.J.," I grumbled.

She shrugged nonchalantly. "Maybe I put it in your box after you left, Tori. I can't remember." Her coughing put a stop to my arguing with her.

I figured I might as well get it over with. I picked up the telephone again and called the home number of Marvin Bumbaugh, president of the borough council.

"Tori. How nice of you to call," he boomed. "P.J. said you would. I'm real excited about this project, and I hope you can do a nice article for us. We're looking for donations."

"A new Tunnels and Trails project is always cause for excitement," I said, stifling a yawn and checking my watch. As my stomach had suggested, it was already noon.

"So how about today?" he asked.

"What about today?" I retorted.

"To take a look at the tunnel. I'm free. We could be there in half an hour."

"I suppose I could go."

"Wonderful. Have you eaten?"

I felt a swell of excitement. Maybe he was going to buy my lunch. "Why no, I haven't."

"Well, you just go and get a bite to eat. I'll pick you up at the office in about twenty-five minutes."

I didn't want to go to the drugstore for lunch, not so soon after Mr. Eshelman's death, so I went to the Waffle Shoppe. Fortunately, neither Haley nor the offensive man who'd once ground a cigarette out in my pecan waffle were there. I ate quickly and was back in the office with five minutes to spare.

Marvin was already there waiting. He finished his coffee, shook hands with P.J., handed a folder to me, and said, "You can look this over on the way. It's background info for the article."

Even before we reached the door, P.J. had her desk cleared off. I hoped she was going home to get some much-needed rest before Monday.

Belted into the front seat of Marvin's Toyota, I leafed through the folder, but I have a tendency to get carsick when reading in a moving car, so I wasn't able to get more than an idea of what our field trip was all about. "Why don't you tell me what we're going to see?" I asked. "It would be better to have it in your own words for the paper. Your constituents would really appreciate it more that way."

Marvin looked pleased and told me the history of the Tunnels and Trails movement. It was similar to Rails to Trails, in that it supported taking something that was no longer used for its original purpose and turning it into a recreation area. It was also unique to Pennsylvania, which, because of its mountainous terrain, has a lot of old tunnels. Marvin explained that he was the chairman of the Caven County Tunnels and Trails Club. He wanted to be sure I knew it wasn't part of his official duties as a member of the borough council, just something he did benevolently because he felt so strongly that it was a good cause.

"The one we're going to visit today is part of an old Civil War-era railroad," Marvin told me. "The railroad went bankrupt after being in use only a few years, and the tunnel has been deserted ever since. We've been hoping it would become available for a long time. Now all we need is enough money to buy it. That's where the paper comes in. Your article will kick off our fund-raising campaign."

It took longer to cross the valley than it should have, for PennDOT was repairing the roads. Marvin's car crept through narrow lanes designated by orange and white striped barrels. Eastbound traffic was stopped dead. A police car in the median strip watched over the turmoil, but the officer inside was making no effort to help. There was really nothing he could do, I realized. We were fortunate to be going west, for the traffic kept moving, although slowly.

Thank goodness, Marvin turned off the highway onto a dirt road headed up the side of a mountain. The views from every hairpin turn were spectacular when I could bring myself to open my eyes and look. Once, I grew so frightened I had to wipe perspiration from my forehead.

Marvin glanced at me and assumed, incorrectly, that I was too warm. He slid open the moon roof an inch or two. "I'll let in some air. You aren't nervous, are you?" Marvin asked, rounding a curve too fast.

"A little. Could you slow down? Please? If I didn't know better I'd say you were trying to kill us."

"Sorry." He slowed down to about ninety or so miles an hour and jovially pointed out landmarks. "You can see the whole borough. There's the landfill. Looks damn nice from here, doesn't it? In another fifty or hundred years that's going to be one swell recreation area. And look at where Lickin Creek meets up with two other rivers. In the old days, they used to float barges all the way down to the Potomac."

I managed to uncover my eyes long enough to take a peek

at the lovely vista below. From way up here, the valley looked like an aerial photo.

"Ought to bring you up here at night," Marvin said. "It's spectacular then. Hey, here we are." He slammed on the brakes, skidded too close to the edge of the road, and backed up. I saw an even narrower dirt road heading even farther up the side of the mountain, and hoped that wasn't where we were going. Of course, it was.

Marvin pointed out a few remnants of the old tracks. "Mostly, though, they've been carried off by souvenir hunters." He rounded a bend, and the entrance to the tunnel loomed before us, a dark, stone-rimmed hole, cut into the mountainside.

"Hardly anybody knows about it," Marvin said proudly. "We're looking to buy the whole mountain. That's why I asked you up here to write an article about it and help us get the donations coming in. We're going to put lean-to cabins over there. For hikers." He pointed to a fairly flat area off to our right. "Over there, a ballfield for day picnickers. Some trails up the side of the mountain as well as one through the tunnel. It'll be a nature lover's dream."

I put my hand on the door handle. "Shall we walk in and take a look at it?" I asked.

"Heavens, no." Marvin drove forward into the tunnel. "It's no place to be walking. Not till we've had a chance to clean it out."

Driving slowly for a change, he turned on his lights. I saw that the rough, curved walls of the tunnel were carved out of solid stone, which glistened from water seeping through tiny cracks in the stone.

I think I'd expected the tunnel to be short, but ahead I saw nothing but blackness. "How long is this tunnel?" I asked.

"Couple of miles. Damn." He rolled his window halfway down and appeared to be listening to something.

"What's wrong?"

"The engine. It's making a weird noise. Can you hear it?"

"No."

Suddenly the car stopped, and in the silence all I heard was the sound of water dripping onto the tunnel floor. Marvin pounded on the steering wheel in anger. "I took it into Hoop's last week and told the mechanic there was a funny noise under the hood. Whatever it was, he sure didn't fix it." He fiddled with the key, turning it back and forth, only eliciting an occasional weak gasp from the engine. Then, finally, nothing.

"That does it. Tori, I'm sorry, but I'm going to have to leave you here and go for help." While he was speaking, Marvin got out of the car. As soon as he opened the door, the headlights went out. I'd never imagined darkness this black.

"I'll go with you."

He spoke through the half-open window on his side. "No way, Tori. Not with you wearing those sandals."

"I can walk just fine in sandals," I protested. I really didn't want to be left alone in the blackness.

"It's not the walking I'm worried about, Tori. It's the snakes."

All I heard was the word I hated most, *snakes*. A snake had killed my little brother. Snakes were evil incarnate. I loathed snakes. I feared snakes. More than anything in the world.

But I still wasn't convinced I should wait for him. "What kind of snakes?" I whispered. I wouldn't like it, but I could handle garden snakes.

"Rattlesnakes. The tunnel's full of them. I'll be back in half an hour. No, better make that an hour. It's a long hike back to the highway. I'm wearing boots and jeans, so I should be safe." And on that cheery note, Marvin faded away.

The radio. I'd turn on the radio for company, I decided. Of course it didn't work. And Marvin had taken the keys, so I couldn't even tell if the problem lay with the battery or something else.

I pulled my legs up to my chin and wrapped my arms around my knees. It wasn't cold. On the contrary it was stifling hot, but I'd heard the word *snake,* and I was shaking as if I were freezing.

Sing. Sing a happy song, Tori. Pretend you're not scared. The only song I could think of was "Follow the Yellow Brick Road," from *The Wizard of Oz,* and once I was past the first five "follows" I couldn't recall any more of it. I sang, "Follow, follow, follow" a few dozen times until I'd bored myself, and then sat quietly waiting for Marvin to return.

After an interminable length of time I glanced at my watch, but couldn't read the dial in the dark. How long had it been? An hour? Fifteen minutes? I had no idea.

And then I heard a thud on the roof. It had to be a snake. What else could it be? I remembered that the moon roof was ajar. And without the car key there was no way to close it. I scrambled to my knees and felt around the back seat, hoping to find something, anything that I could use to plug the opening. There was nothing in there. Marvin kept his car spotless.

I pulled off my T-shirt and jammed it into the opening. I was safe now. Nothing could get through.

Even as these comforting thoughts raced through my mind, the hair on the back of my neck stood on end. Of course something could get through. The window on the driver's side was halfway down. I frantically pushed the button that would close it, but it wouldn't work either, without the ignition on. I huddled next to the door on my side of the car and removed one of my sandals. If anything came slithering through the window, I planned to beat it to death with a flimsy piece of Italian leather.

Ten more minutes passed. Then five more. Maybe I should get out of the car and make a run for it, I thought. But I couldn't bring myself to do it. Not with the tunnel full of rattlesnakes. Even one would have been enough to keep me in the car.

I realized that at last there was some light in the tunnel, and it was getting brighter all the time. Trying to keep one eye on the open window, I looked out the rear window and saw two headlights approaching. Marvin must have reached the highway and gotten help, I realized with relief.

I waited, sandal in hand, until the vehicle pulled up close behind the Toyota. "Get in," a masculine voice called.

Fear kept me glued to my seat. I could not bring myself to leave the safety of the car. After a minute or two, the other vehicle, which I saw now was a van, pulled forward and stopped right next to me. Its side door slid open, and the voice called out again, "Get in."

"I can't get my door open with you parked there," I screamed.

"The window. Climb through it."

I eyeballed the half-open window for size. I really wasn't sure I could fit through, and there was no way to open it any wider.

I stuck my head through. Are people like cats? I wondered. If the head fits through an opening will the body fit? I squirmed and twisted until I got my arms and shoulders and even my chest through the opening. But the hips hung in mid-air, refusing to go anywhere.

"I'm stuck," I cried. "I can't get through." I was practically standing on my head by that time, nearly bisected by the window glass, so I couldn't see whoever it was who was tugging on my shoulders. "Stop pulling. You're hurting me."

The pressure eased. "Don't panic. Your pants are caught," the voice said. "I think if you unzip them, you'll slide right out."

"I can't reach them," I said weakly. By now the blood rushing to my head made it hard to hear him. And my arms had grown weak from bearing all my weight.

"I'll do it." I felt a hand fumbling around with the waist of my shorts. "Now!" he commanded.

With a sharp jerk on my arms, I was pulled through the window and landed in a heap on the back seat of my rescuer's vehicle.

He climbed over me to reach the front seat, and the car accelerated, pinning me to the velour upholstery.

Slowly, I managed to roll over and saw sunlight streaming through the windows.

"We're out," said the driver, gradually coming to a stop.

I sat up and was face-to-face with my rescuer, Haley Haley.

"What on earth are you doing here?"

"I just happened to be driving by and saw your car go into the tunnel. When I saw the driver walk out without you, I got worried."

"I'm not stupid, Haley Haley. I know you didn't just 'happen' to be driving by. Not up here on a deserted mountain road. You were following me, weren't you? In fact," I said as light dawned, "you've been following me for weeks. This van is dark green, isn't it?"

"Here," he said, handing me his JAILBIRDS FOR JESUS leather jacket. "Put this on."

For the first time, I realized I was close to naked. I'd left my T-shirt and shorts and one sandal back in Marvin's car. I grabbed the jacket and put it on. "Thanks," I said, ungraciously.

"Why don't you come up front?" Haley asked, patting the seat beside him.

I moved up to the front and buckled the seatbelt over the jacket, then turned to him and demanded, "I want an explanation."

"You're welcome," he said.

"For what."

"That's what a person says when another person thanks him for saving his life."

"You needn't try to make me feel bad, Haley. Why have you been following me?"

The van began to move. "We'll have to go back through the tunnel," Haley said. "The road dead-ends here. If you want I can let you get back into the car to wait for other help to come."

I shuddered at the thought of being left in the snake-filled darkness again. "Don't even consider it."

Haley made a U-turn and headed back into the tunnel. I held my breath until we were through.

"Place is full of snakes," Haley said, as if telling me something I didn't already know. "Everybody in Caven County knows not to go in there. What was Marvin Bumbaugh trying to pull?"

"Nothing. He was simply showing me the area marked for recreation, so I can write an article about it."

"Only a damn fool would want to buy a tunnel full of rattlers."

Since I agreed with him wholeheartedly, I couldn't think of a retort, so I asked again, "Just why have you been following me?"

"Because I've been worried about you. You're a sweet gal but way too vulnerable."

"The very idea. I am not. I am perfectly capable of taking care of myself. Didn't I survive for ten years in New York City without being mugged once?"

"The country's a lot different, Tori. How many tunnels full of snakes have you seen in Central Park?"

"You left the notes, too, didn't you?"

"Notes?" He was too innocent.

"You know what I'm talking about. You sneaked into my house, my office, and left frightening messages."

"I didn't mean them to be frightening, Tori. I wanted to show you how easily someone could get to you. And I was trying to make you feel protected. Show you someone was keeping you safe."

"Knowing someone has been pawing around in my underwear drawer does not make me feel safe or protected, Haley. You are a creep. And where did you get this van, anyway? I thought you only had a motorcycle."

"I borrowed it from a friend." His jaw tightened, but didn't take his eyes from the road. Haley might be a creep, but I realized I was an idiot for talking to him like this when we were alone. I tried to change the subject by saying, "I'm surprised we haven't seen Marvin hiking along here somewhere."

We had already come down the mountain and Haley had slowed down to turn right onto the highway.

"Maybe he hitched a ride," he mumbled, turning into a very slow single lane of traffic.

"Construction." The word sounded like a curse.

I felt better now that we were off the mountain and back in civilization, even if it was represented by a line of eighteen-wheelers and cars.

After a few minutes of stop-and-go driving, I saw a police car ahead in the median strip, and I placed one hand on the door handle. If traffic stopped again, I was prepared to jump out and run for help.

Luck was with me. The line of vehicles once again ground to a halt. I flung open the door before we'd come to a complete stop and ran between the van and semitractor. The driver tooted his horn, and I realized I had little on other than Haley's leather jacket. But I didn't care at that moment. I ran as fast as I could with only one shoe on, fully expecting Haley to reach out and grab me from behind. At last, I reached the black-and-white car and pounded on the back of it, screaming, "Help me. A stalker's after me. Help."

Why wasn't the state trooper paying any attention to me? He faced forward, not moving a muscle. I looked at the line of traffic, didn't see Haley coming after me, and ran around to the driver's-side window. The trooper sitting so still in the front seat of the car was nothing more than a dummy.

"He's called Cardboard Charlie," Haley said, close behind me. "Don't scream, Tori, or make a scene. I've got a knife. Charlie's not going to help you. And the truckers out there think you're my girlfriend, and we've had a fight. Now come with me, quietly. The line's starting to move."

Haley put one arm around me, and with his other hand, pressed something against my side. He led me back to the van, waving at a couple of truckers who smiled and tooted in reply.

Haley opened the driver's-side door and told me to get in. "Don't try anything stupid, Tori."

I slid across the seat.

"Don't forget your seat belt," Haley said.

I snapped it over my chest and glared at him.

Haley tossed a ballpoint pen onto the seat.

"There's your knife," he laughed. "You should know I can't carry a weapon, being an ex-con. And you didn't really think I would hurt you, did you?"

"If you don't want to hurt me, take me to the Lickin Creek police station," I demanded.

"That's just what I was planning to do. We need to tell them Marvin's lost out there. He could need help."

I was ashamed that I hadn't once thought about Marvin Bumbaugh in the past nightmarish hours. The poor man could be lying hurt in a ditch by the side of the road. Or even worse, he could still be in the tunnel.

Although I still half expected Haley to carry me off to a secret place and turn me into his sex slave, he drove straight to Hoopengartner's Garage, where he insisted on coming inside with me. I wanted to laugh at the look on Luscious's face when we walked into his office. "Your clothes," he gasped, turning beet-red. "Where are your clothes? Oh no…it was you."

"What are you talking about?" I asked.

"About twenty minutes ago something came in on the scanner about a half-naked woman running down the highway. I never dreamed…What on earth was you doing out there, Tori?"

"I was trying to get the attention of the state trooper parked in the middle of the road."

"You didn't need to take off your clothes to do that," Luscious said slyly.

"I'll say. Not when it was just a stupid dummy."

"Cardboard Charlie," Haley said by way of explanation.

"Oh yeah. Everybody knows about Cardboard Charlie, Tori. State Police don't have enough troopers to have one sitting there watching traffic all day, so they done put a dummy in a cruiser, hoping it'll scare people into slowing down. Trouble is, everybody knows he's not a real trooper, so it don't work. Why did you take your clothes off?"

"There's a simple explanation," I said. "I left my clothes in Marvin Bumbaugh's car in a tunnel somewhere."

"Not that Tunnels and Trails place Marvin wants to buy?"
I nodded.

"He oughta be ashamed of hisself, taking you there. It needs cleaned out bad."

"I know that now."

"Where is Marvin?" Luscious asked, peering around the room as if expecting to see the borough council president hiding in a corner.

"We don't know," Haley said. "His car broke down in the tunnel, and he left Tori there while he went for help."

Luscious looked at Haley, seeing him for the first time. "Aren't you Reverend Haley?" he asked.

Haley smiled ever so modestly and inclined his head.

"It's a real pleasure to meet you, Reverend." Luscious was out of his seat, shaking Haley's hand. "Won't you please sit down. I've heard a lot of good things abut you'uns and your ministry."

Haley took the chair Luscious had practically thrown at him and held it for me. "Tori's had kind of a bad day," he said. "I think she needs to rest."

After I sat down, Luscious threw a blanket over my bare legs. Considering that I was showing less flesh than the garage receptionist usually did, I thought that was both unnecessary and amusing.

"Excuse me," Luscious said when the phone rang. He answered, listened quietly, then said, "You don't need to worry about her. She's here. Yup. Brought in by that minister fellow what has the Church on the Go." He hung up and retrieved his hat from the tarnished brass rack by the door.

"That was Marvin," he said. "He's in the Carlisle Hospital emergency room."

"Why?" Haley and I chorused.

"Evidently he had a bad fall and was knocked unconscious. Some trucker found him on the side of the road and brought him in. I'm going down to get him."

"Can you please drop me off at Ethelind's house on your way?" I asked.

Luscious glanced at Haley. "Okay with you, Reverend?"

"I don't need his permission, Luscious," I said, but he paid no attention. Luscious was so impressed by having Haley in his office that I knew there was no point in telling him Haley had been stalking me. He would never believe me.

NINETEEN

I NEEDED TO CONFRONT Alice-Ann with something that had been bothering me for a while. It had been Alice-Ann who had begged me to keep secret our discovery of a corpse, and I had done as she wished until our corpse's fiancée had turned up dead in a trunk. However, when I took Luscious to the springhouse to show him where we'd found the body, she'd been noticeably absent from the scene. And she'd been silent throughout the rest of the week, leaving me to deal with criticism from my boss and disapproval from my landlady, the police, and just about anyone who ran into me on the street.

When I called to ask if I could drop by, Alice-Ann was her usual cheery self. "Come on over, Tori. I can use your help."

I drove out to Silverthorne, the estate where Alice-Ann's deceased husband's family home was located, and parked next to the sandbox. Her son, Mark, waved at me but was too preoccupied with his miniature crane and tractor to come over and give me a hug.

The front door was open, and I walked in without knocking. Alice-Ann sat on the floor of the living room amidst an enormous heap of pinecones and a tangle of florist's wire.

"What are you doing?" I asked, kneeling on a bare section of braided rug.

"Making pinecone pigs to sell at Lickin Creek Day." She must have seen the disbelief on my face. "Don't give me that superior 'New York' look, Tori. Pinecone pigs are very popular. Grab a pinecone and do what I do. It's not difficult once you get the hang of it."

I thought I "got the hang" of making pinecone pigs rather quickly and made three or four before Alice-Ann remarked that they looked too amateurish to sell and suggested I give up my efforts and get us some iced tea instead.

My fingers were sticky with pine sap and sore from the prickly ends of the pinecones, so I didn't object to stopping. In the kitchen, I found a pitcher of iced tea in the refrigerator. After opening a few cabinet doors, I located some tall glasses, filled two of them with tea, dropped a pinch of calorie-free sweetener in each, and carried them back into the living room.

"I'm glad for the break," Alice-Ann said, as we sat side by side on the sofa, facing the tall windows. Poplar leaves danced in the summer breezes and splintered the sunlight into dappled splashes of brightness and shadow on the sloping lawn. I could barely make out the tips of the towers of historic Silverthorne Castle in the distance, on the far side of the pond.

"You're upset with me, aren't you?" Alice-Ann asked.

I was relieved that she had brought the subject up. "You left me in the lurch," I said. "You deserted me when I needed you. I said I was going to tell the police about our discovery, and I asked you to be there, and you weren't."

"I'm so sorry. It's that I felt like such a complete idiot. I kept thinking about how it would sound: first we found a body, and we hid it and didn't tell anyone, then we lost the body and we didn't tell anybody about that, either. If that wasn't bad enough, another body turned up, and I knew we really should tell about the first body, but I thought maybe we'd broken the law by keeping it a secret, and we'd be thrown in jail or something...I'm a single mother, Tori. What would happen to Mark if I went to jail?"

"So you let me face the consequences alone."

She hung her head and peered up at me through the streaked hair that had tumbled in her face. "I wouldn't have let you go to jail alone, Tori. I'd have 'fessed up if it had come to that. 'I'll kneel down and ask of thee forgiveness: and we'll live, and pray, and sing, and tell old tales and laugh at gilded butterflies…' Am I forgiven?"

"Of course. I'll always 'laugh at gilded butterflies' with you." Who wouldn't forgive a best friend who could apologize with a quotation from *King Lear?* Alice-Ann had been an English literature major in college where we first met, and her ability to dredge something appropriate up from her memory for every occasion was truly amazing. The only reason I knew this particular quotation was from *King Lear* was because she'd used it on me several times before. And each time I'd excused her behavior. Sometimes you just have to accept a best friend for who she is, instead of who you'd like her to be.

That dispute settled, Alice-Ann took our empty glasses into the kitchen and brought them back full. "I've been worried about you," she said, as she placed the frosty glasses on the table.

"Why?"

"You've got to be really upset about your father. People are saying that's why you went kind of crazy out on the highway and…"

"What did you hear?"

"That you were found running around the highway with no clothes on and Reverend Haley rescued you. There are some people who said you must have been high on cocaine."

"That's absolutely not true," I stammered. I knew that even if I told Alice-Ann the whole story, the Lickin Creek Grapevine would perpetuate the more interesting version. However, I still felt I had to make an attempt at clearing myself, so I told her about being stranded in the snake-filled tunnel while Marvin Bumbaugh went for help, and of Haley finding me there after following me everywhere I went.

She was more interested in learning why I was naked than in hearing about my terrifying ordeal. She actually seemed a little disappointed when I told her I hadn't been naked at all, but had on my bra, panties, one shoe, and a leather jacket.

"That's not the only thing that's happened to me," I pointed out. "I was shot at a few days ago at the BL Deer Hunting Preserve."

"Oh, my." Alice-Ann's hand fluttered around her heart for a moment, then dropped to the table where it picked up her iced tea glass. "Odd things do seem to happen to you. Like finding Wilbur Eshelman dead in the creek. I've never found a dead body." She corrected herself. "Except for Rodney Mellott. I guess I should have said I've never found a *freshly* dead body. Would you like some cookies? I baked this morning."

I was so used to Alice-Ann's sudden changes in topic that I found nothing unusual in her thinking about cookies in conjunction with dead bodies.

"I'd love some," I said.

While she was out of the room, I thought about what she'd said, not about her never finding bodies, but before that when she'd said odd things happened to me.

When Alice-Ann came back with a pewter platter piled high with chocolate chip cookies, I said, "Odd things *have* been happening to me lately, and they've not only been odd but also dangerous. I can't help but think there have been too many odd events."

"Other than finding Wilbur, what?"

"My father's embassy has been invaded, and he and his family are trapped God-knows-where. And I've been stalked, shot at, and left alone to fend off deadly serpents."

"Serpents? When did they change from snakes to serpents?"

"It doesn't matter," I snapped. "Also, I think it's very peculiar that the one time I go by the drugstore at night to fill a prescription I find the pharmacist has been murdered. And he just happened to be one of the few people in town who has always been kind to me. If you look back, you'll see it all began with us finding Rodney Mellott's skeleton in the cave at Morgan Manor. Which was odd enough without everything else happening."

"Do you think there's some connection?"

"I can't see how, but it does seem strange that all these things have occurred at about the same time."

"Let me get this straight. Are you suggesting somebody shot Wilbur Eshelman to hurt you? Isn't that a rather far-fetched idea? I don't think anybody in Lickin Creek dislikes you enough to shoot one of the borough's favorite citizens just to irritate you."

I sighed. "I know…I know. But I keep thinking it has something to do with me. I just don't know what."

Alice-Ann helped herself to a cookie. "I don't like to worry you, Tori, but it sounds to me as if you're turning paranoid. It isn't always about you, you know."

The beehive on the end table by the sofa rang softly, and Alice-Ann lifted it and uncovered the telephone. She listened a moment, then said, "Just a second," and handed it to me.

I heard Ethelind's voice screech out of the telephone. "Tori, is that you?"

I moved the receiver away from my ear and said, "I often wonder why you bother with the phone, Ethelind. At your decibel level, you could simply hang out the window and converse with people in the next town."

"Sorry," she said, a little more softly. "You had a weird phone call from a truly hysterical-sounding female, and I thought I should let you know right away rather than waiting until you come home. I think she said her name was Jenny."

"Jenny Varner?" A mental alarm went off.

"Yes, I do believe that's what she said. She was carrying on so I could hardly understand her. But she said something about being locked in her bedroom while her ex-husband was trying to break into her house. She couldn't reach the police. Said she was scared to death of what he'd do to her if he got in."

"Thanks." I hung up quickly and dialed Hoopengartner's Garage. According to the receptionist, both Luscious and Afton were out. When I told her that Vonzell Varner was back in town and trying to get at his wife, she said she already knew about it and was doing her best to reach Luscious.

"Did you call the state police?"

"I know what I'm doing," she snapped and hung up.

I glanced at my watch, and thought about what it must be like for Jenny Varner, huddled alone in her bedroom, hiding from her crazy husband. "I've got to go." I said. "Maybe I can scare Vonzell away by driving up to the house."

"I wish I could go with you, but I can't leave Mark."

"That's all right. I wouldn't ask it of you. Do you have a gun?"

"Heavens, no. I wouldn't consider having a gun in the house with a small child around. Why do you need one?"

"Vonzell Varner is on the FBI Most Wanted list. He's not going to give up easily."

"Wait a minute." She ran from the living room and a few minutes later returned with a Swiss Army knife. "Take this." She said, holding it out.

Although I doubted it would be of much use in subduing one of the country's most dangerous criminals, I thanked her and stuck it in the pocket of my jeans.

"Be careful, Tori. Don't try to play Wonder Woman."

"I'm always cautious."

Her laughter followed me to the truck.

Since it was Sunday morning and most good Lickin Creekers were attending church, I was able to drive across the borough in record time.

When I reached the little street of old but neat row houses where Jenny Varner lived, I found it unusually quiet. There were absolutely no signs of life anywhere, which was decidedly odd, I thought. Surely not everybody was in church. There were cars parked along the curb, but the agents or agents in the black pickup were gone.

I drove slowly down the street and saw the front door of Jenny Varner's house stood open. This alarmed me. If she'd been as terrified as Ethelind had described, she would never have left her door open. I abandoned the truck in the middle of the street, jumped out, and ran up the steps to Jenny's front porch. Before I was halfway to the porch, I could see that the door had been kicked in.

"Hello," I called, cautious, afraid to enter. "Anybody home?"

There was no answer, but I didn't know if that was a good sign or a bad one. I glanced over my shoulder in the hope that a neighbor or two would appear, but all I saw was a gray cat strolling slowly across the street. I knew I'd have to go inside. Jenny could be in there hurt…or worse. I pushed the door wide open with one foot, waited a moment, then edged through the door.

The living room showed signs of a fierce struggle. Furniture was overturned and broken, curtains had been pulled from the rods, broken knickknacks were strewn across the floor. And the house was so silent I was sure there was nobody alive in there. Still afraid for my own safety, but more frightened for Jenny, I ran into the kitchen. Everything looked normal there. I went back into the living room, and looked at the stairs leading up to the bedrooms. My stomach churned when I saw a few drops of what could be blood on the worn carpet.

I went upstairs. Off the landing were three bedrooms. Two appeared to be children's rooms, with neatly made bunk beds and no toys in sight. The door to the third bedroom was splintered and hung from just one hinge. Although I was positive there was no one in the house, I took Alice-Ann's Swiss Army knife out of my pocket and unfolded the large blade. It didn't look particularly threatening, so I popped it back into place and pulled out the corkscrew, which I thought might be more useful if I were attacked.

The bedroom with the broken door was obviously where Jenny had been trying to hide from her husband. The telephone, which she must have used to call for help, had been jerked from the wall. The dresser was upended, lamps broken, even pictures pulled from the walls.

But where was Jenny? I felt no fear at all now, only urgency. I had to find her. I refused to let myself think that she was already dead. But after several minutes of throwing open closet doors, checking under beds, looking behind smashed furniture, I realized Jenny Varner was no longer in her house.

Outside I looked desperately up and down the street, hoping to see someone, anyone, but it was still deserted. I ran next door to a house that would have been identical to Jenny's, if Jenny's small front lawn had been littered with toys, and pounded on the door. After an eternity, a woman's voice called through the door, "Who's there?"

"My name is Tori Miracle. Something's happened next door. Can you let me in?"

I heard the metallic clink of a lock being turned, and the door opened just enough for me to see that it was on a chain. A woman peered through the crack at me. "You'uns is that girl from the *Chronicle,* ain't you?"

I nodded impatiently. "Jenny Varner's been hurt. Maybe kidnapped. Did you hear or see anything this morning?"

"Just a sec." The door swung nearly shut, the chain rattled, and then the woman opened the door wide enough to admit me. She slammed it shut behind me and relocked it.

The layout of the house was similar to Jenny's, but the similarity ended there. It was filthy where Jenny's living room was spotless, or at least had been spotless before her husband had rampaged through it. Despite the summer heat, the windows were all closed, and the hot air reeked of dirty diapers and spoiled formula.

"Sorry 'bout the mess," she said, vaguely waving one arm in the air. "I wasn't expecting company."

"I am not company. I'm only here because Jenny's in danger."

The woman's eyes avoided mine as she busied herself with moving toys off the couch. She knew something, I was sure.

"What happened over there?" I demanded.

"I heard him yelling for her to open up. Then he kicked the door in. There wasn't nothing I could do to help her."

"You could have called the police."

"I tried, but all I got was the answering machine. Vonzell's a real nut case. Always has been. I was scared he'd come here and hurt my kids, so I herded them all upstairs and shut them in the bathroom. Then I got on my knees and watched Jenny's front door through my bedroom window. After a little bit, I saw him drive away with her, but when I heard you knocking, I thought maybe it was him come back."

"You saw them leave the house? Was Jenny walking or was he carrying her?" Maybe he hadn't killed her after all.

"He half dragged her out the door and shoved her into the van, but she was on her own two feet."

"Can you describe the van?"

She nodded. "Dark green. Not real new but not a clunker, either. Had those dark windows you can't see into."

"What about the federal agents that were out there? Did you see them?"

"They've been gone for a coupla days. Jenny told me they had to get back to Washington. Guess they thought it was safe to leave since he hadn't showed up."

I dropped onto the orange-and-brown velour sofa, ignoring the dust cloud that arose from it, and buried my head in my hands. Gone. I'd been too late.

"Try the police station again," I said. She went into the kitchen, and after a moment I heard her leaving a message. I decided right then I was going to the next borough council meeting to protest the budget restraints that kept Lickin Creek from getting a real emergency phone system.

Where were they? Where would Vonzell take his wife? And as I asked myself these questions, the answer came to me. His log cabin in the forest. The police had checked the cabin thoroughly after I'd been there and found no signs of him. He'd feel safe going there now that the feds had left the area.

"Keep trying to call the police," I ordered. "Tell Luscious I think they've headed to Vonzell's cabin. If you can't get him, call the state police. I'm going up there."

Her eyes bulged with fear. "I wish you wouldn't," she whispered. "You don't know what he might try to do to you. The word on the street goes, he done killed his own mother when he was a teenager. Only the family made it look like an accident so he wouldn't get arrested or nothing." She added, unnecessarily, "He's one crazy man."

I FIGURED there must be a road through the forest to the Varner cabin, but I also didn't want to waste time trying to find it, so I drove around the barricade and straight down the Appalachian Trail. Within a few minutes, I saw the cabin. There was no sign of the green van Vonzell was supposed to be driving. I tore across the meadow and was out of the truck almost before it came to a stop. The front door of the cabin was open, revealing a few inches of dark interior. I fingered the Swiss Army knife as I shoved the door open. After listening for a minute or two and hearing nothing, I worked up my courage and entered the cabin.

Someone had been here since my last visit. Things had been dislocated ever so slightly, and one of the beds was rumpled. I moved into the kitchen where I saw several open cabinet doors and some bottles and cans of food on the counter.

Neither Vonzell nor Jenny was there. Where had they gone? What was the point of coming here and then leaving suddenly? Had Vonzell been interrupted by something or someone? I moved back into the kitchen and tried to figure out what he'd been up to. A bottle had been knocked to the floor, and without thinking I stooped and retrieved it and identified it as a maple syrup bottle with about an inch of liquid left in the bottom. Just as I started to lift the lid of the metal trash basket to discard the bottle, I noticed a few ants on it and stopped. An unpleasant association had just popped into my mind.

Syrup. Sugar. Sugary substances attract insects. Especially ants. Ants. Anthills.

I was afraid I knew what Vonzell was up to. I drove too quickly down the trail until I reached the area where the anthills were located. The hills near the trail were undisturbed, but, of course, he wouldn't have done anything where he might be seen by hikers. I'd have to go deeper into the pine forest to look for what I hoped I wouldn't find. I left the truck on the dirt trail and hiked into the woods, marveling at how quickly it became dark once I was beneath the trees.

A faint noise stopped me. An animal? A bird? I stood still and listened. Nothing. I began to walk again, trying to keep quiet, but the leaves and pine needles beneath my feet crunched with every step. There it was again. A mewling sound. Coming from my left, where the undergrowth was thick and treacherous with thorns.

The branches caught my clothes, scratched my arms and legs, and threatened to blind me, but I forced my way through the thicket until I came to a small clearing. And there I saw what I had dreaded seeing. A shapeless bundle, enshrouded by a moving blanket of ants, lay between two of the largest anthills. I knew immediately that this frightening black lump must be Jenny Varner, although it was nearly impossible to recognize a human form beneath the insects. The shape shifted and a low moan drifted toward me. That was all I needed. She was alive. I crossed quickly to her side and began to brush ants from her face with my bare hands. The pain was excruciating, so I grabbed a fallen tree branch and began to swat them away with one end.

Someone approached from behind me. I heard the rustle of leaves, but I didn't dare take the time to turn around. I only hoped it wasn't Vonzell.

Thankfully, it was a woman's voice that said, "Stand aside. I have gloves on."

I spun around and recognized Brunhilda, the ant expert, who immediately took charge of the rescue operation. She had dropped her backpack and told me to find another pair of gloves in there. With them on, I was able to help her brush enough ants away from Jenny to see bare skin. Her hands and ankles were bound with duct tape.

"Help me get her on my back," Brunhilda ordered. She knelt down, and I grabbed Jenny by the arms and swung her over Brunhilda's shoulders. The Amazon stood up as if Jenny weighed nothing at all.

"Come on," she yelled, heading off in a direction that didn't involve brambles and thorny thickets. We soon reached the trail, and I saw the truck about fifty yards ahead of us.

Brunhilda gently laid Jenny in the truck bed and climbed in next to her. "Turn around and drive to the ranger station," she said. "It's near the entrance to the trail. I'll keep working on getting the ants off her. My God, she's all covered with something sticky."

"Maple syrup," I said, running toward the driver's-side door.

The ranger assessed the situation quickly and called for an emergency rescue vehicle. While we waited, he gently hosed the rest of the insects from Jenny's now-still body, and I used the Swiss Army knife to cut the silver tape away from her ankles and wrists. I feared she was dead, but Brunhilda found a weak pulse.

The ambulance arrived quickly, and the pair of Emergency Medical Technicians had Jenny on a stretcher in a blink of an eye. While one EMT received instructions on the radio from a hospital emergency room somewhere, her partner deftly started an IV in Jenny's arm. Soon they had her stabilized and took off down the gravel driveway with Jenny in the back of the ambulance.

And as they disappeared in a cloud of dust, the Lickin Creek police cruiser pulled into the parking lot and Luscious leaped out. "Car radio's broke," he yelled. "I just heard about this when I stopped for coffee."

"Day late, dollar short," I muttered, but luckily he didn't hear me. His face was flushed as he grabbed me in a tight bear hug. "Thank God, you're okay" he said with a catch in his voice. "Please don't take off like that again. You could have been killed."

"But I wasn't." I extracted myself from his grip. "And if I hadn't come up here when I did, Jenny Varner would probably have been dead in a few more minutes."

Brunhilda nodded in agreement.

"We've got to catch him," Luscious muttered, his face now a dangerous-looking purple. "He can't get away with this."

"People say he's invisible," Brunhilda said.

"I'm beginning to wonder…" Luscious said, his voice dangerously quiet.

His face blurred as his voice faded away, and I suddenly turned ice-cold and began to shake. Luscious and Brunhilda realized before I did that I had gone into mild shock from the pain of the ant stings and the deep scratches I'd garnered while pushing my way through the bramble thicket.

I spent several hours that afternoon and evening in an emergency room cubicle being treated for shock, separated by a blue drape from Jenny Varner.

"I'm sorry about your uncle," I managed to say to Brunhilda before she left the hospital. In the excitement, I'd forgotten she had been related to Wilbur Eshelman.

She squeezed my hand gently, so as not to irritate it any more, and thanked me. "My uncle was a good man," she said. "I'll miss him."

Luscious insisted on waiting while the ER doctor checked me out. "You'll need a ride home sooner or later," he said.

"I think they'll want to admit me," I moaned pitifully.

"No they won't," Luscious said almost cheerfully, ducking under the curtain. "You'll be ready to go in fifteen, twenty minutes."

I was sure I was too ill to go home, especially when the doctor told a nurse to give me antibiotics in an IV, so while she was plugging it into my arm, I asked her if I would be staying.

She smiled. "You'll be sleeping in your own bed tonight. I'll be back in a few minutes to check on you."

After she was gone, I whispered, "Jenny? Jenny, can you hear me?"

A groan issued from behind the drape on my right.

"How arc you feeling?"

"Awful."

"Who did this to you? Was it your husband?"

I could barely hear her reply. "Yeah."

"Jenny, did he say anything? Anything at all that can help the police find him?"

"He said…he had his eye on me…that he'd be back."

"Where were the federal agents who were supposed to be protecting you?"

The nurse had entered sometime during our exchange and now glared disapprovingly at me. "The poor woman needs to rest."

LUSCIOUS drove slowly all the way back to Lickin Creek, so as not to "jostle" me. I'd taken a couple of pills for pain and probably wouldn't have been uncomfortable on a roller coaster, but I did enjoy the attention. I took advantage of our time together to ask him why the federal agents hadn't been protecting Jenny.

He told me they'd been called off the case because there was no evidence that Vonzell was in the area. "There's a lot of hot spots in the country these days that need protection."

"Didn't anybody but me see the stolen van he's been driving around town?"

"Apparently not, Tori. Least not till today."

"Do you think they'll come back, now?"

"I don't know. Nobody's talked to me about it. I'll bet they would have been in touch with Garnet if he was still here."

"You're doing a fine job, Luscious," I said.

"You really think so?" He managed to sound both aston- ished and pleased.

"Of course you are. I've heard lots of good things about you."

"Who from?"

"Oh…you know…around town."

His naturally stooped shoulders squared and he seemed to grow a couple of inches taller. "It would be nice if you could mention that to Garnet when he's back here for the wedding. I'm scared he thinks I'm goofing off on the job."

I think he continued to talk, but after he mentioned Gar- net's name I didn't hear another word. Until that moment I had given no thought to Greta's wedding or the fact that Gar- net would be here for it, although now that Luscious had brought it up, it did seem perfectly reasonable. The time was fast approaching when all of Lickin Creek would know that Garnet and I were no longer a couple. My position in local society was precarious already, and I knew I was tolerated only because of my relationship with a member of one of Lickin Creek's oldest families. I'd be persona non grata once the word got out.

It was the noise the cruiser's tires made on Ethelind's gravel driveway that brought me out of my thoughts and back to the moment.

"Are you okay?" Luscious asked. "You look kind of odd."

"Must be the pain medication. I'm fine."

With a hand under one elbow, he walked me to the back door and guided me into the kitchen, where Ethelind looked up from her lipstick-smeared sherry glass. Her mouth fell open as she caught sight of me.

"You poor dear," she gushed. "You sit right down here and let me get you a sherry." She disappeared through the arch- way into the dining room where she kept her liquor in a ma- hogany sideboard.

"Scotch, please. I'd rather have Scotch."

But she must not have heard me because she returned with a huge glass full of thick brown liquid. "You sip that slowly, dear, while I fix us a nice cup of tea."

Luscious stood awkwardly in the doorway while all this was going on, and I wondered why Ethelind hadn't offered him a drink. This apparent lapse in manners was explained when she said, "You're needed downtown, Luscious. Maribell Morgan has disappeared from the Sigafoos Home. There's a search party out looking for her right now."

TWENTY

ON MONDAY MORNING I awoke early, sore and slightly puffy, but with no other side effects from yesterday's adventure. While Ethelind fixed my breakfast, I made a telephone call to the hospital in Gettysburg and learned that Jenny Varner was in serious but stable condition. After that I called P.J. and told her I'd be in late. She'd already heard what had happened, of course, and voiced her concern about me, but I noticed she didn't tell me to take the day off.

Ethelind sat across from me and watched solicitously while I drank three cups of coffee in rapid succession. The painkillers I'd taken yesterday in combination with Ethelind's sweet, strong sherry had left me with a slight hangover.

"I'm afraid I have some bad news for you," she said gently once I'd eaten a platter of bacon, eggs, and fried tomatoes.

I waited, coffee mug in hand, dreading what was to come.

"According to the morning news, the embassy was entered by a Red Cross team yesterday." She didn't have to say which embassy. I knew it was my father's embassy.

"They found bodies."

Blood pounded in my head and blurred my vision. I heard my coffee mug shatter as it hit the floor.

"But there was no sign of your family, Tori. That's good, isn't it?"

I nodded, although I was thinking that there are times when death is preferable to the alternatives.

"A man called from the State Department early this morning. Wants you to call him back. I thought it would be best if I told you what was going on before you talked to him."

She pressed the phone into my hand, and I punched in the phone number. The voice from Washington repeated what Ethelind had already told me. "We believe they're being held for ransom in an undisclosed place," he said.

"How much ransom?"

"We haven't heard from anybody, yet."

"Then what makes you think they're being held for ransom? They could be dead, lying in the bottom of a ravine, or even hacked up and fed to dogs. Maybe they've been sold for slaves. You really don't have any idea what's happened to them, do you?"

"We will keep you informed of any developments as soon as we learn of them."

"I can find out what's going on a lot faster from television than waiting for you guys to call," I snapped. "What the hell do you pay intelligence people for, anyway? Maybe you should start watching CNN." A click told me he had hung up.

I gladly accepted the two aspirins Ethelind offered, washed them down with a half glass of sour grapefruit juice, and then went upstairs to get dressed.

I've always done some of my best thinking in the shower. After the initial shock of the water hitting my sore skin, I relaxed and let the needlelike spray pound away some of the pain and anxiety I felt. As yesterday's dirt went down the drain, the events of the day replayed themselves in my mind like a bad television commercial. When my thoughts finally went back to the part of the day I'd spent at Alice-Ann's house, I recalled that she'd said something to me that now struck me as odd. "It's not always about you, Tori." And then she'd said something else. What was it? I remembered: "You're turning paranoid."

I turned off the water and wrapped one of Ethelind's luxurious English towels around me. Wasn't there a humorous saying about paranoia? "Just because you're paranoid, doesn't mean someone isn't out to get you." No, that wasn't quite right. "Just because you're paranoid, doesn't mean *everyone* isn't out to get you." That was it. It really did seem like everyone had been out to get me lately.

Ethelind looked questioningly at me as I came into the kitchen carrying my fanny pack. "I've got an errand to run, then I'm going to the office," I told her. "I need to keep busy."

"Of course you do, dear. That's why I told Bruce Laughenslagger you'd go to Community Concert with him tonight."

"You did what?"

"He called while you were showering. I didn't want to disturb you."

"I can't believe you did that."

"He's quite a catch, Tori. Absolutely loaded. Do you have any idea how rich he is?"

"I don't really care about a person's money."

"He was a wonderful husband to his first wife. They married right out of high school. It was a real love affair."

"What happened to her? Did one of his employees shoot her?"

Ethelind looked aghast. "How could you say such a mean thing? She died of pancreatic cancer about ten years ago. Very tragic. He hasn't dated anybody since."

I was about to call Bruce and tell him I had other plans, but my hand stopped an inch above the receiver. He *was* very attractive, I remembered, even if he was almost as old as my father. And I certainly hadn't had anybody else ask me for a date. Unless I counted Haley Haley, and I didn't. If I showed up with Bruce at Community Concert, a place where everybody who was anybody in Lickin Creek society was sure to be, the word would finally get out that I was *not* engaged to Garnet Gochenauer. That would save me from having to do a lot of explaining when he came back for his sister's wedding. The more I thought about it, the more it seemed like a good idea to keep the date Ethelind had made for me with Bruce Laughenslagger.

A BODY FOUND at Morgan Manor. The corpse's bride-to-be discovered soon afterward. And now, Maribell Morgan, a sick old lady, had disappeared from a nursing home. There had to be a connection. I needed to find out what it was.

But before I worked on that problem, there was something else I had to clear up. I made a stop at a convenience store where I purchased a copy of the Hagerstown *Morning Herald*, then continued south and pulled into the truck stop before nine, practically the middle of the night for me. The Church on the Go was still there, although somehow I'd almost expected it to have vanished. It seemed deserted. The back doors were tightly closed, and no music rang from the little steeple. A new sign on the side of the truck announced that the church would be participating in the Venison Ministry in the fall. I pounded on the driver's-side door, and after a minute or two, Haley's face filled the window.

At first he looked confused, then taken aback when he recognized me. His frown was quickly replaced by a broad grin, and the door swung open.

"Come on up," he said, extending a hand. I had to accept his assistance since I could barely reach my leg up to the floor of the cab. He hauled as I jumped, and we tumbled together into the front seat.

I sat up quickly, trying to regain my poise, and lost it again when I realized Haley was wearing nothing but a pair of plaid boxer shorts.

"Black Watch," I blurted out, then regretted it. I really didn't care what pattern his underwear was.

His blank expression told me he didn't know what I was talking about, and for that I was grateful.

"Coffee?" he asked.

I nodded, and he reached into the cubicle behind us and retrieved a large steel thermos.

"Only got one cup," he said, as he poured. "Hope you don't mind sharing."

After we'd done the coffee ritual, Haley said, "I'm real happy you're here, but I'm wondering why."

I searched for a shred of courage, found it, and said, "I want to know where Vonzell Varner is."

"What makes you think I'd know that?"

"I'm not an idiot, Haley. You've been stalking me in a green van you said you borrowed from a friend."

"I already done told you I wasn't stalking you. I was only watching over you to keep you safe."

"You were in my bedroom. Looking through my underwear drawer."

"That's because I wanted you to know just how vulnerable you really are."

I decided to drop that conversation and return to the original subject. "You have been driving a green van just like the one Varner stole from a car dealer in Maryland last week. Only you said you borrowed it from a friend. You also said you'd done time in Graterford Prison when Varner was there. To me, the connection is obvious; Varner is the friend. I'm just trying to understand why a man of God like you would protect a slimeball like him."

"It's Graterford SCI," Haley corrected. "State Correctional Institute, not prison. And don't forget Genesis four: nine, 'Am I my brother's keeper?'"

"I don't care what the prison is called. You're avoiding the subject, which is where is Vonzell Varner? And I'd say if Vonzell is your brother, you are not doing a very good job of keeping him."

"I did know Vonzell," Haley admitted. "We went to AA meetings together at Graterford. That's were I found God, you know."

I sighed. "You told me that story. What about Vonzell?"

"He repented, Tori. He fell on his knees and begged forgiveness. He wanted to atone for all his sins. Jesus said, 'Joy shall be in heaven over one sinner that repenteth, more than ninety-nine just persons which need no repentance."

"Obviously, he has had a relapse."

"'Judge not, that ye be not judged.' Matthew seven: one."

"Didn't you hear what he did to his wife yesterday?"

"I didn't hear nothing. What happened?" Haley's voice was cold and flat.

"He beat her badly, kidnapped her, drenched her with maple syrup, and tied her up on top of a giant anthill. She would have died if I hadn't come along when I did. Here. You can read about it on the front page of the paper." He caught the newspaper I tossed at him and quickly scanned the article.

His face and chest turned red, then faded to a ghostly bluish white. "God, grant me the serenity to accept the things I cannot change…"

"Haley, prayer isn't going to stop him."

"The courage to change the things I can…"

"Tell me where he is. Before he does something worse."

"And the wisdom to know the difference."

"Haley?"

"You will have to believe me, Tori, I don't know where he is. I'd tell you if I did."

I had to be satisfied with that.

"Any chance you'd go out with me again?" he asked, as I climbed out of the cab. "I think we could be friends if we got to know each other better."

"Haley. The only thing I want from you is Vonzell Varner, trussed up like a Thanksgiving turkey."

BACK IN LICKIN CREEK, I parked behind the drugstore and looked over the embankment at the place where I'd found Wilbur Eshelman's body. Whoever had shot him had had to be standing close to where I was now. I turned around and stared at the backs of the Victorian buildings. Most of them, I knew, had been chopped up into apartments, and many of those apartments had windows overlooking the parking lot and the creek.

Surely someone had been drawn to a window by the sound of gunfire. There was a good chance that a witness to Wilbur's murder was looking down upon me right now.

An hour later, I'd visited more than a dozen spacious apartments, reminders of the days when wealthy shopkeepers lived above their businesses. But nobody admitted to seeing anything. Yes, many said they'd heard a sound that could have been a shot, Friday evening around six-fifteen or six-thirty, the dinner hour, but everyone living near the square had become so used to hearing fire crackers being shot off to scare away crows that nobody had thought anything of it. It had not been a sound that would have drawn anybody away from the table.

At the last apartment, an elderly woman told me Luscious had asked the same questions right after the shooting and wanted to know why I was bothering her again. I was glad to hear Luscious was on the job, but I also was slightly irritated that he hadn't shared his knowledge with me. It would have saved me a lot of time and embarrassment.

I walked to the *Chronicle* office in the next block and checked my box for assignments. When P.J. came in it was afternoon, and I was finished.

"I understand you've got a date for Community Concert tonight," she said, with a knowing grin.

"How did you know…" My voice faded away, as I recalled the infamous Lickin Creek Grapevine.

"No magic. I had lunch with Ethelind, and she told me. Since you're going, would you please take notes and write a review of the performance? It'll save me from having to sit through it."

"I don't mind," I said. I was rather excited about going. Community Concert tickets were sold in advance, during a one-week period each spring, and somehow I hadn't known they were on sale until too late to buy one. This was another thing that only native Lickin Creekers seemed to know about. Tonight was the first of this season's four concerts, and it would also be the first I'd had the opportunity to attend.

When I went home to get ready, I found a box on the kitchen table addressed to me. Curious, Ethelind hung over me while I sliced through the packing tape with a steak knife and found ten copies of my new book, *The Albert Einstein Horror Ship,* sent by my publisher. I should have been excited. Seeing your book in print for the first time is considered by most authors to be a thrill akin to giving birth, but in this case, after all that happened recently, it seemed anticlimactic. I let Ethelind take a book out, closed the box, and went upstairs to change for the concert.

TWENTY-ONE

SINCE I REALLY didn't care what Bruce Laughenslagger thought of me, I hadn't planned to wear anything special for my date, but while I was showering I thought about the people who were going to see me with him and realized I needed to make an impact. I should wear something that would show the townsfolk I wasn't pining away for a lost love. Therefore, I pulled out the black cocktail dress I'd purchased about a year ago at a shop in the Village called Gently Used. The shopkeeper hinted it had previously been owned by a celebrity and had been worn only once, to the Tony Awards. It was low-cut and sparkly, and I knew it was going to make me stand out at the concert tonight.

Bruce had left word he'd pick me up at six-thirty for the seven o'clock concert, but he'd warned me not to eat much dinner since we'd be going to a party afterwards.

While Ethelind fluttered around me, I ate the Lebanon bologna sandwich she'd fixed "to tide me over." When the front door bell rang, I thought Ethelind was going to burst with excitement. "You can't wear that jacket, not with that dress. You look just beautiful. He's going to fall head-over-heels for you. Don't trip on those high heels, now. The carpeting in the auditorium isn't all that great."

Bruce pursed his lips and whistled silently when I opened the door. "You look as pretty as a big-racked buck," he said, and I took that to be a compliment. After helping me into my coat, or rather Ethelind's velvet evening wrap from Harrod's, he took my arm and gallantly escorted me to his SUV.

"Up you go," he said cheerfully, as I stood on my tiptoes and tried to lift my rear end up to the seat. One of my shoes fell off in the process, and he retrieved it and handed it to me.

"Just like Cinderella," he said. "Only there's no surprise over who the princess is because I saw you lose it."

The high school was only a five-minute drive away from Moon Lake, but it took about ten minutes for Bruce to find a parking spot, and another five minutes to hike from the side street to the high school. People were just beginning to file into the auditorium. I looked in vain for a coatroom, then realized I was the only one there with an evening wrap, so I slipped it off, draped it over one arm, and fell into line next to Bruce.

I sensed people staring and knew the dress was getting the attention it deserved.

It was a good thing Bruce was holding my arm, for the carpet in the auditorium was indeed treacherous. We eventually found two empty seats on the aisle near the center of the vast room and sat down.

Tonight's performance was by a very large brass band from Chicago. It alternated patriotic music with jazz and occasionally threw in a Sousa march, and before long I had the headache of the century.

"Isn't it great?" Bruce asked, as we were swept into the outer hall for intermission. "You don't hear music like that every day in Lickin Creek."

Thank God for that, I thought as I nodded and dug through my purse until I found two Tylenol. "I'll be right back," I said, and set off in search of a drinking fountain.

The concert finally dragged to an earsplitting conclusion, and the band received an enthusiastic standing ovation from the audience, which was about half the size it had been before the intermission.

After a silent ride, I was shocked when Bruce pulled into the parking lot behind the Benjamin Koon Funeral Home.

"Are we in the right place?" I asked.

Bruce chuckled. "I wouldn't lead you astray, Tori. It's a tradition to have the post-concert parties here. Lots of room and plenty of parking. What more could you ask for?"

"A party without dead people would be nice," I said.

Goldie Koon, wife of the owner, greeted us at the front door, took my wrap, and murmured that I looked lovely. I caught a glimpse of myself in a pier mirror and thought, too, that I looked pretty darn good. Especially compared to most of the other women there, who wore plain cotton sundresses.

There were two large and lofty public rooms on either side of the front hall, which I knew from the house tour were usually used for viewings and services. Tonight the folding chairs were gone, and in the room to my right a long table sagged under the weight of the party fare. Beef roasts, turkeys, hams, and oyster casseroles vied with salads, Jell-O molds, and pasta dishes.

A bar had been set up in the room on the other side of the hall, and men clustered around it. Bruce pushed his way through the throng and emerged a few minutes later with drinks, Scotch for him, white wine for me. If he'd bothered to ask what I wanted, he would have been carrying two Scotches.

He led me through an archway at the back of the hall that opened into the family's private quarters. It hardly seemed possible, but here the rooms were even larger than out front. Despite the summer heat, gas logs burned in marble fireplaces in every room.

As with most gatherings, at least half the attendees were crowded into the kitchen. We pushed in, and I saw Greta, Garnet's sister, staring at me in astonishment. I waved and kept moving.

After introducing me to a balding gentleman with a smile that spread over his chin but didn't quite reach his eyes, Bruce excused himself to "look for the little boys' room." I watched him walk away, thinking he had a great build for a man his age. If he wouldn't use such corny expressions, he'd be darn near perfect.

The gentleman whose name I hadn't caught quickly exhausted his repertoire of cocktail chatter and moved away, leaving me to either stand awkwardly alone or search for a group to join. I didn't have to stand alone for long, because Greta was suddenly at my side.

"I'm so surprised to see you here," she said. "How come you didn't buy your Community Concert ticket from me?"

"I didn't buy one from anybody, Greta. I came with somebody."

"Not Bruce Laughenslagger? I saw you walk in with him. I thought maybe you'd met up with him in the parking lot. It's certainly nice of him to take you under his wing while Garnet's away." She stood back and studied me as if seeing me for the first time. "That's not what you're planning on wearing to my wedding, is it?"

Preparing to defend my almost-new designer dress, I nodded. "Why?" I asked.

"Because it's…" She paused as if struggling for words, and I cringed as I waited. She frowned, and then her blue-green eyes, so like Garnet's twinkled. "Because it's so pretty, everybody will be looking at you instead of me." She grinned broadly to show me she was joking. "Oops. Buchanan's been cornered by Bob Higgins. Bob's always looking for free legal advice. I'd better go rescue him."

I wandered from one group to another, trying to think of something to say that wouldn't be too annoying to people. After offering a few non sequiturs, I realized I'd be wise to keep my mouth shut and listen.

The conversations didn't vary much. Other than how wonderful tonight's concert had been, there were three subjects: the house tour, Mr. Eshelman's murder, and the discovery of the bodies of Lickin Creek's long-lost lovers. Of the three topics, Rodney and Emily seemed to be most popular. Despite the lack of any real information in the newspaper, the Grapevine had done its job because everyone knew about Rodney being found in the cave, disappearing, and eventually turning up in Funkhauser's tire pile.

I inched forward, glass in hand, determined smile on my face, and pushed my way into a clutch of people who all stopped talking as soon as they noticed me. "Please don't stop on my account," I said. "Just pretend I'm not here."

They took me at my word and resumed their conversation, which happened to be about Rodney Mellott and Emily Rakestraw.

"It's obvious Rodney killed Emily," offered one woman.

"Sure he did, then he walled himself up inside the cave, and stabbed himself in the back until he died," another said. "Don't make me laugh."

"He couldn't have done it," a man said. "Rodney disappeared first."

"He could have been hiding, waiting for just the right time." The first woman wasn't about to give up.

"I think Emily killed Rodney, then committed suicide because she felt so guilty." This was from someone who had just joined the group.

"By climbing into a trunk and having someone else padlock it? Give me a break." I couldn't tell who said this.

"Maybe somebody killed them both."

That was the first thing that made any sense.

As if there was a signal I couldn't hear, the members of the group turned away from each other and formed new groups. I wandered from one to another trying to find an opening, and as I passed a group dominated by Ben Koon, I heard him say something that drew me in. "She wasn't really dressed in the wedding gown, you see. That was tossed into the trunk with her. What she was wearing was white shorts, a white T-shirt, and tennis shoes. I'd say the young lady was just leaving for a tennis date or returning from one."

"Did you have an opportunity to see this for yourself?" I asked.

Ben turned and glared at me as if wondering why I'd been allowed into his house. "Of course I did. The coroner brought both bodies here. Believe it or not, Emily's body is still in the trunk. I'll prepare them for burial when the police give me the go-ahead."

"Can I see them?"

Several people looked shocked and backed away from me as if I had a loathsome disease. Others merely stared curiously at me, as if wondering whether I really was the big city pervert I was rumored to be.

"There's no harm in taking you down," Ben said. "Let me just grab a drink first."

What he grabbed was a nearly full bottle of champagne. He picked up a glass, then turned back and picked up a second one. "Let's go," he said.

I now knew that looks couldn't really kill, because if they could, Goldie Koon's look would have taken us both out. Ben acted as if he hadn't noticed and led the way to the front of the building where the public rooms were. There, in the back of the front hall, hidden behind a velvet drape, was a steel door, which Ben unlocked and held open. The stairwell was well lighted, but the circular staircase was the scary kind that causes vertigo because the steps and risers are made of steel mesh you can see through.

I clung to the railing and tried to keep my eyes focused on the bald spot on the back of Ben's head. At long last, our feet were firmly set on the concrete floor.

"This way," Ben said, holding open a door. I walked into a large chamber, dominated by several shiny steel embalming tables.

"Do you want to see them both?" Ben asked.

I shook my head. "Just Emily, please."

Ben pulled a drawer out of the wall, and as it rolled out,

I saw the trunk that had driven Ramona Houdeyshell into therapy.

"I was hoping you'd still have the trunk," I said.

"We're keeping it all together for evidence," Ben said.

"Can I look?"

"Help yourself."

I moved closer. The padlock was still locked in the hasp, but that didn't matter since the hinges had broken when the trunk lid shattered.

I looked inside and felt a wave of nausea sweep over me at the sight of the yellowed bones mingled with satin and lace.

What I wanted to examine, though, was not Emily Rakestraw's mortal remains, but the inside of the trunk itself.

I needed to see if the story I'd heard second- or third-hand about Emily trying to scratch her way out of the trunk was true. Unfortunately, it looked as if that was exactly what had happened. The satin lining had been torn away, and there were hundreds of scratches on the wood facing of the interior. Emily had been alive when she'd been locked in the trunk. What must her last hours have been like? It was too horrible to contemplate.

Ben leaned into my back and stared over my shoulder into the trunk. "Nasty way to die," he said. "Drink?" He pressed a flute of champagne into my hand.

He was too close, and I stiffened. "I don't think so," I said, looking for a place to put the glass down. "Could you please back up?"

He didn't move, except perhaps to press harder against me.

"I said…back up."

He touched the side of my neck with his free hand. "You share my interest in the macabre, I see," he murmured close to my ear.

"I do not. Get away." I tried to push myself away from the drawer, but he had me pinned against it. "Let me go, or I'll scream."

"Nobody's going to hear you. Maybe you'd like to see Rodney's remains."

"I found him, remember?"

"I'll bet you didn't notice his feet, though."

"What about his feet?"

"He didn't have any. Cut clean away. Right above the ankles."

"Get the hell away from me." I pushed with all my might, and he fell back so suddenly that I almost toppled over.

I spun, prepared to run, and was shocked to see, not Ben, but Bruce.

"Come on," Bruce said, extending a hand. "Let's get out of here. Don't trip over the garbage."

He was referring to Ben, who lay on the floor in a fetal position.

"Is he...? You didn't...?"

"All I did was give him a chop in the kidney. Something I learned to do in Nam. He'll be almost good as new in a few minutes."

I took his hand and followed him meekly out of the mortuary chamber.

Back upstairs, we closed the door behind us and tried to look as if we'd never been away.

"Obviously, you're not local or you'd know better than to go anywhere alone with Ben," Bruce said with a grin. "He's Lickin Creek's best-known lecher."

I looked across the room, to where Goldie Koon stood, looking tall, thin, blond, and rich. She was everything I'd ever wanted to be, but now I knew her life was not what it appeared to be. I might be short, dark, and dumpy but at least I wasn't involved with an adulterer. Or anybody else, the little voice in my head whispered. That's good, I told the voice. I can be my own woman. Do what I want, when I want, with whomever I want. Another minute of thinking like that and I'd have had myself believing it.

The front door burst open, and in came the brass band

from Community Concert. Everyone began to applaud, welcoming them to the party. Goldie Koon looked around for her husband, and not seeing him, stepped forward and greeted the large group. They were led into the other room for drinks.

"They're going to perform with the Downtown Businessmen's Association Band in a few minutes," Bruce told me. "It's an annual tradition. If you want to leave, we'd better do it now."

"Aren't you going to join them?" I asked.

"My musical days are far behind me. I'll get your coat."

In his SUV, Bruce turned the radio on to a country-western station. "I really like this a lot better than what we heard tonight," he said.

"Me, too."

"I had a feeling you didn't enjoy it."

"What gave you the clue? Was it when I put the wet paper towel on my forehead? Or when I made ear plugs out of Kleenex?"

He smiled and pulled out of the parking lot. It was eleven o'clock, and the local news came on the radio. Bruce reached forward to switch it off, but I put my hand on his arm, "Let's hear what's happening," I said.

After a brief rave review of the concert, the reporter announced that a woman who had wandered away from a local nursing home had been found. No further details were provided.

As the radio began to play a Garth Brooks number, I thought about what had happened down in the mortuary. Not only had I discovered that Emily really had been alive, but the news about Rodney's missing feet had caught me completely by surprise. What did it mean?

I suddenly realized that Bruce was talking to me. "What did you say?" I asked.

"I still feel terrible about what happened to you at my hunting preserve. I'd like to make it up to you."

"You took me to a concert and a nice party," I said. "And

rescued me from a fate worse than death at the hands of a randy mortician. I think that's enough."

"I'm going out of town on a business trip. Leaving tomorrow. Why don't you come with me?"

I thought about it for a second or two. "The prospect of looking at deer on an Amish farm somewhere in Ohio is not my idea of fun. Thanks for the offer."

"Not Ohio, Tori. Cancún, Mexico. Sun, surf, Mayan ruins, scuba diving."

"Oh my." Cancún sounded great, but I could not picture myself there with anyone but Garnet.

"I can't," I said regretfully.

"I'd like to get you away from here for a while."

"I've got Greta's wedding coming up."

"You'll call me in the morning if you change you mind?"

At first, I was relieved when he didn't try to kiss me goodnight at the door. However, when I got inside, I thought, maybe if he had I might have agreed to go to Cancún with him.

"Stop it," I scolded myself.

"Stop what?" Ethelind asked. She must have been lurking in the front parlor, just waiting for me to come home so she could interrogate me about the evening. And interrogate me, she did. "How was the concert? Did you have a good time? He's nice, isn't he? Are you going out with him again? My mother always said it's as easy to fall in love with a rich man as a poor man."

"Did you hear anything about Maribell Morgan's whereabouts?" I broke in during a lull. "The radio said something about a woman who'd wandered away from a nursing home being found."

"Of course I did. Everyone's talking about it. She really must be senile. Why else would she try to go home?"

"Home? You mean she was found at Morgan Manor?"

"Indeed she was. In the attic, yet, with a broken hip. You know what they say about old people and broken hips, don't you."

"Not really," I said.

"They don't break their hips by falling down, the hip breaks by itself and *that's* what makes them fall."

My head was spinning. What had made Maribell Morgan risk her health by running away? As far as I could tell, there could be only one reason for her to be in the attic. She was looking for something there. Had she found it? Whether or not she had, I was sure it had something to do with the murders of the long-dead couple. I needed to discover what it was she was seeking.

TWENTY-TWO

ALL THROUGH THE NIGHT, I thumped my pillow and wrestled with my sheet while drawing comparisons between Bruce and Garnet. Bruce was rich; Garnet was not. Bruce was well established in business; Garnet was well respected but unsure of the direction he wanted to take. Bruce had asked me to go to an exotic place with him; Garnet went to an exotic place without me. Bruce was a gentleman; Garnet was rather rough around the edges. And most important Bruce was here, while Garnet was not.

As the first gray light of morning brightened the sky outside my window my heart and mind came to an agreement, and I fell into a deep sleep only to be awakened a few minutes later by my alarm clock. Without hesitation, I turned off the clock, rubbed Fred's tummy for good luck, and placed a call to Bruce.

He sounded a bit sleepy but also pleased to hear from me. "Are you calling to say you'll go to Cancún with me?" he said, and I could envision his tanned skin crinkling pleasantly around his bright blue eyes.

I took a deep breath and said, "I really called to say thank you for a nice evening last night."

"Except for the episode with Ben in the mortuary," he reminded me.

I couldn't help laughing a little. "And I also wanted to thank you for saving me from a fate worse than death."

"You did that last night. Now, why don't you tell me why you really called?"

After another deep breath, I said, "Bruce, I know you only asked me to go on a vacation with you, and that's not exactly a commitment, but I'm not a person who takes things like that lightly. I really like you, and I enjoy being with you. But I am still in love with Garnet Gochenauer, and that's why I can't see you again."

There was silence on the other end of the line, then Bruce said, "I thought he was out of the picture."

"Physically, yes. Emotionally no."

"I see."

"I'm sorry, Bruce."

"No problem, Tori. I appreciate hearing this from you. In my younger days honesty was a trait I admired and strived for. It's something that has kind of slipped by the boards in the past few years. I thank you for reminding me of it."

I didn't know what to say, so I kept my mouth shut.

He added. "I don't take things lightly, either, Tori. Not when they have to do with people and relationships. I had hoped we might…well, never mind…Tori, please be careful. I'm worried about you."

"No need to worry about me," I told him. "I survived for a decade in New York City, and some of it was in the pre-Mayor Giuliani days." I wondered why he was worried, but he didn't elaborate.

I felt better after my phone call, even though I still wasn't one hundred percent sure I'd made the right decision.

Ignoring Ethelind's declarations that I was going to wither up and blow away if I didn't eat breakfast, I skipped the kippers on cold toast and drove to the Sigafoos Home for the Aged where Maribell Morgan was recovering from her mysterious nighttime visit to her old home.

After I parked in the nearly empty lot, I walked under a long awning to the front door and entered an unbearably hot reception hall. The scent of floral air freshener did not quite cover the odor of urine, rubbing alcohol, and cafeteria food that pervaded the air. A young woman sat behind a glass window with a little hole in it, as if she were a bank teller, and told me I'd find Maribell Morgan in the nursing section. She directed me to an elevator hidden behind a thriving rubber plant, and told me to turn left on the third floor and go through the double doors.

The doors were closed and also locked, as I found out when I pushed on them. I rang the bell on the wall under a sign that said RING AND STEP BACK. The doors swung open toward me, and I darted through them before they could knock me over or close me out.

A nurse sat inside a circular desk, writing something on a chart. After a long wait, I cleared my throat, startling her but getting her attention.

"Maribell Morgan?" she said in response to my request. "Down that hall, last door on the right. But you'll have to wait outside until someone comes out. She has two visitors with her now. You are a relative, aren't you? That's all she's allowed to see."

I wiped my eyes and nodded. "How is she?" I asked, hoping I sounded like a concerned relative.

The nurse gave a noncommittal shrug and answer: "As well as can be expected."

"Did she have anything with her when she was found?" I asked. "A package or something that I could take home for her?"

The nurse shook her head impatiently. "Nope."

"How was she found?" I asked.

"Evidently Miss Morgan switched on the attic light when she went in, and a neighbor saw it when it got dark outside. She knew nobody was living there, so she called the police."

"That was a lucky break," I said.

"Yup." The nurse turned back to her paper work, obviously finished with me, so I found my way down the hallway to a row of chairs and chose one covered with turquoise vinyl. There, I sat facing Maribell Morgan's door and waited for it to open.

At long last it did, and a stooped man in a black suit stepped out. It was Father Burkholder, who'd been at St. Mary's Catholic Church since the beginning of time. It was well known that Father Burkholder suffered from severe osteoporosis, which caused him always to walk with his head hanging forward as if he were an archaeologist scanning the ground for clues. When he saw my feet, he twisted his neck enough to see who was attached to them.

He smiled when he recognized me. "Why Tori, I didn't realize you were related to the Morgans?"

I smiled at him and hoped that fibbing to a priest by omission wasn't as serious as an out-and-out lie. Even thought I'm not Catholic, and my only religious training was from the brief period when my mother embraced Zen Buddhism, I do try to show respect for other people's religious beliefs.

"She's not…dying, is she?" I asked, fearful she might be gone before I questioned her.

"Oh no. But she's not doing good. Not at all," he said, sounding depressed. At least he wasn't wishy-washy about her condition like the nurse at the desk had been. "She's undergone a terrible ordeal for a woman her age. The good Lord was looking out for her, though. Her hip isn't broken, after all."

"Morgan Manor is several miles from here. How did she get there?"

The priest allowed a slight grin to stray across his lips, then his face again turned somber. "She stole a nurse's car keys and drove."

"That was certainly resourceful of her," I said.

"Maribell was always a take-charge type of woman. I really must be going. I do hope I'll see you at our summer fair next week. We could use some publicity."

He left after I'd promised to cover the event for the newspaper.

A few minutes later, J.B. Morgan came out. He had his glasses in his hand and was cleaning them with his handkerchief, so he didn't see me. He jumped when I greeted him.

"What are you doing here?" he asked, rather rudely, I thought.

"I heard about your aunt's accident. I wanted to express my condolences."

"I didn't realize you knew my aunt."

"I…I feel like I know her…from the house tour, you know."

"I think you'd better leave now," J.B. said.

"Can't I just pop in and say hello?"

"She's sedated." He took my arm and escorted me through the locked doors, rode in the elevator with me, and finally released me in the parking lot.

"By the way," he said, "I've had a chance to review your loan application, and it looks like a mistake was made by the credit bureau. If you stop by the office, I think we'll be able to approve your home loan." He smiled down at me in an avuncular sort of way, and added," And please don't pester my aunt with any questions. I assure you she knows nothing about Rodney's and Emily's deaths."

Feeling vaguely as if I'd been bribed, I watched him walk toward the bank building on Main Street, and when he was out of sight I got into the truck and drove in the opposite direction. Maribell had been looking for something in her home, something I felt certain had to do with Rodney Mellott's murder, and if I were going to discover what it was I'd have to get out there before someone else came to the same conclusion.

First, I stopped at Alice-Ann's house. I was pretty sure she'd be home, since she worked Saturdays and usually had Tuesdays off. A look of doubt crossed her face. "I don't know if I should…"

"Just give it to me, Alice-Ann. We owe it to Rodney to find out who killed him. And the answer has to be there in the house."

"Why do we owe him anything?"

"Because we found him. You and I. Together. It's just like the old Chinese belief that if you save a man's life you're responsible for him forever."

"But we didn't save his life, Tori."

"Close enough. We found him. Now he's our responsibility."

"I'm not supposed to…"

"Give me the key. I know you still have the keys from the house tour."

With the key to Morgan Manor clutched in my right hand, I drove out to the house, parked behind the barn where I thought the truck would be invisible from the road, and opened the front door.

A house empty of humanity can become soulless. That is what had happened to Morgan Manor since the day of the house tour. Memories had long ago danced out the windows in a whirl of dust motes, leaving a nothingness in their place.

What am I doing here? I asked myself, as I mounted the staircase to the second floor. Certainly not listening to my inner voice, the one that was saying I was once again acting foolishly. But I kept moving forward because I had to know what had drawn Maribell Morgan back. I had to discover what she was searching for in the attic, and I hoped I found it before someone else did.

Hollow footsteps echoed through the downstairs rooms. I stopped breathing for a minute. Listening. Perhaps the house wasn't empty after all. But there was nothing to hear, and I knew it had only been the reverberations caused by my own feet on the staircase. I took another step, on tiptoe this time, and the echoes silently passed me by and waited for me in the long hallway upstairs.

When I was one riser away from the landing, an invisible hand shoved me toward the railing. I'd forgotten the dangerous slope and grabbed the banister to steady myself. A tightness seized my chest, then rose in my throat, brought on by the spookiness of the empty house and my fears of the unknown. With my eyes closed, I waited for my panic attack to subside.

I was alone in the house, I knew, and yet as I stood there

hanging on to the railing, trying to regain my equilibrium, the old building seemed to spring to life. Stairs creaked, air rushed through hallways, and a ray of sunlight streamed through the window at the top of the stairs and settled on my shoulders like a shawl of golden gauze.

"Is anybody here?" I called softly, terrified of how I'd react if someone or something answered. Thank goodness there was no reply, and after a few long minutes, I slinked down the hall to the attic stairs doorway.

No bats, please, I whispered, as I swung open the door. The enclosed staircase was dark, but I was reluctant to turn the overhead light on for fear of attracting the attention of the neighbor who had found Maribell. I shuddered when my fingers came in contact with things soft and squishy as I groped my way up the stairs.

After climbing forever, I came into the enormous attic, its gloom only partially broken by faint rays of light streaming through dirt-covered windows in the bays at either end of the expanse.

The dust-covered random planks of the floor creaked beneath my feet, and from the darkness above came faint squeaks from creatures hiding in the rough beams that supported the roof.

Where slate tiles had broken away, thin slivers of light shone through the roof. There were four chimneys of crumbling brick piercing the room from floor to roof, but no walls to divide the great space.

What really caught my attention were the stacks of furniture, steamer trunks from bygone days, cardboard boxes, and several wardrobes from various eras, ranging from ornate Victorian to knotty-pine rustic and cheap Giant Big-Mart pasteboard.

How on earth could I ever determine what Maribell had been looking for in this antique treasure trove? I recalled Alice-Ann telling me that she'd found the box containing

Rodney's scrapbooks and diary in an antique wardrobe, and I spotted a trail of footprints on the dusty floor leading directly to a walnut Victorian wardrobe, not far from the top of the stairs. I followed it, and in front of the ornate cabinet I saw the story of Maribell's fall and the arrival of the EMTs plainly written in the dust.

I swung open the double doors of the wardrobe and was dismayed to see only empty cardboard boxes. Perhaps Maribell had found what she was looking for just before she fell, but even if she had, it struck me that she wouldn't have been able to take it with her. And that could only mean that someone had gotten here before me.

I pulled out the empty boxes, one by one, and beneath the bottom one found an old-fashioned reel tape recording. I doubted whether it meant much. If it had it probably would have been taken, too, but I popped it into my fanny pack just in case it had some importance.

I heard someone behind me.

"Who is it?" I asked, looking around for a weapon I could use to protect myself. An old drum major's baton lay on the floor of the wardrobe, and I seized it without much thought.

I spun around to see a mop of silver curls appear at the top of the stairs, level with the attic floor. The mop rose higher, revealing a smiling pink face beneath it. "Oh, there you are," the face said cheerfully. "I saw your truck from my bathroom window. After what happened to Maribell, I was worried, especially when that van pulled up behind your truck, and I didn't see any lights come on inside."

So my ploy of not turning on lights for fear of attracting attention had been as attention-grabbing as turning on the lights had been for Maribell.

The woman was all the way into the attic now, and I saw that she was very frail and that I probably could have taken her out even without the baton. "Who are you?" I asked.

"I'm Sara Meminger, from next door. Who are *you?* What are you doing here?"

"I'm Tori Miracle, and I'm looking for something Maribell lost here. Was it you who found Miss Morgan?"

"Oh yes. Me and her have watched out for each other for years and years. After my husband passed, she took good care of me. I been sort of keeping an eye on her place since she went into the nursing home." The curls bounced as she shook her head. "Don't know who's going to be watching out for me, now. Maybe I'll have to go into Sigafoos, too."

"Perhaps you'll get some caring neighbors when the house is sold," I said.

She looked dubious, but only for a second or two before a broad grin split her face. She didn't seem to be a woman who played the "poor me" game. "That would be nice."

What she had said earlier just then registered with me. "Did you say a van pulled in behind my truck? Was it dark green?" Was Haley stalking me again?

"I couldn't tell the color, just that it was dark. My eyes done grew dim about six years ago." I saw then that the pupils of her eyes were rimmed with ice-blue circles. Cataracts. Poor woman.

"When I stepped out on my porch it drove away."

"Could you tell if a man was driving?"

"I couldn't see nothing. Anyway, it had them black windows you can't see through. Is you'uns ready to go? I'll lock up after you." She glanced around the attic as if checking to see if I'd looted. The tape in my fanny pack weighted heavily on my waist and in my conscience, but I consoled myself with the knowledge that there was no way she could know it was there.

I meekly followed her down the stairs and waited while she tried seven or eight keys before finally managing to lock the front door.

As anxious as I was to listen to the purloined tape, I knew I first had to drop by the office and pick up my assignments.

Because a street fair and sidewalk sale blocked Main Street, I had to park about six blocks north of the *Chronicle* and walk the rest of the way. A pleasant breeze stirred the trees that lined Main Street, and the temperature had dropped by ten or fifteen degrees, making it a pleasure to be outside. I purchased a fruit-ice from a vendor and made my way past the exhibits of handmade crafts. It felt good to be outside. Back in New York, I'd walked everywhere, and I felt that the lack of exercise since I'd come to Lickin Creek might be one of the reasons I'd put on some extra pounds in the last few months.

Everything sparkled; even the fountain in the square had been freshly painted, and the little mermaid's tail was now a bright metallic green. The summer water shortage hadn't prevented the fountain from flowing, and the bronze rim of the basin was encircled by red geraniums, courtesy of the Lickin Creek Garden Club. I crossed the street there, passed the Old Lickin Creek National Bank, and paused for a moment in front of the drugstore because my fruit-ice was melting quickly.

A hand-lettered sign in the window said CLOSED TEMPRA-RALEY. And so another Main Street business was gone. I wondered if it would ever reopen, and if it did who would the new owner be? And where was the Old Boys' Club going to get together from now on?

I finished my ice, crumpled the paper cone, tossed it into a mesh trash basket, and took a few steps before something nagged at my mind. Mr. Eshelman had been shot in the parking lot behind his store. To get to the parking lot, he'd had to come out of the side door of the drugstore and walk halfway down the alley. I wondered if Big Bad Bob, who'd been living in the alley since spring, might have witnessed the murder. He was the unseen man in Lickin Creek, the bum who was overlooked by everyone. Perhaps the killer hadn't realized he was there.

I ducked into the alley and called his name.

There was no answer, but that didn't surprise me. I figured he'd probably be asleep in his favorite window well, the one he'd emerged from to scare me half to death. But it was empty. The only evidence that he'd ever been there were an empty whiskey bottle and some candy wrappers.

I checked all the wells. All empty. I was becoming alarmed. As far as I knew Big Bad Bob had been living in this alley for months. It seemed really strange that he'd suddenly leave it. I hoped no harm had come to him.

A slight noise from above caught my attention, and I looked up the brick wall of the drugstore and saw a second-floor window, partially open. What I'd heard was a curtain flapping in the breeze.

I quickly ran to the back of the building, where there was a doorway that opened on a narrow, stale-smelling flight of stairs going up the apartments on the second and third floors. I'd visited them before, when I was asking if anybody had witnessed Mr. Eshelman's murder, but I hadn't then thought it necessary to ask if any of the residents knew where Big Bad Bob had gone.

I tapped on the door of the apartment on the left, the one I figured must look out on the alley. Nobody came to the door, but I could hear a television blaring inside and guessed there must be someone in there.

After I'd knocked three or four more times, I heard a man's voice yell, "Hold your horses. I'm coming, damn it."

The door was swung open by a man dressed in jeans and a sleeveless undershirt that revealed several tattoos. I immediately remembered the description of Vonzell Varner's tattoos, but quickly realized these were not the same. No bloody head. No map of Pennsylvania.

"My dreams done come true," he said, flashing a mossy-green grin. "I been hoping you'd show up again."

Now I recalled I'd interviewed this same man during my first visit to the apartments overlooking the Lickin Creek. I let myself take a deep breath before I asked, "May I come in for a minute? I have a couple of questions I'd like to ask you?"

"Be my guest." He stepped aside and let me pass by him into the small, overheated living room dominated by a super-sized television set. His smirk annoyed me. Did he really think I'd found him so attractive the last time I met him that I climbed that nasty flight of stairs to his nasty apartment in the hope of being seduced by him?

He waited till I was seated on the orange-and-green plaid sofa, and said, "I done told you last time I didn't see nothing. You and the cop, both. Maybe you forgot."

"I remember." I searched my memory for his name. "Mr. Fleegle, isn't it?"

His half smile told me he wasn't used to being called Mister. "Call me Wrigley," he said.

"Okay, Mr. Flee—I mean Wrigley, let's just go over the events of the afternoon Mr. Eshelman was killed, see if there's anything that might have come to you afterwards." That really wasn't why I was there, but I thought with Wrigley Fleegle the direct approach might not be the best.

He stared into space in a pretense of thinking, then shook his head. "Can't think of nothing. I already done told you I heard the shot, but I thought it was those damn Boy Scouts scaring off crows, so's I didn't even get up to look out."

I let him see me write that down in my notebook. Allowing the pages to close, I hoped I appeared finished with my questioning and stood up.

As if it were an afterthought, I said, "By the way, have you seen Big Bad Bob lately?"

"What's it to you?"

"It's just that I usually run into him in the alley, and today I didn't see him there."

Instead of answering my question, Wrigley rubbed his lower back with his dirty left hand and grimaced. "Got a damn herniated disk. Can't do nothing without pain."

"I'm sorry about that," I said.

He rubbed some more and said, "Can't even work. If it wasn't for SSI I'd be out on the street with Bob."

"I am sorry," I repeated.

"It barely pays enough to keep a roof over my head. Sometimes food is short. Right now I ain't even got enough cash to buy gas for my car."

Like being hit on the head with a sledgehammer, it finally dawned on me what he wanted. No wonder I wasn't getting anywhere with him.

I opened my fanny pack and pulled out the red nylon wallet Alice-Ann had given me for Christmas two years ago and hoped it held something. There was a ten-dollar bill in there, which I purposely hadn't broken to make it last longer. I pulled it out and handed it to Wrigley. "For gas," I said.

He sneered at the bill. "Not even half a thankful." But he could see there was no more where that came from.

The bill disappeared into the pocket of his jeans before he said, "Yeah, I seen Bob."

"Since the shooting?"

"Yeah. Later that same night I done found him in the stairwell. Drunk as a skunk and acting scared to death. Shaking so hard he couldn't hardly stand up. He asked me to give him a ride out to the water tower."

"And did you?"

"Yeah. Why not?"

It really wasn't surprising to hear Bob had wanted to be taken to the water tower. The tower, which had been built next to Lickin Creek's oldest cemetery because the land was cheap there, had become a beacon for local addicts and winos.

"Thanks, Wrigley. I'll look for him there."

"Don't tell him I told you where he was. He didn't want nobody to know."

"I'll be discreet."

"Huh?"

"I won't tell nobody," I translated.

It was a relief to be back in the fresh air, and I continued on my way to the *Chronicle*. Since I was running late, I was prepared to face my boss's anger, but when I burst into the office P.J. smiled as if she were actually pleased to see me.

"See what I've got," she said, swiveling her chair so I could get a good glimpse at what she held.

"My new book!" I exclaimed. "Where did you get it?"

"Your publisher sent me a copy; it just arrived. Good job, Tori. Very imaginative concept. I think this one could be a success."

"After the immediate disappearance of my first book, that would be nice."

"If you're planning any promotional appearances, just let me know. I can probably arrange for some time off with pay."

"Pinch me," I whispered to Cassie when I stopped by her desk on the way to mine.

"I've never seen her this impressed," Cassie said. "Here's your assignments for the next few days."

It all looked easy. Not Pulitzer material, but easy. A car wash opening, the ceremonial weeding of the geranium pots around the fountain, the closing of another small downtown business. I could take care of it all in a few hours.

I quickly wrote a review of Community Concert, trying to come up with synonyms for loud. Deafening, blaring, roaring? I gave up and settled for enthusiastic.

As I handed it to Cassie, I asked what was the fastest route to the town water tower. She drew one of her infamous maps on a piece of scrap paper and handed it to me. Fortunately, I already had a general idea of how to find it. Otherwise I'm sure I would have been thrown by her instructions to turn right where the Dairy Bar used to be.

The cemetery next to the water tower had a beautiful wrought-iron fence around it and was entered through an archway, over which was written in scroll work, HARGELROAD ETERNAL LIFE CEMETERY, PERPETUAL CARE.

The grass I could see through the fence was knee-high, the tombstones cracked and toppled, and crypts were missing their doors. Perpetual care here had meant only as long as the original owner was alive. Visitors were now more apt to discover empty syringes and cheap wine bottles on the graves than flowers or plastic wreaths.

A summer storm was moving in, darkening the sky and piercing it with lightning. Wind bent the trees in the graveyard and swept trash discarded by patrons of the neighborhood convenience store down the middle of the street.

The white tower glowed pale green in the eerie light. I prowled around in the weeds beneath it, hoping it wouldn't draw a lightning strike while I was there, and looked in vain for signs of Big Bad Bob. What did I hope to find? I had no idea.

I called Bob's name, but my voice was lost in the wail of the rising wind. I'd just decided I'd better get back to the truck, when I thought I heard my name.

"Mizz Miracle…" There it was again, only this time it was punctuated by a clap of thunder as rain began to fall in nearly solid sheets.

"Help…me…"

"Where are you?" I couldn't see anything through the driving rain.

"Help…"

A flash of lightning lit the sky momentarily, long enough for me to see a man silhouetted against the wrought-iron fence that circled the cemetery. In that brief moment, before he was concealed by the darkness, I sensed desperation in the way he clung to the iron bars, almost spread-eagled against the fence. It all happened so quickly, I almost doubted what I'd seen.

If I'd taken time to think about it, I probably would not have rushed forward toward the menacing figure.

As abruptly as it had started, the rain stopped, leaving the ground beneath my feet a muddy mess. I could see the fence clearly now, and there was no man standing against it.

Feeling relieved, I turned to walk back to my truck, and then I heard again, "Mizz Miracle."

I ran through the open gate and followed the voice to a bundle of rags at the base of the fence. When it shifted, I knew it was my mysterious figure.

I knelt down beside it and gingerly moved pieces of soaking wet, stinking cloth until I came upon a face.

"Big Bad Bob, what are you doing here?"

The man was in no condition to answer. In fact, it was some sort of miracle that he'd ever managed to stand up or call my name.

"Come on," I said. "We've got to get you out of here. Try to stand up."

I pulled on his arms. His eyes opened wide, and he screamed. "No. Scared."

"Nothing to be scared of, Bob."

He began to cry, great gasping sobs punctuated by hiccups and wet coughs that seemed to originate low down in his chest. If I left him there, he'd die from alcohol poisoning or pneumonia or a combination of both. I had no choice but to move him.

I turned my face to one side, inhaled some fresh air, and held my breath while I pulled him to his feet. Standing close to me, he smelled even worse; he reeked of cheap whisky and vomit.

Somehow I managed to drag him to the truck and boost him into the front seat. He lay there sprawled out facedown, and I had to use all my strength to shove him over enough to make room for me behind the wheel.

Now what? I wondered. It was a fifteen-mile drive to the nearest hospital in Hagerstown, Maryland. And I wasn't sure he needed to be hospitalized.

"Bob," I said, nudging one shoulder. "Do you want to go to the doctor?"

His reply was muffled by the car seat upholstery, but I heard his "no" clearly.

"Scared," he muttered.

"I'll take you to my house," I said, as I turned on the truck engine.

His answer was a snore.

I knew I didn't need to worry about Ethelind's reaction, for Ethelind was a rescuer. Just as she'd taken me in and kept me when I had no place to go, she'd find a place for Big Bad Bob and nurse him back to health.

That was exactly what happened. Ethelind was in the front yard, gathering up tree branches felled by the sudden storm. She dropped what she was doing to help me get him upstairs.

In one of the elegant, antique-filled bedrooms, she stripped the rags from Big Bad Bob, sponged him off, and actually got him to take two or three spoonfuls of chicken soup.

His greasy head flopped back on the pillow, and he peered up at us. "Don't tell no one I'm here," he said, just before he fell into a deep sleep.

Noel jumped onto the bed, sniffed delicately, then jumped off the bed in disgust. Fred, on the other hand, seemed to be delighted with the smelly stranger in the bed and curled up beside him with a contented sigh.

"Bloody fool," Ethelind said, and I knew she wasn't speaking of Fred. "I told him years ago he'd come to no good if he kept drinking. Now his liver's probably ruined. Next time you drive by a grocery store, stop in and pick up a dozen bottles of one of those sports drinks with nutrients and vitamins and all that rot."

In the kitchen, I picked up the telephone and placed a call to Greta Gochenauer.

"What am I doing?" she answered ungraciously. "I'm making ribbon roses to decorate the ends of the aisles. You do remember that I'm getting married this weekend, don't you?"

It had slipped my mind, but I didn't say so. "There's someone here at Ethelind's house who needs your help," I said.

"I don't have one minute to spare."

"It's a twelve-step call like you've never had before," I said, knowing Greta would never turn her back on an alcoholic in need of assistance.

"Twelve-step? Who?"

"Big Bad Bob. He's sleeping off the mother of all benders here."

"I'll be there in twenty minutes."

"Don't tell anyone he's here," I warned. "He seems to be afraid of something. Or someone."

I started a pot of coffee, which was done about the same time Greta arrived. "Don't give him any coffee," she ordered upon seeing the pot. "Last thing we need is a wide-awake drunk. Lead me to him."

TWENTY-THREE

MAGGIE, THE LIBRARIAN, had often complained about her out-dated audio-visual equipment; now I was going to see just how old it really was.

"No problem," Maggie said, looking at the old-fashioned reel-to-reel tape I pulled from my bag. "We've got a half a dozen antique tape players in the basement. Come in the office and have a cup of coffee, and I'll get a page to run down-stairs and find one."

She poured coffee and opened a package of Oreos. After only a few minutes a teenager brought in an enormous black leather box, which she set in the middle of the table. "Want me to show youse guys how it works?" she asked with a smart-aleck grin, as she released the clasps.

"I *am* the librarian," Maggie sniffed.

It took us a few minutes to figure out how to put the tape on the machine, after which we celebrated our success with another cup of coffee and a couple of cookies.

"I don't think the tape is going to be anything important, or it wouldn't have been left behind," I told her, but I remembered the shocking contents of Rodney's diary and didn't re-ally know what to expect. "We can't be too careful."

Maggie seemed to understand, for she closed and locked the door to the office before turning the tape player on.

The first few minutes were apparently a recording of a vi-olin lesson. The student's playing sounded pretty good to my uneducated ear. "Nice. Very nice," a man's muffled voice said, periodically.

"That's got to be Rodney," Maggie whispered. I agreed.

He sounded far away at first, then his voice grew louder as he obviously moved closer to the tape recorder. "Take off your shoes. I'll clean them for you while you do it again."

A young male voice answered, "I'd rather not."

"You do want to be first violin, don't you?"

The boy's reply was inaudible.

"Good. Now, try it one more time. This time with passion."

The violin music began again. The man, Rodney, sighed and said hoarsely, "That's so good. Keep going." After a few minutes, the music stopped, but there were other sounds, little moans and sighs that sickened both of us.

I turned off the machine. I could tell by Maggie's expression, she was as nauseated by what we'd heard as I was.

"Don't you want to listen to the rest of it?" she asked.

I pulled the copies of the yearbook pictures from my bag and placed them on the table. "I've heard enough, Maggie. There's no doubt in my mind who killed Rodney."

"Who?"

"Look," I said, pointing to the orchestra picture. "J.B. was first violinist, just like the tape said he'd be if he cooperated. He not only had motive, but he also had access to Morgan Manor at any time because his aunt lived there. I think he must have lost his cool, killed Rodney, and hidden him in the springhouse, where he'd still be if Alice-Ann hadn't fallen into the cave."

"You're probably right, Tori. Everything does point to him."

I looked down at the young teenager's face in the picture and felt pity for J.B. "I hope the law doesn't come down too hard on him. After all, he was just a kid."

"It would be heard in juvenile court, I'm sure," Maggie said solemnly. "Even though the man's in his fifties now, he was very young at the time."

"Criminal Court for murder," I said. "But there certainly are extenuating circumstances to be taken under consideration." I gathered up the yearbook pictures and put them back into my fanny pack. "I'm going to run over to Hoopengartner's Garage and tell this to Luscious," I told her.

I was there before I realized I'd left the tape at the library. No need to be concerned, I told myself. Maggie knew it was important evidence and wouldn't let anything happen to it.

Luscious listened patiently while I made my case against J.B. When I was through, he leaned back in his desk chair and said, "So if he committed murder, as you say, to stop Rodney from molesting him, why did he also murder Emily? And how did he do it?"

I hadn't thought about that. There was no reason I could think of for a young boy to kill the art teacher, no matter what her fiancé might have done. Besides, while J.B. had unlimited access to Morgan Manor, I doubted the fourteen- or fifteen-year-old boy would have been able to go in and out of the Bride's House so easily.

"I don't know, Luscious. Maybe the two victims weren't murdered by the same person. Maybe it was just a coincidence that they disappeared so close together."

Luscious laughed so hard, he had to pull a white handkerchief out of his shirt pocket to mop his eyes and blow his nose.

I felt my face flame as I waited for his mirth to subside. My theory about J.B. still made sense, but because I hadn't thought it through I now had to suffer well-deserved humiliation.

"I'm going to show you something, Tori. I think it will set your suspicious mind at rest." Luscious passed a yellow lined legal pad to me. "This explains everything."

The front page of the pad was covered with neat script and was dated with today's date. I began to read it silently, then stopped after the first paragraph, confused by who the narrator was.

"This 'I' person. Who is it?"

"Look on the last page."

Miffed I hadn't thought of that, I flipped several pages until

I came to a page only partially filled in. There was a blank space, after which someone had signed it with a shaky hand. "Maribell Morgan?"

I placed the tablet on the desk and glared at Luscious. "That may be her signature, but the preceding pages are definitely not in her hand."

"You stopped too soon," Luscious said.

I picked up the tablet again and read what was written two lines below the signature. "'As dictated to and transcribed by J.B. Morgan.' Give me a break, Luscious. You don't really believe this, do you?"

"Keep reading," he said patiently.

"Witnessed by Father Burkholder." My jaw clamped shut. "Guess I'd better read the whole thing," I said, returning to the first page.

This time I read aloud.

"Because of the recent discovery of the body of Rodney Mellott and the confusion caused by the discovery, I want to tell the world what really happened to him.

"When Rodney moved in with me as a border, I was still young and vain enough to think I could be attractive to him. He became a friend, an escort, and then my lover. I was even presumptuous enough to assume he would marry me. Imagine my shock when Emily Rakestraw announced her engagement to the man I loved.

"For many nights I could not sleep, as I lay in bed plotting ways to get even with him. When I confronted him, he only laughed at me and called me 'a foolish old woman.' I snapped. The anger I felt was so strong it was terrifying. I wanted revenge.

"On the morning of his wedding, I followed my plan. I left a note for him in the kitchen, where we always had breakfast together, asking him to come to the springhouse to help me with a water problem there.

"We'd had water leaking in before, and I knew that he

*would rush right over before the instruments he kept there
were ruined. When he came in, I was there waiting for him by
the door. I had my sharpest kitchen knife with me and struck
him in the back with it as he entered.*

*"When I was sure he was dead, I dragged him down the
stairs and hid him deep inside the small opening in the wall.
Earlier that week, I had my gardener, Raul, fill in the cave entrance with stones and mortar. After he had done so, I sent
him home and removed some of the stones before they had a
chance to set. After hiding Rodney's body in there, I replaced
the stones. Nobody knew for over forty years what had happened to him.*

*"It is now time to clear my conscience. Because I am quite
elderly and in poor health, I have good reason to believe that
my days are drawing to a close. Therefore, I have made my
wishes known to my nephew and have dictated this document
to him."*

I reread it, then laid it on the desk and glared at Luscious.
"You believe this?"

"What's not to believe?"

"I don't even think she dictated it. I think J.B. made it up
to cover himself."

"You're forgetting that Father Burkholder witnessed it."

"What about his feet?" I demanded.

Luscious looked blank, so I explained that I knew Rodney
Mellott's feet had been severed just above the ankle.

"Probably happened in the tire dump," Luscious said. "An
animal could have done it."

"The bones were in a heavy plastic bag. No animal got into
that. There was no sign of a hole."

Luscious was looking less and less sure of himself as I
spoke. As he put the legal pad in his top drawer, he said, "I'm
going to talk to Henry again."

"There's one more thing," I said.

He sighed, "What?"

"You didn't like my theory about J.B. being the murderer because I couldn't explain why or how Emily was killed."

I didn't need to elaborate further. Luscious understood what I was getting at. "Maribell didn't confess to it, either," he said thoughtfully.

"There are more questions to be asked. More answers to be sought."

"I know. I know."

I stood, preparing to leave. "By the way, Luscious, I want to swear out a restraining order against someone. How do I go about it?"

"You fill out this form," he said, pulling a paper out of a side drawer of his desk. "And you give it to me. Who's bothering you?"

"It's Haley Haley," I said, purposely leaving off the title Reverend. "He was following me for several weeks, even broke into my house to leave some scary messages. I confronted him, and he said he'd stop. But this morning…" I stopped because I didn't want to admit to Luscious I'd been snooping around Morgan Manor when Haley's van was seen following me. "I'd rather not say where I was, but he was seen there by someone, and he left in a hurry."

"You said *this* morning?"

"Yes."

Luscious dropped the form back into the file drawer. "Impossible. My mom went to a tent revival this morning in Greencastle, and—"

"And Reverend Haley was the minister?"

"Absolutely. She called me right after lunch and said he gave one of the best sermons she done ever heard."

"Maybe he wasn't there all morning," I said, but I knew that wasn't possible. Someone had followed me in the green van this morning, and it hadn't been Haley Haley. That left only one person I could think of. Vonzell Varner, the man who'd stolen the van. My name had been mentioned prominently in the TV news reports as the person who'd found and rescued Jenny Varner. I feared Vonzell had transferred his rage to me.

I told Luscious of my suspicions, and he promised to keep an eye out for Varner, but I knew there was only so much the two-man police force could do. My safety was my own responsibility.

On my way to the truck, I was so engrossed with my thoughts that I walked right into someone.

"Bruce! What a surprise. I thought you'd be on your way to Cancún by now."

Bruce Laughenslagger clutched a cardboard carton close to his midsection. "Did I say today? I meant tomorrow."

"Have a great trip," I said.

"I wish you...no, I'm not going to say that. What I am going to say is thank you."

I couldn't help laughing. "That's the first time anybody has thanked me for *not* going away with them."

Bruce didn't even smile, which made me feel rather foolish. "You remind me a lot of my wife," he said. "She was a decent person, like you."

"That's very kind," I murmured, feeling uncomfortable and wishing I could leave.

"She was honest and forthright like you. Spoke up when she saw things were wrong, even when she knew there'd be consequences that could hurt her."

"Sounds like a wonderful woman," I said. "You must miss her."

"More than I ever thought I could."

"I've got to get going. Have a good trip." If he hadn't been clutching the big box in front of him, I would have stood on my toes and kissed his cheek.

"Heard anything from Garnet?" he asked.

"I'm not changing my mind, Bruce."

He shrugged and smiled for the first time. "Can't blame a

guy for trying." We stared at each other for a moment, then I broke eye contact and continued toward the truck.

At home, Greta and Ethelind were sitting at the kitchen table drinking tea from Spode mugs and giggling like a couple of teenagers.

"I'm glad you're here," Greta said. "Bob's been asking for you."

"How's he doing?"

"Not too bad, considering the shape he's in."

I accepted a mug of steaming tea from Ethelind and blew on it. "Did he tell you what he wants to talk to me about?"

Greta shook her head. "Not exactly, but he did ask for you right after I gave him my 'You're only as sick as your secrets' lecture."

"I'll go right up."

"Wait a minute," Ethelind interrupted. "Maggie called from the library. She wanted you to call her as soon as you came in. Said it was urgent."

"MAGGIE? TORI. What's up?"

"It's the tape. I listened to the rest of it after you left. I think you should hear it."

"Put it on and hold the receiver near it."

"Here we go." Maggie had rewound to about where I'd given up. "It doesn't go on much longer. Pretty much of the same. Until... Well, you have to listen to the very end." She must have moved the telephone closer to the tape player because the music, which had begun again, grew louder.

As Maggie had said it would, the music went on for a few minutes with no interruptions. It came to a stop, and I was about to say, "I don't hear anything," when I thought I did.

"Did you hear it?"

"Play it again, Maggie. Just that last little bit."

She did, and there was no doubt this time what it was.

"Did anyone else hear this?" I asked.

"No, I was alone."

"Do you have some place where you can lock up the tape?"

"There's a safe in my office. I'm the only one who knows the combination."

"Put it in there, and whatever you do, don't tell anyone about this."

After I'd disconnected, Ethelind asked, "Something important?"

"I'm not sure." I finished my tea in one gulp, squared my shoulders, and ascended the back staircase.

"Don't let him talk you into getting booze for him," Greta called after me.

I was back downstairs in less than ten minutes. The two women looked surprised. I grabbed my keys and bag. "Don't wait dinner for me," I told Ethelind. "I've got three, maybe four, stops to make, and I don't know when I'll be back."

I paused in the doorway. "Don't tell anyone Bob is here. It's a matter of life and death."

TWENTY-FOUR

GARNET WAS BACK in the borough for his sister's wedding. He'd called three times since arriving on Thursday, and I'd pretended not to be home each time. Fortunately, there had been no wedding rehearsal because Greta said everybody involved should know what to do, so I hadn't yet had to face him. I dreaded our meeting tonight at the wedding. What if he came with a date? How would I react? This and many other questions surged through my mind as I put on my black cocktail dress.

I examined the dress in the mirror. Why was it so tight across the hips? Could I have gained another five pounds? I vowed that without fail I would start my diet again in the morning.

"Tori, come downstairs immediately." Ethelind's voice, coming up the front staircase, was shrill and urgent.

I slipped into my sandals, having given up on high heels, and ran down the hall. "What is it?" I called, as I raced down the stairs. During the past few days, I'd had several anonymous phone calls threatening me with a fate worse than death if I didn't "lay off the snooping." I hadn't taken them very seriously, but now I feared someone had actually done something.

In the living room sat two young women, one black, one white, and three black men, ranging in age, I'd guess, from twenty to sixty. The white woman was petite and blond and very pretty, much like my mother had been once. She held a small baby in her arms. I stared in disbelief at the group. "Tyfani?" I asked, even though I knew she must be my father's wife. "Billy? Oh my God, you're safe."

She passed the baby to the black woman and stood up. She looked scared. "I didn't know where else to go," she said.

In two steps I was at her side, hugging her, while tears soaked both our faces. Then I took the baby and clasped him tight to my chest, paying no attention to what he might be doing to the silk and sequins.

We sat close together on the couch, while Tyfani explained how her trusted servants had helped her escape. It had involved tunneling out of the American embassy, a moonlit trip across a river in a canoe, hiding in caves, and eventually seeking sanctuary in the embassy of another country, which had secretly arranged for their get-away flight. "These people saved my life," Tyfani said, indicating the four Africans with a sweeping gesture. "If they stayed behind, their lives would have been in peril. I knew they had to come with me."

"Where is my father?"

"He chose to stay. He said it was his job to be the last man out. He's in hiding and safe. I can't tell you where."

The pain and worry I'd lived with for weeks rushed from my body so fast it left me shaking. Tyfani placed her hand in mine. "I'm so glad to finally meet you," she said. "Your father talks about you all the time."

I wanted to believe her.

Ethelind, who had been beaming down at us through all the emotion, now spoke. "Do you have family in this country? Some place you can go to?"

Tyfani shook her head. "Nobody."

"Then you are going to stay here. No arguments. I have plenty of room."

"Thank you," Tyfani said. "I'll take you up on it. Finding a place for five people and a baby to live isn't the easiest thing in the world."

Even as I felt joy at finally getting a chance to know my stepmother and baby brother, I also felt a tremendous sense of loss. My dreams of a little house to call my own had flown out the window. I could not move out of Ethelind's house, leaving her with my family.

Tyfani then introduced us to her entourage: the amah, who was married to the young man who was the gardener; the chauffeur; and the oldest man, who was the cook.

"I will cook for you wonderful meals like you have never had before," he said, and I noticed his accent was French.

"Oh my," Ethelind sighed. "I can't wait."

I thought French and African cooking would be a nice change from Ethelind's usual British fare.

"Look at the time," Ethelind said, bringing us back to the moment. "We've got to get going to the wedding. Let me show you your rooms. We'll buy a crib tomorrow. In the meantime, I think there's an old bassinet in the attic you can use for the baby." Still talking, she led the adults out of the living room, while I held Billy and gazed into his face trying to recognize familiar features there.

BECAUSE THERE WAS no church in Lickin Creek large enough to hold all of Greta's and Buchanan's friends, their wedding was to be held at the Social Hall of the Lickin Creek Volunteer Fire Department. When I pulled in to the parking lot, a full hour before the ceremony was scheduled to take place, there were already fifty or sixty cars there.

I went, as previously directed, to the back door and knocked twice. One of Greta's many Great-aunt Gladyses opened the door a crack, determined I was not a spy from the groom's camp, and admitted me.

After a lot of hugging and kissing, we were given a quick orientation by Greta. Then I was assigned my position in the lineup according to height. Greta made a few last-minute adjustments to her dress and refreshed her makeup, and at last the portable keyboard in the hall struck up "Here Comes the Bride." The double doors burst open, revealing a huge crowd of people sitting on metal folding chairs, their backs to us. But there must have been a secret signal because they all turned as one to watch the bridal procession.

I was second in line, right behind Buchanan's niece, the six-year-old flower girl, so I had a perfect view of the make-shift altar and the wedding party. And who loomed larger than anyone else in the room? Not the groom, who was at least six-six, with an Afro that made him look taller. Not Judge Fetterhoff, who was as thin as a rail and appeared even taller than his six feet. No, even though he was shorter than both men, it was Garnet I saw. Garnet, who never took his gaze off me as I came down the aisle. He was thinner than I remembered and sported a deep tan and sun-streaked hair. I thought he looked a lot like my favorite late-night TV series hero, Don Johnson in *Miami Vice*.

The bride and groom read vows they had written, and swore to take care of each other, the rainforest, dolphins, and anyone who was fighting addiction of any kind. Recited in verse, it was rather nicely done, I thought. Judge Fetterhoff solemnly pronounced them husband and wife and urged the audience to applaud, which it did with enthusiasm.

After they newly married couple exchanged their first wedded kiss, the guests jumped up and began to fold their chairs. Several women from the locals' favorite caterer, Daisy's Bar, Grill and Laundromat, set up folding tables where the chairs had been and more long tables next to the outer wall to hold the buffet.

Enormous containers of slippery pot pie, barbecue, pork and sauerkraut, and baked beans bowed the table. The wedding cake was a masterpiece, topped with a stunning hand-painted scene of dolphins swimming through the ruins of Atlantis.

While congratulations and hugs were being offered, I looked around the group to see whom I knew. I was disappointed to see that J.B. Morgan was present, after everything I'd told Luscious. In fact, I was disappointed in Luscious for not having acted immediately on the information I'd given him. Luscious was not here, nor was Bruce Laughenslagger, who was probably drinking margaritas in a honky-tonk in Cancún right now.

A hand touched my arm, and I knew without looking that it was Garnet. "Why have you been avoiding me?" he asked, guiding me to the farthest, quietest corner of the hall.

"What a dumb question," I sputtered. "You, who never wrote, never called, should know the answer to that one."

"What the hell do you mean I never wrote or called? You're the one who never answered any of my letters. Never called me back."

My heart dropped to my stomach. Inanely I thought, good thing my skirt is tight or it could drop right out. "I didn't answer your phone calls this week, because I have nothing to say to you. Here's the keys to your truck. Thanks for the loan. You'll find it at… Letters? What letters? Are you saying you did write?"

"And call. Several times. You were never in, but Ethelind said she'd give you the messages."

"Something's very weird," I said. "I wrote you right after I left Costa Rica, saying I was sorry for being so demanding of your time. But you never…"

"I never got it. But I did write you and apologize for being so selfish and not spending more time with you. And then I wrote again and again, but I never received an answer. I never gave up, but I think I have the right to know why you didn't respond."

"But I never—"

"I wrote you a dozen letters at least, from Costa Rica. Are you saying you didn't get them?"

"Nor the phone messages. I thought you were angry at me when I left, so I wasn't surprised."

"I thought you didn't care."

"I don't understand."

"Neither do I." He bent down and kissed me. His lips were soft, as I remembered them. "Can we try to work things out?" he asked.

All I could do was nod. He clasped me in an embrace that was familiar and comforting. I put my hands behind his head and pulled his face down to mine.

And at that tender moment, the front doors burst open. A half dozen state troopers stormed through the door, followed by Luscious and Afton. Several minutes of confusion passed, almost in slow motion, as people ran for cover and women and children screamed. The policemen tried to arrest, but then had to wrestle several guests to the floor, along with two tables of food and the wedding cake. And then, as suddenly as they had appeared, they departed, taking an unknown number of handcuffed men with them.

As the doors slammed shut behind them, Greta collapsed, sobbing, next to the smashed wedding cake. I watched in dismay as her hand-sewn, natural, undyed, home-woven-fibre gown turned red from the spilled punch. Buchanan knelt beside her on the food-strewn floor trying to comfort her. At first there was stunned silence, followed by a cacophony of panicky voices screaming questions. "What happened?" "Who?" "What?" "Why?"

Missy Bumbaugh, her face red, swollen and tearstained, pointed at me, and cried, "It's her fault. Damn busybody outsider."

Garnet's arms went around me, but facing the glaring crowd his embrace gave me little comfort.

"I have an idea," Ethelind yelled, getting the attention of the assembled guests. "Let's all go to my house for bacon and eggs. It will be just like being back in high school again. We don't need a cake to celebrate. And we'll ask Luscious to come and explain."

Most of the people groaned with disgust and began to leave. But several dozen other faces brightened at her words.

And that is why a procession of SUVs, pickup trucks, and station wagons drove through the rusty gates of the Moon Lake Colony and parked in side streets when Ethelind's circular drive was filled.

TWENTY-FIVE

ETHELIND assigned me the job of whipping eggs in a copper bowl, while Alice-Ann was ordered to start coffee perking in a thirty-cup urn that had mysteriously appeared in the kitchen. That alone should have made me suspect that Ethelind had planned an impromptu postnuptial gathering all along. Why else would she have ten cartons of eggs in her refrigerator, twenty loaves of bread on the counter, and enough bacon to give coronaries to half of Lickin Creek? She also had several cases of nonalcoholic sparkling cider for Greta and her many AA friends. The only difference between Ethelind's idea of an after-the-wedding party and the reality of the occasion was that her celebration was taking place hours earlier than planned and had to replace the wedding feast.

Friends and relations of the bride and groom filed into the kitchen to heap their plates with food, then carried them into the front parlors. Others, whom I was beginning to think of as my friends, stayed. Alice-Ann was there, of course. So was Maggie Roy, with her fiancé in Civil War uniform, as usual. P.J. and Cassie were there from the *Chronicle*. My realtor, Janielle Simpson, had stayed, even after I'd told her I would not be buying a house after all. The surprise presence at the kitchen table was Big Bad Bob. Cleaned up, he looked almost normal. Even though his hands shook badly, his eyes were clear. Nobody seemed to recognize him.

When everyone had been served, I poured a cup of coffee, walked over to where Garnet was sitting, and placed my hand on his shoulder. He covered it with his. "I think we both deserve an explanation," I said. "And I think I know where to get it. Wait here a minute."

Ethelind was sitting in the parlor. I walked in, slammed my cup down on the coffee table so hard it almost shattered, and jerked my finger at her. "My Royal Doulton," Ethelind murmured. Then she saw the look on my face and followed me back into the kitchen without another word.

"Sit down," I ordered, pointing to the empty chair Garnet had saved for me. Ethelind perched next to Garnet and tried to make herself look small.

"Why didn't you ever tell me Garnet had called?" I demanded.

When she began to make excuses, I held my hand up. "Tell the truth, Ethelind. It will be easier that way."

She gave a barely perceptible nod. "He doesn't deserve you. I thought if I intercepted your letters and kept the two of you from talking, eventually you'd realize he wasn't the man for you and find someone more appropriate."

All along, I'd felt Ethelind cared too much for me, had tried to mother me when I didn't need or want another mother, but this...this was beyond belief.

"What happened to the letters I wrote to him?"

"I took them out of the mailbox after you left for work. I've got them all upstairs, in my dresser. You can have them back."

"And my letters to Tori?" Garnet asked.

"Same thing. They're in my dresser."

I think we were both in too much shock to respond, so she took our silence to mean she should go upstairs and fetch our correspondence.

Garnet took my hand. "I should never have doubted you," he said, and his voice was low and throaty.

"It was all my fault," I said, surprised to find myself crying. "I should have known something was wrong. I should have called."

"I have something to tell you," Garnet said, his face close

to mine. "I thought about what you said at the airport in San José, and you were absolutely right. I was letting the job take over my life. I'm not going back, Tori. I'm staying here where I belong, in Lickin Creek with you."

I didn't have time to absorb what he had said before Ethelind reappeared with many envelopes clutched in each hand. She placed them on the table and busied herself with washing the pots and pans in the sink.

"I don't have to read them now," Garnet said.

"Me either."

The people gathered around the table clapped heartily as he leaned over to kiss me, and the noise of their applause and laughter drew Greta and Buchanan into the room. They helped themselves to coffee and joined us. They had both changed from their ruined wedding finery into jeans and T-shirts with whales on the fronts.

"We're leaving for the Amazon first thing tomorrow," Greta announced, raising her coffee cup. "Figure we'll do better with no sleep than just an hour or two."

"Why the Amazon?"

"We're meeting a group of environmentalists in Iquitos," Buchanan said, "to hike into the rainforest with them."

"Be sure to watch the news next week," Greta said with a grin. "We have some interesting things planned."

A burst of chatter from the front rooms interrupted their description of their unusual honeymoon plans. After a minute the noise died down, and Luscious and Henry Hoopengartner appeared in the doorway.

"Garnet!"

"Luscious!"

"Thank God you're here."

"Man, it's good to see you."

All they needed was the sound of violins to make the reunion complete. The two men pounded each other on the back until it seemed certain someone was going to get hurt.

Henry greeted Garnet with less physical enthusiasm, but the way he pumped his hand made it obvious that he was happy to see him.

"I'll get coffee," I announced.

"Don't." Luscious blushed and stammered, "What I mean is, I'm really here to have you tell me everything you know about this case."

"Isn't it a little late? You've already made the arrests."

"I have hard evidence to back my position. But I need to know how you found out what you did."

"I don't know where to start."

"How about at the beginning," Garnet urged. "I'd really like to know what went on tonight. One minute there's a wedding reception going on, and the next minute the judge and half the borough's best-known citizens are being hauled away in a paddy wagon. What did you have to do with what happened at my sister's wedding?"

He was already beginning to sound like the old Garnet, the one who was in charge of every situation. Luscious brought in two chairs from the dining room for himself and Henry and looked at me expectantly.

"Should I start with Maribell Morgan's confession?"

Luscious nodded. "Good a place as any."

"It was obviously made up to cover for her nephew. Anyone could see that. It was just too convenient having her dictate it to J.B. just as suspicion was pointing at him. No man, not even a close relative, is worth sacrificing yourself for…" I felt Garnet stiffen next to me "…so to find out what really happened, I visited Father Burkholder and asked him about witnessing it. He said he'd been outside in the hall when the document was dictated to J.B. He was asked in to sign when it was finished. He assumed it was a last will and testament. If you look at the last page of her confession, it reads like the end of a will. That was all he saw. That's why he signed as a witness.

"After I'd talked to the priest, I went to see Maribell in the nursing home. I'm really ashamed of this, but knowing she was a good Catholic I used a few phrases like 'immortal soul' and 'eternal damnation.' That's when she told me she had not dictated anything to anybody, and eventually she told me the real story of what happened to Rodney and Emily..."

TWENTY-SIX

MARIBELL USED her right hip to hold the springhouse door open while she hoisted the heavy kerosene heater across the doorjamb.

"I was afraid it might be getting chilly in here, so I brought this heater down from the big house. Don't want you boys taking sick and your parents blaming me for..."

The room was dim, lit only by a pale ray of light streaming through the dusty window. She vaguely made out the seven boys standing before her, and noted the looks of shock on their faces. "What are you boys up to?" she asked jovially, wanting to save her reputation as the "adult who understood kids." Her voice faded away as her eyes adjusted to the darkness, and she saw the nightmare scene in front of her. The door slammed shut behind her. The faces of the seven boys mirrored the horror she was feeling.

Bile rose in her throat, and she struggled to stay conscious even as her head grew light and the room began to spin.

She fell back against the limestone wall, feeling its solid coolness against her back. This couldn't be real. She closed her eyes for a moment, wishing the scene away, but when she opened them it was all still there.

As if she were swimming underwater, Maribell moved forward, her feet making squishy noises beneath her. The stone floor was wet. Water. It had leaked in before. He'd worried about the instruments stored there. No, not water, Sticky and thick. Like the tar on the school playground on a hot September day. The smell was different though. Coppery. Sickening.

She kept moving, kept swimming, until she reached the creature on the chair. She couldn't think of it as a person. Especially a person who had recently shared her bed. Not with that gaping grin beneath its chin.

Not with the blindfold covering its eyes.

Not with bloody stubs where its feet had once been.

The woman held back the nausea she was feeling and reached for its right wrist. She tried in vain to find a pulse. But there was nothing, not even a flutter, and the skin was already cold.

"Rodney," she whispered. "Oh, Rodney."

Today was supposed to be his wedding day. How could this have happened?

She gently placed his hand on his bloody lap and turned to the boys, who hadn't moved.

"Who did this?" she demanded.

They didn't answer.

"Jim Bob," she said to her nephew. "Tell me you didn't do this to him. Tell me you found him this way. Please tell me..." She hated the hysteria in her voice and fell quiet.

Jim Bob, who hated his name and hoped some day to use his initials only, stepped to her side. His feet slipped in the pooled blood, causing him to lose his balance and nearly fall.

He was crying. They all were. Seven fifteen- and sixteen-year-old boys who were the elite of Lickin Creek High School now resembled small children caught making mischief in kindergarten. Except these were not toddlers, they were teenagers on the cusp of manhood.

She lowered her voice an octave and turned to the tallest of the boys. "Bruce, you'll tell me the truth, won't you?"

Instead of speaking, the boy handed her a large book.

She carried it to the window to take advantage of the light and saw that it was a photo album. She opened it.

What she saw there was even more horrible than the bloody body in the chair. After turning several pages, she let it drop onto the floor. The disgusting pictures she'd seen had shocked her even more than seeing Rodney's mutilated corpse.

Now the revulsion that filled her heart was not for the blood and gore she saw but for the perversions her lover had acted out on innocent boys.

She was calmer now. Definitely under control. "Who took the pictures?" she demanded. She swirled toward the shortest boy, her face a mask of anger. "Eddie, who took the pictures?"

When no one answered, she said, "Bennie? It was Emily, wasn't it." That pig, that bitch who had stolen Rodney away from her.

The boys looked at one another, and then Eddie nodded.

"And this?" She waved one arm at the disfigured corpse. "Who did this?"

Bruce began, "We all did. Together."

The others began to speak. "We asked him to meet us here this morning."

"Told him we had a surprise wedding gift for him."

"We blindfolded him. He thought it was a new game."

"We tied him to the chair. More fun and games, he thought."

"We all brought knives with us."

"We took turns."

"I cut his throat so he could never talk dirty again." (Maribell was shocked to hear her nephew say that.)

"He had it coming. He wouldn't leave us alone."

She listened, with mounting dread, as the boys told her of their crime.

"His feet," she whispered. "Why?"

Jim Bob spoke again. "I did it. He had a thing for feet. Now, he doesn't have any." He began to laugh, a tinny sound that ended in a coughing fit.

"With what?"

J.B. pointed to a hacksaw lying on the bloody floor next to several kitchen knives. Maribell was overwhelmed with the horror of realizing that the entire thing, the murder and the mutilation of the body, had been preplanned by the boys. But family was family. The "take-charge" person Maribell Morgan was so famous for being surfaced. The fiend in the chair was no longer someone she had cared for, but garbage to be discarded. "You boys get out of here," she ordered. "Don't ever think about today again. Don't ever talk about it to each other. It never happened. Do you understand me?"

The boys ran for freedom, and Maribell turned herself to the task of disposing of the dead body. She already knew what she was going to do. She was going to make it look like he'd run away rather than marry a woman he didn't love.

Earlier that week Raul, the gardener, had uncovered a small cave in the basement of the springhouse while looking for a termite infestation. The cave, walled up, would be the perfect place to hide the body. It was fairly easy getting him to the lower level. She simply pulled him across the room, then dropped him down the stairwell.

Darkness filled the lower level, and she had to light a kerosene lantern before she could do anything. She tugged Rodney's body over the rough slate floor, and over the pile of rocks pulled from the wall, and dragged him into the cave, placing him against the back wall.

The next few hours were full of backbreaking labor as she rebuilt the wall Raul had so carefully removed, stone by stone.

She was exhausted by the time she finished, but there was more still to be done. She hauled buckets of water up the stairs and scrubbed the floor and walls until she could see no more bloodstains. Then she washed the knives and the saw. The water in the holding pool below the spring ran bright red before she was through.

Satisfied that the place was thoroughly clean, she stepped outside, carrying a small package, and locked the door behind her. She was determined that nobody would ever set foot in there again.

The knives went into her kitchen. The saw into the shed. Nobody would ever have to know where they'd been or what they'd been used for. The package containing Rodney's severed feet went into the garbage where they belonged. In a day or two, they would be buried forever in the borough landfill.

She wasn't finished, though. Raul, who would come to work tomorrow expecting to keep working in the springhouse, had to be sent away. When he did arrive the next morning, Maribell was ready for him.

"I'm closing up the house and moving to Florida," she told him.

He looked as if he didn't believe her, but she didn't worry about that. His English was not up to understanding long explanations. She gave him a briefcase full of cash, more than he'd ever seen in his life. "It's for you," she said, when he tried to give it back. "It's your retirement money. I owe it to you for your faithful service. And I have purchased an airplane ticket to take you to Mexico City. Your flight leaves tomorrow, so you must go home and get ready to go."

She wasn't sure where he was from, but it seemed like a central place, where he could travel onward. And so far away from Lickin Creek. As he sped off in his beat-up pickup, grinning at his unexpected good fortune, she knew she'd never hear from him again. That was what she wanted.

She still had to get rid of the incriminating scrapbook. After tearing out a few of the least offensive pictures, she threw it into the leaf-burning barrel in the backyard and watched as the last tangible evidence of Rodney's crimes vanished in a cloud of black smoke. She wished she didn't have to do that, that she could publicly expose the man for the monster that he was. But that wasn't possible. Not if she were going to protect her own nephew and his friends. As juveniles from prominent families, she felt certain that they would not be charged with murder but be sent away to detention centers. But when they came back to Lickin Creek as adults? They never would be able to. There would never be a place in the tiny community for men who would always be known as teenagers who killed. As she saw it, she had no choice.

Later, Maribell laughed inwardly at the turmoil surrounding Rodney's disappearance. When he hadn't shown up at the church for his own wedding, and the best man came to Morgan Manor looking for him, she voiced the suspicion that he's simply gotten cold feet and left town. People believed her. For several weeks, Maribell watched Emily going about town, her martyred head held high.

But finally, Maribell could stand it no more. She put the photographs she'd taken from the scrapbook into her purse, pulled on her white gloves and best hat, and paid a call upon Emily Rakestraw's mother.

If Mrs. Rakestraw was surprised to find the town's most illustrious matron on her porch, she gave no sign of it and invited her in.

After the ritual of tea and cookies, Maribell came to the point of her visit. She pulled the photographs out of her bag and wordlessly handed them to Mrs. Rakestraw. She watched as the woman turned red, then white.

"I don't understand," Mrs. Rakestraw said, dropping the pictures facedown on the tea table as if they were burning her fingers. "Why are you showing those filthy things to me?"

"Who do you think took the pictures?" Maribell asked her.

"I have no idea.... No. Not my Emily. She wouldn't..."

But Maribell was sure that even as Mrs. Rakestraw denied her daughter's involvement, she knew the truth.

At just that moment, Emily appeared in the doorway, wearing shorts and T-shirt and carrying a tennis racket. "I'm going to meet some friends at Municipal Park for practice," she said. "I'll be home for supper."

"Come in here and sit down," her mother ordered.

Emily flounced in and perched on the arm of her mother's chair.

"What's up, Mumsy? Stop frowning. You know how you always tell me my face will freeze that way and…" Emily realized her words might as well be beamed into outer space for all the attention her mother was paying to them.

Mrs. Rakestraw handed Emily the pictures. Emily turned them over and looked idly at the first one as if she had no interest in someone's old snapshots. Her smile faded immediately. "Oh my God, it's Rodney. Oh no. I can't believe he would…"

"Stop playing me for the fool, Emily. I know you developed these in your darkroom."

The next few seconds were a blur. The mother and daughter leaped to their feet at the same time, crying, screaming at each other, hitting, clawing. And suddenly the girl in the tennis outfit lay on the floor with blood pouring from her forehead where she'd hit her head on the tea table as she fell.

Mrs. Rakestraw dropped to her knees next to the girl. "Emily. Emily. Oh, no. Help me."

Maribell moved Mrs. Rakestraw aside and touched Emily's neck in the hope of finding a pulse. She felt nothing. She stood. "I'm so sorry." She saw Mrs. Rakestraw picking up the telephone. "You fool. Put that down."

"Why?" But she replaced the receiver.

"Because…because you surely don't want anyone to know what Emily was up to with Rodney, do you? Or that you killed your own daughter." That was cruel, Maribell knew. It had been an accident. But because Maribell didn't want anyone to know what Rodney had been up to with her nephew she didn't hold back.

"I…no…I don't know what to do."

"Is anybody home? The maid? Your husband?"

"No… It's the maid's day off. And my husband's at the office." Her eyes grew wide with panic. "He should be home in an hour."

"We'll have to hide her, then. We can take her out later when it's safer and bury her. Where's a good place? The basement?"

"No. The attic…nobody ever goes there…"

"Good. I'll give you a hand. You take her feet, I'll take her head."

With Mrs. Rakestraw sobbing uncontrollably, the two women slowly carried their burden up two flights of stairs to the large attic.

Maribell looked around wildly. They didn't have much time left. Her gaze fell upon an old trunk with rope handles. "Is there anything in that?" she asked.

Mrs. Rakestraw shook her head.

"Then open it up. We can put her in there for now."

"No. Please. I can't do it." It was Mrs. Rakestraw's last attempt at protesting.

"You have to." The take-charge Maribell was back, and nobody in Lickin Creek, least of all the distraught Mrs. Rakestraw, could challenge her authority.

After they'd stashed the young woman inside the trunk, Maribell told Mrs. Rakestraw to hurry downstairs and bring back Emily's wedding dress. "That way, everyone will think Rodney came back and they eloped."

With the dress stuffed into the trunk and nearly hiding the body, Maribell brought the lid down. She was grateful to see there was a sturdy padlock in the hasp, and she locked it securely, checking it twice to make sure it wouldn't pull open. "This way, nobody's going to get curious and open the trunk," she explained. "It's safer that way." They locked the attic door behind them as they left.

Emily awoke in darkness. Where am I? She wondered. She raised one hand and encountered something hard. She shoved against it with all her might, but it wouldn't give. She was inside something. A box. She could hardly move. Her legs were twisted under her awkwardly, and she couldn't straighten them out. She pounded on the surface above her. She tried to claw her way out. She screamed for help. But nobody came.

Maribell was out of the house before Mr. Rakestraw came

home. A few weeks later she took a much-needed vacation, and while she was away she sent postcards to the Rakestraws, purportedly from Emily, telling them of her elopement and her desire to never see them or the gossipy town of Lickin Creek again. She continued the practice of mailing cards to Emily's friends and fellow teachers from various locales over the next twenty years, until travel became too physically challenging for her.

Maribell's intention had been to move Emily's body from the mansion after the talk about her sudden disappearance died down. But Mrs. Rakestraw died, not as some said from heartbreak brought on by her daughter's elopement, but by committing suicide due to the stress brought on by her own guilt. The heartbroken husband and father wasted no time in leaving for Florida. He took only his clothes. His memories were locked in the deserted house, along with his daughter's body.

Maribell grew older, but her conscience was clear. She felt no guilt about protecting her nephew and his friends, and it was with pleasure that she watched the boys grow up, go away to college, and then return to have successful careers and become outstanding Lickin Creek citizens. That, if nothing else, proved she had done the right thing.

Over the years, the fog rolled in slowly. Maribell couldn't remember where she'd left her book or her keys, and often she got lost on her way home from a friend's house. But as she stopped being able to recall what she'd had for breakfast, or even if it was morning or evening, the memories from forty years ago grew clearer in her mind. To her, it was something that had happened yesterday.

She never knew why she was taken by ambulance to an ugly building to stay in an ugly room, but she guessed she must be ill and waited patiently to recover so she could go home.

She didn't know that her nephew, now the administrator

of her estate, had agreed to show Morgan Manor on the annual Lickin Creek house tour.

One day a strange man came to visit her. She had never seen him before but found him pleasant. After a while, though, his chatter grew annoying. He kept claiming to be her nephew, J.B., but she had no nephew by that name. Only a boy named Jim Bob, who never came to see her anymore. And what was he talking about? The house. People going through it? She couldn't allow that. Morgan Manor held too many secrets.

He noticed her distress and took her hand. "What's wrong, Aunt?"

"The springhouse," she whispered. "He's there. Below. In the cave."

Fear enveloped J.B. Morgan. He knew who she was talking about. "I'll move him," he promised. "There's no need to worry."

That night, J.B. entered the springhouse for the first time in nearly forty years. He shuddered at the sight of the circle of chairs, waiting for the students who would never arrive. And for a moment, in the flickering glow of his lantern, he thought he saw something else. Rodney Mellott waiting for him, his pudgy arms open, ready to embrace him. Ready to…J.B. shook the image out of his head.

He went immediately down the stairs. And there, he found the wall, which had been haphazardly reconstructed by Alice-Ann and Tori. It took only a few minutes to make an opening and crawl through. Once again, he was face-to-face with his nemesis.

The wall had obviously been disturbed recently, and he already knew who had been down here. Toby Merkle, that nosy young woman from New York, had come to his office to apply for a loan. While she was there, she'd casually mentioned that she'd been in the springhouse. There was no doubt in his mind that she'd seen the skeleton. He didn't know why she hadn't reported it to the police, but he was sure she would before long. He needed to get rid of the body first, and then he'd deal with Toby Merkle.

The skeleton fell into hundreds of pieces as soon as he touched it. Only the indestructible polyester fabric of the tuxedo had held it together. J.B. swallowed hard to hold down the revulsion he felt and placed the bones, one by one, into a heavy-duty plastic garden bag. It weighed next to nothing when he was done. The moonless sky, lit only by stars, provided the cover of darkness he needed as he drove to the tire dump that had been the bane of his aunt's existence for years, and hid the bag of human remains under a stack of old tires. He knew it would be undisturbed there, for the dump had been deserted for years.

J.B. didn't have much time to feel safe, though. Within less than a week, it was as if the world turned upside down, and he held that meddling out-of-towner Toby, no Tori Miracle, responsible. It started the night of the house tour, when Emily Rakestraw's body turned up in a trunk at the hardware store. How had she gotten there? He had no idea, but he knew that the discovery would trigger more interest in the missing music teacher.

His fear grew stronger the next day when he learned that Tori Miracle had taken Luscious to the springhouse to show him the skeleton she'd found. He allowed himself to enjoy the irony of her standing in an empty cave, looking foolish. Perhaps everything would have been all right, but then his cousin called from Hoopengartner's Garage.

"J.B., I don't know why, but that Tori Miracle has been snooping around Aunt Maribell's house. She told Luscious she found a diary there what might explain Rodney Mellott's disappearance. I heard your name mentioned. Just thought you'uns oughta know."

J.B. had received a lot of useful information from his cousin, one of the part-time garage receptionists, over the past few years. Most of it he had used to his financial benefit. This was far more serious.

He picked up the telephone and called the *Chronicle*. By the time he was finished, P.J. was terrified he was going to call in her mortgages, on the newspaper building itself and on her home. She'd used the money to keep the *Chronicle* going. Without it, the paper would fold. That, he knew, would be enough to make her come down hard on that nosy reporter from New York. But he needed to do more. Something that would permanently put an end to her prying ways.

He made another phone call. This one was to Bruce Laughenslagger at the BL Deer Hunting Preserve.

Bruce didn't like the plan. In fact, he hadn't thought about Rodney Mellott or Emily Rakestraw in a good many years. Now a chill seized his heart as he remembered what they'd done. It had been J.B.'s idea, true, but he hadn't had to go along with it. But they'd been so young. They should have told someone. Now it was too late. Now he had so much to lose. His lodge, his hunting preserve, the respect he'd earned in the community—he didn't want to lose all the things that mattered to him. He told himself it would be like hunting an animal, something he was used to. It was a choice of sacrificing her or himself and six others. The choice was not hard to make.

But by the time the first shot was fired by his employee at the girl, he'd already begun to like her. That was bad news. Sort of like making a pet out of a farm animal, then having to kill it for supper. He couldn't let it happen.

J.B. spat fury into the telephone when Bruce called to report the failure of the mission. He'd have to think of something else. He called Aaron Gelsinger's office.

Over the dentist's sputtered protests, he said, "I don't care how you do it. Get her in any way you can. What she's doing could put us all in jail."

Aaron Gelsinger told his receptionist he had a cancellation that needed to be filled and suggested she call Tori Miracle.

"Her time's flexible," he reminded her, when she argued that others had waited longer.

Everything Aaron did that afternoon went against his professionalism, but he had no choice. J.B. had the financial clout to destroy him. He knew his wife only stayed with him because he was a well-to-do dentist. Lose the money and he'd lose her. He placed a call to Wilbur Eshelman at the drugstore and told him what J.B. wanted them to do. He'd pretend to call in a prescription for an antibiotic; it would be up to Wilbur to substitute a fast-acting, hard-to-identify poison.

Wilbur didn't like it. Didn't like it at all. But he did like Tori Miracle. He wished he hadn't mentioned to J.B. that he'd seen her at the high school looking at an old picture of the group in a yearbook. It was time to put an end to the hiding, the secrecy, the shame. He called the bank and told J.B. he would not cooperate with him. "And if anything happens to that girl, I'll go straight to the police. Straight to them." He hung up, pleased he'd finally had the gumption to confront the man who, as a teenager, had persuaded him to be part of the group that killed Rodney Mellott. No matter what horrors that man had committed, he hadn't deserved to die that way. Not that way.

"I'm going home for dinner," he called out to Mildred, before stepping out into the alley. He nodded to Big Bad Bob sitting in the window well as he passed by him on his way to the parking lot.

J.B. unlocked his desk drawer and took out his gun. He checked it carefully to make sure it was fully loaded. He'd never liked Wilbur Eshelman. Now he despised him. What made that man think he was better than everybody else? He had no right to put them all in harm's way. J.B. left through the back door of the bank, hid behind a clump of bushes, and waited for Wilbur, who, every evening at the same time, made a night deposit at the drive-up window on his way home for dinner.

In the alley, Big Bad Bob saw J.B. come out of the bank alone, look around stealthily, then dart behind the bushes near the creek. A few minutes later, Bob saluted Wilbur as he walked by, lifting his wine bottle. He thought aloud, "What a nice man he is."

Bob watched from the window well as Wilbur walked to his car. He heard the shot that killed him, then saw J.B. step out from behind the bushes, drag Wilbur to the edge of the embankment, and shove him over. Big Bad Bob drew himself low into the well. "Don't let him see me," he whimpered. "Please, God, don't let him see me. If you do that for me I'll quit drinking, I promise. This time I mean it." That night, surprised still to be alive, he got a ride to the cemetery by the water tower where he could hide out.

Marvin Bumbaugh didn't like Tori Miracle. Not at all. She'd meddled in borough council matters too often, and it was because of her that the historical society and the courthouse had been burned down. He readily agreed to do what had to be done. "Don't worry," he told J.B. "I can make it look like an accident. I'll take her up to that rattlesnake pit in the mountains the Tunnels and Trails people want to buy and leave her there. She'll never get out of there alive."

MARIBELL MORGAN tossed in her bed most of the day. She refused the sedative the nurse brought in, because she didn't want her mind any foggier than it already was. That nice man who said he was her nephew asked her if she'd burned *all* the scrapbooks. She clearly remembered burning the one that Bruce had given her, but her mind must be playing tricks on her again because she could not recall burning any others. If there were more, she had to find them and destroy them. Otherwise they'd come and take Jim Bob and his little friends away.

Maribell Morgan got out of her bed, walked down the hall to the nurses' locker room, and helped herself to the night nurse's car keys. For the first time in fifteen years, Maribell

Morgan was behind the wheel of a car. It was like riding a bicycle, she thought. Once you knew how, you didn't forget.

The attic. When Rodney first moved in with her, she'd given him an antique wardrobe in the attic to store his things in. That's where the scrapbooks would be.

It felt good to be back in her old home again. Maybe she'd stay here from now on. She turned on the lights and slowly climbed the stairs. Her breathing was labored as she finally reached the attic. She staggered, caught herself, tottered forward, and then felt something give way in her hip.

She wasn't in her own bed, after all, she realized, when she woke up. She was back in the ugly room in the ugly building, and that nice man was there. "Sign this, Aunt Maribell," he said, putting a pen in her hand and guiding it across the bottom of a piece of paper. "Go away," she muttered, deciding he wasn't very nice after all. "I'm tired."

When Bruce Laughenslagger heard about Maribell's accident, he immediately knew what she'd been looking for in the attic. He found the scrapbooks in the wardrobe, exactly where Rodney had left them many years ago. There were diaries there, also. Despicable details of every perversion. Bruce stashed them in the back of his SUV.

Driving away, he thought about Tori Miracle. She was young and honest and forthright. So much like his wife had been. If she had known what he'd done she would have encouraged him to confess. Maybe if he had, he wouldn't have given up the music he'd once loved so much. Tori made him realize that his self-respect was worth more than anything else.

He didn't want anything to happen to Tori. They'd already made three attempts at taking her life. Who knew what J.B. would dream up next? For her own safety, he was going to persuade Tori Miracle to go away with him. Once she was safe somewhere, maybe in Mexico, he'd come back and turn everything over to the police. The nightmare had gone on too long. It was time to end it.

TWENTY-SEVEN

I TOLD THE STORY as I had figured it out, depending mostly on the facts I had learned from Maribell and Big Bad Bob. Luscious supplied the missing details that he'd learned from Bruce's confession.

The people at the table were stunned. Finally Alice-Ann asked, "What made you go to Maribell?"

"Because everything that had happened pointed to her nephew J.B. Her confession was way too conveniently timed. Because I was sure she was somehow, maybe even unknowingly, covering up for him, and it made me furious. I still believed he was the killer, and I kept thinking, what kind of creep would let his own aunt take the rap for a murder he committed? I admit I was surprised to learn about the others taking part in the killing."

Greta said, "I figured out some of the names from your story. J.B. Morgan, or Jim Bob as he used to be known, was the instigator. Bruce Laughenslagger tried to have you killed, then came around and turned them in at the end. The others who tried to murder you were Aaron Gelsinger, my dentist, and Marvin Bumbaugh, our own borough council president. Wilbur Eshelman was one of them, but threatened to confess so he was murdered by J.B. But you said there were seven boys. Who were the other two?"

"Benjamin Koon and Judge Edward Fetterhoff," Luscious said.

"It's almost impossible to believe," Greta said. "What made you suspect Emily was involved?"

"The tape Maggie and I listened to. There was a giggle at the end. A female giggle. I figured it had to be Emily taking pictures. She even had her own darkroom where it would have been safe to develop them."

Maggie said, "I can't understand how Emily, a nice girl from a good family, could have gotten involved with a rotten pervert like Rodney."

Ethelind sat up straight in her chair. "I went to high school with her, and I happen to know she was not as nice as the legend makes her out to be. In fact, I'd call her pretty wild. She was popular, but that's because she slept with any boy in pants."

Again I wondered from the vehemence in her voice if one of those "boys in pants" had been her boyfriend.

"She went off to Bryn Mawr," Ethelind continued, "and failed at what she thought was the real reason for going to college: getting engaged. It was the fifties, remember? She came back to Lickin Creek because she had no other options. Only trouble was, all the boys she slept around with in high school had gone and married their high school sweethearts. At the ripe old age of twenty-two, Emily Rakestraw was an old maid. I imagine she saw Rodney as her only hope. And the perversions he practiced probably appealed to the wild side of her."

"None of what you told me would stand up in court, you know," Luscious said to me. "It's all hearsay."

My heart sank. After all I'd been through and the arrests he'd made at the fire hall, I couldn't imagine the case not going to court. "Maribell can verify it all."

"She died a few hours ago."

There were whispers of shock and sympathy around the table.

"Then why did you arrest everybody?"

"Because I have hard evidence that backs up everything you done told me. Thanks to Bruce Laughenslagger coming clean and confessing and bringing in the proof."

"So that's what was in the box he was bringing into the police station," I said. "The rest of the scrapbooks. That's not surprising, since Rodney seemed to have kept scrapbooks since he was a kid."

"Diaries, too," Luscious said. "Lickin Creek wasn't the only place he'd done these things. I've left messages at several other police departments."

"What's going to happen to the murderers?" Maggie asked.

"They'll be charged in criminal court for the murder of Rodney Mellott. Additionally, four of them have been accused of attempting to murder you, Tori. And J.B. has also been charged with murder, in the death of Wilbur Eshelman. The other two, Ben Koon and the judge, are probably out on bail by now."

Everyone in the kitchen looked at the back door, as if half expecting the killers to appear there.

Alice-Ann smiled ruefully and said, "Now in addition to all the other things the town blames on you, I suppose you'll be known as the girl who put an end to the Old Boys' Club."

"Not to mention the Downtown Businessmen's Association Band," Greta said.

More questions flew around the table, but I was through giving answers. Tyfani's arrival with Billy in her arms was a welcome relief. She looked only mildly surprised at finding such a large mob in the kitchen. After living in the embassy where there was no privacy at all, she probably didn't see anything odd about it.

"I just need to get some milk for Billy," she apologized. "I won't be a minute."

"Please stay and meet everybody." I proudly introduced my stepmother and baby brother to my friends.

Everyone offered congratulations on their daring escape, and Tyfani immediately credited her servants for saving her life. "I'll be eternally grateful to them," she said.

Ethelind announced, "They'll be staying with me. For as long as Tyfani wants."

I was still angry at the woman for what she'd tried to do to Garnet and me, but her generosity was never at fault.

"You, and she, and the baby could all move in with me," Garnet suggested.

"She's not alone. There are four more people with her. Your house is large, but not that large." Besides, I needed to work out my feelings for him after all this time apart, and I didn't think I could do it if I were living with him. "I think we'll all stay here for the time being."

Garnet's arm withdrew from my shoulder. I couldn't worry about that now.

"Do you hear music?" Alice-Ann asked. "I'll swear I hear 'Amazing Grace' being played on an organ."

"Haley!" I leaped to my feat. How dared he come here? I ran to the front door, followed by everyone from the kitchen, who gathered behind me as I flung open the front door.

Blocking the driveway was Haley Haley's church-to-go, lit up like a Christmas tree, with music blaring from its little white steeple.

"Good God," Garnet grumbled. "What's going to happen next?"

Haley stepped down from the cab, started up the driveway, then stopped when he saw us watching him.

He grinned and waved. "I did what you asked," he announced.

"Me? What are you talking about?"

"I've got Vonzell Varner in there, all trussed up like a Thanksgiving turkey."

I was absolutely at a loss for words and could only stare like an idiot at him with my mouth hanging open.

"Yup, you were right. He was with me all the time. I thought I could save him. Be my brother's keeper. But then I learned from you what he'd done to his wife… And, well, 'the scales fell from my eyes.' Spouse abuse just don't set too well with me. And then when I heard he was following you, I decided that was it. It's back to Graterford for him. I wash my hands of him.'

Garnet had stepped forward to stand next to me while Haley was talking. Haley grinned at me, looking more like Gary Cooper than ever. "Guess you and that police chief dude have patched things up, right?"

"Sort of," Garnet said, looking at me with an odd glint in his eye.

"Sort of? That's a strange thing to say," I said, glaring back at him.

"Uh-oh," Greta said under her breath.

"Come on, Luscious," Haley said. "Let's get that turkey out of my church. I gotta be in West Virginia for a revival first thing in the ayem."

Traditional Pennsylvania Recipes
from the Lickin Creek Chronicle

Red Beet Eggs
2 15-ounce cans whole red beets
1 cup cider vinegar
3 tablespoons sugar
6 eggs, hard-boiled and peeled

Combine beets, liquid from the cans, vinegar and sugar. Heat in a saucepan just enough to dissolve the sugar. Add the eggs to the liquid marinade. Refrigerate for at least 6 hours. Eggs become redder if left to marinate longer.

Red beet eggs are usually served without the beets, as a snack with drinks. Sliced on a salad, they are tasty and colorful. They also make a good substitute for deviled eggs.

Slippery Pot Pie

Dough:
1 cup all-purpose flour
1 egg
1/2 teaspoon salt
1/4 cup milk
8 cups canned chicken or beef broth
4 medium potatoes, peeled and sliced
about 1/4 inch thick

Sift flour and salt together into a bowl. Add egg and mix into the flour with your fingers. Add milk. Knead with fingers until it turns into a soft ball of dough. Roll dough out on a floured board to about 1/8-inch thickness. Cut into two-inch squares. Makes about 22 to 24 squares.

Bring broth to a boil in a 5-quart pot. Drop dough squares into broth, one piece at a time. Stir gently to keep squares from sticking together. Add sliced potatoes. Return to boil, reduce heat and simmer for about 45 minutes, or until potatoes are thoroughly cooked. Makes about 4 servings.

This hearty Pennsylvania Dutch dish is not really a pie but a main dish. Serve in soup bowls. Peas and carrots may be added for color.

Sugar Cakes

1 cup shortening
2 cups sugar
4 eggs
4 cups flour
1 teaspoon soda
1 teaspoon salt
1 cup sour cream
1 teaspoon vanilla
2 tablespoons additional sugar
for topping cookies

Cream shortening, sugar and eggs until light and fluffy. Add flour, soda, salt and sour cream to creamed mixture. Stir in vanilla. Drop from teaspoon onto cookie sheet. Sprinkle additional sugar on top of cookies. Bake at 400 degrees for 12 to 15 minutes, until golden. Makes about 72 sugar cakes.

Although called cakes, these are actually cookies.